ONE SHILLING.

CARACTACUS
champion of the ARENA

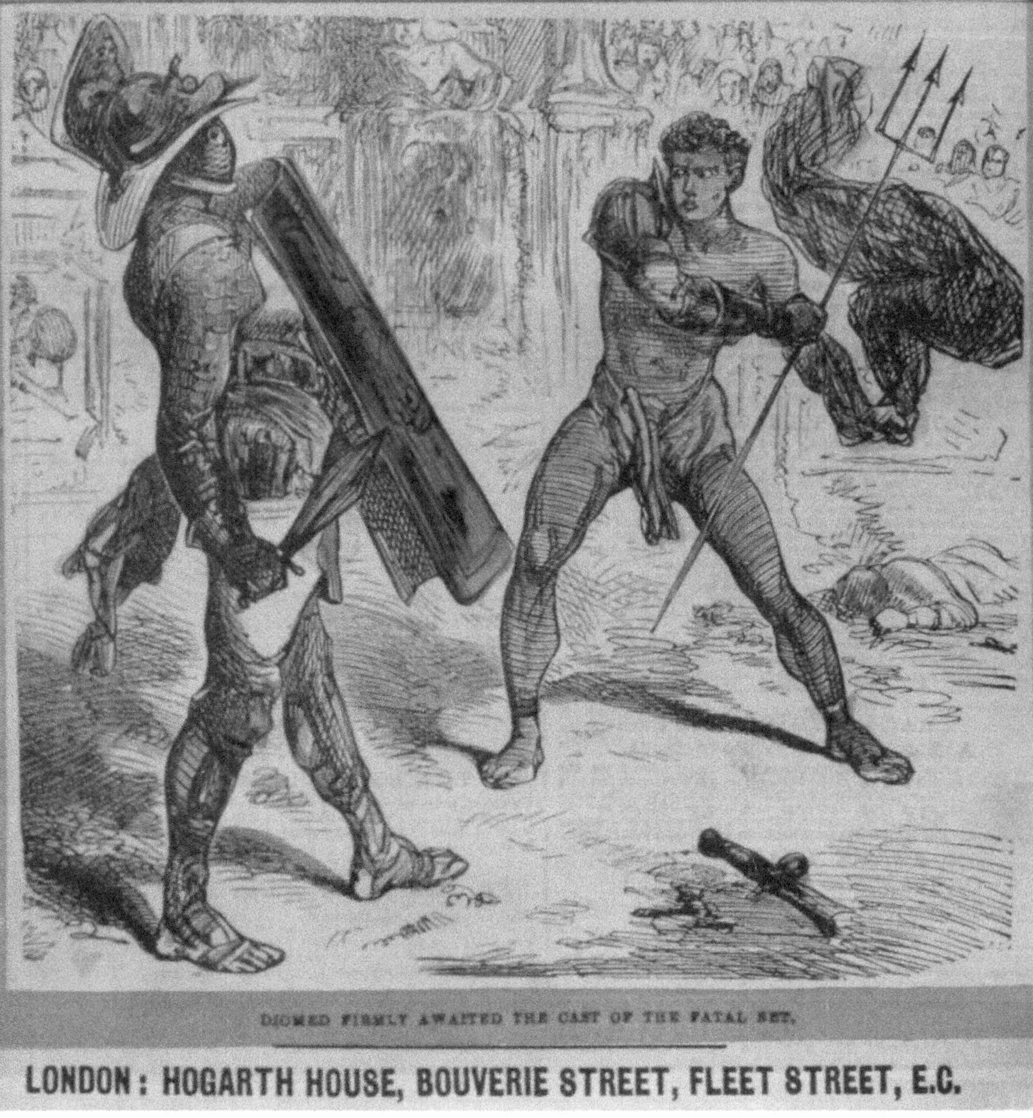

DIOMED FIRMLY AWAITED THE CAST OF THE FATAL NET.

LONDON : HOGARTH HOUSE, BOUVERIE STREET, FLEET STREET, E.C.

CARACTACUS
Champion of the ARENA

"NOW MY SONS," CRIED THE LANISTA, "WHAT THINK YOU OF OUR NOVICE—CARACTACUS?"

CARACTACUS,

THE CHAMPION OF THE ARENA.

CHAPTER I.

THE SLAVE-MARKET.

TOWARDS the close of a hot summer's day in the second year of the reign of the Emperor Claudius, a crowd were gathered in the Roman slave-market, to witness the sale and purchase of a large number of barbarian captives newly imported from Gaul and Britain.

For hours the auction had continued briskly.

Amidst the noise and excitement of the contending bidders, singly or in lots, the human chattels, according to the brutal custom of the age, were stripped and placed on a raised stone, so that everyone might see and handle them, even if they did not wish to buy.

From this practice, it may be mentioned, arose the phrase—*de lapide emptus*, "bought from the stone."

In this manner, men, women, boys and girls, of all ages and various races, had been throughout the day bartered for sordid gold.

Among the spectators of this abominable scene, so degrading to humanity, stood one man, who alone in that hardened throng, betrayed by his looks some proper feeling of disgust and compassion.

He was a Greek, a sculptor by trade, and his name, Philomenes.

He was gifted with the manly grace and intellectual beauty peculiar to his Hellenic breed. His features were as perfect as those of a Phidian statue; his eyes clear, earnest and shining; his hair, of a sunny brown, clustered round a high and noble forehead in crisp, abundant curls.

His dress, though plain and simple, admirably set off his slight, graceful figure.

It consisted of a short tunic of dark woollen stuff, over which was thrown a chlamys or mantle, fastened on the right shoulder with a fibula, a gold brooch set with precious stones. Sandals, and a Phrygian cap, completed his attire, and the only weapon he carried was a small stylus, a steel instrument intended for writing on wax tablets, but not unfrequently used as a dagger.

Philomenes was poor, and, even had his taste been so inclined, he had not the wherewithal to traffic in such costly wares as flesh and blood; yet, as an art student, he found it instructive to pay occasional visits to the slave-market, as to a school where he could meet with the finest living models of manly vigour and female loveliness.

But now the chief interest of the slave sale is over.

The choicest lots have been disposed of.

Men, valuable for their health and strength, or their skill in various handicrafts; virgins, for their budding charms; boys, for their comeliness, had severally fetched big prices, and now what remained to follow?

A miscellaneous "damaged stock," destined to be knocked down at the dirtiest of dirt-cheap bargains.

Miserable wretches from many lands, some of stunted growth, others afflicted by disease or personal defect, riff-raff, doomed to toil under the lash in the mills and cornfields of Sicily, or to sweat and bleed in the dark mines of Spain.

Philomenes moved away, and walked on to a certain part of the market-place which served as a depôt for such slaves as were either reserved for a future day, were claimed by government, or were condemned to fight as gladiators in the bloody arena of the public circus.

On his way thither, the Greek encountered one of the slave-dealers with whom he had picked up acquaintance.

This fellow was a bloated, coarse looking ruffian, armed with a most dreadful instrument of torture, called a flagellum, a whip with three thongs of ox-hide, knotted with bones and bits of iron.

The Greek saluted him gracefully.

"Well met, Torquatus," he said. "How thrives your business?"

"Salve, most worthy Philomenes!" replied the slave-dealer, nodding. "As to the question you ask me, I will own I find no cause to grumble; I have pouched a few thousand sesterces, but I earned them dearly enough."

"How so?"

"How? The labours of Hercules, or the adventures of Ulysses were but child's play to the perils and hardships I encountered on my voyage to Britain. The gods be praised that my foot is once more on terra firma!"

"It was true, then, that you went in the train of our successful general, Aulus Plautius, to whom the senate have decreed a triumph?"

"Yes, and the more fool I," laughed Torquatus, "for, could I have foreseen what I had to go through, I should scarcely have ventured; but I needs must cast in my lot with the rest of the mangones (slave-dealers), who followed the army as the crows follow a furrow newly turned by the plough—why? to pick up the worms."

He laughed gruffly and cracked his whip.

"Those rugged Britons appear to have made a brave defence; they gave your cohorts some trouble," Philomenes remarked.

"Upon my head be it!" was the answer. "The painted barbarians, under their King Cynbolin, fought like lions. All would not do! They were overthrown in a great battle, and thousands of the prisoners were sold on the field. They went as cheap as a haul of pilchards when the weather is hot and there is a glut in the fish-market."

"Then you did a good stroke of trade that day?" suggested the Greek.

"Vah! not so good as you may think, my master," grunted Torquatus.

"No? That is surprising."

"Minime! not in the least," replied Torquatus; "they fought with such desperation, that almost all of them had received hurts—many, fatal wounds; so that in the end not above half of their number were worth removal."

"And what did you do with the rest?"

"What should we do with them?" replied Torquatus, laughing brutally. "We put to the sword as many as we could, but finding that work too tedious, we hurled the rest over rocks and precipices, having received orders to kill all that were not serviceable. But our trouble and loss did not end there, for many of the remainder fell dead or dying on our toilsome march to the sea-shore."

"Merciful gods!" exclaimed the Greek, starting. But he checked his indignation, and murmured bitterly to himself—

"Poor wretches! their misery is past; not they, but the survivors, are to be pitied."

Torquatus either did not hear, or did not heed the remark.

Warming to his subject, he hurried on—

"One custom which is common to the Gauls and Britons, we slave-dealers turned to good account," said he. "Strange to relate, these barbarians take their women and little ones with them to the battle-field. In the heat of the engagement the soldier hears the shrieks of his wife and the cries of his children, and is inspired with undaunted courage."

The Greek's eyes kindled, and the blood mounted his cheek.

"Euge! 'tis a noble plan!" he exclaimed, with a burst of enthusiasm. "The scene passes before me. I see the warrior's tenderest pledges are collected in the field; these are the darling witnesses of his valour, at once beloved and valued. The wounded seek their mothers and wives; undismayed at the sight, the women count each honourable scar, and suck the gushing blood. They are even hardy enough to mix with the combatants when they see the ranks give way, and, by exposing their breasts to danger, restore the order of the battle."

The slave-dealer glared at his companion in astonishment.

"You paint the picture well," he growled rather sulkily, "but what availed the courage and devotion of these barbarian men and women against the superior arms and discipline of our Roman legionaries?"

The Greek's only reply was an expressive shrug.

"Well, beauty is the prize of successful valour," laughed Torquatus; "and I can tell you, Philomenes, that some of the young maids we captured were fairer than the Graces, while many of the boys were fit to serve as cup-bearers at a banquet of the gods."

"I can vouch for that," rejoined the Greek. "This morning I saw a girl sold, who, for grace of form and beauty of feature, might have sat as model to Apelles."

"The girl you speak of belongs to Davus, my former partner in trade, and well deserves your praises," replied the slave-dealer. "She was purchased by order of young Nero, nephew to Cæsar, and fetched a brave price—three hundred thousand sesterces. Meherclé! Think of that!"

"Amazing!"

"You may well say so," chuckled Torquatus, "yet what is she when compared with the British pearl in my possession? Vah! a raven to a swan."

"So, then, you also have found a prize?" rejoined Philomenes, smiling. "Why was she not brought to the auction?"

"I will tell you why, though it vexes me to the heart to think of my ill luck," grumbled Torquatus. "The girl is sick; the horrors of the passage from Britain to Rome have proved too much for her delicate frame. When I saw her just now, drooping in her brother's arms, she looked like a lovely statue cut in alabaster."

"You mentioned her brother: who and what is he?"

"O, Philomenes, a god-like boy!" cried the slave-dealer, uplifting his hands. "His name is Caractacus, a young prince of the Silures, who made havoc in our Roman ranks. He speaks Latin too, having been detained as a hostage by the Roman prefect."

"He must be worth his weight in gold?"

"Not so, worse luck for me," returned the slave-dealer. "By one rash deed he has ruined his own chance for life and spoiled my hopes of profit."

"A crime?"

"Unpardonable! One of the centurions, during the voyage, offered the young chief's sister an insult. Caractacus sprang upon him like a bounding panther—brained him with his fetters. Woe the while! He is now claimed by Cæsar to fight, as a malefactor, with the wild beasts in the circus. My purse is the lighter by two hundred thousand sesterces."

"These Britons, though barbarians, are human, it seems," said the Greek, grimly smiling.

"Sure, and though stolid and patient by nature, it is perilous to play the fool with them," replied Torquatus.

"And the girl is sick?"

"Unto death, I fear! Was ever such ill-luck as mine?" replied the slave-dealer. "But I have called to her aid one Mathias. It is whispered that he consorts with those worshippers of an ass's head, the Christian—but what is that to me? If he can save the life of my slave, I am the better man by twice the price of the girl sold by Davus."

Among the manifold slanders uttered against the Christians at the period of our story, none was more absurd than the imputation that they degraded themselves by the disgusting worship of an ass's head.

"I know the man," said Philomenes; "and look, while we talk of him, he approaches!"

At this moment the physician advanced to meet them.

He was a majestic old man, with prominent features, a noble and benevolent countenance, and a long silvery beard that swept his bosom.

He was dressed in a gaberdine of dark coloured serge; attached to his girdle was a pouch containing his drugs and surgical instruments. In his right hand he carried a long staff, with a head of carved ivory.

"Peace be with you, my brethren," he said, in a mild, pleasant voice.

"And with you, worthy Mathias," responded Philomenes. "Have you forgotten what passed between us at our last meeting?"

A radiant light shone in the old man's bright black eyes, as he replied quietly—

"I am pleased at your question. May God grant the seed then sown may bear fruit unto salvation!"

"Salvation! Ah, good father," sighed the Greek, "the doctrine you preach is new and strange, and I am hard of belief. The storms of life have so hardened my heart, that I fear it is impervious to the good seed that might fructify into hope immortal. Euthanasia! an easy death, eternal rest—there is no more to hope for by wretched man."

"Eternal rest!" repeated Mathias, with a radiant smile; "Ay, but not the repose you mean—dead oblivion—nothingness. No, no; immortal life, eternal bliss, such are the rewards promised the believer by One who cannot lie!"

"Now, by the Sphinx! if you will talk in riddles, I will leave you to crack your conundrums between yourselves," Torquatus broke in, angrily. "I am no Œdipus—I have no brains for the subtleties of the academa. I sent for you, Mathias, to attend my sick slave, and to cure her if you can. Will you visit her, or shall I seek elsewhere for aid?"

"Let us go," said Mathias.

"By your leave, Torquatus, I will accompany you," said the Greek. "As a sculptor, I am curious to see these handsome slaves."

"Do so, Philomenes," the slave-dealer rejoined. "I should like to have your opinion of them."

He led the way down a long stone corridor until they reached an iron-bound door, above which was a grating.

The door was thrown open as they drew near, and a powerfully built, rough-looking fellow came out to meet them.

In one hand he jingled a bunch of keys, in the other he wielded a whip, similar to that borne by Torquatus.

Upon seeing his assistant's rueful looks, Torquatus started and changed countenance.

"How now, Corvus—what is amiss?" he asked. "How fares the girl? See, I have brought the physician."

"He comes too late, I fear, master," replied Corvus. "The girl lies at the point of death."

Torquatus uttered a groan of vexation, and threw wide the door.

Beckoning the Jew and the Greek to follow him, he descended some stone steps.

Upon reaching the floor of the cell, which was lighted from the grating above the door, the three men were brought to a standstill by a sight which moved even the callous heart of the slave-dealer to compassion.

CHAPTER II.

DEATH THE LIBERATOR.

CHAINED to a pillar that supported the roof of his dungeon, Caractacus knelt beside a pallet of straw, on which lay the frail and delicately moulded form of his dying sister.

Supporting her head upon his knee, he gazed upon her white face with the dull apathy of blank despair, bedewing her long tresses of wavy gold with his falling tears.

During several moments the captive Briton did not appear to notice the entrance of his visitors.

His head was bent down, and they could not see his face.

Suddenly, however, he looked up, and confronted them with a bewildered stare.

Though his features were now distorted by anguish, Philomenes and Mathias were at once struck by the youth's remarkable and lion-like beauty.

The rich blood mantled his smooth, fresh cheek, his eyes flashed with fire, his tangles of flaxen hair rolled down in glistening masses on his broad, deep shoulders.

"What cheer, my lad?" growled Torquatus, in rough, but not unkind tones. "How fares it with thy sister?"

The Briton answered quickly, but in hoarse, broken accents, that belied his hopeful words—

"Not dead! she breathes. She spoke but now. She will not die. The gods cannot be so cruel!"

"Courage, boy; your sister shall not die if this good man can save her," replied Torquatus. "He is reputed one of the most skilful doctors in the town."

It was distressing to observe the wild gleam of hope that shot from the eyes of Caractacus as he answered breathlessly—

"Noble master, the gods requite your kindness."

Then, clutching Mathias by the robe, he added, imploringly—

"Do but save my sister's life, and I care not what befals myself. I am young and strong, and can bear the worst the cruel Romans can inflict upon me."

"Stand back, my friends," said Mathias, waving his hand. "Open the door wider. Let in the air."

"Ay, the fresh air," cried the captive Briton, catching at the word. "The free breeze will soon fan the colour back to her pale face, will it not, kind masters?"

The old man knelt down beside the girl without making any reply.

As Caractacus resigned her to the physician's care, he quivered in every nerve with heart-sickening suspense, and hung on every shade of expression that crossed the old man's face, awaiting the verdict for life or death.

Mathias, with professional ease and coolness, loosened the girl's dress from the neck, laid his hand over her heart; he even raised the closed lids, and peered into her glazing eyes.

"Speak," muttered Caractacus. "Let me know the worst."

He broke off, shuddering from limb to limb, and buried his face in his hands.

No answer.

Mathias took a small phial from his satchel, and poured from it a few drops of a colourless liquid upon the girl's lips.

They moved slightly.

Her eyes opened and closed again.

A sigh fluttered from her mouth.

To this faint sound Caractacus responded with a great cry of hope and love.

Mathias sighed, shook his head, and motioned him to be quiet.

Thus rebuked, Caractacus humbly clasped his hands, and looked on as rigidly as though he had been turned to marble.

Philomenes leaned over the old man, and whispered something in his ear.

Tears glistened in the eyes of Mathias as he replied in the same low tone—

"It is God's will. She is beyond all mortal aid," said he. "The sands run low. She has not an hour to live."

While this passed, Philomenes glanced at the face of the British slave, and wondered in his kind heart how the deities could permit one so young and noble to suffer such exquisite anguish.

He laid his hand softly upon the boy's naked shoulder.

"Thou comest of a brave race, and they tell me, my boy, that kingly blood runs in thy veins," he said, very softly.

"I and my sister are the children of the King of the Silures, as brave a warrior, as pure a patriot, as ever struck a blow for freedom," returned Caractacus, checking his sobs, and dashing away the drops from his eyes. "Never till now could I believe my father's son a coward. These are the first tears I have shed since childhood."

"Such grief is natural, and does you no dishonour," replied the kind-hearted Greek. "But you must learn to suffer and be strong. If the inexorable Fates decree that your beloved sister shall be removed from this world of woe, why should you repine? Consider from what shame and misery she will be rescued. Is she not better, sleeping in her restful grave, than living a wretched slave, at the mercy and caprice of some cruel tyrant?"

Caractacus turned from him, and cast an appealing look upon Mathias.

"What does he mean?" faltered the unhappy youth. "Will my sister live or die?"

"Alas! my son, it would be but cruel kindness to deceive thee. The hand of death is upon her," was the solemn reply. "Yet be of comfort; death is but the gate to life eternal. This maiden, though dead, will share in the bliss of the paradise beyond the tomb."

"Iona!" groaned Caractacus, straining the dying girl to his heart. "Ah! my sister, they have murdered thee."

By a feeble movement the girl raised her arm, and placed it around her brother's neck.

Her dark lids unclosed, and she gazed up into his yearning face with a tender, yet dreamy, half-conscious look.

She spoke, but her words came in an almost inaudible whisper.

"My brother, what place is this? All is dark

around us. But see the light yonder! It breaks upon us so bright, my eyes are dazzled."

"I see no light, my sister, but the feeble rays that creep through the bars of this accursed dungeon," replied Caractacus, in anguish.

"A dungeon! No! This is the Druids' sacred grove, which we profane by our footsteps," she replied, clinging closer to him in apparent terror. "Let us fly. But, look! now the light shines brighter still. I see a train of white-robed maidens, the virgins of the sun. They are crowned with garlands of oak and mistletoe; each carries in her hand the mystic bough. They wave me to come to them—I must go."

"Stay with me, dear sister," murmured Caractacus. "Do not leave me desolate."

"I dare not, brother," she answered, tremblingly. "The ghosts of our fathers call to me from the clouds—they will not be denied."

Then there came a flash of returning consciousness.

"A dungeon," she said, abruptly. "Yes, I remember, this is Rome—we are slaves. I know why you look so pale—you think I am dying. I think so too. How cold this place—how dark! Do not let go my hand. Kiss me before I die."

There was a pause.

The dying girl fell back in her brother's embrace.

Caractacus bent his proud head over the white face, for the moment veiling it with his long flaxen hair, and touched with his lips the cold forehead.

As he raised himself, and put back his flowing locks, a smile of loving recognition glowed for one moment on Iona's pale face.

It passed like a summer meteor, and was succeeded by "the rapture of repose."

She was gone!

Caractacus flung himself upon her bosom in an ecstasy of passionate grief.

Philomenes turned aside with a gloomy frown, while Mathias, throwing himself upon his knees, engaged in fervent prayer.

CHAPTER III.

THE DIE IS CAST.

"HO! there, Torquatus, where art thou, man, and where is this British slave?" shouted a deep voice, that rang in echoes along the stone corridor outside the cell.

Then the tramp of footsteps and the clank of arms were heard, jarring harshly upon the solemn scene.

"Whom have we here?" asked Philomenes, turning towards the door.

"I know the voice," replied Torquatus; "it is Ventidius, the lanista, the master, who comes to claim the Briton as a gladiator."

"The poor boy has swooned," said Mathias, glancing pityingly at Caractacus, who lay heaped and senseless on the stone floor. "It is not well that the harsh trainer should find his new pupil in this condition."

"No," rejoined Philomenes; "nor would I have him admitted until we have removed the body of the dead maiden."

Then, turning to the slave-dealer, he added—

"Hark ye, Torquatus; will you do me a favour?"

"That depends on what you ask."

"It is a whim of mine, which, if you will gratify, I will pay you well."

"Speak out then; what do you want?"

"I desire that the ashes of this fair and innocent girl should not be thrown into the common pit. Will you sell me her body, that I may have it buried with decency and respect?"

Torquatus responded with a coarse laugh—

"An odd request," said he. "All that remains of so much beauty is but worthless carrion, but what of that? I cannot accede to your proposal without breaking the Edile's regulations. I must, therefore, ask a fair recompense for my risk and trouble."

"Tush, man! You know I am not rich, but we will not cavil about terms," replied the Greek. "Here is what gold I have about me. When I receive the body at my house, I will add triple the sum."

He emptied his purse into the slave-dealer's greedily extended hand.

The eyes of Torquatus glistened with avarice as he counted the money.

"The next thing is, how can the affair be managed?" he said.

"That is not difficult," replied Philomenes. "Go you and meet Ventidius—detain him under some excuse—invite him to crush a cup of Falernian with you at the nearest tavern; he will not refuse the offer."

"That will he not," laughed Torquatus. "I know the man, he is a staunch worshipper of Bacchus; but in the meantime, how will you proceed?"

"By the help of some of your fellows, I will have the body carried to my house."

"I will send them to you; but take care that it be done as quietly and secretly as possible."

"Trust me for that," returned Philomenes.

"While this is about, I and Mathias will do our best to restore yon boy, and prepare him for his interview with the lanista."

"Go quickly, my friend," urged Mathias, pointing to the door. "Ventidius calls you again, and delay may put him out of temper."

"I go," said Torquatus. "Corvus and his mates shall join you presently to execute your orders."

With these words, he hurried from the cell.

Left to themselves, Mathias and Philomenes gently unwound the arm of Caractacus from the neck of his dead sister; then they drew apart the corpse, composed the stiffened limbs, and covered the face with a handkerchief.

While they were thus employed, Corvus, with Burbo and two other satellites of Torquatus, entered the dungeon.

The ruffians leered at one another, and seemed highly amused that so much trouble should be taken about the dead carcase of a despised slave.

Philomenes saw what was passing in their thoughts, and stung by disgust, he gave his orders in a peremptory tone.

His directions were, that the body, wrapped up in a mantle, should be placed in a suitable vehicle and conveyed to his house, which was situated near the Flaminian Gate.

The men, cowed by his stern manner, mumbled a promise of obedience.

They raised the body from the floor, and carried it forth from the dungeon.

Philomenes and his companion now turned their attention to Caractacus.

The physician applied the proper restoratives, and after a little time the youth was sufficiently recovered to sit up and look about him.

He rolled his eyes around the place in dull wonder, and pressed his hand to his forehead as though to collect his scattered senses.

"Was it a dream?" he gasped.

Then fixing his eyes upon the two men who watched him heedfully, he started to his feet.

"It was no dream!" he muttered; "but the bitter truth. I am alone in my misery."

Seeing that the corpse had been taken away, he asked what had become of it.

Mathias told him what had been done, and he seemed touched to the heart by the delicate kindness of Philomenes.

His face lit up with gratitude, as he grasped the sculptor by the hand.

"Generous friend," he said, "what return can I make you?—none, but the thanks of a helpless slave! but the gods will not suffer your humanity to pass without reward."

"Think not of it—think not of the dead past that can never be recalled."

"Never, never!" Caractacus mournfully assented.

"Rally yourself," continued the Greek, "and be prepared for what is to come. If your brood too deeply over your bereavement, you will lose heart, and forfeit that reputation for courage and endurance that a brave man wins even from his enemies."

The eyes of Caractacus flashed lightning.

"By the altars of Britain!" he exclaimed, "I will teach them to pay me the respect that springs from fear. I am to be trained and armed, and matched to fight as a gladiator in the arena; is it not so?"

"Alas, unhappy boy!" sighed Mathias.

"Unhappy!" retorted Caractacus, with a scornful laugh. "I desire no better fate. For what should I live but to glut my vengeance on those Roman wolves, who have ravaged my country, murdered my kindred, and made me a slave? Iona, I live only to avenge thee!"

"Spoken like a lad of pith and mettle," cried a gruff voice from the door. "Do but keep in that mind, and attend to your training, and the day may come when you will be hailed Champion of the Arena, and crowned with a wreath of palm."

All turned towards the speaker, who stood laughing on the steps at the entry to the dungeon.

"'Tis Manlius, the gladiator," said Philomenes. "The best swordsman in Rome."

"Thanks, noble Philomenes; but I cannot accept so high a compliment," was the reply. "Lycaon, your countryman, fences as well as I, and is my superior in the use both of the trident and the cestus."

"A generous concession," replied the Greek smiling, "showing an absence of professional vanity rare among gentlemen of the blade and buckler. But I know that you and Lycaon have ever been sworn brothers-at-arms. Your hand, lad; I am glad to see you in such splendid fettle."

Manlius advanced and shook hands with the Greek.

The gladiator certainly had an heroic figure, while his dress and arms were magnificent. In the glow of health and bloom of manhood, tall and stalwart, of frank, bold and soldierly bearing, he had black, glossy curls, and eyes that shone with a genial, fearless light.

He wore a brazen helmet, with a golden crest and a plume of red feathers; his deep chest was protected by a shining breast-plate, beautifully engraved with figures of rich design: there were greaves upon his legs, and upon his feet a sort of buskin, strengthened and adorned with brazen pieces; from one shoulder hung gracefully his pallium or cloak, of bright scarlet cloth, and on the other was slung a small light buckler in the shape of a half-moon. A short double-edged sword glittered on his thigh.

Manlius and our hero took stock of each other, and exchanged looks of mutual admiration.

Perhaps in their grim smiles there lurked a touch of—

"That stern joy which warriors feel
In foemen worthy of their steel."

However that might be, their first meeting was cordial enough.

"Salve, my new comrade," said Manlius, heartily. "Meat, drink, and a few months' training in our gymnasium, will make you a challenger fit to contend against Hercules."

"I am glad he meets with your approval," said Philomenes. "I share in your opinion of hi prospects as a gladiator."

"Castor!" laughed Manlius. "Some of ou family will find him a tough customer when it i foot to foot on the sand. But leave the future t take care of itself."

In the meanwhile Corvus returned, and mad Philomenes understand, by a sign, that he ha successfully performed his mission.

"So thou art come at last, old tortoise," said th gladiator. "Bustle, for I am in haste; after partin with Torquatus, my master has returned to ou school in the Via Nova, and I am to bring th novice after him. Strike off his chains."

Corvus brought a mallet and other tools, an soon set our hero at liberty.

"And now farewell, my patrons," said Manlius saluting Philomenes and Mathias. "Away, Carac tacus, I am all eagerness to introduce you to you new comrades."

Our hero lingered a moment to say a few grate ful words to his benefactors at parting. Mathias would gladly have detained the lad, to have given him some pious exhortation, but the circumstance being so unfavourable, he wisely abstained from doing so.

He dismissed him with a fatherly blessing, a the same time promising to seek an early oppor tunity of meeting him again.

Manlius threw a few pieces of silver to Corvus and his mates, and then taking the Briton by the arm he led him from the dungeon. Soon after wards the physician and the sculptor turned thei backs upon the slave-market.

As for some distance their homeward paths lay in the same direction, they wended their way together.

Neither appeared to be in a mood for conversation, so they walked on in silence through the jostling crowd, each wrapped in his own meditation. At length Mathias, as though overwrought by some painful reflection, murmured half-aloud—

"How long, O Lord! how long! This is the appointed day of thy coming. Tarry not longer!"

Philomenes, though somewhat startled at this unconscious outburst, quietly remarked—

"The scenes of the day have made a painful impression on your mind. For my own part, I am saddened when I reflect upon the dreadful fate of that noble-hearted boy, Caractacus."

"A gladiator!" repeated Mathias. "How it is possible that a refined and civilised people can contemplate the horrible spectacles exhibited in the arena, not only without loathing and indignation, but with applause and delight?"

"I own that is a mystery to me," replied the sculptor. "We Greeks, though responsible for many crimes and vices, were little addicted to such degrading pastimes as these; and some of the noblest Romans have protested against them."

"That is true," returned Mathias; "do you remember the words of Cicero, 'Magnificent are these games no doubt, but what delight can it be to a refined mind, to see either a feeble man torn by a most powerful beast, or a noble animal pierced through with a javelin?"

"I agree in the opinion," said Philomenes, "yet, stranger than all, even knights and senators will contend in the arena for the sake of notoriety; while others, maddened by wrong, rejoice in the chance of slacking their thirst for vengeance, in blood. Poor lad, he is lost for ever."

"O, say not so," rejoined Mathias, "nothing is impossible with Him who is omnipotent, and even this unhappy youth may yet be snatched as a brand from the burning."

"It is too late," was the gloomy reply. "I know his resolute nature; for him—*the die is cast!*"

CHAPTER IV.

THE SCHOOL OF GLADIATORS.

MANLIUS the gladiator, and our hero, Caractacus, were standing side by side on the Palatine hill.

On their way to the house of the lanista Ventidius, they had halted at a spot which commanded a magnificent view of the surrounding city.

The day was nearly over, the westering sun was drawing near his goal, and sinking in a sea of molten gold, canopied by clouds of amber and purple—the city lay bathed in his rich soft beams.

Below and around all was picturesque and grand.

Columned temples, gorgeous palaces, graceful terraces and lovely gardens adorned with statuary, all glistening in marble, flanking walls, embattled towers, and masses of chastely designed houses.

Caractacus gazed till his eyes grew weary, and his mind sated with the architectural splendour.

Manlius turned a smiling face towards him, and asked—

"What thinks Caractacus of our city of Rome?"

The young barbarian drew a deep breath.

"By Hertha!" he exclaimed, "at home, in my own land of Albion, I have listened to the songs of our bards, when beneath some wide-spreading oak, and tuning their high harps, they have recited the deeds of my ancestors, and have described the rewards that await the just and valiant."

"Beyond the grave!" said Manlius, thoughtful. "Go on, I should like to know how they depict the Elysian fields."

"They spoke of forests where the summer never fades, the leaves never fall, where the wild beasts of the chase abound, and where the hunter's strength and skill never fail; of banquets, where the mead is poured out into golden chalices by the bright-haired daughters of the sun—but never have they pictured such a scene as this!"

"The poets of your nation draw their ideals from things they have seen," said Manlius. "Certainly Rome is a dwelling for the gods; woe the while that her free-born people should groan under the yoke of demons."

"A curse upon her!" hissed Caractacus, shaking his fist. "'Tis for her very beauty that I hate her—'tis the beauty of the painted tiger or the jewelled snake; beneath all is cruelty and treachery and venom. May the avenging gods consume your accursed city with fire and sword and famine!"

Manlius seized him by the arm and shook him roughly.

"Peace, mad fool!" he whispered, looking nervously around, "you know not who may be listening."

"Nor care," retorted the Briton in disdain, "though it were Cæsar!"

"Again! By Hades! if you are not quiet, I will find means to stop your mouth," growled Manlius angrily. "Come you along, you are too perilous a babbler to walk abroad with."

"Patience, comrade," said our hero. "I will hold my tongue—cursing and railing should be left to women and cowards."

"Now you are reasonable," said Manlius, at once recovering his good humour; "but let us hasten our pace, we have already lingered too long on our road."

They descended the hill and crossed the Campus Martius, in the midst of which loomed an immense stone edifice of great height and circular form.

"What is that mighty building?" asked the Briton, pointing to it in wondering admiration. Manlius laughed.

"Œdepol! you will be better acquainted with it by-and-by," said he, "for on its broad arena you will have to fight for death or freedom."

"Is it the Amphitheatre?"

"It is. But hark, do you hear nothing?"

Our hero paused and listened.

"Yes," he replied, "I hear roars and growls as of wild beasts. What does it mean?"

"This is what it means: a fresh supply of lions, tigers, and leopards, have just arrived from Numidia in readiness for the splendid festival that is to celebrate the birthday of Cæsar," replied Manlius.

Then he added with an impatient gesture—

"Vah! the palmy days of the arena are faded. Our later emperors glut Mars with hecatombs of the slain. There is little true sword play, no fine science—all is brutal havoc, harrying, slaughter—blood—blood—blood! Ah! when I first stepped into the ring it was almost a treat to have one's throat cut by some delicate-handed master of the fence! Ouf! When I think of these things I lose patience."

Thus grumbling he moved away.

Caractacus threw one moody, vengeful glance at the frowning amphitheatre, and followed his comrade.

A few minutes' walk brought them to the Via Nova, and they stood before the house of Ventidius, the lanista.

It was a spacious though modest-looking building, its grounds and gardens surrounded by high walls.

Manlius knocked at the door, which was presently opened by the hall-porter, a grizzly old fellow who had lost an eye and an arm, and whose face was covered with scars—a retired veteran of the ring.

He glanced with surly indifference at the Briton, but as he scanned the youth's noble proportions, his single eye kindled with a spark of the old fire.

"Well, Polyphemus, where is our master?" asked Manlius.

The porter's real name was Hyphax, but the rollicking gladiators nick-named him Polyphemus, on the account of the loss of his eye.

"In the gymnasium," growled the old bear, and shambled off to his den.

"Follow me," said Manlius to the Briton.

He led our hero across a paved court, and up some steps to the gymnasium or training-school.

The walls were hung round with every description of weapon and implement used in the arena.

The athletes, all stripped to the cloth that girded their loins, were engaged in various exercises, some boxing, others leaping the bar, several well-matched pairs fencing with the rudes or wooden foils.

Such quiet and order prevailed as reigns in a well-disciplined academy, under the awful eye of a stern head-master.

Ventidius, who stood near the door, advanced to meet his new pupil.

Though a fine stalwart fellow, his ruddy face and an inclination to corpulence betokened that as far as his own indulgence was concerned, he was no Spartan abstainer from the good things of life.

He measured our hero from head to foot with a rapid but critical look.

"Soh! this is our Briton," he said. "Humph! ha! he'll do!"

Then taking our hero by the arm, he pushed him forwards, and set him in the middle of the room.

"Now, my sons," cried the lanista, "what think you of our novice—Caractacus?"

CHAPTER V.

NOVICE AGAINST VETERAN.

THE gladiators, at their master's call, came trooping round Caractacus.

It required some nerve to endure the scrutiny of dozens of black, keen eyes.

The Briton, however, admirably preserved his self-composure, and was rewarded by the approving murmurs of his new comrades.

Perhaps the lanista's exhilaration might be partly accounted for by the fact that he had been imbibing pretty freely the strong Falernian; at any rate, he appeared to be in high glee at having secured such a fine addition to his "Family."

"Look, my sons," he said, slapping Caractacus on the shoulder, "you see before you the raw material out of which a true gladiator is made."

His pupils assented with a round of applause.

"Yes, my lads, not for nothing have I trained five hundred raw recruits, eighty of whom have been rewarded for their valour and success by manumission or the palm crown." Ventidius went on, with tipsy gravity, "Methinks by this time I should know the form and structure proper for an athlete. Say I well, my lads, or am I boasting? You know I detest flattery—call me a fool if you like, I shan't be offended."

"A Ventidius! Long live our able lanista!" responded his pupils in a half-ironic cheer.

"Very well, then," pursued the lanista, "observe this boy; I say he has all the points about him—a quick, piercing eye, a neck firm and erect, an open chest, broad and muscular shoulders, a length of arm, the belly not too prominent, legs well shaped, without superfluous flesh either on the calf or the foot, well braced with hard and compact sinews."

Another round of applause.

"Hem verbero, ho, you rogue! hold up your head and answer what I shall ask," said the lanista, chucking our hero under the chin. "Let me see, what is your outlandish name?"

"My name is Idris ap Caradoc, but they call me Caractacus," replied the Briton.

"Caractacus be it then," continued the lanista. "So now, Caractacus, let me have cause to be satisfied with you."

"I will do my best."

"It is well spoken," rejoined the lanista. "I shall exact perfect obedience, unremitting attention to your exercises, hard training, abstemious living, and—hic—strict temperance; it is such qualities that make a man—hic—and a gladiator."

His pupils exchanged significant winks and grins.

"Io Bacche!" whispered Pandion, a burly bruiser, in the ear of Manlius. "The master has a skinful; when he prates of 'temperance,' we all know what that means."

"Whist!" replied Manlius, "I wonder if he will try a bout of fencing with the novice."

"The worse for the lad if he does," rejoined the other.

"Ventidius always fences best when he's mellow."

"You hear me what I say, Caractacus?" said the lanista, huskily.

"I hear, master."

"Temperance—my boy, beware the cup of Circe that turns men into swine; take a pattern by your lanista, who never exceeds," continued Ventidius. "And now, attention! In managing your scythed chariots and in hurling the javelin you Britons are reputed to be skilful, but I take it, as a barbarian, you are quite ignorant of the Roman style of fencing?"

"I had some practice while a hostage in the Roman citadel," was the reply.

The lanista's eye glistened.

"It is well," he said; "I will have a bout with you. Automedon, bring the rudes."

The youngest of the gladiators, a mere stripling, brought the wooden swords used in training.

"Take your ground and defend yourself," said Ventidius.

Caractacus grasped the wooden foil and threw himself into position.

The gladiators formed a ring round the two opponents, and awaited the issue of the conflict with much interest and curiosity, not that there existed amongst them the slightest doubt that the skilled lanista would easily overcome an untrained youth, but there was something so free and commanding in the Briton's figure and attitude that he at once engaged their sympathies on his side, and they all expected he would make a good fight of it.

Caractacus placed himself on guard well out of the reach of his opponent's lunge.

"Are you ready?" asked Ventidius.

"Ready," was the quiet answer.

The duel began.

After advancing and retreating several times, they commenced false attacks out of distance, with the purpose of testing each other's skill and style of fencing.

Neither of them ventured to come close enough for his opponent to reach him with a thrust.

Even at this early stage it became evident that the barbarian was no mere tyro in the art of sword play.

Ventidius himself found to his surprise that he was matched against a formidable antagonist, and must look to his own laurels.

"I never saw our lanista fight so carefully," one gladiator whispered to his comrade.

"See the master's eye," returned the other, in the same subdued tone. "He means mischief! Cave! (beware) my novice!"

Setting his features and clenching his teeth, the lanista bounded in upon Caractacus.

By a splendid "parade" our hero prevented the point of the foil from touching him.

The lanista made a feint, rushed in again, and though Caractacus warded finely, beat down his guard, and scratched his sword arm.

"Euge! a Ventidius!" cried the gladiators. "A hit!"

The lanista paused and wiped the sweat from his brow.

"I had thee there, youngster," said Ventidius, with a triumphant grin.

The Briton smiled calmly.

"True, master," he replied, "but with time and practice I shall improve."

"Œcastor! you have made a good beginning, and have shown yourself a lad of great promise," returned the lanista; "but do not fight so closely on the defensive, come at me, put yourself upon your mettle."

"Be it as you wish," returned our hero.

"On guard, then!"

The conflict was renewed with increased vigour, and this time our hero boldly attacked his opponent.

Nothing could exceed the dexterity and elegance of the attitude of the combatants, the intelligence and rapidity of their movements.

As the duel proceeded the on-lookers were l in their applause.

Ventidius made a fearful lounge, which was fully parried by Caractacus.

A rally ensued and our hero retreated, all while parrying the thrusts of his expert antago,

Then the Briton halted, returned to the cha and made an inside thrust, touching Ventidius the right shoulder.

"Habet!" shouted the gladiators, carried away by their enthusiasm. "He has it! One for the novice."

With a muttered curse Ventidius sprang back, and was thrown off his guard.

The Briton took instant advantage of his opportunity.

The wooden swords crossed and recrossed and clattered together.

Ventidius now lost his coolness and self-possession; Caractacus, by a dexterous twist of the wrist, sent his adversary's weapon whirling in the air.

The wooden foil came down, striking its point against the floor and snapping in two.

"Ye gods! It is wonderful!" exclaimed the gladiators.

Many a stiff battle had Ventidius fought, and many a time had he been wounded in the ring, but never before in all his engagements had he allowed himself to be disarmed.

To suffer this disgrace in the presence of his pupils, and at the hands of a barbarian novice. It was too much!

Ventidius was deeply mortified.

However, he thought it the best policy to put a good face on the matter.

He forced a laugh.

"You fence well," he said; "but it is one thing to contend with the rudes, quite another when it is steel to steel."

"Good, my master," rejoined the Briton, with provoking coolness. "Let us try with swords."

Ventidius was a little staggered at this prompt acceptance of his half-challenge, but being game to the backbone, he answered at once—

"Are ye so bold? It will do you no harm to let a little of that hot blood. I will have a bout with you."

Then he gave the command—

"Antomedon, bring the swords."

The youth fetched the weapons.

"Stay, we will take the round bucklers, such as are used by the Thracians," said the lanista.

The shields were brought.

When the antagonists had armed themselves, they stood gravely confronted.

Each threw his warlike shield across his breast, while the fatal steel glistened in each sinewy right hand.

Such a contest in the training school was so unusual, not to say unprecedented, that the gladiators held their breath in astonishment and suspense.

There was a dead hush.

The lanista's voice thrilled clear and distinct through the pervading silence—

"Be cautious, my son," he said. "It is not my wish that either of us should do the other any serious damage. Our blood is not our own, but belongs to our patrons in the amphitheatre. Use caution, do not thrust too fiercely, recover your blade when you thrust, and every touch shall count for a hit. Do you understand?"

"I understand, and will be careful."

"Good, then—engage," said the lanista, clashing his sword against his shield.

For the first time, the Briton's face lit up with the stern joy of battle.

This was no mere sport.

He was armed for a contest which nothing but his own forbearance could prevent from ending fatally.

Warily, and with gliding, cat-like steps, the antagonists approached each other.

Clash!

Their swords met—the highly-tempered steel emitted sparks.

Ventidius received a lunge from the Briton full in the centre of his round target.

The lanista repaid the thrust with interest, aiming a swashing blow at his opponent's head, which the latter neatly stopped with his shield.

After a few more passes, swift as a lightning's flash, Ventidius dashed in, and whipped his sword through the fleshy part of the Briton's arm, causing the blood to spout in a crimson stream, but in the very instant our hero made such a masterly feint that the lanista threw wide his arms and left his bosom exposed.

The gladiators uttered a cry of fear and horror; but though they saw their master's danger, they were powerless to save him, as there was not a second's space for interference.

Caractacus just touched the lanista's breastplate with the point of his sword, and then, turning his hand backwards, struck him a blow with the haft of the weapon that sent him reeling to the ground.

Caractacus instantly bestrode the prostrate body of the lanista.

Then the barbarian spirit broke forth.

"Ha! Roman," he shouted, "I have you at my mercy."

With a triumphant laugh, he flung away his sword and retired.

———

CHAPTER VI.
THE GLADIATORS' DARLING.

THE gladiators beheld this unexpected termination of the contest with the utmost amazement.

Several of them ran to their defeated master, and helped him to get on his feet.

Ventidius rose, and shaking the dust from his clothes, darted a quick look of anger and vexation at the Briton.

"Vah!" he hissed, spitefully, "the cat-a-mountain fights like a savage, as he is. I'll tell ye what, my sons, while I was yet a gladiator, and before I set up a training school, I got my right arm broken by a fall. Since then I have always suffered from a weakness in the wrist, otherwise I should not have so easily succumbed to mere brute force."

"Be not angry with the boy, noble master," said Manlius. "You yourself provoked the contest, and you, for all your weakness, made some splendid play. It would have gone hard with the novice if you had been in earnest. Look how he bleeds."

"Did you hear, noble master, of the boast of your rival lanista, Phorbus?" rejoined Pandion, good-naturedly, wishing to aid and abet Manlius in our hero's defence.

"What tell you me of Phorbus?" scornfully retorted the lanista, snapping his fingers. "A man of straw, a wind-bag, who brags louder than Thersites, and is as big a coward. Could he ever stand against me in the ring? Answer me that, my sons."

"Never, master, never," chorussed his pupils.

"Well, Pandion, let me hear what he had to say," said Ventidius, his professional jealousy aroused.

"It came to pass in this way," rejoined the gladiator. "I met him the other day in the Circus Maximus."

"Was he alone?"

"No, he was surrounded by a crew of betting-men—all gentles, knights, senators, officers of the Prætorian guard—and amongst those present was your rich and influential patron, Narcissus, freedman of divine Cæsar."

Ventidius started.

"What say you—my patron Narcissus, was he of the company?" he asked, frowning.

"Upon my head be it."

"Well, proceed."

"The talk was of the Essedarii—the Britons and Gauls who fight from chariots."

"Indeed they are a novelty, and all the rage just now with the fickle populace," said Ventidius.

The gladiator continued—

"Phorbus was boasting that he had lately bought in the slave-market a youth from Britain whom he would back to drive the chariot of the sun."

"I know the boy he means," said Ventidius, "and must own he is a fine lad."

"The question arose whether or not he surpassed your novice here in strength and comeliness."

"There could be no question in the case," returned Ventidius, doggedly. "Caractacus is worth a thousand of him."

"So Narcissus maintained."

"I am glad of that," chuckled the trainer, rubbing his hands, "for Narcissus is a liberal man—a prince of patrons."

"Phorbus was obstinate in his opinion," continued the gladiator, "and offered to wager his fair slave, Nepthele, against your patron's Thessalian courser, Xanthus, that his Briton would vanquish every opponent of his own nation."

"What would you have? To anoint an ass's head is a waste of pomatum," sneered Ventidius. "Never mind, at the next munus (show of gladiators) I will pit my lad against his, and then we shall see who has the laugh."

Soothed by the subtle flattery of the two gladiators, Ventidius forgot his defeat, and recovered his good humour.

He turned to Caractacus.

The Briton stood with placid face and folded arms, supremely indifferent to the pain of his wound, or the crimson flow of the blood which trickled down his white flesh.

"By Pluto, thou art a gallant lad, Caractacus," he said. "I did not mean to hurt thee so much; but it was partly thy own fault."

"'Tis nothing," replied the Briton, smiling, "a mere scratch. I will bind it up, and to-morrow I shall feel no more of it."

"Here's money for thee, lad," said Ventidius, placing a purse in his hand. "Spend it among thy new comrades; but no excess. Get you to the fountain, and wash away the blood. Some of the boys will bandage your arm."

Then he added—

"Ilicet! you are dismissed for to-day, my sons. Don't abuse my indulgence."

"Long live our noble lanista!" shouted the gladiators.

Amid these cheers, which were as exuberant as those of a pack of schoolboys et loose for a holiday, Ventidius retired.

Relieved from the presence of their lanista, the gladiators abandoned themselves to leisure and enjoyment.

The brawny athletes flung away their weapons, resumed their apparel, and leaving the gymnasium, trooped out into the atrium.

This hall, or rather courtyard—for during the summer months it was open to the sky—was surrounded by an arcade, the roof of which was supported by square pillars, painted with foliage, as if in imitation of climbing plants, placed upon a pluteum or dwarf wall, surrounding the court.

In the midst of this open space, and planted about with myrtles, oleanders and flowering shrubs, was a marble basin, for the reception of rain-water, and further supplied by a fountain.

Meanwhile Manlius, Pandion, and several more came round our hero to congratulate him on his recent victory.

Most of the gladiators spoke high in praise of the Briton's skill and intrepidity.

Manlius alone looked grave, and shook his head.

"You are a good swordsman, my Caractacus, but a poor courtier," he said.

The Briton's frank face expressed the surprise he felt at this remark.

"I do not understand you," he replied; "have I done aught amiss?"

"I do not blame you; your conduct was natural enough," returned Manlius, with a shrug; "but then you might have done better."

The Briton's cheek grew red.

"I fought as well as I could, what more could you expect of me?" he retorted, "a barbarian, as I am styled by Latin insolence, newly come amongst you, and matched against such a practised fencer as Ventidius? Give me time. Remember your own adage, 'Rome was not built in a day.'"

"How you mistake me!" returned Manlius. "What I blame you for is fighting too well. Who ever heard of a novice defeating his own lanista, and that in a first trial?"

The Briton smiled disdainfully as he replied, "I am a captive and a slave; Ventidius bought me body and blood, to fight for his profit like a man and a gladiator, and not to fawn upon him like a spaniel."

Manlius coloured under this rebuke.

"By the gods, barbarian, in this you show a noble spirit," he said; "let it pass. Keep your tongue within your teeth; as yet there is no harm done, I trust. There are worse fellows in the world than Ventidius; he has some generous points about him. But come, my lad, you are losing too much blood—let us attend to your wound."

"What am I to do with this?" said Caractacus, holding up the purse; "it is of no use to me, the Roman dross! it will not pay my ransom."

He flung the purse away in stern contempt.

Pandion caught it as dexterously as the conjuror catches the flying ball.

"By Plutus!" he laughed, "you will learn the value of money soon enough, my hero. Say, shall I not disburse a few denarii on an amphora of Scian and Falernian, that your new comrades may drink to your health and good fortune? It is a custom amongst us, that if a recruit has money, he should 'pay his footing.'"

"Do with it what you please," returned our hero, smiling; "you have already taught me not to despise hard cash, since it gives the means of pleasing one's friends. Procure the wine; as for myself, my drink comes from the well-spring."

"Ho, Silo, there!" shouted Pandion; "where art thou, furcifer?"*

The man he called for was one of the inferior class of slaves, who waited upon the gladiators, helped to clean their armour, cooked their meals, did the household drudgery, and so forth.

The fellow, who was slightly lame, came limping up.

"Who calls so loud?" he said; "is it you, bully Pandion? what do you want now?"

"Hark ye, knave," said the boxer, "dost think thou couldst find the wine shop at the corner of the Via Planca?"

"What, the 'Dancing Faun,' kept by bottle-nosed Hilarus?" chuckled the fellow, drawing his sleeve across his lips; "I can find it in the dark."

"I believe thee there; thou hast found it when thou wast blind as well as lame—blind drunk, I mean," growled the athlete. "Dost mark what I say, thou man of three letters?"†

Silo nodded and grinned.

"I mark thee, Muscles," he retorted pertly; "I am to go the 'Faun' for a pitcher of Sabine."

"Sabine is swill for such pigs as thou, dishclout," responded Pandion; "we gentlemen of the ring drink nothing cheaper than Lesbian or the rough Falernian."

"Whose pigeon have ye plucked lately?" grumbled the saucy varlet.

"Shall I crack this empty egg-shell?" growled the boxer, laying his hammer fist on the slave's bald pate. "Wilt go and earn an obolus, or shall I give the commission to Demus?"

"I'll go to the Pillars of Hercules in thy service, illustrious patron—that is, for fairer words and better pay," returned Silo. "Make it a diobolus."

---

* From furca, a kind of stocks in the shape of the letter V, worn by slaves for punishment.

† That is, fur—the Latin for a thief.

"Fly then, my Mercury, fetch an amphora of the best Falernian, and the sooner you get back the safer for every bone in your body."

Pandion gave him some money, and the slave hurried off as fast as his lameness permitted.

Caractacus, accompanied by several of the gladiators, went to the fountain and washed the blood from his arm.

Manlius examined the cut and found it deeper than he expected.

"This may disable you for some days," he said. "I will get Callias, our surgeon, to look to it."

While he was speaking, a sweet, girlish laugh rang on the air.

Manlius raised his head.

His dark eyes softened, and a pleasant smile crossed his face.

"Hark, comrades," he said, holding up his finger, "do you know that music?"

"Yes," rejoined his fellows, "it is our little darling, Virginia."

"Yes, by Cupid's arrows!" cried one, a Greek, named Parmenio. "Where is she hiding?"

"The little witch! she has come for a peep at our new comrade," replied Manlius. "Go and seek her."

"Look where the wanton creeps from pillar to pillar, like a sunbeam," remarked Diomed, a dandy of the first water, and a man of sentiment.

Parmenio ran to one of the columns and dragged forth a young girl, blushing and laughing.

Caractacus just glanced at her.

On the moment the Briton felt an electric thrill—half pain, half pleasure—run through his veins, his cheek went deadly cold, and his heart fluttered.

The little blind archer had hit his mark!

Virginia, the lanista's daughter, though not more than fourteen or fifteen years old, possessed the development of maturer age—she was preeminently beautiful.

Her hair had the true blue-black gloss of the raven's plumage, she had fine eyes, full, black, well-fringed and melting; features regular and delicate; and a clear complexion was united to her other charms.

Her form was of an exquisite contour, though rather below than above the regular height.

Her feet were delicately small and pretty, as our hero watched them, cased in sandalled slippers, emerging from her robe of pure and spotless white.

As laughing and struggling she tried to release herself from Parmenio's clasp, every attitude, every motion, every gesture, was graceful in the extreme, and yet without affectation, for all appeared perfectly easy and natural.

"Soh! I have caught thee, my pretty bird," laughed Parmenio, dragging her along; "come, your struggles are useless."

"Virginia! Virginia!" cried the gladiators. "Stay with us awhile, pretty one."

The girl blushed like a rose, and pouted her witching lips.

"For shame, Parmenio; let me go, pray do," she pleaded. "You know I have no business here; it is against the rules. If my mother knew it, O, how she would storm! Now, would you, would you get me a beating?"

"Out on the old Hecate! Harsh as she is, she has not the heart to lay a finger on thee!" returned the gladiator. "Be a good girl, and stay with us just long enough to sweeten our wine with one touch of those honied lips, and we will open the net and let thee fly. Will you not drink success to our new comrade, the Briton?"

"Where is he—will he bite?" she asked slyly. "Are these Britons such very wild animals?"

"Let him answer for himself," replied Manlius, pointing to our hero. "There he stands."

Virginia raised her eyes, but upon meeting the Briton's steadfast, ardent gaze, she withdrew them, while her neck and face glowed with blushes.

Caractacus tried to speak, but he could find no words to express the new and wild sensations that stirred the very depths of his soul.

Surprised at his silence, Virginia again timidly raised a glance, and for the first time observed the bleeding gash on his arm. She turned white as death.

Then she looked fiercely round, her eyes sparkling like black diamonds.

"Who has done this?" she exclaimed in burning indignation. "Ye cowards! Is it thus ye entertain a lonely and unhappy stranger?"

"Fairest maiden," rejoined Caractacus, recovering himself, "do not blame my comrades, from whom I have received nothing but kindness. I got this slight scratch while fencing with our lanista, Ventidius."

Virginia looked at him wistfully, and a sigh escaped her lips.

She pressed her dainty little hand against her forehead, as though to crush down some painful thought that flashed through her brain, but instantly afterwards a smile broke over her sweet face like sunshine breaking through an April cloud.

"How well he speaks Latin!" she said naively; and added, "Will you tell me your name?"

"Caractacus."

"Juno! how harsh!" she said, with a pretty frown. "Yet no! it is a name fit for a warrior, it has a warlike sound like the clashing of shields."

She approached him, and continued in accents of enchanting softness—

"Let me look at your wound. I am a gladiator's daughter (woe the while!), and do not sicken at the sight of blood."

She laid her taper fingers on his sinewy arm; his youthful frame thrilled at the soft, warm touch.

The Roman maiden uttered an exclamation of pity.

"It is a savage wound," she faltered. "I have acquired some skill in surgery, let me dress it for you."

She dipped her handkerchief in the fountain and bound it over the cut.

"Wait," said she, "I will go and fetch some healing herbs that Callias gave me. I will return upon the instant."

She waved her hand and lightly tripped away.

With yearning eyes, Caractacus followed her sylph-like form as she retired.

"Charming Virginia!" "Dear, kind-hearted girl!" "Queen of all our hearts!"

These, and like expressions of genuine feeling, burst from the gladiators.

The Briton alone was silent.

His heart was stirred by emotions of gratitude and incipient love, too deep for words.

Silo now returned, bearing on his shoulder a huge stone jar.

"Evoe Bacche!" cheered the gladiators. "Here comes the wine."

"Demus, bring goblets," cried Pandion.

The slave thus named brought in the cups on a tray.

While this was going on, one of those brief and sudden storms, so frequent in southern climes, passed overhead.

Thick clouds lowered and the air grew dark.

"Now, comrades, fill up," said Manlius; "but first give me the sacred chalice, that I may make the libation due to Pluto."

It must be understood that upon their enlistment the Roman gladiators always devoted themselves to Pluto and the infernal deities.

A large, curiously shaped goblet, made of blackened iron, was filled to the brim, and handed to Manlius.

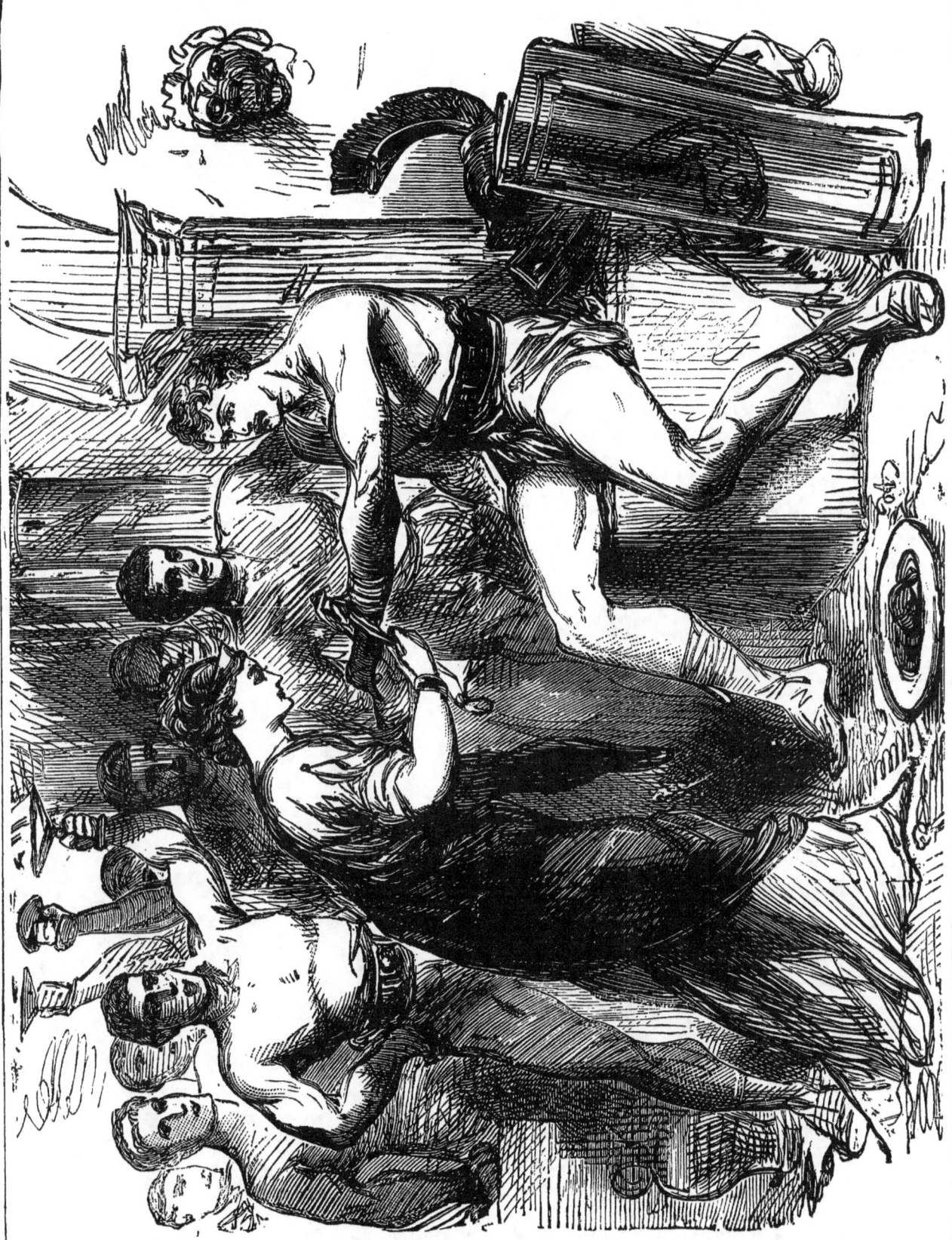

"LET ME LOOK AT YOUR WOUND. I AM A GLADIATOR'S DAUGHTER, AND DO NOT SICKEN
AT THE SIGHT CF BLOOD."

No. 2.

The gladiator placed himself in their midst, and his comrades fell back, forming a ring around him, and standing with folded hands and downcast eyes in a reverential attitude.

Manlius raised the goblet and held it at arm's length.

"O, Pluto, dark and inexorable god!" he prayed, "ruler of the realm of ghosts and shadows, whither all mortal footsteps tend, be propitious. Protect us, gladiators doomed to die, and dedicated to thy mystery. Thou Stygian Jove! sovereign of Fates and Furies, of all the invisible powers that rule the destinies of man;—accord us triumph in battle, fortitude in defeat and death. Freely as this wine is flowing so freely will we pour forth our hearts' dear blood to thine honour."

He emptied the goblet, and the rich red wine splashed on the ground like a stream of blood.

Scarcely had he uttered his terrible invocation when a vivid flash of lightning set earth and air in an electric blaze.

Regardless of this the gladiators chanted their solemn responses.

"Ater Dis! Thou dark god, hear and aid thy votaries."

The closing words were drowned in the loud, deep diapason of the rolling thunder.

Quickly as the scene shifts in a theatre, the aspect of nature changed, the storm cleared away as suddenly as it had come on, and the sun shone forth in unclouded effulgence.

"Did'st thou note, Manlius," asked Diomed, in an awed whisper, "how the thunder sounded from the left? That is a bad token."

"Absit omen!" returned Manlius; "why trouble yourself about signs and portents? let us eat and drink, for to-morrow we die! Cups round!"

The reckless gladiators were now laughing and gossiping as merrily as though they had not a care or a sorrow in the world.

They seized the wine-cup.

"A health!" cried Manlius; "let us drink to the health and happiness of the fair Virginia."

His comrades chinked their goblets together and responded with a hearty cheer—

"Virginia! Virginia!"

CHAPTER VII.

THE POWER OF LOVE.

VIRGINIA came back, bringing with her the simples and bandages she required.

She made the Briton sit down on the base of one of the columns whilst she dressed his wound.

Cup in hand the gladiators gathered round the youthful pair.

When she had finished her task, Virginia fixed her eye—dark, true, and tender, half languor and half fire—upon the Briton's stern but noble countenance.

She took a gold chain, with a pendant gem, from her neck.

"This is a sardonyx given me by a priest of Isis," she said. "It is a sure talisman against hurts and wounds. Wear it in the arena, for my sake."

"Sweet Virginia," he said, his lip quivering, "never shall I forget your kind attention—never while I draw the breath of life will I part with your precious gift."

"Virginia!" It was the first time he had called her by her own beautiful and appropriate name; she veiled her eyes with her dark lashes, and the mounting blood diffused a rosy tint over her milk-white shoulders.

Then, springing to her feet, she turned from Caractacus, and addressed the others—

"Adieu, brave companions; I must begone, or I shall get into trouble."

"Not till you have kissed the wine," said Parmenio, detaining her.

Virginia took a goblet and just touched the rim with her lips.

"Your health, gladiators!" she said, bowing. "May victory crown your arms."

"Hist! cave! beware!" cried Pandion, in a fright. "Here comes the Domina!"

"My mother!" gasped Virginia. "Then I am lost!"

She screamed and let fall the goblet.

Her terror was not unreasonable.

Many of the gladiators slunk off, and those who had the firmness and chivalry to remain looked sheepish and crestfallen as Lupa, the lanista's wife and their dreaded mistress, bounced into the atrium.

The "Domina," as she was always styled by the gladiators, was certainly a daughter of Titan, being fully six feet in height, and stout in proportion; but she was none the less a fine handsome woman, having a superb figure, a comely face, and a clear though dark complexion; her hair was raven and abundant, arranged upon her high, clear forehead in massy bands; her eyes were black, and sparkled with anger, and "vixen" was stamped in the contemptuous curl of her full, scarlet lips.

"Oh! the mighty gods," she cried—"can I believe my eyes?" she half shrieked. "You here, Virginia? Immodest wretch! how oft have I forbidden you to look at, much less speak to, any of your foolish father's gang of scurvy ruffians—scum of the shambles as they are? Yet here in the very midst of such loose companions I find you cheek by jowl, giggling, ogling, sipping, and smirking like a shameless—— Chaste Dian, dost thou see my blushes?"

"Dear mother, forgive me," pleaded Virginia, trembling violently. "I meant no harm."

"Not a word, minx—in with you," cried Lupa, seizing her daughter by the hair, and hauling her along. "I'll tame your wanton blood if there's any virtue in eel-skin."

Among the Romans a dried eel-skin was in common use as an instrument of domestic or scholastic chastisement.

Burly Pandion, the boxer, interposed between the enraged matron and the terrified culprit.

"Be patient, noble Domina," he growled, in what he meant for a soothing tone. "Just listen to——"

"THAT!" shrieked the termagant, fetching him a box on the ear which sounded like a clap of thunder, and sent him reeling half across the atrium. "Darest thou brave me, cut-throat? Oh! that I were a man!"

"I wish you were, Domina mia," groaned the boxer, as she clawed his face.

The Briton flung himself upon the enraged dame, and caught her wrists in such a vice-like grip that she screamed with pain, and crouched down upon her knees.

Caractacus nodded and smiled at Virginia, who took the hint and fled.

She found refuge with her father, and he, poor hen-pecked veteran, hid her away in an upper chamber, and kept watch and ward over her to save her from her mother's vengeance.

Lupa, astounded at the Briton's audacity, glared up at him in speechless wrath.

But he held her tight, and she cowered under his steadfast eye.

"Fair mistress, be just," he said, in firm but respectful accents. "If anyone is to blame, it is I. If you must strike someone, strike me—I alone am at fault."

He had called her fair, he spoke so gently, was so young and handsome, and more than all, she felt so powerless in his iron grip.

What could she do?

"You belie yourself, barbarian," she gasped. "I don't believe you."

"Not so; look at my arm. I got a hurt in a bout with the lanista. The gentle Virginia came to bind up the wound—Virginia pitied me. How can I fight for you, mistress? How can I win pearls for that raven hair, gems for those lily fingers, if my sword-arm is disabled?"

"Who did it, say you?"

"Ventidius."

"The fool! to damage his property in this way," she hissed, spitefully. "Well, you are a civil-spoken lad, but nevertheless, I will make my girl smart for her disobedience. Let me go. Do you hear me?"

"I will, mistress, when you have promised to overlook Virginia's offence."

"Gods! dares this slave to dictate terms to me?" she raved. "Why, 'tis but a boy, and I will teach him who has the mastery."

She made a desperate struggle to rise, but the Briton was too strong for her.

She writhed upon her knees, and wrestled in vain to release herself from his hold.

"Villain, would you murder me?" she shrieked, in impotent fury. "Rogues, dastards—help me! Ho, Ventidius, help!"

"Rescue the Domina! Down with the wolf of Britain!" roared several of the gladiators.

A dozen of them seized Caractacus, dragged him away, and dashed him against one of the columns.

With threatening gestures and infuriated looks the gladiators, excepting Manlius, Pandion, and a few others, swarmed round the Briton with intent to tear him to pieces.

Then, wonderful, but woman-like, Lupa interfered in his behalf, and kept his assailants at bay.

"There, there, that is enough. Keep back all of you," she said, swinging round her white, comely arm. "Don't be too zealous. Let us have no brawling. He is but a wild colt, as yet untamed. Leave your lanista to deal with him. Let the boy alone till you have to tackle him on the sand; then look well to yourselves."

The gladiators slunk back.

Lupa fixed a curious glance on the stalwart Briton—admiration struggling with a sense of defeat.

"Tell me, thou barbarian," she said, "in your native country do the men treat their wives with harshness and violence?"

"The gods forbid," answered Caractacus, with dauntless assurance. "There the husband loves and rules, and the wife renders loving obedience."

"Ha! whence came you?"

"From Britain."

"Ye lie!" she retorted, with a deep, bell-like laugh. "You must have fallen from the moon, for sure I am there is not a spot on earth where such a state of things prevails. Vah! what does a brat like you know about husbands and wives? Wait till you are married, if that may ever be."

She moved off a few paces, then stopped and looked back at him.

"Do not think because I spare you this once that I am not angry—that I have forgiven your daring insolence," she said, putting on a frown. "You are my husband's slave, and he and his belong of right to me. Beware!—my fingers itch—"

"Mistress," interrupted the Briton, with studied humility, "I will submit to any punishment from your fair hands, so you will not let Virginia suffer for her kindness to me."

"Well, well, I was ever too indulgent, and I will hear what excuse the child has to make for her misconduct, but never more let me hear you mention her name," said Lupa.

After a pause, she added briskly—

"You spoke just now of ornaments you could win for me by your prowess as a gladiator. I hope you may make good your boast. By Venus! you have already given me a pair of bracelets—

precious black ones. Had my husband an arm like yours—— But no matter—it is better as it is."

Then turning to the gladiators, she went on impressively—

"Do you hear me, knaves?—no tricks with the novice. Allowance must be made for such untutored barbarians."

She once more addressed our hero—

"Soh, Briton, farewell. When I have an hour to spare, perhaps I may send for you, as I am curious to hear more of your strange country and its extraordinary customs."

Gathering up her robe, with the mien and march of Juno she swept away.

When she was gone, Pandion, the boxer, burst into a roar of laughter.

"Ha! ha! ha! 'those fair hands.' Ho! ho! ho! 'pearls for that raven hair!' Oh! Momus and Jocus, this is a jest for the gods!"

"What say'st thou now, Manlius?" rejoined Diomed, smiling. "Is our Briton no courtier?"

Manlius joined in the laugh—

"I recal my words," he said. "Caractacus is champion of us all, for if he can tame yonder she-wolf he will subdue lions."

"Here comes Demus in hot haste!" rejoined Parmenio. "What's in the wind now?"

"Where's the Briton?" asked the slave, out of breath with running.

"Here," said our hero, quietly.

"The Domina has sent to know if, through neglect, you have not been offered food to-day. If such be the case, you are to go to the kitchen, where a repast is prepared for you."

"Miraculous!" cried Pandion. "In three hours thou hast scored three triumphs—Ventidius vanquished, Virginia enamoured, and the Lupa tamed. Oh! lad, thou art the very favourite of fortune."

He had scarcely ceased speaking, when the sound of trumpets and the acclamations of the populace rang upon the air.

The gladiators started like war-horses at the cry of battle.

"What does that mean?" asked Caractacus.

"Death to most of us," replied Manlius, gravely, "victory to a few!"

CHAPTER VIII.
THE PROCLAMATION.

TWO men belonging to the "Family" now came in from the vestibule, and were heartily greeted by their fellow gladiators.

The one who entered first was a tall man, whose lithe, graceful figure and sculptured features bespoke his Greek origin. He was handsomely dressed in a tunic and mantle of scarlet cloth, and wore a helmet and breast-plate of brightly polished brass. He carried under his left arm a small bundle of wooden foils, neatly bound together with a green ribbon, and in his right hand he held a scroll of parchment.

His companion was of a very different appearance, being short and thickset, with flat features, swarthy complexion, and a mass of coarse black hair tumbling upon his round, brawny shoulders, which were wrapped in a shaggy bear-skin.

Manlius stepped forward and shook the Greek by the hand.

"Welcome, Lycaon," he said. "What news from the circus? What was all that shouting about? The town-criers, I suppose, have been reading the *editor's* proclamations of the coming games; is it not so?"

Lycaon seated himself upon the marble rim of the impluvium, and wiped away the beads of sweat that lay like dew-drops on his rich clustering locks of silky brown.

"Yes," he answered, languidly. "The Furies seize the scurvy rabble—I thought they would have torn me to pieces. I was lugged hither and thither like so much paunch in a den of growling hyænas. I pray the gods that I have escaped the itch. Ouf! I am poisoned by the stink of garlic. Ask our sybarite, Diomed, to lend me his comfit-box to sweeten my breath."

"Here, lad, wash your mouth out with a draught of this elixer," said Manlius, handing him a goblet.

Lycaon drained the cup, and smacked his lips.

"Body of Bacchus! the real red Falernian!" he exclaimed. "You are in luck, comrades. Who's the patron?"

"Never mind that now," rejoined Manlius, impatiently. "Open your budget—let us hear the news."

"Ay, ay, your news; what of the games, Lycaon?" chorused the other gladiators.

The Greek, however, being hot and tired, displayed no inclination to be hurried.

He refilled the cup, and passed it to the companion of his expedition into the city.

"Drink, Gordian," said he. "We should have pierced a wine-skin on our way hither," he explained to the others, "but were prevented by the importunities of the rascal mob."

"No doubt great excitement prevails amongst the lower orders with regard to the coming show," Manlius remarked.

"Are you advised of that?" laughed the gladiator. "Why, look ye here, comrades, this is the sort of torment I have had to endure under a sun hot enough to melt the stones of the Capitol."

He went on with such pantomimic gesture and mimicry as would have made the fortune of a comic actor, causing great laughter amongst his comrades.

"First I was seized by a fat butcher fresh from the slaughter-house, all blood and grease, who bellowed in my ear like one of his own bull-calves—'What ho, bully Lycaon, give us the straight tip. Shall I take odds on the red scarf or the green?' Ere I had time to answer, I was pulled away by a little bleared-eyed cobbler, with a pair of girl's sandals in his hand. 'O, Lycaon,' he piped, "is Parmenio in good form? Is he matched against Manlius? Are they to fight to the death? Because——' Before he could conclude, I was pricked under the ear by a half-starved tailor, the mere shadow of a man. 'The gods bless thee, Lycaon,' he wheezed, while an earthquake cough shook his gaunt ribs. 'I am poor, miserably poor, but I have saved five hundred sesterces to lay on my favourite Pandion, the boxer. Is he to fight with Gallus? and which is the better man?' I was forced to shoulder my way out of the throng as best I could. 'Mercy, illustrious patrons,' I shouted. 'Hearken to the crier, and he will satisfy all your demands.' Then, having got clear, I fled home on the heels of Hippomones, pursued to the very door by the clamorous crew."

When the laugh had gone round, Lycaon raised his eyes, and asked with some curiosity—

"Who was that Briton I heard so much talk about? They tell me our lanista has brought in a novice of whom wonders are anticipated."

"Here is the lad," said Manlius, laying his hand on our hero's shoulder. "What do you think of him?"

The Greek gazed at the stalwart proportions of the British youth with frank and unfeigned admiration.

"One of the Dioscuri!* one of the twins of Leda!" he exclaimed. "Can he speak Latin? I see he has old scars on the front, but where got he that newly-bandaged wound?"

The gladiators vied with each other in their eagerness to explain, and, several speaking at once, gave a brief relation of our hero's encounter with Ventidius.

"Oedepol! what a feat for one so young and inexperienced," said Lycaon.

Then he added, with a genial smile—

"May I shake hands with you, young comrade?"

Caractacus warmly grasped his hand.

"Fortune was not blindfold when she fell in love with you, my lad," said the Greek, kindly. "Deserve well of her, and she will load you with favours. Bene vobis! I drink your health."

"But your news, Lycaon," cried the gladiators, fretting with impatience. "Come, let us hear about these games."

"Well," replied the Greek, "the munus will be given on the name-day of divine Cæsar, and if the proclamation may be trusted, they will be conducted on a scale of unexceptional magnificence and splendour; but there is the libellus, read it for yourselves."

As he spoke he carelessly tossed the parchment scroll towards them.

These libelli were something like our modern play-bills, containing the number, description, and frequently the names of those who were to fight.

"Let Parmenio read it," suggested Manlius. "He is the best scholar of us all."

The gladiators crowded round their comrade, as in a loud voice he read the momentous announcements, in which every particular was fraught with the import of life or death to his attentive audience.

"Three thousand gallant blades," commented Diomed, "on foot, on horseback, with war-chariots, blindfold, half-armed with net and trident, noose and cestus—was ever heard the like?"

"Never, since the days of Augustus," responded the others.

"Here figures your name, my Manlius," continued Parmenio.

"Ho! and against whom am I matched?"

"Against Telamon, trained by Antipas."

"A good fencer that," returned Manlius, thoughtfully. "What are the weapons?"

"Sword and buckler, and no body-armour allowed—only a light helmet."

"Good; I would have it so."

"Then for the secutores, who fight in arrayed numbers," continued Parmenio, still reading. "No less than four hundred pair of swordsmen, matched to fight at one and the same time. What do you think of that?"

"Euge! Bravo!"

"As for beasts, just listen: Ten Lybian lions, three tigers from Numidia, four elephants and a rhinoceros; and then, the bestiarii, some will be armed and fight for pay, but the greater part, it seems, are condemned criminals, refractory slaves, and the like, who will be exposed naked and unarmed to the fury of the savage animals."

"Vah! let that pass, I hate such brutal butchery only suited to glut the blood-hankering appetites of the mob," said Diomed. "Come to something else."

"Well, here is what will interest you, seeing it concerns yourself."

"Let us hear it."

"You are to fight as retiarius, with net and trident."

"That is no news. I have been practising how to cast the net for months past," replied Diomed. "But who is the mirmillo, my antagonist?"

"Ermanricus, a Dacian," replied Parmenio.

"I have never heard of him before," said Diomed.

"What have we here?" resumed his comrade, and went on reading—

"Essedarii: Arvirargus, a Briton, trained by Phorbus, will fight from a war-car in the manner of the Gauls and Britons, against an unknown youth, also a Briton, introduced by Ventidius."

---

* Dioscuri: Castor and Pollux, the twin sons of Jupiter and Leda. They were the patron gods of the gladiators.

"That must be you, Caractacus," said the gladiators.

The colour mounted to our hero's forehead, and his eyes glared with vengeful fire.

"Arvirargus!" he exclaimed, drawing a deep breath. "By the Stone of Judgment, this is indeed good news!"

"Do you know him?"

"He has been my rival and enemy from childhood," answered Caractacus. "It was his father, a chief of the Brigantes, who betrayed me to the Romans."

"Well, lad, you will find this a good chance for avenging your wrongs," said Parmenio, "for I see the battle is to be fought sine missione—to the death!"

A sudden change came over the Briton; his cheerfulness vanished in gloom, he bent his eyes upon the ground in moody thought. The mention of Arvirargus and of British warfare recalled to his mind all his past struggles and sufferings; the death of Iona, and his deep-sworn vow of vengeance.

The slave who had been sent by Lupa pulled our hero by the arm.

"Now, my Trojan," said he, "what message am I to take back to the Domina? Do you want any supper?—yes or no?"

"Do not decline the invitation lest you give offence," whispered Manlius.

Caractacus roused himself.

"I will go," said he, "for, to tell the truth, I am as hungry as a wolf in winter."

Our hero left the atrium in company with the slave.

Parmenio having finished reading the proclamation, the gladiators broke up into small parties, talked over the great event at hand, and discussed the merits of the different competitors for death or glory.

Manlius and Lycaon, linking their arms together, strolled leisurely up and down the shady colonnade.

Manlius observed a fine emerald ring that glistened on a finger of his comrade's left hand.

"What gem is that, my Lycaon?" he asked, smiling. "A new love-token from a new lover?"

Lycaon's cheek grew red, and he laughed with ill-feigned carelessness.

"No, it is the gift of my fair pupil—the Lady Julia," he answered.

"So your fair and illustrious patroness still continues to take lessons in fencing?" said Manlius.

"She does," replied his comrade, "and, I can tell you, is making rapid progress."

Manlius laughed.

"'Tis strange, this new rage amongst our Roman dames for masculine and war-like exercises—women have even fought in the arena during the present reign," said Manlius. "'Tis shameless and unwomanly, I like it not; yet I could not but admire the beauteous Julia, when to-day I saw her driving through the Forum in her chariot, drawn by milk-white steeds. She looked to the life a queen of Amazons."

"By Artemis! it would require another Theseus to vanquish such an Hypolita, when her blood is up, and all her quick wit, and womanish, neat dexterity, brought into play," laughed Lycaon. "You know my old thrust, comrade—thus! well, it would amaze you to see how quickly she has caught it up. I narrowly escaped a lunge that would have shamed me for ever, but a woman's weakness and vanity saved my credit."

"How so?"

"Vah! she should have come in under my arm—so—but Julia would rather perish than strike one graceless attitude. Posture—comrade! do I look well? how do I look? 'Tis that sort of vanity ruins them for fencers."

"Yet renders them invincible," returned Manlius. "Now tell me, Lycaon, what you think of an incident that came under my observation this morning. As Julia's chariot crossed the Forum, a dark litter, carried by Nubian slaves, passed by, the curtains close drawn. Julia bade the charioteer draw rein; the litter was also stopped at the same moment. A woman's white hand was thrust from between the curtains; I saw the proud Julia bend down from her chariot, and press the hand to her lips with every token of respect."

Lycaon changed colour, and glanced nervously around.

"A dark litter borne by Nubians?" he said. "Cannot you guess whom it contained?"

"Though it looked but a mean affair, no doubt it carried some lady of distinction," returned Manlius. "The marked deference and respect paid to its occupant by a haughty patrician lady, proves that; besides, now I remember, the white taper fingers I caught a glimpse of, sparkled with gems."

"It was no other than the new empress Agrippina," replied Lycaon.

"The gods! Can it be possible?" exclaimed Manlius, much astonished. "But why should she venture abroad in the streets of Rome, disguised and with such a retinue, for the slaves who carried her litter were meanly dressed, and glided along with a hurried and furtive step."

A peculiar smile flitted across Lycaon's handsome face, as he retorted quietly—

"Why do you ask me such a question? What should I know of the secrets of the palace, or the private intrigues of imperial personages?"

Manlius smiled in turn.

"I am not ignorant, Lycaon, of your own intrigue with that little black-eyed beauty, Nyssa, who is one of the slaves of the empress," he replied. "She sometimes lifts a corner of the veil that hides the mysteries of Cæsar's establishment. You break no confidence in imparting to me some of the curious knowledge you acquire so pleasantly, for are we not sworn brothers; when was I known to betray my trust?"

"Never, comrade, never; I know that I can trust you," returned his friend, gripping his hand. "And therefore I will whisper in your ear something that I would not for my life confide to any man breathing, save yourself."

"Thanks, Lycaon."

"Know then," resumed the Greek; "that there dwells in one of the lowest and most obscure purlieus of the city, a certain woman, named Locusta, one who deals in philtres, love-charms, and slow poisons. To her the empress frequently resorts, but for what purpose I leave you to guess."

"It appears, then, that Cæsar's new consort is likely to prove a fitting successor to the licentious Messalina," remarked his comrade. "But what could be expected? Agrippina, his own neice! No good can come of such an incestuous marriage."

"No good at least to Cæsar," replied Lycaon. "And that reminds me—I saw him yesterday."

"Where?"

"Walking in the gardens of the palace."

"How looked he?"

"Poor wretch! Bloated and flabby, his gross but enfeebled frame seemed the repository of every loathsome disease," answered the Greek. "He limped along at a snail's pace, supported on either side by two of his freed-men, a eunuch and a physician."

"Even in his youth, Claudius was an invalid, and little better than an idiot," rejoined Manlius. "Who ever could have predicted that he would one day wear the imperial purple!"

"Depend upon it, Manlius, it was to his want of capacity that he owed his elevation."

"No doubt," replied his comrade. "It is reported that the late tyrant Caligula, when he put to death so many of his kindred, saved Claudius for a laughing-stock."

"Yes," rejoined the Greek, "and I have been told that the kindest word even Augustus bestowed upon him was, 'Misellus' (poor wretch). This example was, of course, followed by the parasites about the court. It is said, moreover, that when Claudius came to table, no one showed him the least civility, and when he slept, as he sometimes did after meals, they would amuse themselves by pelting him with the stones of fruit, or by rousing him with the blows of a rod or whip."

"Woe to the empire ruled by such a man!" sighed the Roman. "Nevertheless, he is a good patron to us gladiators, provides rare shows, and handsomely rewards the victorious."

"Enough—let us cease this dangerous talk," said Lycaon; "it grows quite dark, and look, here Demus comes to light the lamps. I shall retire early to rest, for I must be up betimes in the morning, as I have business at the circus, where I have to assist in the preparations for the approaching spectacle."

"You are wise; let us drink one parting cup, and then good-night."

"No more, I do assure you," protested the Greek. "So good night, my Manlius."

"Good night, comrade."

CHAPTER IX.

A DREAM OF EVIL OMEN.

MEANWHILE Caractacus followed the slave, who conducted him to a neat little chamber near the kitchen, which was situated in the back part of the house.

Here the Briton found a plentiful repast spread out for him, consisting of a piece of kid's flesh, bread, and a cake of dried grapes, supplemented with a jar of rough Sabine wine. With keen appetite the youthful barbarian attacked this plain but wholesome fare, and made a hearty meal. He had scarcely finished when he heard a light foot-fall, and a titter of girlish voices. He turned towards the door.

Two saucy bright-eyed maids, slaves of the household, peeped in.

Caractacus was in no mood for fooling, his heart ached and his brain was oppressed by care and anxiety, yet his natural good-humour and gallantry so far prevailed, that he got up, and, stalking to the door, exchanged a few words with them and paid them some simple compliment.

Then, bowing his proud head, he strode past them with lion-like gait.

Bold and saucy as they were, the two girls were rather abashed by the Briton's cold, though courteous bearing—they blushed a little and laughed nervously, as they looked after his receding figure, so tall, handsome, and majestic.

"By the girdle of Venus! there goes a pretty fellow," lisped one of them. "What fine eyes, and then his hair! as bright as gold, and abundant as the locks of Hyperion."

"Vah, Chloris! you Greeks don't know how to judge a man," returned her companion, who was of Roman birth. "He is well enough, but there are handsomer lads in the school. Take Manlius for instance."

"No, I would rather leave him to you, my Lucia, who, I know, admire him so much," retorted Chloris, maliciously. "I confess him to be a splendid animal, but this Caractacus is a demi-god."

"Proh Puder! for shame," returned Lucia, trying to blush. "I will tell him what you say."

"I care not."

"Well, every one has a fancy," retorted Lucia. "He is not mine. Ugh! the barbarian, how vilely he speaks Latin."

"I like his accent," retorted Chloris; "it is like the rough flavour of a fresh plucked nectarine."

"You will dream about him to-night," rejoined Lucia, tossing her head.

"Then I shall lie the longer abed," laughed Chloris, "for I like pleasant dreams."

In the meantime, Caractacus, unconscious of the impression he had made, and heedless of all remarks, whether complimentary or otherwise, retired to the spacious chamber where the gladiators slept.

Some of them had already retired to rest, and our hero following their example, stretched himself upon his hard pallet, and soon sank into a slumber—profound indeed, but not undisturbed by distressing visions.

His dreaming ear rang with the uproar of battle: the shouts of the combatants, the clashing of weapons, and the thunder of the war-cars, the yells of the flying, and the screams of the wounded.

Once more he led the ranks of the British warriors against the Roman foe.

The trench had been crossed, the ramparts carried, and the fair-haired warriors, with their double-bladed axes and long biting swords, had penetrated the very heart of the hostile camp. The battle raged round the Prætorium, or general's tent.

Then his eyes were dazzled by the glare of flames, and amid blood, fire, and smoke, the dreamer fought on, until he felt a sharp pang in his arm, as a gold-crested Tribune dashed in upon him, with a swift and savage lunge. Then the whole scene passed away like a burning scroll, and in chains and gloom, the captive wept over the pale, cold corpse of his beloved sister in the dungeon belonging to the slave-market. Once more "a change came o'er the spirit of his dream," and Caractacus found himself watching on the moonlit banks of the Tiber for the coming of the fair Virginia.

At length a white-robed figure drew near, and he sprang forward to clasp his darling to his heart. Chill as ice, heavy as lead, the wasted form sank in his arms—the veil fell back, disclosing the up-turned features—it was the dead, ghastly face of the murdered Iona! A cry of horror burst from the lips of Caractacus, and he started from his sleep.

Raising himself upon his elbow, he glared around him in bewilderment.

The first grey beams of dawn struck in through the openings in the roof which admitted light and air, and dimly revealed the brawny figures of the gladiators, couched in every attitude of sound and healthy repose. The silence was unbroken except by their deep and regular breathing.

Caractacus shuddered violently, and cold beads of sweat bedewed his forehead.

"Iona—my sister," he gasped. "Well-deserved is thy reproach! Can I have so soon forgotten my deep-sworn vow of vengeance for thy death! Rest, gentle spirit! I will crush down every feeling but deadly and eternal hatred to the oppressors of my country, the murderers of my kindred. The tyrants may fetter my limbs, but they cannot enslave my heart. Roman beauty shall not entice, nor Roman valour subdue the free soul of Caractacus?"

The Briton pillowed his head upon his arm and tried to sleep again.

But sleep had fled his eyelids, and he lay with his eyes glowering upon his unconscious companions, and his brain oppressed by gloomy and slaughterous thoughts.

Gradually it grew lighter, and soon the gruff voice of Ventidius was heard, shouting to his pupils to awake, arise, and betake themselves to their daily exercises.

Like soldiers started by the trumpet-call to arms, the gladiators sprang up.

They stretched their sinewy limbs, yawned like rousing lions, then laughed off their drowsiness, and in all the glory of their manly health, strength, and high training, prepared to commence the labours of the day.

Heavily that day passed with Caractacus.

His wound was painful; but he could endure pain.

What rendered him miserable was that his sword arm was disabled, and he was fain to be a mere looker-on where he so ardently yearned to be a competitor.

Hurling the quoit, wielding huge clubs of heavy weight, vaulting the high bar, racing, fencing, and wrestling, in such exertions hour after hour quickly passed away.

The welcome meal-time came, and the athletes devoured, with the keen zest that is the best of sauces, an ample though rough meal of half-raw beef and lentils, drinking nothing but spring-water. Then all naked as they were, they stretched themselves in the shade upon the cool marble pavement of the atrium for a nap through the hot Italian afternoon.

Towards evening their toils recommenced and lasted till it grew dusk.

Then they were dismissed by the lanista, and dispersed, some remaining at home to spend the evening in gossip and jest, or joining others to stroll about to the taverns to hear the current news and enjoy convivial intercourse.

Among those who remained within doors, the conversation, naturally enough, turned upon the subject that all had most at heart—their chance and prospects in the approaching show.

"It will be your first performance with trident and the net, will it not, Diomed?" asked Manlius of that gladiator, who sat with folded arms, looking rather gloomy and depressed.

"Yes," replied Diomed, smiling faintly; "but I would to Hercules I had to contend with some other weapons."

"Still, in my opinion, the net-thrower, with his net and three-pointed lance, stands a better chance of escape than his enemy the secutor, for all his heavy armour and powerful sword," said Manlius.

"You may be right, and I have reason to think so," was the reply. "Never but once did I engage as secutor, and never was I so near meeting my death. My antagonist was a young noble of high birth, named Sextus Cornelius, who fought from motives of jealousy."

"When was that?" asked Pandion.

"It was in the reign of Caligula," replied Diomed. "If you like, I will tell you the story."

The gladiators willingly assented, and forming a ring around their comrade, listened with interest to his narrative, which deserves another chapter.

CHAPTER X.

DIOMED'S ENCOUNTER WITH THE PATRICIAN.

"THEN know, my comrades, that what I am about to tell you took place in the last year of the late reign, and shortly after I joined the 'Family' of our lanista, Ventidius.

"On one occasion, I gained great applause in the amphitheatre, and attracted the notice of a patrician lady who had won a heavy stake by betting on my skill.

"The Lady Camilla was a widow, young, wealthy, beautiful, fond of gaiety and pleasure, and inspired by an intense passion for the sports of the ring, gambling freely on her favourite gladiators.

"After my victory, I was sent for to her house.

She received me with the most flattering kindness, and proposed that I should give her fencing lessons—the ladies then, as now, having a strange liking for engaging in athletic sports and exercises. Of course I gladly embraced the offer, and my fair patroness would spend hours in wielding the dumbbells, throwing the discus, or fencing with wooden foils.

"As you may suppose, a lady of rank, beauty, wealth and independence, like Camilla, would not want for suitors.

"They came in throngs, the richest and noblest patricians of the empire, but she turned a deaf ear to all their solicitations. It was rumoured that her first husband, whom her guardians compelled her to wed, and who was a sour-tempered senator, old enough to be her father, had treated her with harshness, and that after his death she had made a vow never to marry again.

"At one time I flattered myself it was love for me that caused her to remain single.

"'Ah! Diomed,' she would often say, 'how cruel is Fortune! Why are you a slave and a gladiator, you whom I prefer to all my rich and high-born lovers? and what is the use of all my wealth and influence, that suffice not to purchase your freedom?'

"This was but too true, for, like so many others, I was the property of the state, and condemned to live and die a gladiator.

"Amongst her suitors was Cornelius, a tribune of the Prætorian guard, a very Apollo for beauty of face and perfection of form. To him she showed most favour, and he took it ill that I should visit her so frequently.

"One night, as I was returning homewards after dark—I had been carousing at a tavern with some of my companions—I was attacked by a gang of ruffians, at the head of whom was a fat eunuch, whom I recognised as his freedman, Narbo.

"I defended myself as well as I could, and fortunately my comrades were within call; they came pouring out of the wine-shop, and flew to my rescue.

"My assailants were easily beaten off; they took to their heels, leaving two of their number dead.

"The next day, unable to curb my rage and thirst for vengeance, I hastened to the mansion of Camilla, and, though denied access to her, I flung the slaves to the right and left, and rushed madly into the atrium.

"Here I found Cornelius and Camilla seated together on the same couch, and seemingly on the most amiable terms with one another. I afterwards learned that he had proposed marriage, and that she had accepted him.

"Trembling with rage, I bearded the tribune, and charged him with treachery and cowardice.

"Camilla seemed to be overwhelmed with confusion and indignation at what she termed my daring insolence.

"The tribune, on the contrary, was perfectly composed.

"He rose with dignity.

"'Friend Diomed,' said he, 'you are under a mistake. That Narbo, my freedman, and some of his myrmidons attacked you in the cowardly way you describe, I cannot deny; but it is the besetting curse of men in my station to be surrounded by wretches who hang upon their looks and seek to win favour by their detestable officiousness. I give you my word, as a soldier and patrician, that I knew nothing of this affair until the mischief was done. Nevertheless, I am willing to make you such reparation as lies in my power, either by a present of money or by fighting with you in the arena. Make your choice.'

"I eagerly accepted his challenge, for jealous passion made me unreasonable; besides, I thought of the glory to be got by vanquishing so high-born and distinguished an adversary.

"It was arranged that he should fight as a retiarius with the net and trident, I as a secutor armed from head to foot.

"I promised myself an easy victory.

"The appointed day came round. When shall I forget that day?

"The amphitheatre was packed with spectators, and the greatest excitement prevailed as we stood face to face—the gladiator and the patrician.

"Why should I describe the fight to you who know so well my style of fencing?

"Thrice I avoided the deadly cast of the net, and thrice chased my antagonist round the ring, amid thunders of applause.

"At length I thought of triumph, for what I had done before I thought I could do again.

"Yes, Diomed firmly awaited the cast of the fatal net. I made sure I could avoid it, rush in, and lay the proud tribune at my feet.

"How much was I mistaken.

"I felt the treacherous coils of twine enmesh me, and I was dashed helpless and hopeless upon the ground.

"My life was spared.

"Cornelius flung away his sword, and scornfully retired, regardless of the outcries that doomed me to death.

"His high position saved him from the consequence of this breach of the rules. The noble Roman broke off his engagement with Camilla, and, following Ostorius to Britain, fell with his face to the foe."

"Accept this moral, comrades: Beware the net and trident!"

CHAPTER XI.

CARACTACUS ENCOUNTERS AN ANCIENT ENEMY.

IN the course of a week, the Briton's wounds had healed up, and he was able to take part in his exercises.

One day Ventidius brought home with him a new recruit, a condemned slave, presented to him by a military tribune.

This man, whose name was Varro, had been one of the legionaries serving under Ostorius in the British campaign, but having committed some offence, he had been dismissed the army in disgrace, and delivered over to Ventidius in order that he might be trained to fight as a gladiator.

He was a dark-visaged, hang-dog looking fellow, but of most formidable appearance.

He towered by a head above the rest of the gladiators, being of well-nigh gigantic stature and of herculean mould and build.

Ventidius pitted the sturdiest of his pupils against him for wrestling and boxing matches.

He wrestled in admirable style, but excelled chiefly as a boxer.

Even Pandion, the acknowledged champion with the cestus, sustained a defeat in a set-to with the new aspirant.

Varro was not popular with his new comrades, who were repelled by his surly and taciturn disposition.

From his first introduction to the "Family," Varro had cast an evil eye upon Caractacus, whom he had formerly met in Britain.

Our hero in return regarded him with undisguised abhorrence.

"So, my bold barbarian," sneered Varro, one morning, as the gladiators were resting after some severe exercise with the clubs and dumb-bells, "it seems that you have not forgotten me?"

"Forgotten you!" retorted the Briton. "No, by the sun! You are the ungrateful traitor who betrayed my brave band to the Roman cohorts."

"What is this?" asked Manlius, interposing. "Have you met before?"

Varro laughed brutally.

"Ask him," said he. "I think I have given him some cause to remember me."

"What does he mean?" Manlius inquired of the Briton.

"I will tell you," replied Caractacus, and you shall judge for yourself of his conduct."

"Let us hear, Caractacus," said the gladiators.

"Our British warriors had surprised the outposts of the Roman army in one of the rocky passes of our Silurian mountains," replied Caractacus. "The invaders were repulsed, and utterly routed. They fled, leaving the narrow valley and the mountain brook choked with their wounded and slain. Well, by the order of the king, my father——"

"Your father a king!" interrupted the gladiators, rather incredulously.

"Ay, king of the ancient nation whom you Romans call the Silures," said Caractacus.

"Is this true?" asked Manlius, addressing Varro.

The Briton's cheek reddened, and his eyes flashed.

"Do you think I lie?" he rejoined, fiercely. "My forefathers reigned as kings through long ages ere Romulus and Remus were suckled by their congenial foster-mother—the she-wolf."

"Let Varro speak," said Pandion.

The Roman glanced at the Briton, and answered with a spiteful leer—

"It is not unlikely that they were the progenitors of our founders' wet-nurse, for they are more like wolves than men."

"By Hercules! you speak from mere spleen and malice," said Manlius, generously. "If this lad be a fair specimen of his breed, the race he springs from resemble lions rather than wolves."

"Vah! you have not seen them at home, or you would not say so," Varro retorted, secretly enjoying the torment he was inflicting upon the Briton. "Poor squalid wretches! they dwell in wattled huts, and run their wilds and marshes half-naked, or sparely covered in the skins of wild beasts, hardly less brutal than themselves. Kings! All are kings where there is but one degree of wretchedness. For my own part, I tell you flatly, comrades, I would rather serve as a common scavenger in Rome than flaunt the Cæsar of all those fog-bound, barren islands."

"Thou art no better than a base, lying slave, live where thou wilt," hissed the Briton, his eyes flaming with scorn and defiance. "But thy lies deceive no one. How much blood and treasure has it cost thy robber-race to subdue my fair and noble country? Is it yet subdued? And can you deny that the sacred and unerring oracles have foretold that the time will come when this despised Britain shall bear sway over an empire undreamed of by your bragging Julius in his lust of conquest."

The gladiators laughed at the barbarian's extravagance, as they thought it to be.

"Heed them not, my Caractacus," said Pandion. "Go on with your story."

"'Tis simple, and soon told," returned our hero. "After the battle, our warriors, flushed with victory, began to slay the wounded against my father's orders. I did my best to save the weak and helpless from the fury and revenge of their conquerors. While thus engaged, I came upon that wretch, who, covered with blood, and sinking with exhaustion, had dragged his limbs to the verge of the mountain stream that he might slake his thirst."

Every eye was now turned upon Varro, and our hero's narrative was listened to with much interest.

"Ere I could reach him," pursued Caractacus, "he was surrounded by a party of our soldiers, hot with wrath and carnage. They seized and dragged im from his hiding-place among the rocks, he the while shrieking for quarter.

The gladiators, whose code of honour enjoined them to "welcome the steel"—to meet death with a smile, laughed at the picture of the cringing wretch in the hands of the ferocious savages pleading for his life.

The blood rose to the Roman's brow, and his black, deep-set eyes scowled with shame and anger

"Thou liest, barbarian!" he growled, doubling his fist. "I neither asked for nor expected mercy."

"One at a time," remonstrated Pandion. "Let the lad finish his story, and then we will hear what you have to say."

"I threw myself between the enraged warriors and their intended victim," continued our hero, "when one of our chiefs, who, from his vast stature, was called Torquil the Giant, aimed a blow at him with his battle-axe. I interposed my target, which was shattered like glass, Torquil's axe cutting my shoulder to the bone."

"See, the scar remains," Manlius remarked, pointing to a blue mark on the Briton's smooth, white flesh.

"When my excited clansmen perceived that their prince was hurt, they were immediately cowed into obedience," resumed our hero. "By my command they formed a litter by interlacing their spears and covering them with their folded mantles. On this they laid the wounded Roman, and bore him gently to our camp. Here he was kindly entertained, our women dressed his wounds, the best fare our homely means afforded was set before him, and thus for weeks he dwelt amongst us, sleeping in my own tent. Was it manly, then I ask, or even Roman-like to requite our hospitality with treason and ingratitude?"

"No. The gods forbid. Such conduct were unworthy of the Roman name," responded the gladiators unanimously.

"Yet such was the return made by this caitiff Varro for all our kindness," rejoined Caractacus, with lofty scorn. "Honoured and trusted as a welcome guest, we set no watch upon Varro's movements, he was allowed to come and go at his own pleasure. After some time he disappeared; we became alarmed for his safety, thinking he might have fallen into some ambush, or have lost his way among the misty hill-tops; we scoured the country round in search of him, but found him not."

"Humph! I can guess the reason," muttered Pandion.

"Hear the end," continued the young British chief. "One moonless night our camp was surprised by the Brigantes, a hostile tribe, whose queen, the false Cartismandua, had formed an alliance with our common foe, the Romans. The first to break into my tent, sword in hand, was Varro, our traitor guest. I felled him with my axe. Then rushing forth, I rallied my warriors, and fighting our way through the burning tents we escaped to the mountains.

"The camp was plundered, and the Brigantes started on the homeward march, but with my warriors I overtook them, put them to flight, and recovered the spoil."

Most of the gladiators agreed in expressing their detestation of Varro's treachery, but a few, from motives of jealousy and envy of Caractacus, took the Roman's part.

Words ran high, and a brawl might have been the result, had not Ventidius appeared in the nick of time and put an end to the squabble.

Ventidius smiled grimly, and was not altogether displeased when he heard the case in dispute.

Since the defeat he had sustained at his hands, the wily training-master had formed the highest opinion of the Briton's skill and bravery.

It was a crotchet of his to think that two gladiators who bore a grudge against each other always fought better when brought hand to hand and foot to foot in the ring; he believed that they displayed more spirit and vindictiveness. Probably he was right.

Early the next morning he came into the gymnasium, and bade Caractacus and Varro prepare themselves to engage in a wrestling match, to be conducted with unusual formality.

As Varro stripped for the contest, the Briton eyed him with some misgiving.

The Roman was a man of such superior build and strength that even our hero's friends were doubtful of the issue of the contest, whilst his enemies chuckled at the prospect of his defeat.

Though somewhat daunted at the formidable appearance of his antagonist, Caractacus put on a bold front, trusting to his skill and agility for baffling mere brute strength.

As the combatants approached each other, the Briton's partizans uttered an encouraging cheer.

The wrestlers, before they began the combat, were rubbed all over in a rough manner, and afterwards anointed themselves with oil, which added to the strength and flexibility of their limbs, but as this unction, by making the skin too slippery, rendered it difficult for them to take hold of each other, they remedied that inconvenience, sometimes by rolling themselves in the dust of the ring, sometimes by throwing a fine sand upon each other, kept for that purpose.

Thus prepared, the wrestlers began their combat.

In these combats the whole aim and design of the wrestlers was to throw their adversaries to the ground.

Both strength and art were employed for this purpose.

Varro and Caractacus seized each other by the arms, drew forwards, pushed backwards, used all sorts of distortions and twistings of the body; locking their limbs into each other's, throttling, pressing in their arms, struggling, plying on all sides, lifting from the ground, dashing their heads together like rams, and twisting one another's necks.

The most considerable advantage in the wrestler's art was to make himself master of his adversary's legs, of which a fall was the immediate consequence.

One of the most difficult and skilful of the tricks consisted in stooping down to seize the antagonist under the soles of his feet, and raising them up to give him a fall.

Varro and Caractacus contended long and strenuously, the Briton baffling his more powerful foe by his superior nimbleness, but gaining little advantage on account of the herculean fellow's immense strength.

The contest provoked great excitement among the spectators, who now shouted for Varro, and again loudly applauded the swiftness and dexterity of Caractacus.

Varro, ashamed of being so long kept at bay by a mere stripling, began to lose his temper and his presence of mind.

Grappling Caractacus in a bear-like hug, he lifted him off his feet and was about to dash him to the ground, when the supple lad, slipping through his arms, caught him unawares by seizing his leg and tripping up his heels.

The gigantic fellow went down heavily, and lay half-stunned.

The gladiators, completely carried away by the Briton's success—as success is, in all ages, the god of popular idolatry—set up a shout of applause.

When Caractacus left the ring, he received the hearty congratulations of his friends Pandion and Manlius.

But what was more to the purpose, Ventidius shook his hand, swearing by all the gods that our Briton was the most promising novice he had ever trained, and with a little practice would become the Champion of the Arena, and win a cap full of money.

As for Varro, deeply mortified by his defeat, he rose and sneaked away unheeded, revolving in his mind a thousand schemes of vengeance.

This victory appeared, at the first blush, to be of great advantage to our hero; but he had made a dangerous and implacable enemy, and the time came round when Caractacus discovered that his triumph had cost him dear.

CHAPTER XII.

ZABA THE ETHIOP.

"WHAT HO! my noble Caractacus!" cried Manlius, one sunny afternoon, as our hero lay fast asleep under the shady colonnade of the atrium; "uprouse thee, sluggard, and come abroad with me and Pandion."

Caractacus sat up and rubbed his eyes, which were somewhat dazzled by the bright sunshine. Throwing back his yellow locks, he smiled cheerfully.

"What say'st thou, Manlius?" he asked. "Whither am I to go with you?"

"First to the amphitheatre. I want to see how the masons and workmen are getting on with the improvements and decorations of the building," replied Manlius. "Afterwards we will pay a visit to the vivaria, and have a look at the lions, tigers, ostriches, and other wild beasts and birds just imported from Africa."

Caractacus was on his feet in a minute.

"I am ready," he answered. "There is nothing I more desire than to see these things."

"Well said, my hero," returned Manlius. "But first go, and, having washed yourself and combed out that tawny mane of yours, put on the new clothes you will find ready for you in yonder room. Demus will help you to dress. This done, follow me to the entrance-hall."

"I'll be with you in the twanging of a bowstring," said the Briton.

He retired to one of the small recesses or apartments on the left and right of the atrium, where, assisted by Demus, he made his toilet, and viewed with pleased surprise the handsome raiment provided for him.

A light-blue tunic bordered with gold, an egg-shaped helmet of shining steel, sandals of gilt leather, and a short mantle of snowy white. Such a costume suited the blue-eyed, fair-haired Briton to perfection.

Lupa herself had chosen the garments.

"For money is to be made by that young barbarian," she argued, when discussing this matter with her husband, "and fine feathers make fine birds. The handsomer he looks, the more likely are our patrons to back him. They hang the white steer with garlands, you know, when they send him to be sacrificed."

"True, my dear, and serve up a calf's head with a lemon in its mouth," chuckled her obsequious spouse. "You are always right. The boy shall look as brave as a Prætorian trumpeter."

Caractacus, thus gaily apparelled, and looking quite princely, made his way to the vestibule or entrance-hall.

As a matter of fact, the vestibule did not properly form part of a Roman house, but was a vacant space before the door, forming a court, which was surrounded on three sides by the house, and was open on the fourth to the street.

Here Caractacus found Ventidius and Virginia conversing with the strangest and ugliest looking being he had ever beheld.

He was a dwarf, and an Ethiop black as night. His hunched yet brawny shoulders overhung his squat form and bandy legs; his huge head and hideous features were perfectly demoniac in their deformity and malignity of expression; his hair, that hung down to his waist in rugged elf-locks, was black, coarse, and lank, and without gloss; his little pig-like eyes glinted with a blood-red gleam; whilst behind his enormously thick lips his teeth flashed like polished ivory.

He was clad in a short garment made of a faded leopard-skin stained with blood and wine-droppings. He carried a heavy whip loaded with bits of lead.

At his feet gambolled a beautiful little lion-cub, not larger than a good-sized kitten, which from time to time he stooped to fondle.

"And is it possible to tame such creatures?" asked Ventidius, pointing to the cub. "Of a truth it looks harmless enough now, but when its teeth and claws are grown, I should scarcely care to venture near it even with two feet of good steel in my hand."

"Zaba loves such creatures, and they love him," returned the dwarf, fixing a gloating look upon Virginia that caused her to shudder with loathing, and cling closer to her father's arm. "Wouldst thou have it for a plaything, sweet mistress. I will train it till it will follow thee and fawn upon thee like a dog."

Virginia turned away her head.

"The gods defend me against such treacherous playfellows," she said; "as cruel as they are beautiful."

"Beauty is often cruel," returned the dwarf, rolling his glistening eyes over her lovely form; "but cruelty and beauty may be subdued. There is my tigress, Atropos—she hated and feared me once because it has pleased the gods to make me ugly and misshapen."

"If you are the gods' work at all," growled Ventidius, shrugging his shoulders. "And it is almost blasphemy to think so."

Zaba's eyes glittered like a snake's, and quite as snake-like was the hiss in which he retorted.—

"Yet, noble patron, there be men who pride themselves upon their strength and comeliness who would be glad to find in those they cherish the obedience I command from my favourite. Do you mark, Atropos has killed thirty men and women, yet she cowers at the slightest frown, or stern word from me. Well some tigresses are untamed," he added, with a horrible grin, pointing towards the door from which emerged the stately form of Lupa.

Ventidius started, flushed, and looked confused upon seeing his wife.

"Well, Ventidius, what is all this now? Why are you all here whispering and conspiring together?" she asked, in a shrewish voice. "For no good, that I'll be sworn."

"No harm, sweet chick, no harm in the world," replied Ventidius, drawing his daughter closer to his side, while he stared into vacancy to avoid his wife's keen, angry glance. "We were chatting with Zaba here about his mode of taming wild beasts—nothing more."

"He, the abortion!" retorted Lupa, turning away in disgust. "Send him off, it makes me ill to look at him."

"Do you in truth feel ill, mistress?" sneered the dwarf. "Some do who look on Zaba."

"Avert the omen!" gasped Lupa, waving her hand in disgust. "Send him away; he has the evil eye—the very sight of him makes me feel sick."

"Take thyself hence, thou hunch of deformity," growled Ventidius. "Await in the street, my lads will join thee presently."

The goblin-like dwarf made a low obeisance, cast one lingering look at Virginia, and then, shouldering his whip, slowly retreated.

"Now, where is Pandion?" asked the lanista's wife, briskly.

"Here, mistress," returned the gladiator, stepping forwards.

"I hear that one of your children has been sick," she said, not unkindly.

The gladiator, the mere man of blood, whose very trade was slaughter, how his grim face softened into almost womanlike tenderness at the matron's remark on his child.

"'Tis too true, mistress," was the reply. "My least of the little ones, our pet Phillida, has been sick almost unto death, but under the care of a worthy physician named Mathias, she is fast recovering."

"Well," rejoined Lupa, "I will send Demus round to your house with some comforts for the child, and mayhap, will pay your wife a visit in the course of the day."

Pandion thanked her for her kindness.

With all her faults of temper, the lanista's shrewish wife was not without her good points; she was free-hearted and liberal in her favours to those to whom she took a fancy, and frequently showed great kindness to the wives and children of the married men belonging to the "Family."

Virginia stole a bashful, timid glance at the noble young Briton, then blushed and looked down.

Caractacus gazed upon her with a fixed and inscrutable countenance, but his cheek went pale and his breast heaved.

Lupa scanned our hero's gallant figure with eyes that sparkled with bold and undisguised admiration.

Turning to her husband, she whispered something at which he smiled and nodded assentingly. Virginia watched her parents, and though she did not catch her mother's words, she guessed their purport. An irrepressible shudder shook her whole frame.

They were speculating on their chance of gaining so much sordid pelf by the outpour of the blood of that majestic stranger, every drop of which was dearer to her than all her own.

So brave, so beautiful he looked—but then so cold and indifferent, he would not cast one look her way.

"No wonder if he hates me," she inwardly sighed. "That he should hate all of my race, is but just and natural."

Now Virginia was a Roman maiden, with a Roman heart. War she looked upon as a reasonable and proper pursuit for a man of spirit. Without a murmur she could have armed her hero and sent him forth into the battle-field to do or die—to win renown or find a soldier's grave; but that he should be exposed like a slave and malefactor in the brutal, the degrading arena, to make sport for the blood-hankering mob, it was horrible.

"Ay, my Lupa," she heard her father say, "he is every inch a gladiator."

The hated word rang like a knell upon her heart, and she felt quite sick and faint with loathing and resentment.

Her father observed her start and change colour.

He threw his arm around her, drew her closer to his breast, and patted her cheek.

"How now, what ails thee, my pretty pigeon?" he asked, smiling fondly. "The lily has chased the rose from thy cheeks. Why art so pale?".

"Am I pale, my father?" she asked, smiling faintly.

"Ay, truly art thou, wench—thy face is as white and pawky as the face of yon statue of Eurydice just stung by the serpent."

"'Tis the heat of the sun, perhaps," she answered; "but I am better now."

"Go in, Virginia," rejoined her mother, sharply. "This is no place for you. Hence to your chamber."

Virginia made no reply, but instantly retired—not, however, without looking wistfully back at the Briton, who remained in the same position, his arms folded and his eyes bent upon the ground.

When she was gone, the training-master turned to the three gladiators.

"Now, my children," said he, "away with you to the amphitheatre, where you will meet my patron, Narcissus, who is to act as editor in the games. To you, Manlius, I entrust this letter, which you must place in his own hands; do it secretly; make a sign to him by lifting your hand —thus. He will comprehend you, and take you to some private place where you may confer in freedom. Do you understand me?"

Manlius nodded.

"He will send back an answer," continued Ventidius. "Be discreet, and above all, take no more wine than is good for you."

The gladiators went their way, while the lanista and his wife re-entered the house.

Virginia, in the meantime, had crossed the vestibule, and ascending a staircase, opened a little door at the top, which gave admission to her sleeping apartment.

The room was small, and its scanty furniture was of the most ordinary description, yet the whole formed a picture of simple elegance, which spoke well for the refined taste of its fair occupant.

On one side stood a low truckle bed, the pillows and coverlet as white as drifted snow; opposite to this was a small window covered by a kind of lattice or trellis work, and screened by a half-drawn curtain of spotless white bordered by a tasteful Greek pattern in dark blue. Hung in the sunshine, a bird was singing in its gilded cage, beneath which was placed a vase filled with fresh-gathered flowers that filled the place with their fragrant perfume. A chair, a clothes' press, and a table containing most of the articles of a lady's toilette, and ornaments, including a mirror of highly polished steel, completed the inventory.

Virginia softly closed the door, and stepping to the window, drew back the curtain.

The window looked out upon a kind of square, surrounded on three sides by buildings, some of them handsome enough, but others common lodging-houses, many stories in height and of squalid appearance, rented by persons of limited means.

Of such rookeries, Juvenal humorously says, "that broken ware flung out from the upper stories, would break one's head or indent the pavement." The poet Martial describes himself as living up three pair of stairs.

While Virginia was watching from the lattice of her bower, Manlius, Pandion and Caractacus issued from the house and stalked across the open square, followed at a modest distance, and with slinking gait, by the hideous black dwarf.

All unconsciously, Virginia had plucked a rose-bud from the vase of flowers that stood in the window, and as the gladiators passed, she knew not why, dropped it from her lattice.

The rose fell fluttering down on to the hard pavement below.

Absorbed in conversation, neither of the gladiators observed this little incident, but moved on arm-in-arm together.

Not so the Ethiop, Zaba.

His little ferret eyes at once sighted the blossom which dropped in his path.

He snatched the flower from the ground, and leering up at the window, grinned, salaamed, kissed, or rather munched the flower, and then dropped it into his sooty bosom.

Shuddering violently, Virginia withdrew from the casement, and flinging herself upon the bed, burst into a passion of tears—her heart torn by a tumult of conflicting emotions—hate, love, maidenly self-reproach and bitter mortification struggling for mastery.

DIOMED FIRMLY AWAITED THE CAST OF THE FATAL NET.

CHAPTER XIII.

A VISIT TO THE VIVARIA.

AT the exact moment when the rose fell from Virginia's casement, our three gladiators were walking abreast, Caractacus in the centre.

The Briton halted and turned half round. Pandion, who was in high spirits and in the full flood of conversation, impatient at being interrupted, tugged at his arm.

"Mehercle! what now, my skittish barbarian?" growled the boxer. "You fret and start as I have seen a hot-blooded Parthian shy when the meta is grazed by the chariot-wheels."

These meta were gouls which the chariots turned round in the races. The Parthian breed of horses were very highly esteemed by the Romans.

"I crave your pardon," replied Caractacus, a little confused, but instantly recovering himself. "You were remarking, and I agree with you, that there are worse trades than a gladiator's."

"None better," was Pandion's hearty reply. "What says the poet? 'With impartial foot, black Death strikes at the palaces of kings and the hovels of the peasants.'"

"True enough," replied Caractacus. "But what has that to do with our lanista, Ventidius, of whom you were speaking just now?"

"No more than this: it is a question whether a sudden and quick despatch in the heat of action be not preferable to the lingering miseries of old age or a dying bed," rejoined Pandion. "Ventidius ran the risk of such a death in fifty battles, yet came off conqueror at last. What was the result? He obtained his freedom, and what is he now?"

"A man of wealth and influence, if I may judge from what I have seen," replied the Briton.

"Are you advised of that?" said Pandion, with a chuckle. "Ask Manlius else."

"It is the truth," rejoined his comrade, thus appealed to. "Few men in Rome are more courted and dreaded than the trainers of gladiators, who have at their command bands of picked men ready for any mischief."

"Well, then, the same good fortune that favoured him may attend ourselves," resumed Pandion. "Who knows but that some fine day we may either remain in town and set up as contractors for the shows, or retiring into the country, spend our remaining days in peace and quietness."

"May the benign gods fulfil your wish, my Pandion," replied Manlius. "In the meantime we have rough work before us."

"You may well say that," was the response. "The age has not seen such a show as that promised for the birthday of Cæsar. The people are a tip-toe with expectation. In the fora, the streets and squares, multitudes assemble to quarrel and fight about their different favourites."

"Those whom the gods are resolved to destroy they first afflict with madness," returned the Roman, gloomily. "The sober, frugal spirit of the old republic has departed, and now-a-days the people spend all their earnings in drinking and gaming, in spectacles, amusements and shows. The Circus Maximus is their temple, their dwelling-house, their public meeting, and all their hopes. The gods alone can tell what the end will be."

"I must confess that I shall be glad when all is over," said Pandion; "for though I care not a jot for myself, I am anxious on account of my wife and children."

They had now reached the Campus Martius—so called because dedicated to Mars—enclosed by a bend of the river Tiber, and bounded by the Capitoline and Quirinal hills.

It had originally been used as a place of exercise for the people, but at the period of our story was occupied by buildings, the most important of which were the Mausoleum of Augustus, the Temple of Minerva, built by Pompey, the Pantheon, and the Amphitheatre.

Zaba, the dwarf, now came forward and took the lead.

Followed by the three gladiators, the Ethiop skirted the high, dark walls of the mighty amphitheatre, till he came to a wide yawning entry that led down by a steep incline, made for the passage of heavy vehicles into the vaults below the arena.

Here he stopped, and knocked at an iron-bound gate.

The loud barking of dogs now rang through the hollow passages within, followed by the dull and distant roar of the wild beasts immured in the subterranean dens; the noise waked the sleeping echoes, and they reverberated like thunder.

Then a heavy footstep was heard, accompanied by the clanking of keys and the continuous barking of the dogs.

"Back, Pluto!—down, Medusa!" thundered a deep base voice. "The Furies seize the brutes! Lie down, I say."

Then was heard the slashing of a whip, a howl, and the rattling of chains.

Someone then rapped on the inside of the door.

"Who is there?" was asked from within.

"'Tis I, Cimber; do you not know my voice? Zaba, the beast-keeper. Make haste and throw open the door."

"I could hear nothing for these infernal dogs," replied he, gruffly. "They scent a stranger—you are not alone."

"No, I have friends with me who come on business."

"Who are they?"

"Gladiators, belonging to the Family of Ventidius."

"Good, they are expected; wait a moment and I will let you in."

With much clashing of bolts and creaking of hinges, the folding-doors were at length thrown wide open, showing a broad, arched tunnel.

A man advanced, holding a flaming torch in one hand, a loaded whip in the other.

He was a tall, huge fellow, with a fierce countenance and a shock of yellow hair; his only garment was the loose hanging hide of a lion, the head of which was drawn over his shaggy locks like a cap or hood.

An iron chain girthed round his waist, and from it depended a heavy bunch of keys.

"So you have come at last, Zaba," said the gate-keeper, looking over the black dwarf's hobgoblin head at the three splendid specimens of humanity that accompanied him. "I am glad you have brought the lads with you; one you wot of awaits them with impatience."

"Where is our patron?" asked Manlius.

"In the editor's saloon over the Gate of Death," was the reply.

By this grim name the entrance was called, by which the combatants entered the arena.

"Wait here a moment and I will call for Pollio, the locarius, who will conduct you into the presence of my lord."

The locarii were attendants at the amphitheatre, whose duty was to conduct the spectators, according to rank, to their allotted seats; to keep order, and so forth.

Cimber moved off, and turning the corner of one of the maze of vaulted passages, disappeared.

Thus left to themselves, the gladiators remained silent and thoughtful, not a little impressed by the gloomy surroundings.

The darkness was made visible by the red glow of a solitary and half-extinguished torch stuck in an iron socket fixed to the rough and dripping wall.

"Ouf! a breath of fresh air," muttered Manlius. "This place is stifling."

"The mouth of Hades!" responded Pandion, holding his hand over his mouth and nostrils.

Zaba, the Ethiop, alone appeared in his element. He fondled the lion-cub in his bosom, and droned to himself some monotonous, dismal tune.

After the lapse of a few moments, which seemed to them an age of miserable suspense, the gladiators hailed the returning light.

Holding a torch aloft, Cimber approached with the locarius, who wore as livery a handsome scarlet tunic broidered with gold, and having the monogram of the reigning Cæsar embroidered on his breast.

Pollio seized the boxer's hand and shook it cordially.

"Eja, my Pandion!" he exclaimed. "How goes it with you, my hearty? You are making too much flesh. I trust you will pull off the next combat as well as you did the last, for you know I am your constant backer."

"I starve myself and train hard, Pollio, but I am not so young as I was," replied the boxer. "Yet I pluck up heart of grace, and trust I shall give a good account of myself."

"Euge, well said, my Trojan," returned Pollio, slapping him on the shoulder. "But who is this fair-haired lad you have brought. By Ajax, he will prove a handful for somebody!"

Pandion was about to expatiate on the merits of the novice, but Manlius interrupted him hastily.—

"We trifle time," he said. "Conduct us at once to the patron."

Cimber looked askance at the Briton.

"Does your new comrade speak Latin?" he asked.

"Yes," replied Manlius, "almost like a native."

"Is he to go with us?"

Manlius pondered a moment.

"I received no orders in that regard," he said. "But though bondsman to Ventidius, he has not yet taken the oath of initiation as a gladiator. I think it will be better that he should wait here until our return."

During this conversation the black dwarf had sat crouching on the floor, teasing the lion-cub as one might play with a kitten; he now raised his head, and turned his repulsive face towards our hero, darting a peculiar and mischievous gleam from his red eyes.

"Shall Zaba, just to beguile the time till your return, show the noble youth the vivaria? They contain many strange animals—beasts, birds and reptiles—which it is not likely he has seen before."

The Briton eagerly caught at the suggestion.

"Thanks for your kindness," he said. "There is nothing I more desire."

"Be it so, lad," said Manlius. "It is a strange and instructive sight. Meet us here in an hour's time."

Manlius and Pandion then departed with the locarius.

The Ethiop lighted a torch. "Come, my Phœbus," he said, with a fiendish grin. "Let me present you to some of the monsters with whom you may be one day brought face to face in the arena.

CHAPTER XIV.
HECATE.

ZABA, the Ethiop, led Caractacus down a long stone corridor, at the end of which was the partly open door of a chamber in which a light was burning.

As they drew near this door, deep growls were heard from within, and were repeated again and again by many-voiced echo.

The Briton paused, and laid a hand on the dwarf's hunched shoulder.

"Take care!" he said, in a half whisper. "One of your wild beasts has broken loose."

"Are you afraid?" asked Zaba, with a harsh, grating laugh. "'Tis only my pantheress, Hecate; she is so tame that she follows me like a dog. She will do you no harm while I am with you."

Zaba pushed open the door, and, followed by Caractacus, entered a vaulted stone room, lighted by a lamp suspended to the blackened roof by a rusty chain.

Scattered at random about the floor lay iron chains, spiked collars and long iron rods set in wooden handles. In one corner stood a moveable bronze tripod on which a charcoal fire was burning, shedding a dull, crimson glare and intense heat, and thrust into the embers was an iron rod glowing red hot. In a deep recess was a pile of skins, apparently serving as a bed.

Near the fire lay crouching the long, lithe form of a pantheress, her greenish yellow eyes fixed and glaring brightly.

At the entrance of her master with our hero, the tawny brute raised herself, and dragged her body along like a serpent, her belly close to the ground, her tail swaying like a pendulum in the air, her black muzzle convulsively wrinkled, her white fangs glistening.

As though distrustful of the presence of a stranger, she uttered a low, deep growl.

The dwarf stooped, and seizing the brute by the back of the neck, dragged her forwards.

"Come hither, Hecate," he said, imperiously. "Make friends with our guest."

But without heeding the visitor, the huge brute rubbed herself against her master, arching her back and tail and purring like a great cat.

"She's a beauty," chuckled the Ethiop, stroking the pantheress as she fawned upon him with sheathed claws. "I have had her since she was no bigger than that."

He pointed to the lion-cub, which was now gambolling about the place with all the mingled grace and agility of a playful kitten.

"She appears fond of you," said our hero.

"Yes, and I love her for her mother's sake," replied the dwarf, with a horrible grin.

"Did you tame the mother also?"

"Tame Atropos!" laughed Zaba; "Hercules would have failed in such a task. She was as fierce as one of Bellona's war-dogs—you see I know something of these Roman gods and goddesses. Had I pleased, I could have tamed her by a fetish of my own god, Obeah; but that was not my plan. I put a spell upon her though, and she got me my revenge."

"Your revenge! Upon whom?"

"Upon a bragging gladiator who had abused me," said the dwarf. "I went with him into her cage. By a secret power I possess, I made her crouch at his feet; he set his foot upon her neck, he thrust his arm between her jaws, he spurned her with his foot."

"And the savage brute offered no resistance?"

"None; I had cast a spell upon her," returned the Ethiop. "Encouraged by her submissiveness, the gladiator thought to distinguish himself by confronting her in the circus. His challenge was accepted. Ugh! how I exulted when I saw her tear him limb from limb!

"Poor Atropos!" sighed the dwarf. "She was pitted against an elephant, and the huge unwieldly monster trampled her to death. When I heard her bones crack, it went through my heart like a dagger."

The dwarf paused, and set his teeth hard, as he went on, savagely—

"I was not ungrateful to her memory—she had her revenge. I crept into the elephant's pen, one night, and killed him with a poisoned arrow."

"Come," said our hero. "Enough of this—you promised to show me the vivaria."

"I did, thou valiant youth, and I will be as good as my word," returned the Ethiop. "Follow me."

Carrying the torch, Zaba paced on before Caractacus till they reached a huge iron gate, or rather grating, through which some faint rays of daylight struck in.

Zaba extinguished the torch, and thrust it through his belt.

"What think you of this music?" he said, as he unlocked the grating. "I like it better than the singing of birds or the twangle of lutes."

The pair passed through.

They were deafened by an uproar of howls, yells, and roarings.

Caractacus felt his pulse beat fast, and his eyes sparkled with pleasure and curiosity as they passed the dens of lions, tigers, panthers, and other ferocious beasts, which roared, howled, raced and ramped in their narrow prison.

At length they came into an immense vault beneath the podium or gallery in which the spectators sat to witness the games.

It was lighted by large gratings in the outer wall of the amphitheatre.

Here the untutored Briton beheld beasts and birds of rarest kinds and infinite variety, such as he had never dreamed to exist upon the face of the earth.

It may be remarked that the exhibition of wild beasts was one of the most popular amusements in Rome.

The number of wild beasts killed in the arena during one day of the games, is truly wonderful, and were it not well attested, one might be incredulous as to the possibility of so many being supplied.

When Pompey dedicated his theatre, there was the greatest exhibition of beasts ever known.

There were seventeen elephants, six hundred lions, which were killed in the course of five days; five hundred panthers, and other beasts too numerous to mention.

On one occasion there were turned into the arena one thousand ostriches, one thousand stags, one thousand ibices, wild sheep, and other animals, as many as could be fed or found. At the period of our story—that is, in the reign of the Emperor Claudius—we find in Pliny mention of the boa-constrictor. He gives it the name of boa, and tells us that Claudius had one killed in the Vatican Circus; in the inside of this serpent a child was found entire.

The same author's description of the giraffe or cameleopard, exhibited for the first time by Julius Cæsar in his third dictatorship, may amuse the reader.

"The Ethiopians call it Nabis," he states. "In the neck it resembles a horse, in the feet and legs an ox, a camel in the head, and in colour it is red, with white spots."

It may be added that the ancients far surpassed the moderns in the art of taming and training wild animals.

Elephants were taught to walk and dance on tight-ropes, and Mark Antony actually yoked lions to his carriage.

No apology is needed for this slight digression, as it has a direct bearing upon our story, inasmuch as it will show that descriptions to be given in future chapters of the scenes in the amphitheatre and the hippodrome are by no means exaggerated or over drawn.

Caractacus wandered from cage to cage and den to den, lost in astonishment and admiration.

Quite an army of slaves and keepers to feed and tend the animals; while the flesh, grain and other provender consumed, would have sufficed to supply the whole population of a provincial town.

"By the Logan Stone!" exclaimed Caractacus. quite bewildered at all he saw; "I did not think there could be so many and such wondrous creatures in the world."

"Vah! this is nothing to the number and variety exhibited by the late emperor Caligula," returned the dwarf. "I remember in those days, when butchers' meat was very dear, the noxii, or criminals sentenced to death, were brought here in hundreds, and flung alive into the wild beasts' dens. But let us go forth into the open air. I will show you the pits, tanks, and aviaries."

CHAPTER XV.
THE LIONS' DEN.

LIKE one walking in a dream, the Briton followed his weird guide, who, throwing wide an iron gate, led him into a garden planted thick with trees and shrubs.

Passing down a broad walk under a shady avenue of forest trees, they came to a sort of enclosure ornamented with rock-work, in the midst of which was a pit surrounded by a low wall.

"Look down," said Zaba, pointing with his whip. "Here is kept the biggest and fiercest of the lions; they call him the 'Terror;' he has slain thirty men. Here, too, are his lioness and cubs."

Caractacus seated himself on the parapet-wall, and looked down into a spacious area flagged with stones, having on one side a covered den, and in the centre a pool or tank of water.

It was an imposing sight.

In all his colossal proportions, the lordly lion stretched his tawny length along, his thick matted mane buried between his outstretched fore-paws. Beside him, seated on her haunches, a gaunt lioness was gnawing at a large bone, while the offspring of the majestic pair, a brace of beautiful cubs, were rolling something over and over in their graceful play.

But why did Caractacus recoil, suppressing a cry of horror, while the blood rushed with a great throb to his heart, leaving his limbs trembling and bedewed with a cold sweat?

It was the sight of the remnants of the ghastly meal on which the monarch beasts had been feasting, at which his gorge rose, his blood ran cold.

Around were scattered human remains, fragments of dress and of hair, and a few bones crushed and broken.

Now and then the lion-cubs would stop in the midst of their gambols to lap from a little pool of blood, while the white, round, crackling, hollow thing they made their foot-ball was a human skull.

"Avenging gods!" ejaculated Caractacus. "This is horrible! Tell me, Zaba, what unhappy wretch is this who has met with such an awful fate?"

The Ethiop leaned over him, and hissed in his ear—

"So much for beauty and shapeliness—such will you be when the time comes that came to him. I hated him!"

"Was he a condemned malefactor?" asked our hero.

"No," returned the dwarf, grinning malignantly. "He had youth, and limb, and beauty."

"A gladiator?"

"Even so," retorted the dwarf, with a horrible grin. "He was a fine lad, about your own age and stature, and one who, like yourself, could boast of standing high in his lanista's favour."

A dark suspicion crossed our hero's mind.

"You say you hated him?" he said, frowning.

Zaba shrugged his huge shoulders.

"There was little waste of love between us," he replied. "He spurned me because I am what it pleased the gods to make me, and I returned him hate for scorn."

"I blame you not for that—the feeling was natural," said the Briton. "But how came he here?"

"How should I know?" sneered the dwarf. "Was I his keeper? Florus was one of those arrogant meddlers who could never learn the prudence of letting sleeping dogs lie. While provoking the imprisoned brutes, his foot may have slipped, and he may have fallen into the lions' den. This is a mere guess; what matters it to me?"

Caractacus turned upon him with indignation, and fixed upon him a penetrating look.

"Monster!" he exclaimed, "with mind as tortuous and depraved as thy body is filthy and deformed, thou hast done this."

The Briton was standing on the very edge of the wall that enclosed the lions' lair, and he tried to shift himself into a safer position, but the Ethiop placed himself before him and barred his way.

"Prove your charge, or it may go hard with you!" hissed the dwarf through his yellow fangs "What the gods have denied me in comeliness they have made up to me in strength; so look to yourself."

"Incubus! dar'st thou threaten me?" retorted Caractacus, with lofty disdain.

"What should I not dare? I have you in my power," sneered the dwarf; and he went on with an eldritch shriek, half-rage, half-triumph, "you think me a loathsome thing, an eye-sore to my fellow-creatures. I am to be shunned like some noxious reptile. I am to be buffeted, spit upon, abhorred. Hah! is it not so?"

"No, by the gods you wrong me altogether!" returned the Briton, with generous warmth. "That you have been afflicted by the inexorable hand of fate and nature, is no fault of yours—you cannot alter that; but the mind is your own, and given to you as a garden, which you may sow with poisonous weeds or plant with flowers."

"Flowers! rose-buds!" chuckled the dwarf, catching at the word. "Trust not too much to a fair face. 'Tis a wise saying, women have strange fancies; think you not the eyes of Beauty will ofttimes smile on her extreme contrast? There is a sculptured group in the Forum of a lovely Bacchante borne in the arms of a horned and hairy satyr more hideous than myself, while the blind Cupid runs laughing by."

This idea amused Caractacus mightily—he laughed outright.

"You! you!" he exclaimed. "Can any girl be in love with you?"

"Ay, and one for whose favours the proudest noble might humbly plead; yet see, she throws them at my feet," laughed Zaba. "Ecce sigmun!"

He pulled the rose out from his bosom, and waved it mockingly in the Briton's face.

"Where got you that?" asked Caractacus, turning deadly pale.

"It was bestowed upon me by the white hand of the fair Virginia," returned the dwarf.

Hot with passion, Caractacus threw himself upon him and seized him by the throat.

"Thou lying slave!" he ejaculated, shaking him.

"Two can play at that game," growled the dwarf; "and here I have the vantage-ground."

Caractacus felt the sinewy ape-like arms of the Ethiop twine around him, and he was lifted from the ground as light as a feather.

Our hero struggled might and main to recover his foothold, but in vain.

He was amazed at the immense strength displayed by his deformed antagonist.

Zaba pushed him forward to the margin of the pit, and held him there at arms'-length.

Excited by the angry voices and the scuffle above them, the lion and lioness sprang up, raised themselves upon their haunches, and scratched at the wall with a burst of frightful roaring.

Our hero was borne backwards, and his foot slipping, went over the wall, and he preserved himself from being precipitated into the lions' den by clinging with a convulsive grasp to the dwarf's shoulders.

"Confess yourself vanquished, and ask your life," snarled the dwarf, "and then I will spare you."

"Never, monster of spite and treachery!" cried the Briton, writhing to force his adversary back. "I am not vanquished yet."

By a violent effort, the Briton succeeded in freeing his right arm.

Then doubling his fist, he dealt the vicious little monster such a violent blow between the eyes as sent him reeling to the ground.

Zaba did not relinquish his hold, but clung to the Briton with the tenacity of a bull-dog.

They came to the ground together, and rolled over and over in the dust, the dwarf snarling, biting, and scratching like a wild beast.

For an instant the Briton was uppermost. Again and again he dashed the Ethiop's head against the stones with as little effect as if it had been a ball of solid iron.

Zaba entwined his arm in the Briton's long, yellow hair, and clutched it close to the scalp; then, extricating himself by dint of kicking and struggling, he sprang to his feet, and uttering a yell of triumph, dragged his adversary towards the den.

"Soh, my invincible champion!" he shouted, "I have you now. To the lions!"

But his triumph was premature.

A resounding blow fell upon his shoulder, which made him howl with rage and pain.

In the same instant, a pair of strong hands were laid upon his shoulders, and he was pushed off from his victim, and sent staggering backwards.

"Hades and Phlegethon! what is this brawl?" growled the deep voice of Pandion the boxer, as that worthy bestrode the prostrate Briton and kept the dwarf at bay. "Advance a step at your peril."

He helped our hero to rise.

Caractacus was much exhausted by his terrible encounter with the dwarf.

Some moments elapsed before he could recover his breath to speak.

Meanwhile he looked round to see who it was who had come so opportunely to his deliverance.

Beside him stood Pandion the boxer, and Pollio the locarius.

Gnashing his teeth, and shaking his fist at his intended victim, the Ethiop turned and tried to slink away.

But Pandion caught him by the arm, and held him tight.

"Not so fast," growled the boxer. "You shall not go till you have answered for your share in this business."

Then, addressing Caractacus, he added, sternly—

"Shame, comrade! I did not expect this from you. Are you aware of the seriousness of the offence you have committed?"

"Or the punishment to which you have rendered yourself liable?" supplemented Pollio.

"What offence? what punishment?" asked our hero, with indignation.

"Offence! Is brawling within these precincts no offence?" grumbled Pandion. "You may thank your stars that only friends have witnessed your misconduct."

"Yes, by Jupiter!" returned Pollio, "or you might have been tied naked to a post and scourged to death."

"What I did was done in self-defence," replied our hero, recovering his composure. "Withhold your censure until I have explained how this affray came about."

"Speak, lad," said Pandion. "I'll be sworn this

lump of malignity was at the bottom of the mischief."

"But first let me thank you for having saved my life."

"Your life!"

"Yes, that treacherous monster would have consigned me to a horrible death, but for your interference."

"Believe him not, worthy Pandion," said the dwarf. "I did but jest with him; but the splenetic barbarian is too brutally stupid to understand a joke; he flew at my throat like a tiger, and see how he has mauled me."

"You shall judge for yourselves, comrades, what kind of trick this villain would have played me," said our hero.

Caractacus then explained how the dwarf had attempted to fling him into the lions' den.

"What have you to say to this, abortion?" growled Pandion, shaking the dwarf till his teeth rattled again.

"I have no more to say than what I have told you already," was the sullen reply. "I was but jesting with the thick-witted fool; he took it in ill-blood—our tussle was the consequence."

"He lies," retorted Caractacus. "Ask him upon whom he last played a similar jest; ask him what has become of a man of your acquaintance, named Florus."

Pollio started.

"Surely you cannot mean Florus, the gladiator, whose sudden and strange disappearance has given rise to suspicion?" asked the locarius.

"Doubtless the same."

"Accursed slave!" growled Pandion, tightening his clutch upon the dwarf. "Florus was my sworn comrade, and if he has met with foul play, your life shall pay the forfeit."

"Release me, you ruffian," screamed the dwarf. "By my gods, I swear I know nothing of the man, or what has befallen him!"

"A reward has been offered for the recovery of Florus," said Pollio, speaking to the Briton. "Do you know where he is?"

"He is there!" replied our hero.

He pointed to the lions' den.

With awe-stricken faces the gladiators drew near the margin of the pit and looked down. When they caught sight of the remnants of the lions' grisly feast, the blood, the half-gnawed bones, the grinning human skull, they drew back with a cry of horror.

"It was an accident. I am not guilty," screamed the dwarf; "let me go, Pandion—I shall do you a mischief."

"Wretch!" cried the gladiator, in a voice hoarse with concentrated rage and vindictiveness, "you have done mischief enough already, but your last trick is played—you are caught in your own trap."

And seizing the malignant little monster by the waist, he hurled him over the wall of the den.

Zaba fell in the midst of the growling lions.

"All the gods!" gasped Caractacus; "what have you done?"

"An act of just retribution," replied Pandion, doggedly.

"An act of madness!" rejoined Pollio; "you will suffer for this."

"I care not if they serve me the same," retorted Pandion. My comrade is avenged, and I have rid the earth of a monster."

As though moved by a common and uncontrollable passion, they shudderingly approached the margin of the pit, and gazed down upon the awful struggle that was passing below.

With furious bound the lion and lioness sprang towards the prostrate dwarf as he lay half-stunned, bruised, and groaning on the pavement of the den.

The lion seized him at the instant he was recovering himself, and rolled over and over, holding the unfortunate wretch in his teeth, whilst he savagely tore his sides with his claws.

But quick as lightning Zaba drew a knife from his bosom.

The breathless spectators saw the knife glitter in the air; when it waved again it was crimson to the haft in blood, and a howl told that it had been driven home.

The lion abandoned his victim, roaring and licking his wound.

Zaba was on his feet in an instant.

He stood his ground calm and immovable.

His clothes hung about him torn to ribbons, but fitting tight to his skin glistened a shirt of steel tissue, as pliable as cloth, as hard as diamonds.

The lioness now came crouching towards him, swaying her tail, and preparing for a spring, while the lion came limping and roaring after her.

A bound, a yell, a scuffle, and then to the amazement of the on-lookers, the Ethiop, with the agility of a baboon, clambered up the rough masonry of the opposite wall, while the lions leaped and ramped after him.

"By Pluto! he has escaped!" exclaimed Pandion, wiping the sweat from his brow.

Zaba staggered a few paces, and then dropped on the very verge of the pit, and lay motionless—an inert, bleeding heap of humanity.

CHAPTER XVI.

CARACTACUS IS INTRODUCED TO A GREAT MAN.

"LET me get at him! The treacherous monster shall not live! I will fling him back into the den!" Thus growled Pandion, as Zaba, the beast-keeper, recovering himself from his swoon, and slowly raising himself upon his knees, turned towards the two gladiators, and shook his fists at them with a grating laugh of triumph and derision.

Pandion would certainly have fulfilled his threat had not the Briton caught hold of him and held him fast.

"Let him go, my comrade," said Caractacus, soothingly; "remember the caution you gave me about engaging in a brawl within the precincts of the amphitheatre—do not get yourself into trouble on account of a thing so vile."

"You did not know Florus," returned Pandion, shaking his head and drawing a deep breath; "he was a man to love and honour, so frank and free, so bold and noble-hearted. Look you, Briton, once I had him down—I fought as a Samnite then—it was before I took to the cestus. When he lay sprawling on the sand and held up his hand to ask the cruel mob for mercy, I made signs to some of my backers in the equestrian benches to spare him. No! the stony hearts! They only laughed and jeered, while the lanista stamped and tore his hair at seeing me display such disgraceful feeling—moral cowardice —as a fine Greek sophist told me afterwards. But never mind, we got well out of that trouble, for see you what I did. 'Up, Florus,' quoth I, 'grapple me once more—I cannot kill thee thus for Phillida's sake'—that's my youngest, dearest—she was so fond of him, and you too must be her playfellow, my hero."

He paused and brushed the tears away that sparkled on his long black lashes.

The Briton let him go, for he saw that Zaba had gathered himself together, and he was pleased to think the villain would decamp while the garrulous Pandion was finishing his story.

"He took me at a word," continued Pandion, with a laugh, "and bare-fisted we had such a merry encounter, boxing and wrestling, that the rabble were inspired with good humour, and let him off with a cheer."

Once more he glanced fearfully down into the lions' den, but instantly drew back, shuddering with horror.

"Come away," said Pollio, taking him by the arm. "This affair is too dreadful to bear contemplation. The Ethiop's turn will come, he cannot always escape you, some day you will get your revenge."

"You may rest assured of that," growled the boxer; "I will not be satisfied until I have hunted him down."

"We are wasting time," said Pollio—"look where Manlius comes to seek us."

The gladiator was seen approaching, and the three advanced to meet him.

"How now, comrades, what means this delay?" asked Manlius, sharply. "The chariot of Narcissus tarries at the gate to convey him back to the palace."

"Has he asked for us?" questioned Pandion.

"Aye, more than once," returned Manlius; "he grows impatient. Where is this Briton?" he said. "Why does he not attend at my command?"

Our hero looked up in surprise.

"Was this spoken of me?" he asked.

"Of you," replied Manlius; "wherefore else was Pandion sent to find you? Has he not explained?"

The boxer gave a brief account of Zaba's treacherous attempt upon our hero's life, and Manlius shared in his comrade's wrath and indignation against the malignant dwarf.

But there was no time for discussing the matter or forming any scheme of revenge.

"Let us make haste," said Manlius; "and do you, my lad, prepare yourself for an interview with a very great and influential personage. Narcissus is freedman and secretary to Cæsar himself, and consequently—a notable patron—one who can make or mar your fortune."

"Is he a Roman?"

"No, a Greek, with all the craft and subtlety of his race," was the reply. "They say he has amassed immense riches by plundering the Roman citizens—but that concerns not us."

"What does he want with me?" asked our hero, bluntly.

"Why, mark you this, my Caractacus," rejoined the Roman, laying his hand on our hero's arm and sinking his voice to an impressive whisper, "you are now one of us, and will be initiated in some of our secrets."

"You have secrets then?" said the Briton smiling.

"Aye, lad," returned Manlius, drawing himself up proudly; "can you believe that we gladiators are not a power in the land?"

"Why no," returned the Briton: "thousands of highly trained warriors—devoted to death—ought to have very great power, if they but knew their own strength and how to use it."

"Say you so?" chuckled Manlius. "But do not speak so loud. Trust me, the lanista who trains a large 'family,' like that to which we belong, is courted by patricians of the highest stations. Our master, Ventidius, is a client of Narcissus, who shows him great favour."

"But what is that to me?"

"You are a novice of whom report already speaks highly," answered the Roman. "Narcissus has already heard of your skill as a fencer, and wishes to see and interrogate you, whether from a motive of mere curiosity or for some weightier reason, I know not. That you must learn from his own lips."

"Let me advise you, lad," said Pandion, "to curb your proud spirit, for it is most important you should conciliate this great man."

The Briton made no reply, except such as was conveyed by an expressive shrug of his brawny shoulders.

While this conversation was passing they had mounted an immense stone staircase behind the podium, or gallery for the spectators, and now entered a long stone corridor, along one side of which was a range of doors admitting to the apartments at the back of the pulpit or tribunal where the emperor sat.

These were used as retiring rooms, whither the emperor and his chief nobles might betake themselves at pleasure, when fatigued by the sports, or in need of refreshment.

Before the largest of these doors a couple of lictors were on guard, with their fasces and secures on their shoulders.

The fasces were rods bound in the form of a bundle, and containing an axe in the middle, the blade of which projected from them.

These public officers always attended the chief Roman magistrates as a guard of honour.

It was always the duty of the lictors to inflict punishment on those who were condemned, especially in the case of the Roman citizens; for foreigners and slaves were punished by the carnifex, or common executioner.

The lictors likewise commanded persons to pay proper respect to a magistrate passing by, which consisted in dismounting from horseback, uncovering the head, standing out of the way, and so forth.

A richly attired slave now threw wide the folding-doors, and beckoned to the three gladiators to enter.

Bowing their heads the three comrades stepped into the apartment.

It was splendidly furnished. The entrances to various ante-rooms, on either side, were screened with silk hangings of the richest dyes, the walls were adorned with pictures, statues, lamps, and vessels of gold and silver, while the seats, tables, and couches were gilded and covered with silk and velvet.

Narcissus sat writing at a table, while four attendants stood at a modest distance awaiting his orders.

Narcissus was a tall, well-built man of about forty, but looking older. His profile was handsome, and wore an expression of great intelligence; his eyes were dark and penetrating, but his long curly hair and beard were quite grey, and the lines across his forehead and about his sunken eyes betokened the ravages of care and anxiety.

His tunic was of the finest material, and dyed with the richest Syrian purple; its border and loose sleeves were ornamented with a deep fringe of bullion gold.

A naked sword lay upon the table.

Its sheath, together with a princely mantle, were thrown upon a couch.

As our hero and his comrades entered the room, Narcissus threw down the stylus with which he had been writing, and rose to greet them with a courteous smile.

"Salve, illustre!" said Manlius. "According to your order I have brought into this presence the new member of our family—Caractacus the Briton."

CHAPTER XVII.

THE BRITON SCORNS A BASE REVENGE.

NARCISSUS regarded our hero with a keen, scrutinising glance, but with a Greek's instinctive admiration for beauty, wherever found, and in whatever form, his brow cleared and his face lit up with an approving smile.

"By the gods!" he exclaimed, "those murky isles of Britain produce a breed of heroes; who shall say but in some future age this noble race may not extend their empire far and wide, and set an example to the world of magnanimity and free institutions?"

He took our hero by the hand, and his eye kindling, surveyed him from head to foot with increased satisfaction.

"It is well," he muttered to himself; "this young Achilles will suit my purpose admirably."

He asked the Briton several questions regarding his birth and antecedents, to all of which he received modest and frank replies.

"And this kingly boy!" resumed Narcissus, speaking rather to himself than to Caractacus, "what has he done to deserve so harsh a fate? A slave—without rights—devoted to death!"

"True, illustrious," replied the Briton, "but though I am a slave, it was by the chance of war that I became so, and I am not alone in my misfortune."

"Alone!" Narcissus repeated bitterly. "In Rome a few are masters, but the mass are slaves. I was once a slave myself, and well I know how heavy are the galling chains of servitude—yet," he added, with a sigh, "I know not whether I have exchanged my yoke for one more light."

And in truth, Narcissus had sufficient reason for viewing his position with anxiety and apprehension.

Though the freedman and secretary of Claudius, the Greek had lost the favour of the giddy mob, and was cordially hated by the proud patricians, who envied him his immense ill-gotten wealth, despised him on account of his lowness of birth, and were perpetually conspiring to bring him to ruin.

His most violent and dangerous enemy was Cæsar's wife, Agrippina, a profligate and revengeful woman, the mother of that future tyrant and scourge of his country, Nero the Cruel.

She feared him, partly because he opposed the interests of her son, and partly because he had procured the divorce and destruction of the former empress, Messalina, a name that has become a byeword for all that is guilty and depraved.

By Messalina the weak and half-witted Claudius was urged on to commit the most frightful cruelties, while her debaucheries exceeded all that had ever been known, even in dissolute Rome.

With such audacity did she perpetrate her crimes that she compelled Caius Silius, her paramour, to divorce his wife, and to marry her, with all the usual solemnities, in the most public manner.

Claudius was at this time at Ostia, and such was Messalina's influence over him that his courtiers were afraid to inform him of the enormity she had committed.

At length Narcissus made bold to state the facts to the emperor, and, having roused his sluggish resentment, induced him to return to Rome.

The arrival of the emperor dispersed in an instant all the libertines and parasites who had thronged around Messalina; but, though thus deserted, she resolved to dare the worst, and sent to Claudius demanding to be heard.

As for the emperor, when his first outburst of rage had subsided, he appeared to be inclined to pardon his faithless consort.

Narcissus, however, fearing the effect of her presence on the weak mind of her husband, despatched an order, as if coming from him, for her immediate punishment.

The order found her in the gardens of Lucullus.

She endeavoured to destroy herself, but her courage failing, she was put to death by a tribune, who had been sent for that purpose.

When the news of her death was brought to Claudius he appeared to take no notice, and even inquired some days after why Messalina did not come to supper.

By this vigorous measure Narcissus gained great power and influence, but he failed in his attempt to persuade Claudius from contracting a second marriage with the infamous Agrippina, and, in consequence incurred her hatred and resentment.

Such was the man to whom our Briton was presented.

"Thou hast a soul above thy fortune, my lad," he said. "I like thy looks, and it may lie in my power to do thee service. I would speak a few words with thee in private."

He waved his hand to our hero's comrades and to his own attendants to leave the room.

The signal was instantly obeyed, and Narcissus and our hero were left alone together.

Caractacus was naturally rather astonished at this strange proceeding.

"What can this exalted Roman have in common with me, a barbarian and a slave?" our hero asked himself. "What can he want with me?"

The wily Greek put on his most serene and condescending air.

"No doubt you are aware that your lanista, Ventidius, is devoted to my interest," said Narcissus. "He and his maniple of gladiators which—I confide this to you—he is daily increasing at my expense."

"True, my comrades have told me that Ventidius is your client," replied our hero, "and that to him and to all his 'family' you have proved a noble and generous patron."

Again Narcissus smirked and rubbed his hands.

"I am pleased to find that he is not unmindful of the goodwill I bear him," he went on. "And there is not one of his brave fellows for whom I would not strain my power to the utmost to do a good turn—most of all for yourself, Caractacus, to whom I have taken a liking, none the less, but all the more sincere, because it is spontaneous."

This was very fine, but there was something in the Greek's oily tones that had a false ring.

Frank and ingenuous as he was, the Briton felt this to be the case.

He therefore answered coldly—

"Thanks, illustrious."

"It is a pity that one so young, and with personal advantages so great as you possess, should be given over to the brutal and degrading trade of a common gladiator."

"No, by the sun!" returned Caractacus, drawing himself up to his full height, "I would not have it otherwise. Since I must be a slave, at least it is some consolation to me to live and die a warrior. It grieves me to think that too often I shall be pitted against comrades from my own training-school, or against others whom I have no cause to hate. But I am told that it is a growing custom for the flower of the Roman nobility to contest in the arena with professional gladiators."

"Even so," returned Narcissus, grimly smiling. "Many of our patricians seek to win questionable honour in the circus."

"It is with such I long to do battle," replied Caractacus. "I shall consider it a proud day when I can set my heel upon the neck of such a Roman."

"You would do much for freedom?" rejoined Narcissus, giving our hero a peculiar look.

"That would I, indeed," replied the Briton.

"And much for revenge?"

"Yes, perhaps more."

"What say you then," rejoined his tempter, "if I could show you how by one bold stroke you may secure both revenge and liberty?"

Caractacus turned pale—then his heart gave a great bound.

"Speak, my patron," he faltered, "say what am I to do. I am willing to undertake the boldest deed that a man may achieve with honour."

Narcissus started at the last word, and a shade of displeasure crossed his face.

But he instantly smoothed his brow, and answered softly—

"Honour! What deed can be more honourable or more glorious than to avenge the wrongs of your country?"

"None, my lord."

"That is well said," rejoined Narcissus. "I will shew you how you may rid your native land of its most powerful and implacable foe."

"To whom do you allude?" asked our hero.

"To him who has laid waste your fields, burned your villages, and led your people into captivity," replied Narcissus.

"Can you mean the Roman general, Aulus Plautius?" returned the Briton, his brow darkening at the name.

Narcissus caught the fierce look, but entirely missed its meaning.

"The same—your inveterate foe and mine," replied Narcissus.

He paused, and there was an embarrassed silence.

At length, seeing that he was required to make some answer, Caractacus looked up and said boldly—

"Go on, my lord—I do not yet understand what deed you wish me to perform."

"Are you so dull-witted?" retorted Narcissus, restraining his anger. "Well, I will speak out plainly—I wish the man dead."

"Not more than I do, who have most cause to wish his death," replied Caractacus. "Would I could meet him face to face on the battle-field!"

"What matters where you meet him?" urged Narcissus. "If the wolf prowls in at your open door, if the serpent is found basking on your hearthstone, do you spare such guests? Is not your first thought to slaughter the one, to crush the other? Is it not a triumph, by your own hand and by an unaided blow, to destroy the destroyer of your country?"

"But how am I to strike such a blow?" asked our hero.

The eyes of Narcissus glistened at the question.

"He yields, he is mine!" such was the thought that flashed through the schemer's brain, as, clutching the Briton by the wrist, he hurried on in a low, excited whisper.

"Go to! I will tell you how it may be done with safety to yourself—a deed that will win you eternal renown, while it will make you free, rich, and happy for the rest of your life."

The Briton felt a cold tremour run through his veins, as he began to see the drift of his tempter's suggestion.

But Caractacus remained cold and calm, determined to hear more.

"Mark me! I could have chosen some other agent," continued Narcissus, "but I have selected you as one that wears the impress of a man capable of great enterprises. You are a Briton fired by a thousand wrongs. What in me would seem an act of baseness and treachery, in you would be heroism and patriotism. You would shine forth as a Brutus, a Scævola, another Harmodius."

"If I remember rightly those were men who slew tyrants?"

"Each one of them; and see how their names are honoured."

"By the great sun-god! not by me," returned Caractacus, breaking out at last. "They slew their enemies by a coward blow—took them unarmed, unwarned. Such is not a Briton's mode of warfare."

The Greek was cowed by our hero's look of lofty scorn, and it was a moment before he could recover himself.

"You fool!" he hissed. "I will put Aulus Plautius helpless into your hands—a ship shall be ready, loaded with treasure, to waft you home to Britain. One thrust—flight—escape!—how easy. Think of your murdered kinsmen, your enslaved countrymen. Fling womanish scruples to the wind, and think only of the brave man's compensation for every bitter wrong—sweet revenge!"

The Briton shook back his yellow locks and laughed in proud disdain.

"Pardon me, illustrious," he replied. "If you can set me hand to hand, and foot to foot with Aulus Plautius, either I will kill him, or he shall kill me. If you can restore me to my native land, at the head of a few hundred of my clansmen, I will assail his legions; but I am no hireling cut-throat, no secret stabber—I cannot do this thing."

Narcissus was taken aback: he studied our hero's countenance, and read there nothing but high and firm resolve.

He inwardly cursed himself for having broached his design so rashly to a stranger, though one of the band of Ventidius. His first impulse was to call in the guard and have the daring and noble-hearted youth slain on the spot.

A moment's reflection, however, sufficed to convince him of the danger and impolicy of such a course.

His only alternative was but to dissemble, and he was a master in the art of dissimulation.

He pretended to be overwhelmed with delight and admiration at our hero's magnanimity.

"I thank thee, great Jove!" he exclaimed, "that I am vouchsafed this sure evidence that the spirit of honour yet survives in this degenerate age, though it fires only the breast of a barbarian, from a far obscure island. Embrace me, thou noble youth; believe the great general Plautius is my bosom friend, and my proposal but a foolish device to test your integrity."

Our hero was not in the least degree deceived by these inflated protestations, but he called to mind the warning that his comrades had given him, and made a cautious reply.

"Your secrets, my lord, and those of my master, Ventidius, are safe with me," he said, fixing his steadfast blue eyes boldly upon the Greek's agitated countenance. "Think not the worse of me because, in this instance, I cannot execute your orders. You have spoken kindly to me. In aught else I am devoted to your service."

There was a tone of common-sense and straightforwardness in the speech which made more impression upon Narcissus than if our hero had affected to believe in his excuse.

The Greek felt that his confidence would not be betrayed.

He paid the Briton a hundred compliments, assured him of continued favour and protection, and would have forced a heavy purse of money upon him, but our hero steadily refused to accept it.

He then called for Pandion and Manlius, and told them to make much of their comrade, swearing that he was the finest lad he had met for a lustre, and would be sure to make his mark as a gladiator.

Then, throwing a meaning look at Caractacus, he put the purse, which our hero had rejected, into the hand of Manlius, who received it with a grin of delight.

He then dismissed his visitors, who left the amphitheatre—Manlius and Pandion in high glee and loud in their praises of so liberal a patron—Caractacus silent and thoughtful, his heart oppressed with a dull foreboding of evil to come.

Left to himself Narcissus paced about the room in violent agitation.

"A curse upon my folly!—shall I not call it madness—in revealing my dark purpose to this rugged barbarian?" he gasped, striking himself upon the breast. "Yet it is a noble boy—I do not think he will betray me. No matter for that—he refused my gold, I am in his power. He shall not live! But I must proceed with caution. It will not do to give offence to Ventidius and his gang. It shall be done quietly, secretly, how I know not yet; but one thing is certain, the lad is too honest to live—he must die!"

CHAPTER XVIII.

THE INSTRUMENT OF TREACHERY.

TIME passed, and Caractacus did not find it pass heavily with him; nor was his condition so wretched and hard to be borne as he had anticipated.

It was fortunate for him that, slave and exile as he was, he had fallen in with a master, who, though somewhat coarse in manners and rough in temper, was genial and kind-hearted, whilst our hero's bluff yet unassuming manner had won the good will of nearly all his comrades.

The training was hard and severe, but no member of the family complained of it, knowing full well that their very lives depended upon gaining that perfection of form and dexterity of eye and hand that alone could save them when the fatal hour arrived.

That hour drew nearer and nearer.

Vast preparations were being made for the gladiatorial show.

Besides the usual combats between man and man, and man and beast, there was to be a naumachia or naval engagement.

Born on the rugged coast of Wales, our Briton had always loved the sea, and had braved many a storm in his light coracle, and he felt the liveliest curiosity to know how such aquatic warfare as a sham fight could be conducted within the comparatively narrow limits of the amphitheatre.

The amphitheatre was so constructed as to be easily filled with water.

Some of the emperors erected buildings on purpose, which were called "Naumachia."

Two of the largest were built by Cæsar and Augustus. Suetonius speaking of the former tells us that a lake was dug in the form of a shell, in which were war-vessels of all sizes representing the Tyrian and Egyptian fleets engaged, with a vast number of men aboard.

Sometimes sea-monsters were swimming about the artificial lake, while the ships were almost equal in number to real fleets.

As the eventful day approached, Ventidius and his gladiators made it their practice to resort to the amphitheatre, to measure out their ground, perform their evolutions, and to rehearse upon a stage, as actors do, the parts they were afterwards to play in tragic earnest.

On these occasions Zaba, the beast-keeper, took good care to give the gladiators a wide berth, knowing that it was more than his life was worth to fall into their hands.

Nothing afforded our hero greater delight than to stroll through the vivaria and take a peep at the cages, dens, and cisterns in which the strange birds, beasts and reptiles were confined.

On these occasions Pollio, the chief-locarius, generally acted as guide.

About this time a gay young patrician, Caius Licinius by name, came often to the school, and mingled and fraternised with the gladiators in the most condescending manner.

He was a supremely handsome, though profligate-looking man, always splendidly dressed, and flush of cash, with which he was very free-handed.

He was what is called a "knowing character," an old bettor, one who was "up" to every trick and turn of the gaming world—a steady backer of promising swordsmen, familiar with the names and performances of the different competitors, and considered a "sure card" by the sporting fraternity who thronged to him for advice.

He paid great attention to Caractacus, prophesied great things on his behalf, and used all his art to get on terms of intimacy with him.

He even invited our hero to visit him at his country villa near Præneste—a pretty town about twenty-five miles from Rome.

"I cannot offer you such fare, my bully barbarian, as my great patron Narcissus could, though he does not disdain to crush a cup and partake of a simple repast at my humble country-house. For, what would you have? It is by betting on such blades as you that I have lost the better part of my fortune."

"Then, noble sir, the great Narcissus visits your house," said Caractacus, with a slight start.

"He does me that much honour," replied the young patrician; then added with a sneer—

"Though I am not so sure that the honour falls not so heavily on his side as on mine, considering the difference between our origin. Since the great civil war the whole framework of society is turned topsy-turvy, and now-a-days your noble of the Julian or the Mutian blood must dance attendance upon every manumitted slave, every pampered eunuch that springs to power like a mushroom under the sunshine of imperial favour."

"I do not see upon what compulsion a man of noble blood and free spirit must needs associate with those whom he despises," answered the Briton. "If nothing of his patrimony remains, there is yet his good sword. Rome exists by perpetual warfare. Let her impoverished nobles seek wealth and distinction on the field of honour, and not in the ante-rooms of a tyrant's parasites and harlots."

As the bold outspoken Briton uttered such noble sentiments the Roman winced.

The blood mounted to his cheek. His black eyes glowed, and his hand unconsciously wandered to the hilt of his dagger.

But he checked his rising impulse to strike the insolent slave, who had dared to speak truth, dead at his feet, and he laughed with well-feigned good humour.

"Vah!" he said, "I am not made of the stuff that heroes are cut out of, and I own myself rather a votary of gentle Venus than of rugged Mars. I take the world as I find it. Narcissus is rich, and I am poor. Narcissus is high-placed—I vegetate upon the few acres remaining from my ancestral estates. Narcissus is a man of wit, a good drinker, and one whose company I enjoy. So I pay court to him in the style of old Horace—

"At home, thou sipp'st Campanian wine,
 The racy Cæcuban is thine;
Here, juice of rich Falernian vine
 Thou ne'er wilt see."

"Yet none the less to such fare as my means afford thou art heartily welcome. So I say to him, and so I say to thee, my doughty Caractacus."

But our hero respectfully declined this gracious invitation, under the excuse, that, while he was in training, he could drink no wine, nor allow himself any relaxation from his sober, hardy, and regular mode of living.

When this was reported to Ventidius he was very angry.

He sought out our hero and roughly upbraided him for giving offence to such a patron as Licinius.

"Know you not," said he, "that Licinius is a man whom, above all others, we must keep on good terms with? His opinion is regarded as oracular; he is considered the best judge of a gladiator of all the sporting gallants that haunt the schools. He knows every charioteer, every athlete, every lion-feeder in Rome. He invites you, a slave, a common gladiator, to sup with him at his country villa, and you decline the honour. By the Furies! your impudence passes all I ever heard."

"I had my reason for acting as I did," replied our hero calmly.

"Your reasons, slave!" retorted Ventidius, working himself into a passion. "Hear him, ye gods! Why, thou knave, art thou not mine—body and blood as much my property as is this cane with which my fingers itch to beat thee; and dost thou prate to me of 'reasons?' What reason should you have but obedience and dog-like submission?"

Caractacus gave a broad fearless laugh.

"True, my master, and dog-like sobriety. A dog does not besot himself with strong drink; neither does your slave."

"Well, well, you shall find me just," returned the lanista, somewhat softened. "I will give you credit for having paid good heed to my precepts and to the example by which I enforce them. In the matter of temperance I would the rest of my lads were as moderate."

"Good, then," said Caractacus. "Do you not think I should prefer delicate viands and rich wines to the lentils and raw meat I get here—that the velvet cushions of a noble's triclinium are not a softer couch than the blanket and bare boards of our dormitory? I am well and strong, in fighting trim—

way should I impair that health and vigour which I have gained by so much toil and hardship?"

"Tell not me," grunted Ventidius. "Thou knowest well enough that I preach and practise temperance; but all extremes are folly. Thou art now in splendid condition, and a few cups of generous wine, even one night's debauch, would do you no more harm than a few days of rest and abstinence would remedy. Anything is better than passing a slight on such a valuable patron as Caius Licinius."

"One moment's patience," our hero answered quietly. "Do you not think that this haughty young noble has some motive for inviting a felon slave to sup at his table?"

"What motive can he have but to do me honour by encouraging the lads under my care?" returned Ventidius. "Go to, thou knave! I am proud to say that Licinius is my friend. All the world knows he is a spendthrift, and in my time I have done him good service. I have lent him money, and once stood bail for him when he was imprisoned for debt."

"Is it not true that I am matched to fight from a war-car with Arvirargus the Brigantian? To fight to the death. Yes or no?" asked Caractacus.

"Why, yes, it was so set down in the libellus," replied the lanista; "but what of that?"

"Are you aware that Licinius has wagered two hundred thousand sesterces that Arvirargus will kill me?" asked our hero, in the same composed tone.

Ventidius started back.

"It is a lie!" he roared; "the noble Licinius would not treat me so scurvily."

"Ask Lycaon if this bet is not the common talk at the baths, in the atria, in the fora—everywhere throughout the city."

Ventidius was thunderstruck as a new light broke in upon him.

Was it not possible that Licinius might intend to get rid of, hocus, or at least disqualify, the powerful British champion in order to save his money?

Such tricks were not uncommon among the "gentlemen" patrons of the arena.

But he was too much ruffled to abandon his hectoring tone.

"I *will* inquire of Lycaon," he growled, "and if I find what you have told me is true I will reward your fidelity, but if you have belied my patron woe to your head!"

With this he turned sulkily away.

Caractacus was right in his suspicions. The friendly noble was but a spy sent by the treacherous Narcissus to watch our hero's actions, and to contrive some means to destroy him.

CHAPTER XIX.

IN THE JAWS OF A CROCODILE.

THE gladiators of the family of Narcissus were gathered round a large pool or bank in which the crocodiles brought from the Nile had been placed in readiness to be exhibited in the naumachia.

The gladiators were naturally curious to see these ugly and monstrous saurians, as none had been shown since the time of Augustus, who had exhibited at once thirty-six crocodiles, besides several hippopotami.

Ventidius himself was present, accompanied by Caius Licinius and several other nobles.

The tank in which these monsters were confined was of circular form, surrounded by a low stone wall, and at intervals along the water's edge were shelving wooden platforms on which the huge reptiles could rest when so disposed.

There were twelve of them, several over thirty feet in length.

Some of them lay asleep on the platforms, others stretched their scaly lengths along, their ridged blackish-brown backs appearing just above the surface of the water, while others circled slowly round and round, flashing their little red vicious eyes, exposing their greenish-yellow breasts, and snapping their frightful jaws.

Much excitement and astonishment prevailed amongst the gladiators, most of whom had never seen such loathsome creatures before.

"Meherclé! what a sight!" whispered Pandion in the ear of Caractacus. "I wish we had that villain Zaba, the beast-feeder, here. I'll warrant his coat of mail would prove but a slight protection against the tremendous jaws of these harpies of the deep."

Caractacus smiled assent.

And now a messenger arrived calling for Ventidius, and informing him that he had been sent for by Narcissus.

When he was gone Licinius cast a peculiar look at our hero, who stood with folded arms, absorbed in contemplating the sluggish movements of the titanic reptiles.

Licinius turned to Pandion—

"Who are to fight these monsters?" he asked "None of your professional gladiators, I take it."

"The gods forbid!" replied Pandion. "To tackle a lion or an elephant is bad enough, but to fight one of these chimæræ would require the weapons of Perseus, and the invulnerability of Achilles."

"Of a truth it would require one with the strength and courage of Hercules to engage in such a combat," assented Licinius.

"Yet I have seen such a feat performed," rejoined a fine-looking man, with commanding features, scarred brow, and bronzed complexion, and dressed in splendid armour—he was a tribune of the Prætorian guard.

"Where, most noble Honorius?" asked several of the bystanders, speaking in a breath.

"In Upper Egypt!" replied the veteran. "I have there seen a meagre, skin-dried Ethiopian, in the shallows of the Nile, mount the back of a crocodile, larger than any of these, and ride it as you would an unbroken colt, and defy all its efforts to unseat him; then having tired of the sport, despatch the monster with one stab in a vulnerable part, and haul him ashore, with a rope and grapnel."

"Jove! we are not likely to witness such a deed of daring in the amphitheatre," rejoined Licinius.

The gladiators laughed and shook their heads.

"Not likely, indeed, illustrious," they murmured.

"I'll tell you what, now, I will make a bet with any man—with you if you like, noble Honorius," said Licinius, "that amongst all these braggarts there is not one who would venture to swim across this pool. I will bet five hundred thousand sesterces upon it."

"You may safely do that," retorted the tribune, smiling grimly, "for no one would be such a fool as to take up the wager."

Caractacus sprang forward.

"Accept the bet, noble tribune," said he; "I will dare the venture."

"You!" exclaimed the tribune.

"Yes, on two conditions, that I may be allowed a knife, and that you yourself, noble Honorius, will hold the rope by which I may aid myself to get out of the water after I have accomplished my task."

"*I* hold a rope for *thee*!" laughed the tribune. "Why, thou slave—"

"Even the tribune of a Roman legion might think it worth such a slight sacrifice of his honour —five hundred thousand sesterces—will you take the bet?"

"I will," returned the tribune. "But can'st thou be in earnest?"

"You shall see—no matter for the rope—give me a dagger someone."

"Here, take this," cried Licinius, handing his jewelled stylus.

There was a plunge, an uproar of shouts and cries—a surging and plashing of the waters, which now ran thick with blood where Caractacus had disappeared.

CARACTACUS STRUCK MADLY AS THE EAGLE WHIRLED ROUND AND BUFFETED HIM WITH HIS WINGS.

No. 4.

CHAPTER XX.

THE TRAITOR FOILED.

A BREATHLESS silence prevailed, and every eye was strained upon the bloody whirlpool in which Caractacus had gone down.

"He is lost!" muttered Licinius. "Narcissus will applaud my stratagem, and I shall win my wager."

Then followed a loud heart-stirring roar of applause.

Caractacus rose above water, shook back his matted yellow locks, and struck out boldly.

But he was allowed scant breathing time.

The scaly monster came to the surface, distending his monstrous jaws, and lashing the water into foam with his powerful tail.

A furious rush, and again the Briton dived, by a few inches only eluding the grip of the huge saurian.

He sank like a plummet and grovelled about on the slimy bottom of the tank.

Through the green gloom around he saw something glint and glow like a chain of fiery sparks.

He eagerly grasped it—it felt hard, and yet hung loose in his hand; even in that perilous moment our hero felt curious to know what it was.

A huge black shadow floated over him.

The crocodile was diving to seize his prey.

Caractacus darted to the top of the water, still grasping his trophy.

One glance sufficed to show him that he had clutched a treasure—it was in fact a necklace of large and precious rubies, which the treacherous Licinius had thrown into the tank.

The trick was almost successful.

Even in the passing instant occupied by the daring Briton in examining his spoil, a fresh crocodile made a dash at him.

Removing the knife from his mouth, and grasping it in his hand our hero swam quickly round the crocodile, which of course was comparatively slow in turning its unwieldly bulk.

Caractacus made a spurt, and flinging one arm over the monster's hard and rugged back, with his right hand plunged the knife again and again into its belly.

The crocodile in its pain beat the water into a cream, and then plunged headlong to the bottom dragging the Briton down and half drowning him.

Caractacus, however, loosened his hold and returned to the surface as buoyant as a cork.

A third monster now slid down from its resting-place, at the side of the tank, and taking to the water flew in pursuit of Caractacus.

Then followed a most exciting scene.

The Briton darted hither and thither like a fish, while the reptile swept after him with surprising agility; they flew through the water side by side, they plunged and rose again, they crossed and recrossed each other's track with surprising speed and agility.

"By the ferryman of Styx!" laughed Pandion, "If this were enacted in the amphitheatre how the mob would applaud! This barbarian seems amphibious like the monster in chase."

"He was born on the rugged Silurian coast," said Honorius. "The natives of that part of Britain swim almost as soon as they can walk; they take to the water like ducklings, and expose themselves in their light coracles in the roughest weather. They are thorough sea-dogs!"

"Look, he strikes another blow," cried the locarius. "Mehercle! If this goes on we shall not have a crocodile left for the spectacle."

Licinius changed colour and quivered with secret rage and mortification.

"You will lose your bet, my Licinius," said the tribune, turning with a smile to the young patrician.

"That remains to be seen," answered Licinius, sulkily.

Then his face brightened up and he stretched forth his hand.

"At last!" he shouted, with malicious glee. "At last the monster has caught the rash fool. Look! look! he is in the jaws of the crocodile—his thigh is covered with blood."

Such indeed was the case, the Briton grown more bold by impunity, swam right across the crocodile's path, the reptile made a rush at him and made a snap at his leg, just grazing it and causing the blood to flow.

But, by a sudden and violent effort, Caractacus got clear, and made for the side of the tank.

The spectators roared out in triumph, and were so vociferous that they did not hear the Briton call for them to throw him the rope.

Manlius and Pandion at once saw our hero's peril, and in the same instant seized a coil of rope that lay at hand, and threw one end of it into the water.

Honorius remembering his half promise to Caractacus, advanced to assist them.

But quick as thought Licinius interposed.

"Hark ye, my lads," he whispered; "help me to save my money and I will divide it between you. Give me the rope."

Pandion scowled darkly.

"What and leave our comrade to perish!" he grunted. "Not for the wealth of Crœsus!"

Honorius took the rope.

"Let me help you, noble tribune," cried Licinius, eagerly.

"Not for thrice my bet would I have harm befall the gallant Briton."

Honorius gave him a meaning look.

"Not so, Licinius," he said, quietly. "This is my business, not yours."

Meanwhile Caractacus was engaged in a desperate struggle to escape the enraged monsters in pursuit of him.

He was forced to swim round and round, and twice he failed to catch the trailing rope.

The excitement among the spectators now grew intense, they hailed the daring swimmer with encouraging cheers.

At length our hero succeeded in gaining a firm hold of the rope.

A dozen brawny arms were extended to his aid, and in a moment Caractacus was hauled up and stood erect and smiling on the margin of the pool.

His comrades cheered him to the echo.

Though inwardly chafing with rage, Licinius disguised his feelings, and clapped our hero on the shoulder.

"I protest thou art a second Hercules," he said, with well-feigned good humour—"one who would swim the Styx and drag the bull-dog Cerberus to upper earth. Well, I never more fairly lost a wager."

"Here is your necklace," said our hero.

"Nay, keep it, lad," laughed the tribune; "thou hast earned it dearly enough."

"Assuredly," rejoined Licinius, though with an ill grace. "Keep it or give it to the dark-eyed daughter of Ventidius."

Caractacus flushed slightly, but the idea seemed to please him—at any rate he put the gems into his bosom.

"Thou art a noble lad," said Honorius, addressing our hero. "Art a slave, or hast thou taken to the degrading and unnatural trade of a gladiator of thine own free choice?"

"I am a slave, condemned to fight in the arena."

Honorius frowned.

"A criminal!" he exclaimed.

"Even so," replied Caractacus, grimly.

"What was your offence?"

Caractacus sighed.

"Would the deed were to do again," he answered sadly. But the occasion will never more recur—my sister is now beyond the reach of Roman insult."

"Your sister?"

"She is dead. Well, for her, that I have brought myself to think so," replied the Briton, his lips quivering. "While on our voyage from Britain she was insulted by a Roman centurion; I slew the dastard. Had you been in my place, noble tribune, you would have done the same."

"You should have left his punishment to the chief officer of his cohort," replied Honorius. "But yet I do not blame you. Well, I will represent your case in high quarters, but can make no promise of any good result. However, here is gold for thee to broach a wine-skin with thy comrades."

He thrust some broad pieces into our hero's hand.

"Vivat Honorius! Long live our noble patron!" cheered the gladiators.

Ventidius now came back, and seeing Caractacus hurt and bleeding, started aghast, and angrily inquired of his pupils how this had come about. Pandion explained, making the best of the affair.

But the lanista was in no wise appeased. He shook his fist in his novice's face.

"Dog! pig!" he hissed. "Wilt thou cheat me thus? Was it for this I took so much pains with thy training, that I have licked thee into shape as a bear licks her cub, that thou must expose thyself to every hair-breadth 'scape that reckless patrons urge thee too, so that when the time comes for thee to appear in the arena thou wilt be as halt and lame as I was after my fiftieth victory."

Now Caractacus seldom lost his temper with his choleric lanista.

On the contrary, he treated him with a studied, half-mocking deference, that had in it something akin to disdain, and Ventidius, for all his bluster, stood in no little awe of his stalwart and princely pupil.

"Be easy, my master," he said, quietly. "There is no harm done; I have got only a few scratches hardly skin-deep."

"No matter, I will not have you disfigure yourself in this way," retorted Ventidius. "Never again will I trust you out of my sight. To your charge, Manlius, I henceforth commit this wild colt. Look to him, for I shall hold you responsible if he gets into further mischief."

Then pushing Caractacus, he added, sternly—

"Home, you knave! I will take care you come not abroad again."

Honorius interposed, and soothed the lanista's anger by a few well-timed compliments and a liberal present of money.

But Ventidius was not satisfied until he had hurried his refractory novice from the amphitheatre, and got him safely home.

CHAPTER XXI.

THE NECKLACE OF RUBIES.

HYPHAX, the surly, one-eyed porter, opened the door.

"Visitors," he said, gruffly.

"Who are they?" asked Ventidius.

"Philomenes, the sculptor, and the physician, Mathias."

"Good," said Ventidius. "Where have you bestowed them?"

"In the peristyle with the domina."

"I will go to them," said Ventidius. "As for you, Caractacus, go wash the blood from your limbs, change your wet clothes for dry ones, and make yourself decent. I may have occasion to send for you."

Ventidius then passed on through the house till he came to the peristyle, which was situated at the back of the premises.

It was a sort of court-yard, surrounded by Doric columns, and having a small garden in the centre. On the right was the triclinium or dining-room,

adjoining the kitchen, on the left the cubicula and other rooms for the use of the family.

Here the lanista found Philomenes and Mathias seated at a table, with a jar of wine and a basket of fruit before them, while Lupa hovered about, laughing and chattering, filling their cups and acting the part of a hospitable hostess.

Ventidius seated himself at the head of the table, and poured out a cup of wine.

"Bene vobis!" I drink your health, my patrons," he said, heartily. "I am right glad to see you both. If you want models for your sculpture, worthy Philomenes, you will find amongst my lads such form and condition as you will find in no other ludus (training school) in Rome. I never trained so fine a maniple."

"Report speaks highly of them," replied Philomenes. "But there is one youth amongst them—a Briton—who surpasses all the rest."

"You mean Caractacus, and you give him no more than his due," was the reply. "He will serve you as a model for Achilles."

"One object of my visit, good Ventidius, was to ask you to allow this Briton to accompany me home. I wish to make a sketch of him for my new statue, the 'Fighting Gladiator.'"

"I protest to Jupiter that if I do so I shall break my oath," replied Ventidius; "for I swore this day that I would never again permit him to quit my sight. The young barbarian is as wild and untameable as a mountain-cat."

Hereupon he narrated our hero's adventure with the crocodiles.

"Nevertheless," he continued, after he had finished the story, "if you will pledge me your word to restore him safely I will not refuse."

Philomenes gave the required promise.

"Good, I will send for him presently," replied Ventidius.

Then addressing himself to Mathias, he asked—

"And now, doctor, how fares your patient?"

Mathias raised his benevolent countenance, and replied with a gentle smile.

"Your daughter sickens with a disease that lies out of the range of my art to cure," he said. "She is troubled with vague yearnings; her mind is ill at ease."

"What do you mean by that?" cried Ventidius, impatiently. "What can trouble her mind? What wish of hers remains ungratified? Do I not love her? Is she not my child, the apple of my eye, the corner of my heart? Praised be the gods, I am well-to-do, and she is better off than thousands of maidens of her age and station. Have I not promised her trinkets, new vesture, and a trip to Baiæ, if I come off well at the next munus?"

"The puling minx," responded Lupa. "I believe the best remedy for her complaint would be a smart whipping."

"Tush! Do not make folks believe that you are harsh with the girl, replied her husband, with unusual pluck. "It was yourself that first told me how much she is altered, how pale she is, how she has lost her good looks; that's why I sent for our worthy friend, Mathias."

"Oh, of course, Ventidius must needs blame me. If thunder curdles the cream no one but poor me is to blame," sneered Lupa, tossing her head. "Well, the gods rule all. I am his humble slave or his lawful wife—it's much the same thing. Of course, Virginia is not my child—I did not bear her; and equally of course I have no natural love for her."

"Lupa, don't be a fool."

"Your humble slave, Ventidius!" retorted Lupa, curtseying. "If I were not a 'fool' I should not have a fool's patience to endure what I have to endure daily. It matters not. I was saying, courteous friends, that whatever he may think (if he ever thinks at all of me or my feelings), I am very anxious about the child—she is wasting away, she has no appetite."

"Feeds on nothing," rejoined the lanista, "unless her meat and drink be sighs and tears; and then she mopes in her chamber, and if I ask her why she does so—'I am well, father—I love to be alone.' Ouf! May this cup be my last if I know what ails her! If I know, may the furies seize me!"

"All in good time, Ventidius," rejoined Lupa, coolly. "In you, Mathias, I place my hopes, and I will tell you my opinion."

"I listen, mistress," the physician replied. "You are her mother, and in such a case my best guide."

"You are a sensible man," replied Lupa. "Now, look here," she added, smiting her fist on the table, "listen, doctor, listen to my opinion—nay, my conviction—she is bewitched."

"Bewitched!" cried Philomenes, suppressing a laugh. "The gods forfend! By whom and how bewitched?"

"By that pigmy abortion, Zaba, the dwarf," replied Lupa. "Everybody knows he has the 'evil eye.' He has 'overlooked her.' Some time ago he saw him in the porch; since then she has never been herself."

"He cast an evil spell upon her, as you think?" said Mathias.

"Can you doubt that, after all that I have told you?"

"Such a spell must be cast out by a spell more powerful," Mathias resumed.

"Do you know of one?"

"Aye, one that cannot fail," replied Mathias, "though Satan hinder—a hope, a joy, a crown of rejoicing."

"You speak like an oracle," exclaimed Lupa.

"Quite so," rejoined Ventidius, emptying his cup, "and quite as mysteriously."

"Whence does this wretch, Zaba, derive his evil influence, think you?" asked Mathias, looking steadily at Lupa.

"Avert the omen! It is not well to speak of such things," replied Lupa, turning pale with superstitious fear, and clutching the amulet that hung about her neck. "Yet I suppose that it comes from the Larvæ and Lamiæ, the spectres and goblins that hover round the throne of Pluto."

"But you profess to believe in a God greater, more powerful, than the ruler of the infernal regions?" said Mathias.

"Yes, indeed; in Jupiter—most high, greatest, and best," said Lupa, reverently.

"But according to your poets and your oracles, there is an unknown power that controls even the gods themselves, and sways the destinies of men?" continued Mathias.

"Fate, and the three inexorable sisters," assented Philomenes. "Man must endure, as Homer says, 'whatever Fate and the stern sisters spun for him at his birth.'"

"That is true," rejoined Ventidius. "Not to speak it profanely, there is not much dependence to be placed in the help of our gods. I will give you a case in point. I had a comrade once; his name was Ladon, as brave a gladiator as ever trod the sand. He was a man of good life, and pious withal. In his day he had sacrificed a whole hecatomb of black swine to Pluto; yet mark how the deceiving god abandoned him in his extremity. It is well known that even the bravest men are at times subject to an access of panic and fright. Ladon was a man of nervous and excitable temperament, and though he had performed prodigies of valour he always predicted that he would die the death of a coward—and so it came to pass."

"What! did he lose his courage in the arena?" asked Philomenes.

"He did, poor fellow! Disarmed and wounded by the Samnite with whom he had engaged, he took to his heels and fled for his life, among the hootings and jeers of the multitude. He had not got far before he fell to the ground and swooned from sheer horror. I did the best I could for him, and saved him further disgrace by cutting his throat as he lay insensible. You should have seen the rage of the mob! There was a whirlwind of hisses and curses. They spat on his mangled corpse and pelted it with orange-peel as it was hooked off to the spoliarium. So much for putting one's trust in Pluto."

"Do you hear this blasphemer?" cried his wife. "I wonder the earth does not open and swallow him up."

Philomenes here interposed for the preservation of the peace.

Without noticing Lupa's remark he turned to Mathias.

"I think I perceive the drift of your argument," said he. "You would remind us that an all-ruling Providence can baffle the machinations of the evil powers."

"True, I would have the gentle Virginia anchor her hope upon the rock of ages," replied Mathias. "I would have her fix her gaze upon that sun of righteousness before whose bright beams the mists and darkness of ignorance and superstition are dispersed and vanish away. Then she would have no fear of the 'evil eye,' or of any of the pretended spells of witches or wizards."

"Spare me, most learned Mathias. Such speculations are beyond my powers of comprehension," rejoined Ventidius. "One thing is certain—something must be done. A change of scene might benefit the peevish lass. I own a little farm near the country town of Sora, at the foot of the Appenines. I have a mind to send Virginia thither for awhile, only business prevents me leaving Rome just now, and I cannot bear the thought of parting with the child."

"No," though it were to save her life!" retorted Lupa, bridling up. "But I tell you, Ventidius, the poor darling shall not be sacrificed to your selfishness. Do you hear me?" she went on, raising her voice; "she shall go. I have sent Pandion's wife and children to the farm, and the bracing mountain air has restored Phillida, a poor little sick thing, to blooming health. Virginia shall pack off to-morrow, as soon as that morrow dawns."

Ventidius gave a sly wink at Philomenes, and, putting on a frown, said, with pretended roughness—

"Virginia shall do nothing of the sort. She is the sunshine of the house. I cannot endure her absence."

"Let her stay, then, unnatural wretch! Let her stay to sicken and die, and deprive me of my only blessing." And Lupa began to sob.

Ventidius looked scared, but screwed up his courage.

"The girl will do well enough," he growled. "She ought not to be indulged in all her fancies."

"Pardon me, Ventidius," rejoined Mathias; "you do wrong in this. Nothing is more likely to do my patient good than such a change as your wife suggests."

The simple old man thought Ventidius was in earnest in raising objections to a scheme which he had set his heart upon.

He yielded to the persuasion of his guest with much apparent reluctance, and grumbled a good deal.

"You will need an escort," he said, "for the roads are infested by disbanded soldiers, runaway slaves, and robbers of all sorts. I will send a few of my lads to accompany you."

"Let Pandion make one of the party," suggested Lupa. "He is a stout fellow, and, besides, has asked for a holiday to visit his wife and family. And then there is the Briton, Caractacus—you may as well let him go, too. He will be out of harm's way."

"Be it as you will," replied Ventidius; "your wish is my law."

At this moment Virginia came to the door, but seeing that there were guests present immediately withdrew.

Lupa made a sign to her husband, and then rose and followed Virginia.

She caught her by the hand and detained her.

"Whither away so fast, my child?" she said. "You were not wont to be so bashful. Come in, and pay your respects to our guests, who are friends of the house—Mathias and Philomenes."

Virginia looked up into her mother's face with bright blushes, and eyes that sparkled with innocent delight.

"Look, mother," said she, "see what he has given me."

And she held out the necklace of rubies which our hero had snatched for her, as it were, from the very jaws of death.

Lupa clutched the chain eagerly, and uttered a cry of astonishment and admiration as she examined the jewels.

"Juno! These rubies must be of great value!" she exclaimed. "Who gave you this?"

"Caractacus, the Briton," replied Virginia, in a low, sweet voice. "It was presented him by the noble Licinius as a reward of valour."

Lupa put the chain round her own neck, and looked down with complacency on the gleaming blood-red stones as they rose and fell upon her full, white bosom.

"Ah, me!" she sighed; "it is not becoming for such folks as we to wear such showy trinkets, and I hold it presumption on the part of a mere slave like Caractacus to make presents to his master's daughter. He ought at once to have handed the prize over to his lanista. Still it is a gallant action, and I wish he were anything else but a gladiator. Go, child; I will take care of this gew-gaw for you. But mark me, I expressly forbid you from receiving any more gifts from your father's slave. Tell him that whenever such rewards are bestowed on him by our patrons he is at once to hand them over to Ventidius; at the same time you may assure him that in such cases he shall have for himself a trifle for drink-money."

CHAPTER XXII.
THE STATUE.

THE house of Philomenes, the sculptor, stood a little distance from the Flaminian Gate.

It was a small and modest-looking dwelling, but not without a certain neatness and elegance that spoke well for the good taste of its occupant.

Thither came Philomenes and the Briton in the cool of the summer afternoon.

Philomenes knocked at the door, which was opened by a beautiful Greek slave-girl, whose face brightened up at her master's return.

A noble-looking hound sprang forward from the interior of the house, and with a joyous yelp fawned upon his master.

Then the brute hurried to Caractacus, and sniffed at him rather suspiciously.

"A friend, Hylax—one you must learn to know," said Philomenes, patting the dog's head.

The animal seemed to understand him, for he licked the Briton's hand, and then with a loud, sharp bark, raced backwards and forwards as though he would go mad with delight.

Philomenes quieted him, and then turning to the girl he asked—

"Has any one called here whilst I was away?"

"Yes, Philomenes," replied the girl, smiling; "the widow of that gladiator who was killed at the last games. She brought with her a little boy—as beautiful as Eros. She had taught him to lisp thanks to you for your bounty. She was so disappointed that you were not at home; but I knew your wish, and did not send her away empty-handed."

"Hist, Glancé!" said Philomenes, frowning, and glancing at our hero. "Fetch me some wine, the Scian—you know which I mean—and bring it to me in my workshop."

Philomenes then took the Briton to his studio.

Here were found statues, some half-finished, others just begun, with blocks of marble, and all the tools required by the artist.

Among these were a number of mallets of different weights and sizes, many compasses, curved and straight, a great quantity of chisels, three or four levers, jacks for raising blocks, saws, and other implements.

The wine having been brought, Caractacus just sipped from a goblet by way of courtesy, and then partook of some fruit.

Philomenes put many questions to our hero regarding his position and prospects, to which our hero frankly replied.

"I have not much to complain of," he said; "Ventidius, though quick-tempered, is not unkind to me in the main."

"And your comrades?"

"Well, I have made a few enemies, but gained more friends."

"I am glad to hear that," replied Philomenes. "Still, I would to Jupiter that you had met with better fortune. You have not yet made your first essay as a gladiator in the public ring. You have a terrible ordeal to pass through."

Caractacus smiled fiercely.

"It shall be welcome," he replied. "Death is the worst I have to fear; and, as you may believe, to one in my condition life has few charms."

"Alas, no!" assented Philomenes. "But do you never indulge in dreams of escape?"

"Escape!" repeated Caractacus, shaking his head "No, Ventidius has rendered that impossible."

"How so?" asked Philomenes. "He appears to give you liberty enough. Few gladiators are permitted to roam abroad so often and so freely as you do."

"I cannot deny it," was the answer. "But I am bound to his service by a chain which, though invisible, is stronger than adamant."

"You mean that you have made a promise not to attempt to run away?" said Philomenes.

"I have, and he trusts me," answered the Briton. "Would you have me break my word?"

"By no means," replied the Greek. "I should be the last to give you such base counsel. Better death than dishonour."

"More than all this," continued the Briton, gloomily, "I have my sister's death to avenge."

He wrung his hands in grief.

"Dear Iona!" he exclaimed; "and I know not even where they have laid thee. I am denied the mournful satisfaction of weeping at thy grave. And thou, the daughter of a race of kings—it may be thy fair body was thrown into the common pit, the ghastly receptacle for the carcases of vile slaves and felons. Ye gods of Britain, give me some revenge!"

"Do not torture yourself needlessly," answered Philomenes. "I and that holy man, Mathias—for so he is—consigned your sister's remains to a secret but sacred spot, and there she was entombed with solemn and impressive rites. Never mention this, as our proceedings were against the harsh Roman law, and one or all of us might get into trouble. Some day I may show you where she lies."

Throwing himself upon his knees, Caractacus seized the hand of the generous Greek and pressed it to his heart.

"I cannot thank you in words," he sobbed. "Speech fails to express my heartfelt gratitude."

"No more of this, brave Caractacus," said Philomenes, gently. "If, indeed, there be an Elysium beyond the grave be sure your dear sister is now happy. Compose yourself, and come with me. I wish to show you some of my handiwork—sometimes I regard it as my masterpiece."

He rose, and led the way by a passage to a large reception room, adorned with statuary, and furnished with couches and chairs.

Caractacus followed him, little expecting what he was about to be shown.

At the far end of the room was what appeared to be an alcove, screened by closed curtains of rich purple velvet.

"Is it a statue?" asked the Briton.

"You shall see," replied the sculptor, smiling. "Remain where you are, and I will draw the curtains."

Leaving Caractacus standing in the centre of the room, Philomenes approached the wall and drew a silken cord.

The curtains instantly parted and rolled back, disclosing a wondrous statue.

It was the image of a lovely maiden, crowned with a wreath of oak-leaves and mistletoe, and holding in her hand the mystic sickle with which the Druid virgins were wont to lop the sacred bough.

The robe drawn tightly over the person beautifully marked the form, the right arm resting on the breast and enveloped in an exquisite drapery. The countenance was sweet, placid, yet noble; the head fine, the curling of the hair very beautiful—it seemed moulded as if it would yield to the touch.

Caractacus uttered a shout of enthusiasm.

"Iona—my sister! It breathes—it is life itself. Oh, mastery of art!"

The red blood mounted the sculptor's cheek, and his fine eyes kindled at this genuine and impulsive approval of his work.

He let fall the curtains.

"Enough, Caractacus," he said, gleefully. "It is a fine statue, and I am proud of it, though a fool for making such a confession."

From that hour Caractacus and Philomenes became fast friends.

It was a happy thought of the sculptor to select Caractacus as the model for his "Fighting Gladiator," as the arrangement afforded the two friends frequent opportunities of meeting together.

On each of these occasions Ventidius received a small fee. The lanista was fond of money, and even little fish are sweet; besides, he knew that his turbulent pupil was in safe company and out of harm's way, and so all parties were satisfied.

The Briton keenly enjoyed these visits to the sculptor's house.

Philomenes was a man of a genial and sympathetic disposition, of liberal mind, and varied experience. Caractacus set a high value upon his friendship, and grew daily more attached to him.

Mathias was also a frequent visitor to the sculptor's studio.

The good old man's strange, absorbing talk made a great impression upon the young barbarian. Caractacus felt his heart softened, thought less of his wrongs and expected vengeance, and began to be ashamed of his unnatural and bloodthirsty vocation.

Ventidius would not have been very well pleased if he had known what influence Mathias had gained over the young gladiator.

Important consequences might have been the result, had not our hero been called suddenly away to join Pandion and others of the "family" who had been chosen as a bodyguard to escort their lanista's wife and daughter to their temporary home among the mountains.

CHAPTER XXIII.

A ROMAN FARM.—THE EAGLE'S EYRIE.

THE little country town of Sora, which has retained its ancient name, is pleasantly situated on a fertile plain, though the hinder extremity rests against the foot of an insulated rocky hill, while in the background soar the lofty Appenines.

A beautiful stream—the Liris—forms a bend round the city, and meanders through the neighbouring fields.

Juvenal represents it as one of those country towns in which an honest man might reside with comfort in that age of corruption which he satirised.

The farm-house belonging to the wealthy lanista was very pretty and tasteful.

The front, situated to the south-east, formed a roomy portico, resting on Ionic pillars, before which extended a terrace planted with flowers, and divided by box-trees into small beds of various forms; while the declivity sloping gently down bore figures, skilfully cut out of the box-trees, of animals opposite to each other, as if prepared for attack, and then gradually became lost in the acanthus, which covered in its verdure the plain at its foot.

This villa, which was attached to a large farm, had two courts.

At the entrance to the outer was the abode of the villicus, who had charge of the entire farm except the cattle. Over the gateway was the room of the procurator, a kind of under-steward.

The villica, or housekeeper, under whose orders the female slaves were employed in providing food and clothes for the family, had another room.

The inferior slaves lodged in one great room, and the sick had a separate apartment.

The lodgings of the freedmen had a southern aspect.

The inner court of the villa was occupied chiefly by the horses, cattle, and other live stock.

Both the outer and inner court had chambers for the slaves, fronting the south.

The place where offending slaves were kept in chains was underground, and lighted by several high and narrow windows.

This prison-house was called the "ergastulum," and under harsh masters many cruelties were there perpetrated.

The cattle kept in a Roman farm, which had yards like our own, were horses, mules, oxen, and asses.

The geese, hens, pigeons, and peacocks were under the charge of a particular slave.

Deer, hares, and all kinds of game were attended to, and the more opulent of the Romans kept a variety of animals at their villas.

Caractacus did not take up his abode in the villa, but was lodged in a cottage on the farm, which had been assigned to Pandion and his family, where he was most kindly and hospitably entertained.

Marcia, the wife of our hero's comrade, was a buxom, comely dame, the mother of a family of four fine children—two boys and two girls.

With these little folks the good-natured Briton soon contrived to render himself a favourite.

The eldest son, Marcus, was a gentle, thoughtful boy, between twelve and thirteen, slight, delicate, and tall for his age, beautifully formed, and with regular features and dark eyes full of intelligence.

Florus, named after that luckless comrade of Pandion's—the gladiator who had met with such a terrible fate at the hands of Zaba, the deformed beast-keeper—was a sturdy, frolicksome urchin about two years younger than Marcus.

Helen, the elder of the two girls, was a charming little blue-eyed, golden-haired maid of seven, and Phyllida, the youngest, a sweet little creature just able to walk.

The delight of Pandion, at finding himself once more in the bosom of his family, was boundless, and Caractacus long remembered the first happy evening he spent in the humble cottage of that worthy fellow.

The first embraces over, Pandion threw himself on a couch near the window, and gathering his children around him, cried merrily—

"Dulce domum! Home, sweet home! Ah, comrade, would I might win the rudis, and retire from the ring, and spend my life among my own. It is these," he added hugging his children—"it is these that make a man a coward."

Then again he laughed cheerily.

"But why think of that?" said he; "let us make a feast, my Marcia. Be at home, comrade," he went on, shaking the Briton's hand; "you cannot be more welcome, and soh! Marcia, wine, wine! What sings jolly Anacreon?"

"I pray thee, by the gods above,
Give me the mighty bowl I love!
And let me sing in wild delight,
I will—I will be drunk to-night."

"I trust you can be merry and wise too, my Pandion;" answered his wife, her face beaming with joy and affection. I have yet left one jar of Samian, your favourite tipple."

"Body of Bacchus! that is golden news," laughed Pandion; "let Marcus fetch it whilst you spread the supper, and in the meantime I will tip you a stave of my jovial countryman's—"

And he broke forth in a deep bass voice—

"'Tis true my fading years decline,
Yet can I quaff the brimming wine,
As deep as any stripling fair,
Whose cheeks the flush of morning wear;
For though my failing years decay,
And though my bloom has passed away,
Yet like Silenus' sire divine,
With blushes borrowed from my wine,
I'll wanton 'mid the merry train,
And live my follies all again."

Supper over, the hearty boxer entertained his guest with interminable yarns about his battles in the ring.

"And thrice he routed all his foes,
And thrice he slew the slain."

So the merry hours glided away, and, when at last they retired to rest, Caractacus was shown into a neat and pretty bedroom, and flinging himself upon his bed, sank into a deep and dreamless slumber.

He woke with the lark, and stealing forth from the cottage, enjoyed a cool swim in the Liris: then he went afield to see the reapers at work, for it was harvest time.

He had not gone far before Pandion hailed him.

"I am glad to find you up betimes, comrade," said Pandion, taking the Briton's arm. "We could not have arrived here at a better season—we are at the end of the vintage, and to-day the rustics hold their Dionysia, or vintage feast. Yonder goes the villicus. I will call him. Ho, Thyrsus—halt, man!"

The steward at this shout turned towards them his ruddy and cheerful face, and came to meet them.

"Abroad so early, my gallants!" he said.

"Yes, good Thyrsus. We want to see the grape-gatherers and wine-pressers at work," answered Pandion.

"'Tis well; and a bunch of grapes with a slice or two of bread makes a wholesome breakfast," replied the villicus. "I will take you where you may pluck as many bunches as you can carry, and afterwards, if you like, will show you over the farm."

"Thanks, good Thyrsus," replied Pandion. "You have had splendid weather for the vintage," he went on to remark.

"Praise be to Ceres and Pomona, both the wheat harvest and the vintage are the finest we have seen for many a year," was the reply. This, together with the visit of the domina and her fair and gentle daughter, will render our feast to-day a right merry one."

They passed several groups of women and children loaded with the beautiful purple grape. Caractacus suddenly paused and pointed upwards.

"Look yonder," he said; "there flies an eagle—the first I have seen since I left Britain. Among my native glens and mountains I have shot many a one. I would I had my good yew bow with me now."

"If you are a fair marksman I wish the same with all my heart," returned the villicus. "The rascal bird has been a very pest to us all through the summer—has thinned the folds, the poultry-yard, and dove-cotes. I wish we were well rid of her. If you would undertake the task of tracking her to her mountain eyrie you would do a deed deserving of gratitude."

"I will do it willingly," said Caractacus.

"Do not think so," grunted Pandion. "You have got yourself into scrapes enough already. You shall not risk your neck among yon crags and cliffs whilst I can keep you in tow."

Caractacus laughed, but made no answer, for he had fully made up his mind to give his comrade the slip on the first opportunity, and attempt the perilous feat.

They had now reached the vineyard, and saw numbers of labourers—men, women, and children—busily employed in gathering the grapes.

The huge heaped-up wains almost hid the patient, plodding oxen that drew them along.

The balmy air was jocund with laughter, jest, and song, and redolent with the delicious odour of the newly-gathered fruit.

All at once a female shriek was heard, and a woman with streaming hair and outstretched arms came rushing into the midst of the startled group.

"Lydia!" she exclaimed, wildly; "where is Lydia?"

A young and beautiful woman who was on her knees pressing the luscious cluster of grapes into a basket, started to her feet.

"I am here," she exclaimed. "What is the matter?"

"Oh, Lydia!" replied the woman, panting for breath; "your child—your child!"

The young mother turned white, and clutched at the woman's dress.

"My child?—oh, the gods!" she gasped. "What has happened? I left him asleep under the shade of yon chestnut tree."

"The eagle has taken him," cried the woman. "I saw the fell bird swoop upon the innocent and bear him off in its talons."

"To the mountain!" was the general shout.

In another instant many hundred feet were hurrying towards the distant hills.

Disregarding Pandion's warning shout, Caractacus snatched up a bill-hook, the only weapon that lay within reach, and joined the chase.

Swift-footed as the mountain deer, the Briton soon outstripped his companions. Two miles of hill and dale, wood and morass, and many intersecting brooks lay between, but in an incredibly short time he had reached the foot of the mountain.

The eyrie was now in sight, and both the old birds were visible on the rock-ledge.

But who should dare that dizzy and almost precipitous cliff.

Caractacus stood hesitating.

He felt a light touch on his arm.

He looked round and beheld Lydia, with a face perfectly white, and eyes like those of a mad person fixed upon the eyrie.

"Courage!" whispered the daring Briton; "I will save your child or perish."

And without another word he began scrambling up by the brakes and rock-vines, and over the huge stones—up, up, up, as though he were fleeing from the death he really courted.

From boulder to boulder he sprang, as fearless as a bounding goat, every instant increasing his danger of being dashed to pieces.

No stop—no stay. He knew not how he drew breath.

At length he reached a ledge of the precipice, just below that upon which the eyrie was built.

Clutching with hands and knees to the airy verge he glanced fearfully down the steep.

To his amazement he saw that the distracted mother had followed him in his perilous ascent, and stood just below, with white, upturned face and clasped hands.

The sight restored his failing energies, and nerved him to desperation.

By a powerful effort he raised himself on to the upper ledge.

The crumbling rock gave way under his feet, and large pieces of stone rattled down into the dark abyss below.

Then his ear caught the wailing cry of the child, which the eagle had dropped on the summit of a projecting rock.

Down came the fierce rustling of the eagle's wings, and Caractacus struck madly with the bill-hook, as the savage bird dashed close to his head, so near that he saw the yellow of its wrathful eyes and the gleam of its hooked cruel beak.

Then Caractacus leaped upon the eyrie, and seized the child, while the two eagles at once flew to the attack, striving with their beaks and talons to tear his eyes from their sockets, and buffeting with their thunderous wings.

CHAPTER XXIV.

THE RESCUE.

CARACTACUS struck blindly at the eagles, as again and again they flew on rushing wings to the attack. The infant he clasped in his left arm uttered a faint, feeble cry.

Daunted for awhile by our hero's shouts and fierce defence, the eagles soared away to some distance, and hung almost motionless in mid-air, then with screams they shot up high over his head, and beating with their wings seemed to be preparing to swoop down upon him.

The Briton thought it time to make an attempt to descend.

He looked over the verge of the jutting rock on which he was crouching.

Crags, chasms, boulders of granite, and the skeletons of old trees—far, far, down, and dwindled into specks, the crowd running to and fro.

His eye got dim, and his head dizzy, and his heart sick.

But only for a moment. Caractacus was born among mountains; it was only the disuse of habit. He had lived so long traversing plains, crossing the sea, and pent in the city, that his old intrepidity in respect of climbing giddy heights seemed to have abandoned him; but he hardened his heart, and kept his hands firm, and scared away his fears with such defiance that they cleared like a film from his eyes, and his whole secure consciousness came back to him, and the momentary scare passed off.

He looked up—the eagles were hanging motionless in the air.

He slid down the shelving rock, and found himself on a small piece of firm root-bound soil, with the tops of bushes appearing below.

Lydia, who was standing on the narrow brink of a tremendous precipice, uttered a cry of mingled hope and terror, as she saw Caractacus descending, the child clasped to his breast.

With fingers suddenly strengthened into the power of iron, he swung himself down by briar and broom, and heather, and dwarf birch.

Here a stone leaped over a ledge, and no sound was heard, so profound was its fall. There the shingle rattled down, and he hesitated not to follow it.

His body was callous as the cliff.

Steep as the wall of a house was now the precipice. But it was matted with ivy, centuries old—long ago dead, and without a single green leaf, but with thousands of arm-thick stems petrified into the rock, and covering it as with a trellis.

Caractacus bound the baby to his neck, and with hands and feet clung to that fearful ladder.

Turning round his head and looking down, he beheld the crowd below looking up in an agony of suspense. Many of the women had fallen upon their knees, and were praying to the gods for his deliverance.

Overhead frowned the precipice, never touched before by human hand or foot.

No one had ever dreamed of scaling it, and the eagles knew that well in their instinct, as before they built their eyrie they had brushed it with their wings.

But all the rest of this part of the mountain side, though scarred, and seamed, and chasmed, was yet accessible—and more than one of the people from the farm had reached the bottom of the "Eagles' Cliff."

Again the Briton's feet touched stones and earth.

With a sobbing cry Lydia stretched forth her arms. "Take the child," said Caractacus.

He unbound the child and passed it to the mother, who hugged it to her breast, and half-smothered it with kisses.

Then the Briton clung by both hands to the ivy, and swinging himself backwards and forwards, launched himself in mid-air. Lydia shrieked.

But the next instant Caractacus alighted by her side.

She caught his hand and kissed it.

"Thou art some god!" she murmured.

Caractacus laughed in his broad free way.

"I would I were," said he, "that I might fly with you to the plain below, for the descent is very dangerous, but be of good cheer; safety is yet within our reach."

Making a sign to her to remain where she was the Briton scrambled to the ledge below.

At this moment, a she-goat, with two little kids, came springing past him, bounding from rock to rock.

"A happy omen," said Caractacus; "let us follow in their track."

With great difficulty he helped her down to the ledge on which he was standing.

Caractacus led the way, and they followed their dumb guides a hundred yards, among dangers enough to terrify the stoutest heart.

The head of one man appeared—then another, and our adventurers knew that Providence had delivered them and the child in safety into the hands of their fellow-creatures.

Honest Pandion was the first to reach them.

Not a word was spoken—eyes said enough. Lydia hushed her friends with her hands, and with uplifted eyes pointed to Caractacus as to a guide sent her by heaven.

"Do not thank me," said Caractacus, reddening. "It is to the instinct of these pretty dumb creatures that we owe our rescue."

Even now the whole party found it safest to follow the she-goat and her kids.

Small green plats where those creatures nibble the wild flowers became now more frequent—trodden lines, almost as easy as sheep-paths, showed that the dam had not led her young into danger; and now the brushwood dwindled away into straggling shrubs, and the party stood on a little eminence above a mountain stream.

There had been much trouble and agitation among the multitude, while the gallant young Briton and the trembling mother were scaling the cliffs—sublime was the shout that echoed afar the moment our hero had reached the eyrie—then succeeded a silence deep as death while our hero was battling with the fierce birds of prey.

But now all these tremors were followed by the wildness of thankfulness and congratulatory joy.

Overpowered by her emotions, Lydia sank to the ground and fainted away.

"Fall back and give her fresh air," said honest Pandion.

The circle of close faces widened around her, lying as in death.

"Give the child into my arms," cried first one mother, and then another, and it was tenderly handed round the circle of kisses, many of the maidens bathing its face with tears. "There is not a single scratch about the poor innocent, for the eagle, you see must have struck its talons in his clothes and swathing bands."

Lydia started up from her swoon.

"Oh! the bird, the bird, the eagle, the eagle!" she cried, looking wildly around, "the eagle has carried off my darling—is there none to pursue?"

A neighbour put the baby into her breast, and, shutting her eyes and smiting her forehead, the sorely bewildered creature said in a low voice—

"Am I waking? Oh! tell me am I waking, or if this be the work of fever, the delirium of a dream?"

Pandion's wife, Marcia, sobbing joyfully, clasped Lydia to her arms.

"All is well, dear sister," she murmured; "yonder stands the brave youth who saved your child. Have you no word of thanks for him?"

Little Helen tugged at her dress.

"Yes, there he is," she lisped; "we saw him climb the rock, and fight the great bird-thing; give him a kiss. He brought me a squirrel out of the wood."

"He's brave; he's a gladiator like father," rejoined her sturdy little brother, Florus. "He made me a fine bow and arrows."

Lydia knelt at the Briton's feet, and raised her tear-streaming eyes to his frank noble face, with a look of ineffable gratitude.

"Do not think me ungrateful because I lack words to thank you," she faltered; "be assured, noble youth, the benign gods will requite you."

Our hero made no answer; he bent down his proud head, kissed the infant, and stalked away.

But he was not to be let off so easily.

The men of the party surrounded him, shook him by the hand, clapped him on the shoulder, and overwhelmed him with praises and congratulations. Not content with this, they insisted upon carrying him home in triumph.

In spite of his entreaties and even resistance, they raised him upon their shoulders, and bore him back to the house amidst songs, music, and shouts of rejoicing.

For many a long year that day's adventure was talked over by winter firesides, and henceforward the craggy descent from the eagle's eyrie went by the name of the "Briton's Ladder."

CHAPTER XXV.

VIRGINIA'S WARNING.

THE Dionysia—Bacchanalia or vintage feast— went off with extravagant merriment. Hilarity and frolic were the order of the day.

There was a sort of rustic Carnival or Saturnalia holiday, in which, from time immemorial, the slaves on the farm were accustomed to allow themselves, and to be allowed by their masters, a large degree of liberty.

As long as it lasted the peasants and serfs employed in it indulged in a truly Fescennine license of tongue with all who approached them or chanced to pass by, bespattering them with all manner of queer language, and pelting them with doggrel rhymes, without any regard to their rank or condition.

When the wine was all trodden out in the winepress—trodden out by the naked feet of jumping, frolicking, roaring swains—the prime part of the festival commenced, consisting of semi-ludicrous, semi-serious classical processions, after which followed a good repast.

One such procession was really admirable.

Bacchus, instead of being represented in the manner of our vulgar sign-painters, by a fat, paunchy, red-faced, drunken boy, was personified by the tallest, handsomest, and most graceful young man of the party.

His head was crowned with a wreath of vine-leaves, mixed with bunches of the purple grape, which hung down the sides and the back of his neck.

In his right hand he carried a lance tipped with a cone of pine or fir-apple, and the shaft was entwined with ivy and some wild autumnal flowers— the thing being the classic thyrsus, one of the most ancient attributes of the god and his followers.

A clean sheep skin, spotted with the red juice of the grape, in imitation of the skin of the panther or spotted pard which Bacchus is represented as wearing when he went on his expedition, was thrown gracefully over his shoulder.

He was followed by some silent sedate women, carrying on their heads baskets filled with grapes; by little boys carrying in their hands large bunches of the same fruit; by Bacchante of both sexes, who carried sticks entwined with vine leaves; by two or three carri or carts, which had been used to convey the ripe fruit to the wine press—each drawn by a pair of tall cream-coloured oxen with those large, dark, pensive eyes to which Homer thought it no disparagement to compare the eyes of the wife of Jupiter.

In the rear of all came Silenus, a fat, old man with his face and hands besmeared with wine lees, bestriding a fat old ass.

The Bacchante bounded, danced, frolicked, and laughed uproariously.

Silenus lolled and rolled upon his donkey, singing snatches of vintage songs, making all sorts of ludicrous grimaces and gestures, and jocosely, yet loudly, abusing every stranger or neighbour he discovered in the throng.

But Bacchus preserved the decorum and dignity of the true classical character of the god, who was as graceful as Apollo, who shared with that divinity the dominion of Parnassus, and the faculty and glory of inspiring poets with immortal verse.

The merry throng set up joyous shouts—

"Evoe Bacche! Io Iacchi!"

The laughs and shouts of the Bacchante, the songs and jokes of old Silenus, were mingled with the beat and jingle of two or three tambourines, with the rural sound of cow-horns, and occasionally the blasts of a cracked but antique-looking trumpet, and with the clapping of hands and shoutings of all the men, women, and boys of the district.

The hills, which bore the fruit productive of the generous wine which Horace extolled as the drink of Mæcenas, echoed and re-echoed with the joyous sounds, for the scene of the festivity was at the foot of those hills on whose sunny slopes the vines had ripened which furnished this happy vintage.

Sated at length with amusement, and tired of the bustle and uproar, Caractacus strolled out from the "madding crowd," and betook himself, for a quiet walk, to a little belt of forest at the base of the Eagles' Crag.

The Briton wandered on through the green, shady depths of the wood, admiring the sylvan beauties, and listening to the songs of birds and the chirrup of the grasshopper—his mind busy with thick-coming fancies.

"What a paradise might this be," he murmured to himself, "were it a land of freedom! But, alas! the oppressions of the nobles, who wallow in luxury, the miseries and sufferings of their wretched slaves who receive worse treatment than the brute beasts, the cruelty of the blood-hankering mob, such things disgust a stranger. Ah my loved country, home of the brave and the free! shall I see thee again, or will my blood sodden the sand, my body reek in the foul and ghastly shambles! That Great Unknown of whom Mathias spake—'tis He alone can tell; I am in His hands."

Caractacus pressed his hand to his brow.

"Mathias, the Christian—for such he is. The words he spoke still resound in my ears like the mutterings of a distant storm, the rumblings of an approaching earthquake. This unnatural state of things can never last. Rome must fall. Nay, he darkly hinted that the end of the world and the great day of judgment are near at hand. I would I knew more of this strange new faith."

While thus ruminating he was suddenly brought to a stand by the noise of a slight rustle among the bushes, and in the same moment he caught a glimpse of a white fluttering robe, and the graceful form of a young maiden emerged from among the trees.

It was Virginia.

Upon seeing the Briton she drew back, startled and confused, her face rosy with blushes.

Caractacus, on his part, was equally disconcerted.

However, he soon recovered his composure, and, bowing his head, said in a respectful tone—

"Forgive me, fair Virginia, if I have unwittingly intruded on your solitude."

The Roman maid raised her glance, then looked down, as she replied in a low voice—

"I cannot hold you accountable for a mere accident," she said. "Nor am I sorry that we meet for a moment alone."

Then she added, clasping her hands and looking him frankly in the face—

"For, O Caractacus, I have longed for such an opportunity to warn you against a great danger that threatens you."

The Briton smiled calmly.

"Gentle Virginia," he answered, "danger and I are old playfellows."

"True," responded the Roman girl. "But I am not speaking of the hazards you have had to encounter on the battle-field, and will have to brave again in the accursed arena. The peril against which I would give you timely warning proceeds from another and a darker source—the treachery of your own comrades."

"Is it so?" replied our hero, shrugging his shoulders; "I knew I had foes in the 'Family.' Well, let them do their worst."

"But I tell you your life is in jeopardy."

"Well, I can die."

"Do you desire death?"

"No, but I am indifferent to life," replied the Briton, with a sigh. "For what should I live? A slave, a gladiator, torn from my native land, bereft of all I held dear, lonely and despised, what matters where or how I die? Who is there to shed for me one tear of pity or regret?"

Virginia breathed a deep sigh.

"You are not so desolate, so unloved as you suppose," she answered with quivering lip.

Then as if she had been betrayed into speaking too freely, she hurried on.

"Ah, brave Caractacus, if you must perish, at least die as becomes a man and a warrior. Do not suffer yourself to be made the victim of malice."

"Who are these secret enemies against whose designs you so kindly put me on my guard?" asked our hero.

"Beware that man, Varro, who has newly joined my father's maniple," said Virginia, "and more than beware that horrible wretch, the deformed beast-feeder."

"Zaba, the black dwarf?"

"Yes, he and Varro, with some others, have vowed to compass your ruin," she went on eagerly. "They are in league with a certain noble named Licinius, one of my father's patrons, who hates you, but for what reason I know not."

"I can partly guess," replied Caractacus.

"You will wonder how I have learned all this," continued Virginia; "but it came about in this way. Varro is in love with Chloris, one of our household slaves; to her he confided his secret, which she betrayed to me."

Caractacus with fervour expressed his thanks to the noble-hearted girl for her kind interest in his welfare, and promised not to disregard her warnings.

"For Zaba, the dwarf, I have no fear of him; my comrades have a grudge to settle with that wretch, and he will take care to keep out of my way," said Caractacus. "And as for Varro, I have yet to learn that he is invulnerable, or a better swordsman than myself."

"Not for your life!" exclaimed Virginia, turning pale; "do nothing to provoke that dangerous man. Speak him fair when you meet him; avoid him as much as you can, and above all bury this secret in your breast, for the warning I have given you must not be breathed again even to your dearest friend."

"Your command shall be obeyed, sweet mistress," answered our hero.

"My wish it is—I do not presume to command you," replied Virginia.

"Your slightest wish I regard as a command," said the Briton, "to obey which I consider my dearest duty."

"Would to the gods, noble Caractacus, my power were equal to my goodwill," replied Virginia; "then you would be free and happy. But, hark! footsteps are approaching—I must begone. Remember what I have told you; be silent and be vigilant; and so, vale—farewell!"

She waved her hand, and in the next moment had disappeared behind the clustered trees.

"Kind, beautiful Virginia," murmured Caractacus "why should I despise life, or wish to leave a world brightened by thy sweet smile? No, by the gods of my fathers, I will live and conquer for thy dear sake."

He turned and repaced his steps towards the farm He had not gone far before he heard shouts.

"Caractacus, hilloa! where are you hiding, lad?"

Our hero responded to the call, and waked the woodland echoes with his loud cheery halloo.

Pandion and Manlius now came into sight, and hurried to meet him.

"So, comrade, we have unearthed the fox," laughed Pandion.

"What, Manlius!" cried our hero, grasping that worthy by the hand, "I am right glad to see you; what brings you from Rome?"

"I came in search of you, truant," was the reply, "to fetch you back to the city."

"So soon," answered the Briton, sighing. "I thought this respite was too pleasant and happy to last."

"'Tis ever so," rejoined Pandion. "Few are the days in life's calendar that one may mark off with a white stone. Life's a rough journey, make the best of it."

"A mournful truth," assented Manlius. "I remember once seeing in a garden a sun-dial, round which was inserted this gloomy motto—'These hours each in turn wounds, the last kills.'"

"By my faith, you are merry companions," returned Caractacus, laughing. "Have you nothing more cheerful than this to tell me?"

"Yes lad," rejoined Pandion. "Hearken to Manlius, he has stirring news for you."

"Let me hear it then; I am curious to learn why I am so soon summoned back to Rome."

"Know then," said Manlius, "that on the day after your departure from Rome our lanista was sent for by his illustrious patron, Narcissus."

"Ha!" ejaculated our hero, starting uneasily.

Manlius continued.

"Narcissus appears to have taken a mighty fancy to you. He expressed his admiration of the expertness and courage which you have displayed on so many occasions, especially in regard to your adventure with the crocodiles, as related to him by Honorius, the Tribune."

"Noble Roman that Honorius—every inch a soldier," our hero remarked, approvingly; "I am glad to have his good word. Proceed, comrade."

"When told that you were rusticating at this country farm, Narcissus appeared surprised, and blamed Ventidius for trusting you so far out of his reach, and indeed he advised your instant recall."

"I am much obliged to him," retorted our hero, scornfully; "who made this man my master I should like to know."

"You will discover, good lad, if you live long enough, that as, in Rome, one man may possess many slaves, so one slave may be at the beck and call of many masters," rejoined Pandion, drily.

"Then I take it that at the request of Narcissus I was sent for," said the Briton.

"Yes, and for another reason," he continued, "as Horace tells us,—

'There are who round the Olympic goal
Delight the kindling wheel to roll.'

We are to have chariot races, my boy, and the president will be no other than young Nero, the nephew and heir-apparent of divine Cæsar."

Our hero's face brightened up at the prospect of joining in a sport he so keenly relished.

"And am I to drive a chariot with the rest?"

"Yes, and I wish you good fortune."

"To which faction will he be assigned?" asked Pandion.

"The White," replied Manlius.

"Do not smile at my question. You must remember that I am a stranger and have much to learn," said Caractacus. "What and how many are these factions you allude to?"

"The drivers are divided into four companies," explained Manlius, "each distinguished by a different colour, to represent the four seasons of the year. They are each called a faction. Thus the green represents the Spring, red the Summer, the azure the Autumn; yours will be the factio Alba, the White, for winter, no doubt in allusion to the wintry isles you came from."

"And talking of these islands," rejoined Pandion, "startling intelligence has been received from Britain."

"O, let me hear that," cried the Briton, eagerly.

"It is reported that your namesake, Caractacus—"

"The king, my father?"

"Has defeated one of the Tribunes of the army of the prefect, Ostorius Scapula, in a great battle. A whole cohort was destroyed to the last man."

"The gods be praised!" ejaculated the excited Briton; but immediately added in a tone of poignant regret.

"But I not there."

CHAPTER XXVI.

THE WILD BEAST FIGHTS.

"ZABA!"

"Hard at hand, Varro."

"Acheron! what a night! How the blue lightning whizzes! How horrible it makes you look! It exaggerates your deformity, and renders you a very cacodæmon!"

"It has changed you, too, Varro, but in another way. You do not look at all yourself—quite a different man."

"Not like myself! How do I look, then?"

"Handsome! No worse sign than when a man changes like that! They say just before a man dies——

"Avert the omen! why do you speak of death?"

"Because death showed me your double, your fetch—your eidolon, as the Greeks call it—that is the spectral shadow, the counterpart of yourself!"

"Jupiter! when?"

"Just now, while the last lightning flash played o'er the high wet walls of the circus, I saw something pass as like—but look there! Hum! it's a bad omen, say what you will."

"Malignant little beast! you say this to frighten me."

"Are you frightened of death? We must all die, you know, comrade. A man who is not always ready to 'welcome the steel' makes a poor gladiator."

"It is not that—death, a fair brave death, has no horrors for me."

"I am glad of that."

"Why do you say so, and in such a tone?"

"Because you are walking over the spot where you will get your last fall."

"That's a lie. On the other side of yonder frowning wall it might be—but not here."

"By Obi! we shall see."

"Well, good night; the rain begins to fall—no, it is hail. I shall turn into the 'Dancing Fawn' for a cup of rough Sabine and then to bed."

"I must look to my pantheress. She is mad with hunger, but she must starve till to-morrow."

"Well, you understand our compact."

"Yes, the worse for the Briton, Caractacus."

"And Nero is in the secret?"

"Yes."

"He enjoys such sport."

"He does; he will make a brave emperor."

For such as you and me. Have you heard the news from Britain?"

"Yes, Caractacus still holds the Romans at bay; he has thrice defeated the lieutenants of Ostorius."

"So much the better. That king of the Silures is the father of our man. When the Briton falls the mob will rejoice."

"And that shall be to-morrow, as surely as the morrow dawns."

"Well, Zaba, good night. Jove, send us better weather for the games!"

*　　*　　*　　*　　*

The circus maximus was densely crowded by excited crowds assembled to witness the sports, which were to comprise a fight of wild beasts and a chariot race.

The storm had cleared off and the sky was bright and cloudless.

Separate places were marked out for the senators and knights, where each might see the games.

These were called fori. The other spectators were on high seats around a wooden gallery.

At the extremity of the circus were placed the stalls for the horses and chariots, commonly called carceres, twelve in number.

In the centre of the carceres was a large entrance, called the porta pompæ, because it was the one through which the Circensian procession entered.

Near this was the cubiculum or seat of the editor of the games, on this occasion occupied by young Nero, the nephew and heir to the Emperor Claudius.

He was about eighteen years of age, sturdy in proportions, florid in complexion, but extremely handsome, and the manners of the future tyrant gave no indication of his real character, being bluff, frank, and engaging. The young prince, it may be noted, was at this period of his life the idol of the mob, who, as he mounted his gold and ivory tribunal, hailed him with hearty and prolonged acclamations.

He was magnificently dressed, and surrounded by a brilliant retinue of knights and nobles, and a body of stalwart Prætorian guards, with crested plumes and glittering armour.

There was a sudden and deep hush of expectation as the prince rose from his seat, and raising his ivory sceptre gave a sign to the musicians.

Then came a flourish of trumpets loud and long-continued, but silver-sweet, accompanied by the brazen clash of cymbals.

The gates of the porta pompæ were thrown wide open, and a grand procession issued forth.

In it all those who were about to exhibit in the circus, as well as many persons of distinction, bore a part.

The statues of the gods formed the most conspicuous feature in the show, which were paraded upon wooden platforms called fercula and thensæ. The former were borne upon the shoulders of the priests, as the statues of the saints are carried in modern processions; the latter were drawn along upon wheels.

The spectators, impatient for the more serious business of the day to commence, showed little interest in this exhibition, and, though there was some faint applause, all seemed glad when this portion of the spectacle came to an end.

Once more Nero raised his sceptre and gave the

CARACTACUS.

AS CARACTACUS NEARED THE WINNING GOAL A PANTHER SPRANG UPON THE NECK OF ONE OF THE STEEDS.

No. 5.

signal, which was again responded to by the blare of trumpets and the clash of cymbals.

Then commenced the venatio, the hunting or "field sports," but which were, in fact, uninteresting and cruel, and totally warring against our English ideas of fair play.

First five or six antelopes were brought out of cages, so stiff and weak from confinement that they could barely stand.

They were abandoned to the mercy of chetahs and lynxes, which pulled them down without their making any effort to escape.

An hyæna was next turned loose, and pursued and brought to bay by a pack of above twenty large dogs, but the unfortunate animal was muzzled, and was therefore unresistingly mangled for about ten minutes.

The next victim was a bear, which was worried by a troop of yelping curs, several of which he strangled.

Then a gigantic cage was drawn into the arena.

Sundry smaller cells, communicating by sliding doors with the main theatre, were tenanted by every species of the wildest inhabitants of the forest.

In the large cage, crowded together and presenting a formidable array of broad, shaggy foreheads, well armed with horns, stood a group of buffaloes, sternly awaiting the conflict.

The trap-doors being lifted, two tigers and the same number of bears and leopards rushed into the centre.

The buffaloes instantly commenced hostilities, and made complete shuttlecocks of the bears, who, however, finally escaped by climbing up the bars beyond the reach of their horned antagonists.

The tigers, one of which was a beautiful animal, fared scarcely better, indeed the odds were much against them, there being five buffaloes.

They appeared, however, to be no match for these powerful creatures, even single-handed, and showed little disposition to be the assaulters.

The leopards seemed throughout the conflict to jedulously avoid a breach of the peace.

A rhinoceros was next let loose, and the attendants attempted to induce him to pick a quarrel with a tiger who was chained to a ring.

The rhinoceros appeared, however, to consider a fettered foe beneath his enmity, and having once approached the tiger, and quietly surveyed him, as he writhed and growled, expecting the attack, turned suddenly round and trotted awkwardly to the gate, where he capsized Zaba, the dwarf, and several others of the beast-keepers, who attempted to drive him back.

A buffalo and a tiger were the next combatants.

They attacked furiously, the tiger springing at the first onset on the other's head, and tearing his neck severely.

But he was quickly dismounted, and thrown with such violence as to nearly break his back, and quite to disable him from renewing the combat.

A small elephant was next impelled to attack a leopard.

The battle was short and decisive.

The former falling on his knees, thrust his tusks nearly through his antagonist.

Then there was a match with quails.

The birds, trained for the purpose, were placed upon a green cloth, and fought most gamely, after the manner of the English cock-pit.

This was an amusement much in fashion among the Roman nobles, and they bet large sums on their birds.

Elephant fights were announced as the conclusion of the strife.

The elephants, educated for the arena, were large, powerful males, wrought up to a state of fury by constant feeding with exciting spices.

Several of the animals entered the arena, their drivers seated on their backs, which were covered with a strong net-work for the driver to cling to in the conflict.

In attendance upon every elephant were two or three men, armed with long spears, a weapon of which the animals have the greatest dread.

Two of the combatants slowly advanced towards each other from opposite sides of the plain.

As they approached their speed gradually increased.

They met with a grand shock.

They entwined their trunks, and kept pushing, until one, finding himself overmatched, fairly turned tail, and received his adversary's charge in the rear.

This was so violent that the driver was dislodged from his seat, and fell at the feet of his pursuer.

The enraged and gigantic beast instantly trampled him to death, amid the applauding shouts of the cruel multitude.

Five or six couple were fought.

They engaged with the utmost desperation, the result being that another man was killed, while one of the elephants was so horribly mangled, that the spearmen in attendance were forced to despatch him on the spot.

This brought the first part of the entertainmen to a conclusion.

The arena was cleared, and the spectators awaited in breathless expectation, the chariot races.

CHAPTER XXVII.

THE CHARIOT RACE.

VERY gallant looked our hero in his white tunic fringed with gold, his gilded sandals, and the gemmed fillet that confined his fair curls.

He was standing in one of the carceres, or stalls, ready to mount the chariot.

This car was what was called a quadriga, a light carriage drawn by four horses, glorious creatures, full of fire, and of the purest Parthian breed.

They fretted, started, pawed the air, champed the bit, and it was only by main force that the grooms at their head could restrain the impetuosity of their high-mettled charges.

Caractacus was not alone.

He was surrounded by sympathetic friends and enthusiastic backers, who overwhelmed him with advice, and cheered him with words of encouragement.

Among the former were his three comrades, Manlius, Pandion, and Lycaon, while among the latter were Licinius and Honorius.

Lycaon, who had at one time been an auriga or chariot racer, took upon himself to give the Briton his final instructions.

"You see, my Caractacus," he explained, "there is a meta, a gaol, at each extremity of the course; the chariot runs seven times round the course, and that which arrives first at the meta nearest the carceres wins the race."

"All this I know already," answered the Briton with impatience.

"Patience, young fire-eater," returned Lycaon, "it is against this I would warn you; do not drive too close to the spina—the low wall that intersects the course—but when you reach the meta farthermost from the starting place dash in and past the goal as narrowly as you can; 'tis a bold stroke and a perilous one, but if successful brings you off victorious."

"Stand clear," bawled the grooms that held in the horses; "the first trumpet is sounded!"

"Are you ready?"

Caractacus nodded assent.

He leaped into the car.

"Hold!" cried Lycaon, "you have not your cleaver with you."

"What should I want with such a weapon?" asked our hero.

"Understand, you keep within the reins which pass around your back," resumed his instructor; "this enables you to throw all your weight against the horses by leaning backwards, but it greatly enhances your peril in case of an upset."

"I am not afraid of that."

"It is as well to be prepared against the worst," was Lycaon's reply; "take this instrument and buckle it to your waist, it will serve to cut the reins in case of emergency."

Licinius interfered.

"What folly is this?" he said. "I am sure that Caractacus handles the reins too well to need such a weapon."

"Pardon, my lord," returned Lycaon, with respectful firmness; "it is as well to take every precaution."

He hung the implement, which resembled in shape a bill-hook, to our hero's waist.

Licinius frowned and bit his lip.

"Hark! what is that?" cried Honorius, suddenly raising his hand.

"'Tis the roar of wild beasts," said Pandion.

"They should have been removed out of earshot," said Honorius; "they frighten the horses and render them wild and unmanageable."

"Too true," rejoined Lycaon; "look at the Parthians how they sweat and tremble."

"'Tis that villain Zaba," rejoined Pandion, shaking his fist; "he has some design in this. I caught his hideous leering look as he passed me; I knew he was bent on mischief."

"Now it has ceased," rejoined Licinius, "and all is well."

"Soh, Auster! quiet, my beauty," cried Pandion, patting the delicate neck of the nearest horse, which was pawing and kicking at the wooden doors of the carcer, as though impatient to dash through the obstacle in the very wantonness of its strength and mettle.

Caractacus reined back the car, the four steeds trampling, and tossing their manes.

So splendid did he look, so free, bold, and graceful was his attitude, that his comrades and his backers murmured their admiration.

"So looked Phaëthon when he mounted his sire's chariot to drive the flame-breathing coursers of the sun," remarked the sentimental Diomed.

"Avert the omen," grunted Pandion. "That presumptuous youth, if the poets be believed, was thrown headlong from the solar car and drowned in the river Eridanus. We must wish our comrade better luck than that."

"Silence, babbler," said Honorius. "The gates of the carcer will be thrown open presently."

"Tell me, comrades," asked our hero, "to what faction does my countryman belong?"

"To the Green," rejoined Honorius; "you must beware of him—he is the favourite with most of the sporting men."

Caractacus laughed defiantly.

"Give me the libellus," said Licinius, turning to his slave. "Ha! I see here that in this missus (course or heat) Octavian and Miletus are competitors. Well-known names. Veteran charioteers both of them."

"Well, my lad," rejoined Honorius, raising his eyes from the scroll and nodding to our hero, "your horses bear auspicious names, I see."

"What better could they have?" chuckled Pandion, rubbing his hands; "Eurus, Auster, Zephyrus, and Boreas—the names of the four winds."

"May the power and speed of the winds nerve their beautiful limbs," added Diomed.

"Fortune grant your wish."

Varro now stepped up to Licinius and whispered something in his ear.

The patrician started.

"It is well thought of," he said; "bring me the goblet."

Varro retired a moment and then returned with a silver chalice brimming with wine.

"Here, my Caractacus," he said, handing the cup to our hero, "one draught of this fine Lesbian will stimulate your nerves and do you good. Come, drain it off—just to propitiate Bacchus."

The Briton looked at him steadfastly.

"Thanks, noble Licinius," he said.

He stretched out his hand, seized the cup and placed it to his lips.

Licinius and Varro exchanged a rapid look of triumph. But Caractacus had not tasted the wine.

He held the goblet aloft.

"To Castor and Pollux I pour out a libation," cried Caractacus, and he poured half the wine upon the ground, and then staying his hand he continued, "Another to the Goddess of Victory!"

He poured out the rest of the wine, at the same time fixing a meaning look upon Licinius.

Then he threw away the cup.

As it fell to the ground the restive steeds started, reared, and plunged, and Caractacus had some trouble in quieting them.

"The cunning knave suspects us," whispered Varro to his confederate.

"Fool! it was your fault," retorted the patrician, angrily; "why were you so eager to thrust in that villainous face of yours? He caught your eye as you handed me the cup and his suspicions were at once aroused—no, our work is marred."

"Not so," returned the gladiator; "Zaba will not fail, my lord."

"Silence!" cried Honorius, "That is the trumpet. Now for it. Hark to that crash! the moratores are opening the barriers."

Before he had ceased speaking, the folding gates were thrown wide and each chariot, leaving its stall, rolled out upon the level course amidst the roar of a myriad applauding voices—a volume of sound that resembled nothing so much as a clap of thunder.

Guided by the grooms and ring-keepers the chariots were brought to the linea alba—the white chalk line—where the moratores or starters stood ready to set them off.

There was another flourish of trumpets.

Perfect silence now reigned in the circus, broken only by the champing and trampling of the fiery steeds.

Nero stands up in his tribunal, holding in his hand a gold-embroidered napkin.

"One, two, three!"

The napkin falls.

Another deafening shout rends the sky.

"They are off!"

Away dash the chariots with whirlwind speed.

Caractacus sees nothing but his horses, though he is conscious that the serried rows of faces flash past him in a carnation glare, as dim and confused as the picture of a drunkard's dream.

The uproar of cries, shouts, yells, curses, applause, hisses, cheers, ring in his ears like the noise of a storm.

He sways backwards and forwards, tightens or loosens the rein, and plies the lash, while he cheers on his darting thundering steeds with his wild British battle-cry.

"Iero, Iero! vich, Iero!"

Sand spurts about him, the foam flies like spray from the silken coats of his splendid coursers, and they thunder along.

"Arvirargus has passed the meta!" roar the mob.

"Octavian, forward, forward!"

"Miletus, laggard, coward, tortoise!—forward!"

"The Briton! the Briton! He is over!"

Caractacus felt his wheel graze the meta, and a flame shot up from the burning tire.

"Iero—vich—Iero."

The meta is passed, an ivory ball, shaped like an egg, is placed by an attendant on a conspicuous pillar to mark the first round.

Away fly the chariots in a ruck, cheered or cursed by the frantic crowd.

The seventh, the last round.

The wheels of our hero's car are burning, his horses strain in their trace, the slashing of whips, the rattle of wheels, the hubbub of myriad voices, a babel of madness! and then—what means that wild shriek?

"The panther! the panther!"

Caractacus is within twenty yards of the last goal, having outstripped his competitors, when there is a sudden check.

A huge panther springs upon the neck of one of the steeds, the driver foams with rage and dismay.

An instant the car rolls over and the Briton is dashed to the ground.

CHAPTER XXVIII.

HOW THE BRITON SLEW THE PANTHER.

CARACTACUS lay for some moments half-stunned, and unable to move.

One of his legs was crushed under the weight of the fallen chariot, while his hands and arms were entangled in the reins.

It was an exciting scene that followed.

The spectators rose in their places and rent the air with shouts of wrath and consternation at this disastrous termination of the race.

Many of them loudly demanded that the men who had charge of the wild beasts should be summarily punished for their negligence in allowing the panther to escape.

There were some, however, who had bet heavily against Caractacus, and these kept quiet, inwardly congratulating themselves upon having saved their money—for, of course, after such a "foul" their bets would be drawn.

Meanwhile the scene on the racecourse was one of indescribable confusion.

The chariot driven by the Briton, Arvirargus, was the second in the race, and at the moment when the panther sprang upon the horses of Caractacus came thundering up close behind.

Upon seeing the savage beast they backed, reared, stumbled, and two of them fell, the consequence being that the car was overturned and Arvirargus was dashed against the ground, where he lay, bleeding and insensible.

Octavian's car came next; but with great dexterity the veteran whip managed to turn his horses in time, and they dashed back at break-neck speed towards the carceres.

Miletus met with better luck.

The grooms and ring-keepers threw themselves before the horses, and, aiding the driver's efforts, succeeded in stopping them before more damage was done.

As soon as Caractacus was able to gather together his scattered faculties he endeavoured to extricate himself from his trammels.

Our hero might have lain still and awaited the arrival of the attendants, who, led on by his comrades, Lycaon and Manlius, came running up to his assistance.

But Caractacus was exasperated to a pitch of madness by the base trick that had been played upon him, and determined to free himself, if possible, by his own exertions.

He bethought him of the sharp instrument which Lycaon had given him to cut the reins and traces in case of such an accident as that which had befallen.

The Briton who, like most of his race, was enraged and touched with pity when he heard the human like sobs and groans of the suffering steed, and the ferocious growls of the savage panther, as with teeth and claws he rent the living quivering flesh.

Drawing the hooked knife from his belt, Caractacus cut through the tangled leathern bands, and sprang to his feet, shaking the dust and sand from his clothes.

Then grasping tightly the handle of the knife he crept close up to the panther.

The hungry beast was too absorbed in his bloody meal to notice his foe's approach.

He sucked the gore, while his victim, fascinated, quelled, lifted its beautiful head and strained its blood-shot eyes, moaning in dreadful agony.

One fierce, quick, powerful stab, and then a yell of horrible anguish and rage.

The panther left his victim and licked his own wound, then turning the glare of his greenish-yellow eyes upon our hero, approached him with sinuous writhings, and prepared to make the fatal spring.

With perfect calmness Caractacus awaited the shock, poising his body in such a manner as to be able to slip aside when the bound came.

He had not long to wait.

For an instant the panther crouched upon his belly, lashing his gaunt sides with his long powerful tail.

Our hero stood confronting him with steady mien and watchful eye.

A roar, a mad bound, and then a terrific scuffle.

Caractacus and the panther rolled upon the sand together.

But our hero had all the advantage.

In the nick of time he had avoided the charge of the furious brute, by nimbly springing out of his way.

The panther came to earth, baffled, hurt, and dismayed.

Not giving the ferocious animal time to recover himself, Caractacus flung himself upon him, wielded the keen strong blade, and stabbed, stabbed, death in every blow, till the blood spurted over his face and body, and he reeked like a butcher in the shambles.

"Habet! he's got it, the cursed brute!" roared the infuriated mob. "Euge! Well done, Caractacus!"

The panther lay still and dead—weltering in a pool of blood.

Dazed and breathless, the Briton gazed around in dull wonderment upon the dense multitude that packed the immense building.

His comrades came rushing up, almost as spent and breathless as himself.

Pandion was the first to break the silence.

"Speak, thou bravest of the brave!" he faltered. "Art thou hurt? Art thou hurt?"

"Not a scar!" answered our hero, smiling.

"The gods be praised!" ejaculated the hearty boxer.

"But I have lost the race!" grumbled the Briton.

"You have won more than you have lost, believe me, comrade," rejoined Lycaon. "Young Nero has sent for you!"

"Put that poor creature out of its miseries!" said Caractacus, pointing to the dying horse. "Its groans pierce my heart like barbed arrows.'

"In a trice! Though I cannot understand your squeamishness. A horse is but a horse, after all!" responded Manlius, who, with that brutality which lurked in Roman nature, could not understand the Briton's sympathy for a mere brute animal.

However, it was well that the man of blood and iron was merciful enough in stern fact—one thrust in the proper place, and the gallant steed was past all pain.

"This is Zaba's doing," said Pandion, "and I doubt much whether that false patrician, Licinius, was not in league with him."

"I know he was. They tried to poison me, between them," answered Caractacus. "Did you not observe that I rejected the cup of wine that Licinius proffered me?"

"I did not heed—it is so seldom that you touch wine!"

"No; I take example by the 'precept and practice' of our abstemious lanista."

"Who is never drunk more than seven times a-week!" chuckled Pandion. "But don't make me laugh when I am ready to cry with joy to find thee safe and sound! Such a scurvy death to die! But, never mind, we shall have our vengeance on Zaba. The mob will tear him to pieces!"

"Wait till you catch him," said Caractacus.

"That is done already," replied Manlius, as he wiped his sword by plunging it in the sand, and then rattled it back into the scabbard. "Honorius has him fast, and will bring him before young Cæsar."

"I am glad to hear it," said Lycaon. "The monster will no longer live. A libel on humanity."

"Let us go," said Pandion. "The people are irritated, and we had better get out of the way."

Whether Pandion was right or wrong in this opinion the assembly displayed nothing but good will towards the Briton, and cheered him vociferously as he left the course.

The pulvinar—the station for the emperor, or his representative presiding over the games—was placed in the best situation for seeing both the commencement and end of the course, and in the most prominent part of the circus.

At the back of it was a spacious gallery adorned with columns and statues, and reached by a broad marble staircase.

Thither our hero was brought by his comrades.

Here he found young Nero, surrounded by many nobles and military officers of high rank, together with a good number of the ladies of the court, all magnificently attired.

A murmur of admiration arose as the noble-looking Briton stood before the heir-apparent of a world-wide empire, as calm and dignified as though he had been from birth accustomed to the society of princes and nobles.

Young Nero appeared to be as well satisfied with our hero's appearance.

He paid a graceful compliment to the Briton's skill as a charioteer, and also praised him for the courage he had displayed in his encounter with the panther.

"If I am not misinformed, you are the son of the famous Caractacus, the King of the Silures?" said Nero.

"It is so, illustrious," returned the Briton, proudly. "I am his eldest son."

"I think no worse of you for that," answered the young Prince, graciously. "Rome can afford to respect a brave and honourable foe."

Our hero bowed.

"Now," continued the Prince, "we must inquire into the circumstance which marred your triumph, for there can be no question that you would have won the race had it not been for the attack of the panther that broke loose through the negligence of the keepers. Take my word that, whoever is responsible, they shall be severely punished."

"August and mighty!" said Pandion, "there is no one to blame except the deformed slave, Zaba, the Ethiopian beast-keeper. By him my gallant comrade, Florus, was done to death; and this is not the first time he has attempted the life of Caractacus."

"It is my pleasure to inflict shrewd torture on such offenders," returned Nero, with a cruel leer. "Leave him to my power and will, for punishment."

"Not so, illustrious," said the Briton, with that quiet dignity which became him so well. "The villain's base design was frustrated. Let him not suffer on my account—he is *Cœla ictus!* [smitten by Heaven.] Confine him if you will, until he grows into a better frame of mind, but neither torture him nor kill him."

As the princely barbarian made this generous speech, he thought of Mathias as prompting him, and whispering in his ear what to say. The good seed had been sown in fertile soil and began to germinate.

"Your tone is too masterful, Caractacus," retorted Nero, with a scowl that made his handsome face for the moment quite ugly. "You must remember your change of fortune. I do not wish to remind you of it, but reflect—what *I* am and what *you* are."

"Still myself," answered the Briton, proudly. "Though I own my folly in trying to teach mercy to a Roman."

"This is insolence."

"No, indeed, illustrious. Why should you respect my father as a noble foeman, if you cannot hear me, his son, speak my thought?"

"The brave son of a brave father," replied Nero. "I admire your spirit. But think not your generous pleading shall excuse the villain dwarf; on the contrary, it renders his attempted crime the more atrocious."

"Spare him not, heir of divine Cæsar! Spare him not one lash of the whip, one twist of the rack!" cried Pandion, bitterly. "He would have destroyed our Caractacus, the pride of our maniple, the king of all hearts. Let the villain taste sharp torment!"

While he was speaking Honorius approached, followed by some of the Prætorium soldiers, who dragged Zaba along.

The miserable wretch was brought before the young Cæsar, whom he glanced at with a look half-terrified, half-defiant, such as a rat might glint from his wicked black eyes when driven up in a corner.

"Now, thou filth, what hast thou to say for thyself?"

"All-powerful and divine, ask the noble Honorius where he found me."

"Highness! he lay beside the panther's cage, apparently insensible," replied the tribune. "The bars of the cage were broken; he tells me that the beast broke out of his prison, and, striking Zaba down, sprang into the circus. That, at least, is his account of the affair."

"I have told the truth; 'twas thus it came about!" cried Zaba, falling on his knees, and clasping his hands.

This imploring attitude was a great mistake.

It only whetted the incipient tyrant's appetite for cruelty.

"Villain, I am not to be deceived by your lies!" he said, sternly.

Then he went on, with a cruel laugh—

"Gods! the distortion of that Gorgon face under the torture will beat the best fun of a Fescinine farce!"

Little Zaba, like most dwarfs, was full of conceit and pluck.

"Hear me, hope of Rome!" he cried, extending his long, hairy arms. "Spare me, and I will spare you. Though a divinity, you are not immortal. I tell you that you dare not hurt a hair of my head. Remember the fate of Messalina and of Caius Silius!"

Nero laughed till his sides ached.

"The humour of it!" he chuckled. "See, my Sporus," he added, turning to his favourite, a beautiful but effeminate-looking youth. "Mark what weak human nature will do to save itself from pain—to preserve the boon of existence!"

"Imperial!" smirked the fawning slave; "glad am I to see you so amused. But do not get too far—do not provoke a popular outcry. In this case, however, I think you are safe."

"Safe! Hark at the wretches in the cavea, how they howl for his destruction! I will have him torn to pieces by the brutes he feeds. But I do not like this Briton. I will deal with him afterwards."

Looking fiercely at the dwarf, he asked, with savageness—

"Are you prepared for death?"

"No, illustrious, but for the life and reward I dare to claim," answered Zaba. "Can you write, imperial?"

"Write! thou thing too hideous to be mentionable! Thou shalt see. I will set my hand to that which will consign thee to torment. I can write, Adonis, and I will stand by my written bond."

"So can Locusta's man, her scrivener" hissed

the dwarf, drawing a scrap of parchment from his bosom. "Read that! 'tis a copy of a letter from your royal mother, Agrippina."

"O, for the gods, sweet prince! listen to me, and let this fellow go!" cried a sweet girlish voice, and a beautiful dark-eyed maiden stepped out from a group of court ladies and caught Nero by the sleeve.

"What you, my pretty Nyssa!" returned the young prince, very much astonished. "Can it be possible that you should plead the cause of such an abominable miscreant?"

"Do you think it is for any good will I bear him?" she answered, in a low, hurried voice. "Is he an object that any girl would be likely to fall in love with?"

"Scarcely," answered Nero, with a laugh. "But why then do you intercede for him?"

"Because he knows too much," was the reply. "He consorts with that witch, Locusta, who is in the pay of my august mistress."

"The more the pity," answered Nero, frowning. "I marvel that my mother should have dealings with a woman of such evil repute."

"It is not for me to question the actions of my mistress," rejoined Nyssa. "But I am sure it would be unwise to drive this wretch to desperation, lest he should betray dangerous secrets."

"There is reason in what you say," replied Nero; "but I fear I have gone too far now to retract. Many keen eyes are upon me, and if I spare the villain I am likely to excite suspicion."

"There is no need to set him free," suggested Nyssa. "Let him be kept in durance until you can decide how best to dispose of him."

"This is a good plan," assented the prince. "I will take your advice."

He turned to the courtiers.

"My lords," he said, "circumstances have come to my knowledge which render it unadvisable that this wretch should be summarily punished, as was at first my intention. He must be brought to the question. There are other charges against him which demand inquiry."

A subtle gleam of triumph glanced from the dwarf's blood-shot eyes, while Pandion and Manlius looked their disappointment at the miscreant's escape.

"I commit him to your charge, centurion," continued the prince, addressing one of the officers of the Prætorian guard. "Let him be confined in one of the dungeons of the palace. See that no one is allowed access to him until my further pleasure shall be made known. Take him away. I will not hear him speak."

The soldiers closed around their prisoner and marched him off, and soon afterwards Nero dismissed the gladiators and returned to the palace of Cæsar.

CHAPTER XXIX.

THE ORDER ON RELEASE.

ZABA the Ethiop was led to his dungeon by the guard, and went in silence and without a murmur.

He inwardly exulted in the power which he possessed over Agrippina and her son, Nero.

"She dares not kill me!" he said to himself. "One word from me would destroy her. Besides, I am too useful to her. My knowledge of charms and philtres and slow poisons has done her good service. Still, I hate that haughty Nero; there is something false and cruel in his face, which fills me with dread. I will have my revenge upon him, and her too. I will beguile the time until the messenger comes to set me free by thinking how I may best accomplish the task that I have set myself."

He flung himself upon the litter of straw in one corner of the stone cell, and gnawing, and biting his fingers he sat staring into vacancy, a horrible looking object, more like a brooding demon than a human being.

The hours passed slowly by, but no one came to disturb his solitude.

Nothing was heard but the steady tramp of the sentinel pacing up and down the corridor outside the cell.

It grew late in the day, the rosy beam of sunset struck in through the rusty iron grating that admitted light and air.

The rosy ray faded out and it grew dusk, and then the moon rose and poured in a flood of bluish, spectral light that, resting upon the crouching hunchback, rendered him more weird and goblin-like than ever.

At length he was roused by the sound of approaching footsteps, and the loud, stern challenge of the sentry.

The he heard some one give the word, and instantly after he heard a voice that was familiar to him speaking to the soldier.

"Admit me to your prisoner, by order of Narcissus."

"Have you a written pass?"

"Yes, his discharge, under the hand and seal of Nero."

"Wait, noble sir, until I call the gaoler."

"Very good; but make haste."

Zaba, who stood eagerly listening at the door tossed up his arms and cut a caper expressive of delight.

"'Tis Licinius," he muttered, "and I am saved!"

There was a jingling of keys and clashing of bolts, and then the dungeon door was thrown open, and Licinius entered, accompanied by the gaoler, while the sentry stood looking in upon them, leaning on his spear.

Zaba made a cringing obeisance to the young patrician.

"Come forth, Zaba," said Licinius, making him a sign to be cautious as to what he might say in the presence of the others. "I have brought an order for your release."

"Thanks, noble Licinius," said the dwarf, in a fawning tone; "I knew that I could safely depend upon the justice and clemency of such a patron."

"Enough. I trust you will be able to establish your innocence of the crime you are charged with," was the reply. "Meanwhile, without further parley, come you with me."

Again Zaba bowed low.

"To hear is to obey, my lord," he answered.

They emerged into the stone passage.

"There is a secret staircase leading to a door which opens into the palace-gardens—is it not so?" Licinius inquired of the gaoler.

The man started, and looked rather scared at the question.

"That is indeed true, noble Licinius," he replied. "But to that door there is but one key, now in the possession of the empress, Agrippina."

Licinius smiled.

"By whom it has been entrusted to me," he replied, and as he spoke he drew the key from his bosom.

The gaoler and the Prætorian guardsman both appeared thunderstruck, and regarded each other in bewilderment.

"Now show me this secret outlet to the gardens."

"'Tis more than our lives are worth," cried the two men in a breath.

"Your lives are worth little, knaves, if you dare to dispute my command," retorted Licinius, fiercely. "Here is the sign-manual of the all-powerful Narcissus, here the signet-ring of Agrippina, and here the key itself. Are not such guarantees sufficient? Are you not satisfied?"

"If my lord will pledge his knightly word that we shall be held blameless," faltered the gaoler, in a reluctant tone.

"Have I not said? Fear not you. Come, let us have no more words. Lead the way

The gaoler shrugged his shoulders, and, retiring into one of the cells, presently returned, bearing a lantern.

He conducted them down a long vaulted corridor, at the end of which was a small chamber of octangular shape.

The gaoler then pressed hard against one of the marble slabs in the wall.

The stone yielded to the pressure, and turning round upon an iron pivot disclosed a steep spiral staircase ascending from the level of the underground prisons to the earth above them.

The gaoler, lantern in hand, mounted the steep rugged flight of steps, while Licinius and Zaba followed him close.

When they got to the top of it they found themselves standing in a small tomb-like structure without the slightest aperture, while the confined atmosphere was so close as to be almost suffocating.

"We are now in the place described to me," said Licinius. "This cell is built within the thickness of the wall of the palace gardens. I was told that there were two entrances, one opening into the gardens themselves, the other giving egress to a lonely spot outside the palace-grounds and lying near the Appian Way."

"You are rightly informed," answered the gaoler. "By which of these outlets will you go forth?"

"Oh, set us clear of the palace," answered Licinius. "Let us take the Appian Way."

"I will, my lord," answered the gaoler. "But first I must mask the lantern lest the light might attract the notice of some passer-by."

The next instant they were in total darkness.

Licinius and Zaba now heard a harsh grating noise, as though their guide were turning an iron wheel or crank.

Then a part of the wall sank down, leaving a narrow gap, just wide enough for a man's body to pass through.

The cool night breeze rushed in, fanning their heated brows. They saw the bright moonshine tipping with silver the tops of waving trees.

Licinius placed some money in the gaoler's hand at the same time whispering him to keep secret all that had passed that night.

This was readily promised.

The young patrician then sprang out upon the fresh dewy sward, and drew a deep breath of relief.

Followed by Zaba he hurried through a dark grove of trees, and soon reached the famous Appian Way.

The Via Appia was the most celebrated of all the Roman roads; it was made by Appius Claudius Cœcus, the censor, in the fifth century after the founding of the city, and extended as far Brundrosium, three hundred and fifty miles, and cross, the Pontine marshes, the inundation of which from time to time occasioned much damage.

In spite of all that was done to drain them, the marshes still remain. It was of sufficient breadth to allow two carriages to pass with ease. In many places it may still be found entire, after a lapse of more than two thousand years.

The spot where Licinius and Zaba were standing was gloomy and desolate.

On one side of them were the boundary walls of the palace-gardens, concealed by a fringe of dark pine trees; on the other stretched the marshes.

Far and wide pools of water, intersected by clumps and beds of osiers and bullrushes. The hollow, monotonous croaking of innumerable frogs, and the occasional distant boom of the bittern from his sedgy retreat, were the only sounds that broke the solemn stillness of the night.

"We part here," said Licinius. "I am bound for the villa of Narcissus, while you must return to the city."

"But not to the vivaria, I trust, noble sir?" said Zaba. "There I might meet with a rough reception."

"You will be safe enough," replied Licinius,

"under the protection of such powerful friends. I do not wish you to go back to the amphitheatre for some days."

"What will become of my poor Hecate?" grumbled the dwarf. "She will be starved."

"Hecate!" repeated Licinius, with a laugh. "Who is she—your wife? If so, she has a very appropriate name."

"My wife! Why should my wife be a Hecate, or a Harpy, because I am black and hunched? Grimy Vulcan, the bandy-legged, married Venus herself, the goddess of love and beauty!" snarled the dwarf.

"Well, if ugliness is a recommendation in a suitor, your bride ought to be lovely indeed!" retorted Licinius. "But, tell me, who is Hecate?"

"My pantheress."

"I had forgot. I have heard that you have tamed such a creature."

"She will wonder what has become of me," returned Zaba, "and unless someone feeds her, she will go mad!"

"I will give orders that she shall be cared for," rejoined Licinius. "But to-night I have a commission for you to execute."

"I await your commands, most noble Licinius," answered the dwarf, making his usual salaam.

"This is not the time nor place to explain all I wish you to do," said the patrician; "but hasten to the house of Locusta, where you will meet Varro. He will tell you what business I have in hand; it concerns the Briton—Caractacus."

"And bodes him no good," chuckled Zaba.

"Of that you may be sworn," answered Licinius. "Thrice he has escaped me. Narcissus is enraged at our repeated failures, but we shall reach the barbarian yet. Though, by Jupiter," he went on grinding his teeth, "the audacious slave appears to lead a charmed life, and to be protected by something invisible that wards off every blow that is struck against him. It must be he foils his enemies and preserves his life by art-magic."

Zaba raised his glowering eyes, clutched the speaker's mantle, and said in an awed voice—

"Do you know what it is that protects him? I will tell you. It is the fetish—the charm thing he wears about his neck."

"An amulet?"

"Yes, a sardonyx given him by Virginia, his lanista's daughter."

"Tush! an idle superstition," replied Licinius, contemptuously; "I have no belief in other charms or talisman than a quick eye, a strong arm, a ready wit, and a brave heart; though, as I said just now, luck counts for something, and in his case appears quite magical."

"And magic it is—nothing else," rejoined Zaba. "But I will rob him of his fetish, and then he will be at our mercy."

"Be that as you please, but something must be done to satisfy Narcissus," resumed the patrician.

"By Obi! I will cast a spell upon him, and you shall see how he will wither away like a blighted sapling," hissed Zaba. "Locusta shall help me to perform the proper rites."

Then he added mysteriously, and glancing round as though to make sure that there was no one near to overhear him.

"But I shall want a child for my purpose."

"A child! Gods! What for?"

"To sacrifice to Obi. It should be an infant newly snatched from the mother's breast, and without spot or blemish."

Licinius gave a cry of horror, and raised his hand to strike the hideous dwarf, but instantly recoiled with a shudder of loathing.

"Horrible monster!" he gasped. "And do you dare to make this detestable proposition to me!"

He turned upon the dwarf, at the same time quickly drawing his stylus, which sparkled blue in the moonlight.

Zaba sprang nimbly back, and crouched like a whipped hound.

"Pardon, noble master; be not so angry, we can find some other plan," he whined.

"Thou abhored monstrosity!" panted Licinius, again threatening him with the dagger. "If ever again thou dost, in my presence, so much as hint at the black and foul sorceries practised by thyself, and by the witch Locusta, I will strike thee dead."

"I will promise, master, upon my head be it!" cried the dwarf. "We will find some other way."

For some time they walked on in silence, Licinius removing to a good distance from the dwarf, who took his cue and slunk behind.

"Humph! What is that barbarian's life that it should be so hard to destroy?" Licinius said, aloud, but speaking to himself. "The life of a man is as easily taken as the life of a fly, and he is surrounded by no unusual safeguards, indeed, he most recklessly exposes himself to danger and death."

"And he walks the streets, too, illustrious," prompted Zaba, stealing back to the patrician's elbow. "He wanders forth from the city, and often does not return till after dark."

Licinius started.

"Ha! how do you know that?"

"I have watched his movements!"

"You did wisely; let me hear more."

"I dogged his footsteps some days ago, and tracked him through the Esquiline gate," continued the dwarf. "There is a spot on the Appian road where there are many hollows and excavations; perhaps you know the place."

"No doubt you mean the arenariæ, or sand pits, that lie in the direction you indicate," remarked Licinius; "some call them the catacombs, thinking they must have formed some ancient cemetery. I remember how Cicero speaks of them in his Defence of Milo, as a hiding-place and receptacle for thieves."

"He was not far wrong," replied Zaba; "whoever might have haunted them in his day, they now afford a refuge for worse characters than thieves."

"You allude to those blasphemers of the gods—the atheists they call Christians, or Nazarenes?"

"The same," returned Zaba; "I have seen hundreds of them torn to pieces by the wild beasts in the circus."

"Never mind that; keep to the thread of your story."

"I am glad it interests you."

"It does, proceed."

"At a careful distance I tracked him over the barren, sandy plain," Zaba went on. "What surprised me was he carried in his hand a basket containing such chaplets of flowers as they hang on urns and tombs."

"What could that mean?"

"I know not; perhaps the Christians use flowers in their ceremonies."

"Not improbable," answered Licinius; "I half suspect him of being one of that dark sect."

"It was nearly dark when we reached the quarries," said Zaba. "Though I tried my best to keep him in sight he suddenly vanished from view like a flash of wold-fire."

"But why did you not wait his return?" said Licinius. "He might have descended into the catacombs."

"I did wait for him," replied Zaba; "I lingered among the sand-pits and kept heedful watch, and at the end of an hour he reappeared as suddenly and mysteriously as he had before vanished."

"And upon the same spot?"

"No, on quite another part of the plain, distant at least three hundred paces from the place where I stood."

"There are as many holes and burrows there as in a rabbit warren," Licinius remarked.

Then he inquired, as if struck by a sudden thought—

"Did you observe, Zaba, whether he carried the basket of flowers when he reappeared?"

"No; he did not. Wherever he had been he had left the flowers behind him on his return."

"Well, what followed? did you trace him back to the city?"

"I did, and got pretty close to him, for he seemed full of thought and care, and walked with his eyes upon the ground."

"So you came close behind him—ha!"

"Yes; I had my knife with me."

"Why did you not strike?"

"No hare is more quick of hearing, no lynx has keener sight than the Briton. He turned as I drew near and uttered a shout as loud and fierce as the roar of my panthers just before feeding time."

"And what did you do?"

"Not much time was allowed me for consideration," replied the dwarf; "I sprang over a thicket, and rolled headlong into a deep fissure of the sandstone rocks, bringing down a shower of pebbles that well-nigh buried me alive."

"Do you think he recognised you?"

"That is more than I can tell," was the reply. "But I was not disturbed, though I lay half stifled for a full hour before I dared venture forth."

"Then you saw him no more that night?"

"No!"

"Well, I am glad you have told me this," replied Licinius. "You must try and find out when he will pay another visit to the catacombs."

"I will not fail to do so."

"We will lay an ambush for him," said Licinius. "I will take care that it shall be strong enough to prevent any possibility of his escape, and I, myself will lead the party."

"Let me make one," cried the dwarf.

"You shall."

"I thank thee, Licinius."

"Here we must part," returned the patrician. "This is my road, that yours; to-morrow betimes I will send to you at Locusta's."

They parted.

As the dwarf shambled off he laughed and clapped his hands.

"It works well," he muttered to himself. "What care I for these Roman puppets? I will use them all for my own advantage. There is a conspiracy afloat to dethrone, perhaps to murder, Cæsar. There will be a rising in the city. Ventidius scoffs at me—let him look to himself! I hate him and I love his daughter. Who knows that in the midst of the bloodshed, pillage, licence of a revolution I may not snatch the prize I covet? Ah, Virginia!"

CHAPTER XXX.
THE SCHOOLMASTER AT HOME.

IT not seldom happens in the affairs of this mutable life, that disappointments, thwartings, and restraints which we find hard to bear while they last, ultimately turn out to our advantage. Such was the case with our hero.

Nothing afforded the young gladiator greater delight and enjoyment than the liberty of strolling forth to ramble for a few hours whither he listed, after the exercises of the day were over.

He appeared never to weary of visiting the sights and scenes of the mighty capital of the known world, while his visits to the dwellings of his friends. Philomenes and Mathias, were a source much happiness and mental improvement to the cultured but noble-minded exile.

When deprived of these pleasures he felt grievance very keenly.

But Ventidius sternly put his veto upon these excursions.

"I command you, stay within doors, at least until after the games on Cæsar's birthday," he said. "You cannot be trusted from home. You will rush into so many hair-breadth adventures and foolhardy scrapes. Such a wild colt must be kept in the stable!"

It was in vain for the slave to remonstrate the master was inexorable.

Lupa, for a wonder, approved of this measure.

"Believe me, Ventidius," she would say, "some of the black-legs outside have a design against this lad. Don't let him stir out an arm's length!"

Caractacus quietly submitted to what he knew to be inevitable.

But, nevertheless, he inwardly chafed and pined, for confinement was the affliction which his free soul could endure with little fortitude.

He grew silent or peevish, became listless at his tasks, and lost his freshness of colour.

But Ventidius was too much engaged with other and more important affairs to take much notice of this change in his pupil's looks and demeanour.

It was, nevertheless, a fortunate circumstance for our hero that he was obliged to remain at home.

Licinius and his gang were on the watch for him every evening, with the intent to take his life on the first opportunity.

It may here be explained that the object of our hero's journey to the catacombs was to visit the tomb of his sister, the beautiful and unhappy Iona, whose body had been buried there by the good Mathias.

There is plenty of evidence to show that these subterranean excavations were used by the early Christians to hide themselves in from their persecutors.

In the succeeding reigns a decree was made that they should not be allowed to hold meetings nor to enter the places they called cemeteries.

The Christians appear never to have adopted the Roman custom of burning their dead.

This custom conferred an additional sanctity upon the catacombs; and the religious veneration paid to relics is to be traced to this necessity of the living and the dead being brought so closely in contact.

Mathias, having every confidence in our hero's good faith, had introduced him to the community of Christians in their subterranean abode, where he attended their churches and listened with breathless interest to the gospel there preached.

But to return to our story. As before mentioned, the free-born Briton for the first time found himself a prisoner, and then for the first time he felt the galling weight of the chains of slavery—the iron entered his soul.

He hated his home, which before had been tolerable.

Things had reached this crisis when a trifling circumstance wrought a change for our hero.

One morning early, as Ventidius, just risen from bed, entered his vestibule, he was accosted by the surly one-eyed door-keeper whom the lads of the "family" had nicknamed "Polyphemus," on account of his visual defect.

"Master," he grunted.

Ventidius stared at him in some alarm, it was such a rare thing to hear him speak.

"Well, Hyphax?" he asked, smiling.

"A word," growled the bear.

"Two if you like," laughed Ventidius, who was in a good humour. "You don't waste many, old Cyclops."

"No."

"What is it you would say?"

"Zaba!"

"That horrid little dwarf?"

"Aye."

"What of him?"

"Prowls about."

"Where?"

"There!" and he pointed through the door which was open into the street.

"When?"

"Night-time."

"The venomous pigmy! Would I could lay hands on him! What does he want prowling about my doors at night?"

Hyphax shook his head.

"You don't know?"

Hyphax shrugged his shoulders.

"Can't you guess?" asked his master.

Hyphax leered knowingly.

"Speak, you dumb block, or I'll twist out your tongue!" roared the lanista, getting in a passion, and stamping his foot. "What is your guess?"

Hyphax winked and pointed with his thumb over his shoulder.

"The Briton!" he whispered.

Ventidius gave a great start as the force of this hint struck his mind.

"By Pollux! I believe thou art right," he said. "The odious wretch has been suborned to lay a trap for my novice to do him an injury. It must be so, witness the malignant little demon's conduct at the chariot race, when he loosed the panther on Caractacus! And then he should escape unpunished! I should have thought young Nero would have torn him with hot pincers, or had him rent in quarters by wild horses! There is a mystery in all this."

Hyphax made a gurgling noise in his throat, as though he was strangling.

He was actually going to speak again!

Ventidius opened his ear, and after an effort, Hyphax opened his mouth.

Then followed a miracle.

"A plot to kill the Briton—Caius Licinius at the bottom of it. They'll do it, too, or I'm—aw—yaw!"

This was the longest speech Hyphax had been known to make, or was suspected of being able to make, so no wonder that it ended in a yawn of weariness and exhaustion.

"So, so, my fine patrician, who for all thy fine blood hast not a second toga to thy back, and who livest on the scraps thy patrons throw to such spaniels, this is my return for lending thee money, and signing bonds for thee? Never mind, time turns round. I'll cry quits with thee yet! Burst ye!"

And the indignant lanista gave such a violent punch at his "dream-drawn" antagonist, that Hyphax got a narrow escape of a broken head.

Then he patted his servant on the back.

"I'll tell thee what, good lad. If ever again you catch that black Nubian wolf sniffing around my sheep-cote, do you call me up," continued Ventidius. "Call me up, I say, though it be in the dead of the night, and upon my head be it if I do not stop his prowling!"

He paused to regain breath, and wipe the sweat off his forehead, and then went on in a milder tone—

"Thou art a trusty fellow, Hyphax, and I like thee none the worse because thou knowest how to keep a still tongue in thy head. I'll reward thee for this. Go, I'll send thee a wine-skin, presently, but drink with moderation—don't make a beast of thyself. Follow my rule and example in the matter of temperance. But, above all, lock, bolt, and bar! Thou hast but one eye, but that's a piercer. Keep it wide open for the black wolf."

With this, the lanista hastened to his wife, who was in her room, one of the slaves combing out her long dark hair.

Ventidius told her what he had heard, and asked for her advice.

She gave it promptly.

"Send him back to our farm at Sora."

"Well, my lovely one, but even then he will get into mischief Witness his scramble up the Eagle's Crag."

"Bah! that is nothing. He'll not hurt himself that way. Born among mountains, he is as sure-footed as an ibex."

"Well, I'll think it over."

"Don't think, but act. Send him off at once!"

"Well, if that's your opinion—"

"Tush! I am not blind if you are. I have watched

his looks. He is not in good form—he is dull and dejected—he has lost flesh, and that nice, delicate, ruddy colour that used to warm his cheeks."

"On my soul, Lupa!" cried her husband, with a jealous flash, "you take most particular notice of that young slip."

His consort looked him in the face with sublime disdain as she gave the quiet retort—

"If I did not take more care of your property than you do, where would you be, I wonder? Rotting in some debtor's gaol, that's where you'd be. But abuse is the only recompense I expect for my devotion to your interest. Ah, well-a-day! you may do as you like—beggar yourself as well as break my heart."

"Well, no more words. He shall go."

And the poor lanista beat a hasty retreat.

Caractacus could hardly conceal his joy when told to prepare himself to walk to Sora, in company with Pandion.

Walk? Why it was under thirty miles—a mere nothing to two fine athletes.

Arrived near his home, Pandion pointed out the most remarkable features of the beautiful scenery, and amused our hero with many local tales and legends.

With light hearts and unwearied limbs, the two comrades crossed the orchards and vineyards, and entered the picturesque town.

All at once our hero's attention was attracted by the hum of youthful voices, and turning his head, found the noise proceeded from a barn-like structure.

"That place is full of children. What is it?" asked the Briton.

"Why, the school-house, kept by a pedagogue I am acquainted with—a strict, learned man, and one who knows how to wield the rod and the ferula, as most of his unruly brats know to their smart."

"Let us go near and see what is going on."

"So will we, lad. To watch the antics of the mischievous youngsters is better than a play."

As they drew near the house, they heard a woman's shrill voice raised to the highest pitch of anger, and, peeping in at the window, they viewed a strange scene.

A buxom market woman stood near the door, and held in her hand a dead porker, which had been ruthlessly done to death by one of the boys, who had slung a stone at it with deadly effect. Her fury may better be imagined than described. Solemn and stern, the domine clutched the trembling culprit, and flourished the dreadful lash.

CHAPTER XXXI.

A ROMAN SCHOOLBOY.

PANDION and Caractacus were highly amused by the scene they were watching, unobserved by the actors.

The gesticulations of the infuriated market woman, the grim and solemn visage of the school-master, and the rueful countenance of the blubbering culprit brought smiles to the lips of the stern gladiators.

Not that either of them was harsh or hard-hearted, but for the very opposite reason—because there was something in this mimic strife and terror, this tempest in a puddle, that contrasted so strangely with the fearful realities of their own savage trade.

"See the little despot of the victims, how he exults in his authority, how he scowls at the small trembling boy, and twirls the lash," remarked Caractacus. "See the fury of the woman—her blazing eyes, her burning cheeks. She displays as much wrath over her trumpery grievance as though she had suffered some serious wrong. Human nature is the same everywhere."

"Look, too, at the daring youngsters filching the grapes from her basket under their master's very nose," chuckled Pandion. "But after the farce comes the tragedy—the boy will be whipped."

Lads at school in the present day may grumble at the comparatively light punishments they receive, but if they had lived in the "good old times" they would have found real cause for complaint.

Scholastic discipline among the Romans was no joke.

Over the door of a school-house at Pompeii has been found a painting of one boy horsed upon another's back undergoing a flagellation—an ominous indication which might give a hint to our modern School Boards, at their wits' ends to know how to deal with "incorrigible truants."

"The best pig in the litter! One that I meant to keep and to fatten for our own use! My husband, Mopsus, told me only the other day that it was the 'flower of the farrow!'" screamed the irate peasant-woman. "And now look at it, do!—stoned to death by that thief of a boy! Now, tell me this, magister, do you call yourself a pedagogue who cannot control your brats better than that?"

"*Pauca verba!*—quietly, my good woman," returned the preceptor, shaking his head. "*Festina lente!*—be slow to make haste. Remember the words of Aristotle."

"I never heard his words, because I don't know the man. He don't live in these parts," retorted the woman, raising her voice. "But, if his words are worth anything, he will tell you that it is a shameful thing for a poor, hard-working woman to be abused in this way. The wonder is that I was not murdered as well as the pig. Just look at that!"

"Videlicet—a stone!"

"A stone!—a rock I call it."

Here Caractacus whispered to Pandion—

"Don't you observe the prisoner at the bar is your own son, my little playmate, Florus?"

"Yes, I see," answered Pandion, grimly.

"Had we not better interfere and save him from a flogging?"

"Let him alone. He has deserved it."

"Pardon him this once."

"No. The unruly brat gives me more trouble than enough with his mischievous pranks," returned Pandion. "Let him be taught discipline and endurance. If he howls too loud I will thrash him myself when we reach home."

"Hist!" rejoined our hero. "Let us hear what he has to say for himself."

Meanwhile the pedagogue had caught the urchin by the ear and was eyeing him severely.

"What is your defence?"

"I never had none, preceptor; I only had a sling," blubbered young Florus. "I was throwing a stone and the pig came in my way and got hit."

Then he added, grinning through his tears—

"Gemini! didn't he squeal?"

This ingenuous remark raised a loud titter through the school.

The preceptor looked sternly round.

"Silence, you rogues!" he shouted. "Con your tasks, or every mother's son of you shall share his punishment."

"Squeal, young impudence!" cried the indignant plaintiff, shaking her fist. "You shall squeal, too, before I have done with you."

"Patience, good woman. All in good time," replied the preceptor. "Let us proceed calmly and judiciously."

Then, holding out the strap, he asked the trembling lad—

"Do you know what this is?"

"Yes, preceptor, it's the ferula."

"Imo vero! very true. *Experientia docet* Experience is the source of knowledge," returned the schoolmaster. "Now can you tell me what it is made of?"

"Pig skin."

"True again. Woman, and you, my scholars, admire the beautiful fitness of things. The pig us justly slaughtered by my refractory pupil finds a just reparation in the very nature of the instrument which chastises the offender. Florus will for the future take care how he meddles with pig skins."

Then beckoning to the biggest boy in the school, he added in an awful tone—

"After sentence, execution. Balbus, take him up!"

And poor Florus was taken up accordingly.

The strokes fell swiftly and surely.

The injured dame had a long while to wait before she had the pleasure of hearing the culprit squeal; and it was not till he had received a good round number of strokes that he cried out for mercy.

"Enough! let him go," cried the appeased matron.

Florus was set down, and retired to his place, weeping and rubbing himself assiduously.

Caractacus and Pandion now thought it time to enter the school-house.

Pandion shook hands with the country dame, with whom he was acquainted, and asked her whether she was satisfied with the punishment his son had undergone, and offered to pay the price of the defunct porker.

The good dame, now all smiles, declared that she was quite satisfied, and, complimenting the boy for his bravery, gave him a huge bunch of grapes. Payment she would not hear of.

The athlete and the pedagogue exchanged a hearty greeting.

The boys crowded round the Briton; his adventure with the eagles had rendered him immensely popular.

Caractacus made them scramble for a handful of loose coin, and entreated the master to allow them a holiday.

Nothing loath, the pedagogue accepted an invitation to sup with Pandion, and dismissed his scholars.

The urchins dispersed with loud shouts of—

"Vivat Caractacus!"

Our hero spent a jovial evening with Pandion and his guests, and a week passed pleasantly enough.

Yet, go where he might, the daring young gladiator seemed destined to meet with some perilous adventure.

One evening Pandion proposed that he and Caractacus should the next day go for a ride on horseback through the neighbouring forest.

This was just such an excursion as suited our hero's taste.

They rose at the first blush of dawn, and each mounted on a great strong horse descended the bridle path, crossed the valley, and entered the wood.

They were enchanted with the fragrant freshness of the verdant sward and the bright greenwood.

There was something ineffably soothing and exhilarating in the sweet air, and the thousand concerting sounds of birds and insects, and the ever-rushing murmurings and tinklings of the brooks that run on for ever.

Pandion possessed a nice wolf-hound, which came abroad with his master.

The dog seemed keenly to enjoy his boisterous gamble along the greenwood side.

He sniffed about, stopping and pricking his ears as his watchful eyes caught a glimpse of some skulking fox or weasel, then bounding off with a sharp yelp, expressive of thorough enjoyment.

Thus the splendid creature led the way for the riders through echoing glades, by copse and dell.

"By Actæon!" laughed our hero. "What a noble hound! He would be highly prized in the circus. I'll warrant 'tis a fine sight to see him pull down a wolf or a stag."

"That you shall judge for yourself," quoth Pandion.

Over bush and briar bounded the merry companions and their swift coursers.

At length, as they entered a winding glade they came in sight of a large red deer, that was flying crash, crash, through the underwood a good distance ahead.

Off sprang the hound with a mighty bound, the dim woods baying.

"Ho, Castor! have at him, boy!" shouted Pandion.

Away they flew—hunter and hunted.

Honest Pandion laughed and shouted with boy-like glee.

He strove hard to keep pace with the fiery Briton.

But our hero was better mounted, and spurred on his gallant steed at a rattling pace.

Pandion, not being so well mounted, failed to keep up with him, and so fell back in the rear.

Caractacus urged on his course, and did not turn his head to see how his companion was getting along.

At last Pandion set up a loud shout, half-laughter, half-dismay.

Caractacus reined round his horse.

As he did so the horse which Pandion had so lately ridden dashed past like the wind.

Caractacus hurried back to find his friend.

He beheld the stalwart gladiator humbled to the earth.

A large wild boar had attacked him.

His small eyes glowing like burning coals, his stiff bristles set up along his huge black body, his curved ripping tusks gleaming, the monster rushed upon the prostrate Pandion.

To dismount from his horse and to draw his hunting knife was the work of an instant.

Caractacus threw himself upon the monster just as he reached Pandion, and was about to slash him open with his powerful tusk.

One fierce, heavy downright blow and the Briton had buried his dagger to the brisket.

The huge monster staggered, reeled, fell over, and expired.

Caractacus and his comrade rode home to breakfast, laughing over the adventure, and it was agreed between them that nothing should be said about it.

They laid out many plans for future pleasant outings, but their hopes were not to be fulfilled.

At the end of a few days came a message from Ventidius, recalling them to the toils and hardships of the gymnasium.

CHAPTER XXXII.

THE MANDATE FROM NERO.

FOR a fortnight after his return to Rome our hero, Caractacus, remained close within doors. The Briton no longer complained of this enforced confinement, for he felt it necessary for safety.

None who knew Caractacus would suppose that he dared not face the perils that beset his path, or that he would have gone far out of his way even to preserve his own life.

But our hero felt a burning desire to distinguish himself in the arena, and so determined to take as much care of himself as possible until after the games.

The mysterious conduct of Narcissus gave the Briton much subject for conjecture and anxiety.

"Why does he dare to arrogate such power over me?" Caractacus would frequently ask himself.

"He is not my master, neither am I his slave, yet I am compelled to come or go at his slightest bidding. It is because he has revealed to me his secret designs against the general, Aulus Plautius, and thinks himself in my power. He dares not attack me openly, but would cause me to fall a victim to some treacherous stratagem, but I will foil him yet, him and his myrmidons."

Caractacus applied himself with so much renewed industry and diligence that in a very short time he was able to defeat the most skilful of the antagonists opposed to him, no matter what weapons they employed.

THE DOMINE CLUTCHED THE TREMBLING CULPRIT, AND FLOURISHED THE DREADED LASH.

No. 6.

"Give the lad but fair play," remarked Ventidius, "and he will prove himself invincible, the undoubted champion of the arena."

And this verdict was confirmed by the opinions of all the members of the "family."

Even those amongst them who hated and feared the Briton, on account of his superior dexterity and prowess, were obliged to acknowledge the merits they envied.

They contented themselves by hinting that there was many a slip 'twixt cup and lip, and the race was not always to the swift, nor the battle to the strong.

During this time Caractacus saw but little of Virginia, yet she was very seldom out of his thoughts.

Whether it was simply gratitude to one who had shown him kindness, or whether it was some deeper, tenderer feeling, the Briton never felt so happy as in the presence of the fair and amiable Roman maid, never saw her approach without a thrill of joy, nor took his leave of her without a pang of regret.

But the young couple did not come together much. Virginia remained for the greater part of the time at her father's country seat, and when in Rome she kept herself to herself as much as possible.

The fact was, that the mother, beginning to suspect Virginia of being too fond of the society of the princely young stranger, contrived to keep her out of his way.

About this time the gay young noble Licinius began to pay attentions to the young beauty of the Via Nova.

He was strongly attracted by her budding charms, and had an eye to her father's fortune.

"It is true Ventidius is but a retired gladiator, but then he is rich, and stands high in the favour of some of the most influential personages at court," he thought. "His low birth is no doubt a great objection, but in such cases there is always some drawback. Narcissus may be ruined and disgraced at any moment, then what becomes of me? Overwhelmed as I am by debts, I must fall below hope, without his support. Ventidius may be ennobled, and how many now holding high commands in the army are of great importance in the state? As for the girl herself, she is so well educated, and by nature so graceful and refined, that she would do no dishonour to the throne itself."

Possessed with such ideas he paid court to Ventidius and his wife, Lupa, in the hope of obtaining their good will before he attempted to win their daughter's love.

"I am inclined to suspect the foolish girl is fascinated by the fine face and stalwart limbs of the barbarian, Caractacus," he said. "I am told that she dressed his wound and gave him an amulet; no matter for that, he will not live much longer, and even if he did there would be no difficulty; I have but to gain the parents' consent; Virginia is of a yielding, submissive temper, completely under their control, and would never dream of disputing their wishes."

But in this he reckoned without his host.

Virginia had a stronger will of her own than he bargained for.

The fact, as already known by the reader, was that Ventidius disliked and distrusted the patrician for many and forcible reasons.

In the first place Licinius had played him false in many betting transactions, and his designs against such a promising novice as Caractacus were a proof of his black ingratitude to the lanista, who had lent him money and stood his friend on more than one occasion; and, in the second place, the rough old gladiator had no ambition to see his only and dearly loved girl married to one above herself in station, knowing that such marriages seldom result in happiness.

"That vapouring dandy, with all his pride of birth and courtly manners, is a beggar in pocket," the shrewd, money-making Ventidius argued with himself. "He would be fingering at my gold bags, knowing that Virginia will inherit all I have scrambled together in the course of a toilsome and hazardous career. What will he do with my hard earnings that should belong to my precious one, for whose sake I have toiled and suffered so long? He would squander it broadcast, and would certainly despise his low-born wife, and almost as certainly ill-treat her."

But the patrician's crafty plot against Caractacus galled the lanista perhaps more than any other consideration.

Altogether he had fully made up his mind that his daughter should never marry the bankrupt noble.

He sounded her upon the subject in a bantering way, and asked whether she would not think it a fine thing to flaunt at the imperial court as the wife of such a nobly-born husband as Caius Licinius.

He was secretly pleased when Virginia repudiated such a destiny with horror and disgust, vowing that she would rather kill herself than marry such a man.

Ventidius commended her decision, and assured her that it met with his own entire approval. At the same he advised her to disguise her sentiments, to treat Licinius with cool civility, and put him off with evasive answers.

"Take this advice well to heart, my Virginia," he added, in conclusion; "for you must understand that though the wily, double-faced patrician is a traitor to my friendship and a foe to my interests, I cannot afford to quarrel with him just now. Nothing must be done or said that will lead him to suspect that I am acquainted with his true character. A great and startling change in Roman affairs is near at hand. Let the storm pass. When I have weathered it, then the hour will come, and I shall know how to strike!"

Virginia gave the required promise, and no more was said at the time.

With Lupa the young nobleman had better success.

By judiciously flattering her vanity, and making her some handsome presents, he quite won her heart.

She indulged in the brightest day-dreams of the honour and distinction that awaited her child. Nor did she leave herself out of the reckoning.

She retired to her room, hugged herself with delight, and with a proud flush frequently consulted her looking-glass.

"I was younger than Virginia is now when I married Ventidius," she soliloquised. "How often has the girl been taken for my sister! There is not a gray hair in my head, not a wrinkle nor a crow's-foot in my face. I am still in the ripeness of my beauty, and by the aid of art—which, thank the gods! I have never yet had occasion to resort to—I may preserve my good looks for years to come. Why should I not cut a figure as well as the best of them? Imagine it! A gilded chariot, a retinue of well-dressed slaves, a seat in the equestrian benches at the circus, and above all a presentation at the court of the emperor! What a glorious prospect opens before me!"

She called for her slaves, had herself dressed with such care and ceremony that her poor female attendants were almost worried to death, and wondered what new freak their fiery and capricious mistress had taken into her head.

However, they had the fear of the lash before their eyes, and took care to keep their imperious mistress in good humour by loading her with the grossest compliments.

Poor girls! they were not much to blame.

Juvenal gives a harrowing picture of the manner in which the excitable Roman mistresses treated their female slaves.

"Ah, domina mea, what a pity that the hair of our young mistress, Virginia, so fine and soft in quality, is so small in quantity to your own!" lisped the Greek girl, Chloris. "She is obliged to wear it in the simplest fashion, while all these plaits, and rolls. and bands as black and bright as jet, are your own."

"And that Juno-like form, how much better it becomes the graceful new fashion of wearing the silk tunic!" rejoined Lucia.

"Speak rather of Hebe than Juno when you refer to the domina," rejoined the Greek. "Hebe, the goddess of youth! What need for the stibium (black antimony applied on the eyelids) to give brilliancy to those dark shining orbs, so much admired by Licinius!"

Lupa looked round.

"Whither will your saucy folly lead you?" she said, languidly. "Beware the whip! What said Caius Licinius about my eyes?"

"Oh, I dare not tell you, domina."

"Speak! I shall not be angry."

"Oh only this—do hold the mirror straight, Lucia."

"You give her good advice. I have told her before of her awkwardness; the next time—but go on, Chloris, with what you were saying. What said the patrician in his insolence?"

"Only this, most honoured. I had it from Varro," replied the slave. "You knew how sweet Virginia has been rather pale of late; Licinius remarked upon this, but added: 'Virginia is indubitably a very lovely girl, but (and here he swore an oath, madam) her eyes never were so fine as those of her mother, who always looks as young as her daughter.' Then he heaved a great sigh (at least so Varro told me, a rough brute who laughed while he related the story); 'lucky man that Ventidius to have such a paragon of a wife!'"

"Licinius is a fool, and did not know what he was talking about," retorted Lupa, but in such a tone that the two slave girls winked at each other behind her back.

That night, when Ventidius came home to supper, Lupa joined him and appeared to be in unusually high spirits, and in such an amiable temper that Ventidius was quite astonished.

He noticed too how carefully she was dressed.

But the lanista had heard news in the city which filled his mind with uneasiness, and he asked her rather grimly—

"Have you received visitors to-day, my Lupa, that you have put on all your bravery?"

Lupa's black eyes flashed at the tone in which the question was put, but she bit her lip and curbed her temper.

"I have received no visitors to-day, Ventidius," she answered, as mildly as she could. "But, as for my dress, I am sorry you are dissatisfied."

"Dissatisfied! Who said so?" retorted her husband. "I like to see you well dressed, though you always look yourself to me in any gear—beauty, you know, needs no adornment."

"Do you grudge me these few ornaments?"

"Did I grudge you anything when I gave you myself and everything that I could earn for you?" he answered. "Tush! Let us leave this strain! fill up this cup and fill your own, dear wench, and let us drink confusion to the man I hate."

"Do not speak of hatred and strife—let us talk of very different matters."

"What, you refuse my toast?"

"Not now, Ventidius! Such a temperate man as you can set your cup aside for a minute or two, I am sure."

"Temperate or not I will drink this toast," cried Ventidius, in a tone of such startling fierceness that Lupa shrank within herself. "Aye, though the draught may choke me! Confusion to that traitor, Licinius!"

Lupa turned deadly pale, and sank back on her couch.

"Are you mad, Ventidius?" she faltered, as all her dreams of ambition began to fade away.

"Aye, mad enough—the gods give me self-control!" growled Ventidius, greatly irritated. "But

let it pass; we will try to forget the cares of the day. I dismiss them with this libation to Pluto, to whom I consign Licinius and all his gang!"

Lupa, who had very rarely seen her husband in such a humour, felt that for the time her power was gone, and had cunning enough to keep quiet, though in her heart of hearts she promised herself a bitter revenge when his fit of passion had worked off, and her authority re-established itself.

"My dear husband," she said, "what has happened to excite you thus? It was that very Licinius of whom I wished to speak."

Ventidius was now cold and surly—his wife would rather have seen him in a rage.

"Humph!" he grumbled. "What have you to say about the illustrious?"

"Can you be so blind as not to have seen what has been going on?"

"I am not so blind as you may think me," retorted her husband. "I see a great deal more than pleases me."

Lupa stared aghast.

"What have you seen to give you such offence?" she demanded, in a tone of virtuous indignation.

"That which I will put a stop to," returned the lanista, smiting his clubbed fist on the table. "I have seen that fawning parasite, Licinius, whispering at your ear, and casting sheep's-eyes at my daughter, Virginia. I will not have my home invaded and its peace imperilled by such a treacherous traitor!"

"Do not call the noble Licinius a traitor," answered Lupa. "His intentions are honourable."

"How, honourable?"

"He seeks our daughter in marriage," was the reply. "And I confess that I can see no objection to the match."

"And what advantage, pray you?"

"Advantage! Is there none in bestowing our daughter's hand upon the representative of one of the noblest families in Rome?"

"A bankrupt spendthrift, steeped to the lips in debt."

"I grant he is not rich, but what of that? You have money enough."

"Which I have not earned so hard for him to squander," rejoined Ventidius. "It is my money that he wants, and not my daughter."

"You wrong Licinius—indeed, you do," rejoined Lupa. "He is your friend."

"Say you so?" retorted the husband. "Behold a convincing proof of his friendship!"

He took a letter from his bosom and flung it upon the table.

Lupa snatched it eagerly.

"What is this?" she asked."

"Read it for yourself."

Lupa perused the document. and uttered a cry of surprise.

"A mandate from Nero, commanding you immediately to send your novice, Caractacus, to the palace of Cæsar," she said. "Well, what harm is there in that?"

"The fine lad! and after all the pains that I have taken with his training!" groaned Ventidius. "They intend his destruction; it is like sending the lamb to the shambles."

"Then why let him go?"

"How you talk! It is more than my life is worth to refuse to obey a command coming from such a quarter," was the retort.

"Still I do not see how this concerns Licinius," persisted Lupa.

"He and others have entered into a conspiracy to defraud me of the money I have staked. Besides, the patrician is jealous of the gallant fellow."

"Jealous! of what?"

"His favour with Virginia. She is a good and prudent girl, but I know that in her heart she loves Caractacus."

"Shame on thee, Ventidius!" cried Lupa, recover

ing her courage and firing up; "a daughter of mine in love with one of our own slaves!"

"A slave! well what was I before I won the rudis and my manumission?" cried Ventidius, with generous warmth; "a slave and a gladiator like him, but never what he is, a prince in his native land, the son and heir of a king who sets the legions of Rome at defiance!"

"I have nought to say against the youth," responded Lupa; "but do not be blinded by prejudice If our daughter were wedded to a patrician, such as Caius Licinius—"

"Name him not!" retorted Ventidius, with a quiet firmness, the more effective because it was so unusual in him. "You know me, Lupa, or rather should I say, you know me not. In all that concerns myself I have paid the utmost deference to your wishes. I, who should rule, have obeyed. But where the happiness of my precious one is concerned, the apple of my eye, the corner of my heart, I must hold my own; she shall not be sacrificed to her mother's selfish, brain-sick vanity. Rather than see her wedded to your courtly favourite, Caius Licinius, I would bestow her upon the roughest cut-throat in my maniple. I have spoken—let it be enough."

He rose and left the room, slamming the door behind him.

No sooner was he gone than Lupa uttered a piercing shriek, and was seized with a violent attack of hysterics.

CHAPTER XXXIII.

THE PALACE OF CÆSAR.

VENTIDIUS, his brows bent in a gloomy frown, walked straight to the gymnasium, where his pupils were busy at their exercises. At the far end of the hall was set up a wooden figure of a man.

It served as a kind of stock or dummy, on which the swordsmen practised their cuts and thrusts, but during a long course of such ill-usage it had been so cut and hacked about as to be almost shapeless.

The gladiators had formed themselves in two lines, extending from this image almost as far as the door.

They were practising at throwing the javelin.

Each in his turn stepped into the clear space between the two lines formed by his comrades, and hurled a dart at the image.

The success or failure of each cast was hailed by the "family" with a shout of applause or a laugh of derision.

Gordian was considered one of the most skilful in this kind of exercise.

He had just thrown a javelin with such steady aim that it remained quivering full in the breast of the wooden figure.

His feat was applauded with rounds of hurras and clapping of hands.

At the very moment that Ventidius entered, Caractacus had taken Gordian's place to try his skill.

The lanista, who had not been observed, kept back to watch our hero's performance.

The Briton took up his position, shook back his yellow locks, stretched his magnificent limbs, and looked round with a frank, pleasant smile.

"That was a capital throw, Gordian," he said; "I have seldom seen a better."

"Mehercle! you may well say that," rejoined Manlius; "you will find it no easy feat to beat it."

Gordian grinned at these compliments.

"They say, however, that the Britons are famous spearmen and archers," he remarked.

"I'm glad the Romans speak some good of us," laughed our hero.

The lad, who waited on the gladiators, brought him a spear.

"Thanks, Automedon," said Caractacus; "now to try my luck."

He took the weapon, struck the butt on the ground, and shook the truncheon to test its soundness.

"The shafts of your spears are not so good as we make at home from the mountain ash."

"Try another," said Gordian.

"No, this will do, said Caractacus.

Then he threw himself into an attitude worthy of Apollo spearing the Python—the freedom, grace and power of his naked limbs would have delighted a sculptor to behold.

Ventidius heaved a sigh when he reflected that a pupil, of whom he had so much reason to be proud, might soon be cut off, not in fair fight, but by base treason.

The javelin was hurled with a force that made it whistle through the air, and with such unerring aim that it split the shaft of Gordian's spear, driving the blade deeper into the image, but itself snapping short about a foot from the head.

There was quite a storm of wonder and applause. But this moved the stolid Briton not a jot.

On the contrary he looked vexed.

"What did I tell you?" he said, turning to Manlius. "After our tough ashen pikes your Roman lances are no better than straws and bull-rushes."

Ventidius now stepped forward and laid his hand upon our hero's bare shoulders.

"Euge! that was a splendid cast," he said. "But come with me, Caractacus; I have something to tell you."

"I attend you, Ventidius," replied our hero.

Taking his novice by the arm, the lanista conducted him into a small private room adjoining the atrium.

"I have a message for you, Caractacus," he said.

"A message! from whom?" asked our hero, smiling.

"From Nero."

Caractacus frowned.

"Well, master," he said, "what are his commands?"

"He has sent for you to the palace."

"For what reason?"

"He gives no reason—he only gives the order."

"Well, I have no alternative but to obey," said Caractacus. "It is reported that my warrior-father has captured the son of the Roman general, Ostorius, and keeps him as a hostage; they may wish to hold me in durance until he is liberated."

"And then set you free?"

"Who knows?"

"I wish I could encourage you in such a hopeful view of the case," returned Ventidius. "But, alas! I cannot. No matter, you must go. But look well to yourself, good lad, for you are venturing into a nest of scorpions when you enter the court of Cæsar."

"I know it," replied Caractacus; "I will be on my guard."

"The gods protect thee, as they have hitherto shown thee great favour, my son," answered Ventidius.

"When must I go?"

"To-morrow; so prepare yourself. I will take care that you shall be provided with a proper equipment, and I protest to Hercules how sorry I am to lose you."

"Thanks, my kind master."

"Call me your friend."

"You are a Roman! but there's my hand. I would I had you at home in Britain," said our hero.

"And I, that I were anywhere but in this cursed city," growled Ventidius.

They parted for the night.

The young gladiator stretched himself upon his pallet and soon fell asleep, and dreamed of his old dear Britain.

The next day he arose betimes and got ready for his visit to the palace.

He found a handsome suit of clothes provided for

him, and **Ventidius** at parting forced upon him a heavy purse of money, and gave him many cautions respecting his conduct and dealings with his new associates.

He asked the lanista how long they would detain him at the palace, but Ventidius could give him no satisfaction on that point.

Caractacus departed, bright and fearless, yet not without casting one loving, lingering look at the window of the chamber which he knew was tenanted by Virginia.

Caractacus strode along through the busy streets, the observed of all observers, calm, proud, and perfectly self-contained.

Our hero reached the palace, which was built on the Palatine Hill, and covered nearly the whole of it.

Caligula united this mount with the Capitol by a bridge across the Forum.

The temple of Castor and Pollux was transformed into a vestibule to the palace, which was very splendid, and besides the usual costly decorations of such a building, there were within the precincts of it fields and woods, and pools of water.

Before the gates of the reigning Cæsar, by a decree of the Senate, were set up branches of laurel, he being the supposed perpetual conqueror of his enemies.

As Caractacus stood under the glorious portico, he looked about him with a gloomy frown.

"Thus is it," he mused, bitterly. "Whence got the Romans their vast wealth? How came they by such power and magnificence? By the strong hand, the hard heart, the dead conscience, the living will; by the remorseless fiat—Let it be done! And so men and nations prosper, and success condones all."

Forgetful where he was, Caractacus could not repress an outburst of rage, and mortification.

"Oh, how I hate these Romans! Selfish, cruel, rapacious banditti as they are! Robbers and the sons of robbers, who despoiled Greece of her divine works of art, Persia of her riches, Gaul and Britain of her strength and manhood! Yet the day must come, predicted by the Druids, when the Gauls and the rest of the despised barbarians will level this accursed stronghold of tyranny and crime with the dust. Would I might live to see that day!"

Thus pondering, Caractacus crossed the splendid vestibule.

From time to time he paused to admire the fountains and statuary.

At last he came to a large flight of marble steps, which he ascended.

He knocked at the golden gates somewhat imperiously for one of his condition.

The sentinels on guard at the foot of the steps glanced admiringly at the handsome and noble-looking exile, as he gave the word, and was allowed to pass them.

They recognised him as the famous novice of Ventidius, as the son of the hero-king, Caractacus, and the charioteer who had won such brilliant renown in the hippodrome.

They exchanged significant grins, sarcastic but not unkind, at his haughty and fearless demeanour.

Caractacus, however, paid no regard to them, but waited calmly until the doors were opened by half-a-dozen porters in a sumptuous uniform.

An officer, bearing a white wand, advanced and inquired his business.

Our hero presented his credentials.

"This is the man of whom the noble Honorius, tribune of the Prætorian guard, spoke to me?" he said.

"Are you not Caractacus, the Briton?"

"The same," returned our hero. "I belong to the family of the lanista, Ventidius, and am come hither by the express command of Nero."

"Follow me," was the reply.

Caractacus bowed proudly

The old chamberlain paced on before, and conducted him into the aula.

This was a spacious court or hall—a large oblong square — surrounded with covered or arched galleries.

The side opposite the gate was called the tablinum, and the other two sides the alæ, or wings.

The tablinum was filled with books, records, and other documents.

Upon being conducted to this apartment, Caractacus found Honorius surrounded by several of the centurions, and other officers, with whom he was conversing.

He evidently expected our hero's arrival, for he immediately left his companions, and came forward to meet him.

Caractacus bowed with unfeigned respect, for Honorius was a man of blameless character and high reputation, the only Roman, except, perhaps, one or two of his comrades, for whom he felt any regard.

"Thou art welcome, Idris-ap-Caradoc," said the tribune, speaking to our hero in the British tongue. "I have orders to bring thee at once into the presence of the august Nero."

It was the first time our hero had heard his native tongue spoken—except, indeed, in the last faltering accents of his dying sister, Iona—since his arrival in Rome.

"Thanks, noble tribune," he said, while his voice quivered with emotion.

"I know not why you were sent for," continued the tribune, still speaking in British, "but I have had some talk with Ventidius, and have promised him to take you under my wing."

"You shall not find me ungrateful for such kindness," was our hero's reply.

"That scoundrel Zaba is here," said the tribune; "he is now in audience with Nero."

"Is he alone?"

The tribune laughed.

"No, he has brought his sweetheart with him," he answered.

"His sweetheart!" thought the Briton; "What can he mean?"

But he did not think it worth while to ask any more questions.

As they approached the royal chamber, Caractacus was astonished to hear shouts of laughter, screams, and a low deep growl as of some wild beast.

The tribune turned to our hero with a smile.

"Do you guess the secret now?" he asked.

"Hecate!" said the Briton, nodding his head.

"Even so," laughed the tribune, "the black dwarf has brought his tame pantheress, and he is putting her through her tricks, to amuse the young prince."

"A pretty amusement for the future emperor of the world," thought the Briton.

But he had sense enough to hold his tongue.

They entered a noble hall; seated on a curule chair Nero watched the antics of the terrible-looking pantheress, as she placed her paws on the neck of her master, and licked his forehead and hair.

The beautiful and voluptuous Agrippina was present.

The moment she saw Caractacus her eyes sparkled, her colour rose, and rushing up to him she clasped his arm, and exclaimed—

"The horrid monster scares me to death. Thou handsome youth, I claim thy protection!"

CHAPTER XXXIV.

HOW NERO GAVE HIS MINION A TERRIBLE FRIGHT.

CARACTACUS recoiled from the embrace of Agrippina as though a serpent had stung him. A blush of wounded pride, rather than shame, flushed her brow as she fixed her glittering black eyes on his cold, stern countenance.

But whether or not she set down this gesture of

aversion to his youthful bashfulness, or thought proper to disguise her feelings, she smiled quite graciously.

Then she waved her hand majestically.

"No more of this, my son," she said, and pointed to Zaba, who had thrust his ugly black head between the panther's jaws, "put an end to this scene—it wearies and disgusts me."

But Nero enjoyed such congenial sport too much to end it so abruptly, and so he answered with a loud laugh—

"Let him finish, good mother; I think his performance very diverting."

Agrippina shrugged her white shoulders and retired in disdain.

The two ladies quickly followed her, clinging together, and at every step casting terrified glances behind them as though they feared that the savage animal would fly in pursuit of them.

Agrippina, however, had not gone far before she stopped and turning back stood half-hidden by one of the columns, her eyes rivetted upon the noble form of the young gladiator.

"By the girdle of Venus, 'tis long since I beheld such a noble youth," she whispered to one of the ladies who stood beside her; "Lycaon, your fencing master, is a fine fellow, but I must tell you, my Julia, I think this barbarian far surpasses him, both in face and figure. He is a very Apollo."

"Tastes may differ, divine empress," replied the beautiful patrician girl thus addressed, "but there is no denying this to be a model of a man."

"Who is he, can you tell me?" queried Agrippina.

"His name is Caractacus," replied the Lady Julia, "a Briton, reported to be the son of the king of some wild but intrepid people with whom our legions are at war."

"A king's son! I can well believe it," replied Agrippina, first sighing and then laughing. "Had you told me that he was one of the demi-gods I should have believed you."

"Yet, highness, after all, he is but a common gladiator," rejoined her attendant.

"I have been told so," replied the empress. "To what 'family' does he belong?"

"He belongs to the same maniple as my fencing master, Lycaon," was Julia's reply; "they are both trained under the lanista, Ventidius."

"I wonder for what reason he was brought hither."

"That I cannot tell, illustrious," replied the lady. "But I fear he has incurred the enmity of some great personage of the court, and has been decoyed to the palace that he may be at the mercy of that personage; indeed Lycaon hinted so much to me, but all my coaxing would not induce him to mention names."

"Poor boy, would I could save him!" replied Agrippina. "Though I own I like his looks better than his manner, which is somewhat rough and churlish."

"What can be expected, illustrious, of a barbarian sprung from such a rude and savage race?"

"He is a man at any rate," replied the empress, "and his roughness pleases me better than the effeminate courtesies of the minions that flutter around my throne. Yes, he is a noble boy; I will save him if I can."

Then, after a moment's thought, she asked abruptly—

"Do you think Narcissus is his enemy?"

"I do not know, but it is not improbable," answered Julia; "I have heard it rumoured that one Licinius, a creature of the secretary's, hates this Briton, and has more than once attempted to compass his destruction."

A flash of vindictive passion shot from Agrippinas' black eyes.

"It is enough!" she answered; "I will befriend the youth, if only to spite my detested adversary."

At this moment they were interrupted in their whispered conversation by the loud ferocious growling of the panther, and the boisterous laughter of Nero.

Turning, shudderingly, their gaze to the place from whence these sounds proceeded, Agrippina beheld a sight which caused her to shrink with horror and loathing.

The black dwarf and the pantheress were rolling over and over together upon the floor, engaged in a mock struggle.

"Come away, sweet empress," gasped Nyssa, the lady who had not spoken till now, as she knelt beside Agrippina, and clutched her by the hand; "you and the Lady Julia have stronger nerves than I. I cannot bear this sight—I shall faint if we stay here longer."

"Silly girl, there are creatures in the palace more to be dreaded than yonder enslaved panther," replied the empress. "By the gods! It is admirable what a command the hideous wretch has obtained over the fearsome brute."

"It is necromancy!" gasped Nyssa.

"Well, child, let us go," returned the empress; "we will retire to my own apartments and talk further of this peerless youth, Caractacus the Briton."

Meanwhile Zaba, the dwarf, was diverting the future emperor with an exhibition entirely suited to his taste.

Kneeling down the dwarf spread wide his long arms.

The pantheress, with a graceful bound, cleared the right arm, and then the left, and finally sprang over the dwarf's head.

Then she touched him softly with her paws, and lay down beside him, stretching out her gaunt limbs, and purring like a cat.

Nero rose from his chair, and approaching the panther regarded it with a look of astonishment and interest.

Honorius stepped forward, his hand upon his sword, to guard the prince.

"Tell me, thou slave," said Nero, "will thy brute allow any but yourself to approach and lay hands upon him?"

"She will, most mighty," returned Zaba, salaaming to the ground. "That is while I am present and keep my eye upon her."

"Good," returned the prince. "I will put your mastery to the test. Do you think, if I set a man before your pantheress—a coward, mark you—will she spring on him in play and harm him not?"

"Yes, I can call her off. Hecate obeys my slightest nod."

"We will have rare sport, then," chuckled Nero.

He bade one of the slaves in attendance to fetch Sporus.

The man bowed and retired.

"Go, remove thyself and the pantheress behind yonder curtain," said the prince, and he pointed to a silken hanging, embroidered and fringed with gold-work, that was suspended between two of the pillars.

Zaba caught the pantheress by the neck and dragged her on to her feet, then placing himself at the distance of a few paces in front of her he made a motion with his hand.

The pantheress stood still for a moment as though dazed and bewildered by some mesmeric influence, then she shook her head, growled hoarsely, and stretching her long supple body, all nerve and muscle, with united vigour and agility, made a stride towards her master.

The dwarf and the pantheress passed behind the curtain.

A breathless stillness prevailed.

Sporus now entered the hall, and with smirking face and mincing gait slowly approached the prince.

He was a supremely beautiful but effeminate youth

of sixteen, his cheeks shamefully painted, and his hair curled and arranged like a woman's.

He was more splendidly dressed than even Nero himself, and his hands and neck were covered with sparkling gems.

"Come hither, my Sporus," said Nero.

The minion drew near the prince with an air of familiarity, and leaned upon the arm of the curule chair on which Nero sat.

"What is your pleasure, my dear lord?" lisped Sporus, in a drawling tone.

Honorius and the Briton scowled at the unmanly fop with looks that bespoke their scorn and indignation.

"The fawning spaniel!" muttered our hero, under his breath.

The soldiers of the Prætorian guard, drawn up in the background, smiled grimly at each other, and whispered together.

"I think thou lov'st me, Sporus," said the prince, "and would dare much in my cause."

Sporus laid his hand on the jewelled hilt of his toy dagger and glared about with the air of Ajax defying Jove's thunder.

"I am but one man," he said; "but my sweet prince commands my sword."

"His sword!" chuckled one grim veteran, under his grizzled beard; "Agrippina lent him a bodkin."

"But first blunted the point," returned his comrade, "that it might not prick his milk-white fingers."

Nero smiled softly upon his favourite.

"Did I not know thee brave, I should not have bestowed so many favours on thee," he said.

"Art thou not Nero, and what imports that name?" lisped Sporus, "is it not old Sabine for 'strong' and 'warlike?' None but the brave delight the brave."

At this boastful speech, not even the presence of the imperial prince could wholly restrain the scornful merriment of the Prætorian guardsmen, which found vent in a round of smothered laughter.

Sporus drew himself up to his full height, and glanced about him with flaming eyes and burning cheeks.

"What is the meaning of this insult?" he crowed in his weak, womanish voice.

"They doubt thy valour, my dear Sporus, replied Nero, soothingly, "but I will give thee a present opportunity of disproving their doubts, and will put thy valour to the test."

Sporus turned white as ashes; he quaked from limb to limb, and his knees knocked together, for he was well aware of Nero's cruel disposition.

"How, my lord?" he faltered, his teeth chattering.

Nero rose, and clutching him by the arm, pointed to the silk screen between the pillars.

"Go, he said, draw that curtain."

"But wherefore?"

"A panther lurks behind it—take him by the beard and drag him forth!"

Sporus looked at the young tyrant piteously, and answered with a sickly smile.

"My prince is pleased to jest with his poor slave," quavered Sporus.

"We shall see."

Sporus clasped his hands together, his fingers twitching with ill-repressed terror.

"But, sweet prince, I—I am unarmed," he remonstrated.

"Well thought on," returned Nero; "Honorius, lend him your sword."

But the veteran frowned and answered sternly—

"Pardon, illustrious; it is too heavy to be wielded by a hand so girlish. Besides, I wear my sword with pride to defend your sacred person, but not to be used as a wand by a mountebank."

At this rebuke Nero flushed deep red, and bit his lip, while his eyes glowed with a malignant fire.

Nevertheless, he answered with well-feigned humility—

"I meant your priceless sword no dishonour, brave Honorius; forgive the thoughtless impulse of an idle moment. Here, take this."

He drew his own sword, and placed it in the trembling hand of his minion.

"But, my friend, my gracious prince," panted Sporus, "what do you require of me?"

Nero's look was quite terrific as he threw up his arm and pointed at the curtain.

"Go!" he thundered.

Poor Sporus, thus placed "between the devil and the deep sea," had no alternative, but obedience.

With trembling steps he crept nearer and nearer to the fatal spot, his stylus sparkling and quivering in his nerveless hand.

The bystanders watched him breathlessly.

So perfect was the silence, and so quiet the demeanour of the surrounding throng, that Sporus was reassured.

"If there were really a panther behind the curtain," he thought, "I should hear some sound, and it is not likely such a beast would be loose. If there at all, it must be chained up, and I will take care to keep out of its range: no, it is some trick to befool me."

Thus regaining confidence, he braced up his nerves and advanced with a bold, firm step.

No sooner, however, had he approached within a few paces of the curtain, when it was rolled up by a string drawn by a hidden hand.

He stood face to face with the pantheress!

She lay in a crouching attitude, her forepaws extended, her head, flattened like a viper's, her greenish yellow eyes immoveably fixed upon him.

The poor craven wretch leaped backwards, and uttered a yell of terror.

He stood paralysed with fright, shaking and shivering like a reed in the wind.

His eyes dilated, his mouth agape, his body bent, his arms extended.

The stylus fell from his powerless grasp; he stood as though rooted to the spot, unable to advance or retreat.

"To him, Hecate!" growled the harsh voice of the dwarf Zaba.

The pantheress dragged herself along, her belly touching the ground, her glaring eyes constantly fastened upon her intended victim.

Sporus, poor trembling coward, remained passive and unresisting; he moved neither hand nor foot.

Nearer and nearer drew the pantheress, her lithesome body wriggling on the ground like a serpent.

Suddenly she doubled herself and, with a roar, bounded upon Sporus.

Her paws had scarcely touched his breast when he fell like a stone, and lay flat on his back, stiff and rigid.

The pantheress instantly threw herself upon his breast, snarling and growling.

"Enough!" cried Nero. "Call her off."

Zaba stepped forwards, and cracked his heavy whip.

"Hecate, come hither!" he shouted.

"But the brute showed no inclination to obey this order.

She lay upon the breast of the unconscious Sporus, and with her rough tongue licked his cheek till the blood came.

Zaba sprang upon her—slash—slash! fell the heavy whip upon the gaunt ribs of the pantheress, who set up a blood-chilling howl of rage, pain, and fear.

The hideous little African then, with kicks and curses, drove her from her prey.

Hecate slank away, whining and licking the weals on her side, and crouched against a pillar, terrified and subdued.

At a sign from Nero four of the guardsmen left their rank, and raised Sporus from the ground.

His body drooped in their arms, limp and life-less.

"Meherole!" said Honorius. "Poor wretch, the fright has killed him!"

"Vah! the poltroon," returned Nero, contemptuously. "Duck him in one of the fountains; that will bring him to. Take him out of my sight."

The insensible minion was borne away by the stalwart rough-looking soldiers.

Nero rose from his seat.

"Attend me in my library, Honorius, within an hour," he said, "and bring the Briton with you."

"And what are your commands in regard to the beast-feeder?"

"Zaba has amused me," said the prince, and added, laughing "he has a wide mouth, but fill it with gold, and send him packing. Let me know presently whether Sporus is dead or alive."

CHAPTER XXXV.

HOW CARACTACUS WAS LURED BY THE GODDESS DIANA.

HONORIUS, the tribune, and Caractacus, our British hero, conducted by a chamberlain, walked through the gorgeous halls, vestibules, and galleries of the magnificent palace of Claudius Cæsar.

The Briton's eyes were fairly dazzled by the blaze of gold, the gleam of marble and ivory, and the sparkling of gems.

High above him was the richly painted ceiling; on one hand the gilded and frescoed walls, with their rows of gold and ivory tables, marble statues, and bronze candelabra.

On the other hand noble colonnades of majestic pillars, through which appeared lovely patches of garden, vivid with the brightest and darkest tints of green, spangled over with beauteous flowers, and adorned with the finest statues and most graceful fountains.

It seemed as if nature and art combined to exalt and pamper the imbecile who ruled mankind.

Yet amidst all this splendour, a gloomy restraint, an ill-disguised uneasiness, prevailed among the glittering throngs of courtiers, guards, and minions that crowded the various apartments.

Men stole in and out with slinking steps, and conversed together in cautious whispers.

Caractacus looked half-confusedly about him, and felt dizzy and excited by the pomp that met his gaze, half-stifled by the atmosphere so heavily laden with perfumes.

Yet to the free-born barbarian there was an oppressive sense of thraldom, and he yearned more than ever for the free open plains, the shaggy woods, and rugged mountains of his own native land of liberty.

Knowing as he did that a dark plot was hatching against the reigning Cæsar, he envied him not the possession of that wealth, power, and magnificence which wore as transient and unsubstantial as the glories of a fleeting dream.

Still following their conductor Honorius and the Briton at last arrived in a large atrium, full with a splendidly accoutred troop of the Prætorian band, and here they were received by a haughty-looking noble, the præfect of the imperial guard.

Honorius saluted this officer, and together they stepped aside and talked briefly in a low tone, the præfect from time to time stealing a curious glance at the Briton, and soon after quitting his companion, Honorius at length made a sign to our hero to draw near.

"For the present you are safe, Idris-ap-Caradoc," he said, speaking in the British tongue; "at least I have reason to hope that I have so far succeeded in foiling the nefarious scheme of your enemies."

Our hero murmured his thanks.

"Be cautious what you say, and how you act in the presence of Nero," continued the tribune

"Sulpicius, our noble præfect, has gone into the prince's cabinet, and will represent to Nero that the son of Ostorius is in the hands of your father, and that he will keep him as a pledge for your safety."

"By the sun!" returned the Briton, "if you Romans have any wish to save the life of your general's son you will do well to protect me. Caractacus is a man of iron will, and, should my life be sacrificed, the hostage will have to pay the penalty. My father will exact blood for blood."

The præfect, Sulpicius, now came into the vestibule, and announced that he had been dismissed by Nero with orders to send our hero to him at once.

Accompanied by the tribune, the young Briton entered the imperial closet.

The hall in which they found themselves was by far the most splendid of any which Caractacus had yet seen in the palace.

Nero lay stretched upon the velvet cushions of an ivory couch, while three beautiful boys attended upon him.

They came and went, bringing him wine and fruit upon golden salvers.

The perfumed air thrilled with the melody of music, the performers being concealed.

Nero was reading a letter.

At a little distance from the couch stood Nyssa.

Nero having perused the letter, looked up at the beautiful girl and smiled.

"Fair Nyssa, tell my mother, the empress, that her commands shall be obeyed."

Then seeing Caractacus he at once waved her away.

She made a deep obeisance and swept from the hall.

Nero then motioned Caractacus to approach him.

Our hero bowed and drew nearer to the couch.

"I have sent for you, Caractacus, to tell you that you will henceforth remain a hostage in the palace. Start not nor look dismayed. You will be treated with every consideration, and will be attached to my own retinue."

"But, my lord, must I forego my exercises, and abandon the hope of distinguishing myself as a gladiator?" asked the Briton.

"There will be no need for that," was the prince's reply. "Many of the nobles will take part in the games; you may use your own discretion."

"Then I will not disappoint my lanista, who has staked a heavy sum on my success," replied the Briton.

"I approve your choice," replied Nero; "like yourself I take keen pleasure in the sports of the arena, and have myself fought as a gladiator, and have driven a chariot in the races."

Our hero then asked if he might pay an occasional visit to Ventidius and other friends in Rome, or whether he was to consider himself a prisoner.

To this Nero replied, that on the condition that he would pledge his word to return to the palace, and to make no attempt to escape, he might, under certain restrictions, be allowed the privilege he requested.

Caractacus thankfully agreed to this arrangement.

Nero, who appeared to be in a very gracious mood, asked him many questions about his former history, and discussed with him the various merits of the gladiators belonging to the school presided over by Ventidius.

The interview lasted about half an hour, and the prince dismissed him.

Caractacus was glad to escape.

Honorius asked him with a grim smile, whether he would like to take his meals with the slaves and minions of the palace, or whether it would suit him better to dine and lodge in the barrack of the Prætorian guard.

Our hero's decision need scarcely be stated.

He eagerly accepted the latter alternative, and Honorius promised him that he would see that the soldiers behaved towards him with proper respect.

These matters arranged, Caractacus strolled out for a walk through the gardens of the palace.

Caractacus wandered on through the beautiful terraces and parterres enriched with statuary and blooming with flowers.

He chose himself a resting-place in a shady dell, surrounded by dark cypress trees.

In the midst of this quiet dell a fountain shot its glistening spray far up into the air, and fell back with a continuous plash into a marble basin planted round with roses and myrtles.

Scattered about were blocks of marble, while some trees had been felled. It seemed as though some further adornments to the already lovely scene were to be added by the hands of skilful workmen.

Caractacus seated himself upon one of the marble blocks, and his eyes drank in the enchanting beauty of the scene.

"Beautiful, too beautiful!" he murmured. "A bower for fair women, but no abiding place for men who would retain their manly vigour. Give me back the rugged rocks, the frowning woods, the thundering forests, the keen cold blasts that pierce to the marrow. Give me Britain, the home of hardy hunters and fearless warriors! By the spear of Bran! a week's sojourn in this place would undo a twelvemonth's training, and reduce me to the condition of that wretched coward, Sporus."

He sprang to his feet.

"Can it be possible!" he exclaimed. "I feel my strength oozing from my limbs, a languor oppresses me. Idris-ap-Caradoc, art thou lost to thyself?"

As if really giving credence to the morbid impression he seized hold of a block of marble that two ordinary men would have found it hard to lift, and sent it whirling over the green sward.

"Not yet," he said to himself, and laughed a deep laugh. "My thews and sinews are not yet unstrung, but if I remain long in the palace the gods only know what may happen to me!"

As he chanced to turn his head, what was his amazement to see posed upon a marble pedestal, at a little distance from him, the statue of a beautiful girl draped in a robe of dazzling white?

There were plenty of statues in all directions, but the wonder was that this one stood alone, and yet he had not till now observed it.

Caractacus looked at it for a moment in silent astonishment.

Then he drew nearer, saying to himself—

"This is a masterpiece. I wonder why it stands thus by itself."

Then he asked himself whether he was dreaming, or had taken a sudden leave of his senses.

The statue moved.

Impossible! A mere trick of the imagination.

No, no! If he could believe his eyesight he saw it move once more.

Caractacus stared at it—his soul in his eyes.

It was a lifelike image of Diana—so lifelike that it seemed to be alive.

There were the buskins, the silver bow and quiver, and, more than all, a crescent moon gleamed upon the marble brow.

"What have they done to me?" gasped Caractacus, flinging his brawny arm behind his head, and clutching his massy yellow hair. "What have I eaten—what have I drunk, that has driven me mad?"

But whether or not it was an hallucination the bewildered youth distinctly saw the image raise her arm and waving him to approach her.

Uttering a cry of anguish and self-scorn, Caractacus rushed to seize the statue.

The pedestal was void—the image gone—vanished he knew not when or how!

To convince himself of the reality of this astounding fact Caractacus sprang upon the pedestal and stood upon the identical spot lately occupied by the image.

"By the altar of Bel!" panted Caractacus. "So much for trusting to mere human wisdom! I had faith in the teaching of Mathias, the Christian, as in the voice of an oracle; and lo! he is in error. The divinities he derides as false are true living gods and goddesses. This was Diana, the patroness of hunters, and it was because I sighed for my native hunting-grounds that she appeared to me. Must I be befriended by an alien goddess? What matters that? If I invoke her and do her homage, perhaps she will transport me to my native woods and mountains. I will fast, live on berries and drink spring water, lie on the bleak mountain side, fight bare-handed with the wolves, do anything, bear anything, to propitiate the huntress-goddess that loves the chaste and hardy."

A thrill of intense joy—the joy of the fanatic stirred the heart of the ignorant though noble minded barbarian.

He had found a divinity after his own heart, on there could be no mistake about, one he had seen with his own eyes.

Instinctively he gazed towards a clump of dark fir trees, because they so sternly contrasted with the artificial showiness and gaiety of the surrounding scene.

Diana stood revealed to him, stately and graceful, holding in her hand a bunch of oak, with which she beckoned him to follow her.

Inspired by madness Caractacus sprang from the pedestal, and rushed down a mossy bank to pursue the figure, now receding into the dark enclosing grove of pine trees.

"It may be some demon sent to me," gasped the Briton; "it matters not, its power is irresistible; follow it I must and will!"

He sped after the fleeting white figure.

As he entered the pine-wood a breeze sprang up, and the black funereal boughs rustled above his head with a sound stern but familiar, but which gave him nerve.

Outside the grove it was twilight—within the grove it was night, so thickly planted were the trees.

Still the white figure glided on before him.

Caractacus rushed wildly after it.

The phantom reached the centre of the grove.

Caractacus overtook it.

It paused and confronted him.

The face was noble and majestic; the long streaming curls of black hair floated in the evening breeze, the crescent glittered on the high and haughty forehead.

Overawed, the Briton sank upon his knees and clasped his hands.

He tried to offer some words of devotion, but his tongue failed him.

Diana smiled benignly, and shook the oak bough over her votary's head.

Caractacus felt cold drops, as of dew, fall upon his heated brow, but they were as cold as particles of ice.

The dream vanished, the scene faded away, he fell to the earth as senseless as the clod he pressed.

CHAPTER XXXVI.

THE SPELL IS BROKEN.

CARACTACUS awoke. Soft arms were twined around him, a scene of dazzling beauty and splendour floated before his bewildered eyes, his ears were lulled by the sweetest and softest strains of music.

He raised himself upon his elbow, and found himself reclining upon cushions of three-piled purple velvet, stuffed with swans' down, and embroidered with gold.

He looked at his limbs and body, and found them clothed in raiment of the richest hues and finest texture, sparkling with gems.

A wreath of fresh roses encircled his brow, and a chaplet of thick-matted violets hung about his neck

Over and around him twinkled a hundred starry lamps, while kneeling, standing, reclining about him, was a bevy of girls, in mist-like draperies, some dark-haired with glowing black eyes, others with golden tresses and eyes blue as the Italian sky in mid-summer, but all alike, lovely.

"If I am dreaming, oh, let me not awake!—let me dream on for ever!" murmured Caractacus, and he closed his eyes and pressed his head back upon the downy pillow.

A loud chord of music, like the crash of a thousand harps, accompanied by the prolonged trill of a Lydian flute, roused him from his lethargy.

He started to his feet, and gazed amazedly at the wondrous spectacle of beauty and magnificence that remained real and incorporate, in spite of his unbelief in its existence.

"This is no dream," he murmured; "I have crossed the shadowy bourne; I am dead. This is Elysium, and these the bright-haired daughters of the Sun."

And now there approached him, the majestic yet voluptuous form of a tall and beautiful woman, decked in royal robes, a glittering diadem on her lofty brow, a golden sceptre in her right hand. She was followed by a retinue of attendant maidens, while, trailing their resplendent tails, a pair of peacocks strutted by her side.

"It is Juno!" thought the simple Briton—"Juno, the Queen of Heaven."

The beautiful being approached him and stood by his side, smiling down upon him with an august but kind expression.

"Hebe, the chalice!" said the queen, waving her sceptre.

A young and fair damsel, clad in spotless white, bent on her knee before Caractacus, with a gem-incrusted goblet, and presented it to him.

"It is nectar—the cup of immortal youth," said Juno. "Drink, stranger-guest, and welcome to Olympus."

With trembling hand Caractacus took the cup.

"Oh, goddess! I am not worthy," he faltered.

This naive remark caused an outburst of musical laughter from the attendant nymphs.

But Juno checked this levity with an imperious gesture.

"Drink, noble Caractacus," she said. "Your evils, your hardy adventures, your warfare—all are over. Henceforth you will live in peace and bliss. Drink, I command you."

Caractacus raised the cup to his lips, and drank a deep draught.

The wine seemed to fire his blood and brain, and he laughed joyously.

"I have drunk nectar—I am in Elysium!"

Then a thought flashed through his bewildered head, and he exclaimed abruptly—

"If it be so, she must be here."

Then, clasping his hands, he asked, in a tone of fervent entreaty—

"Tell me, benign goddess, where is my sister? Tell me when shall I press her to my heart—dear, dear Iona?"

This provoked another chorus of laughter, which the presiding divinity rebuked with a frown.

"Know, mortal, that in these blissful regions all such earthly bonds are dissolved," she said. "Here is the abode of free love. I, even I, who reign supreme, will be to thee more than a sister—I am thine own."

And she clasped the youth in her arms, and pressed a burning kiss upon his cheek.

The spell was broken.

Caractacus hurled her off, and stood erect, glaring about him with rage and shame, and looking as terrible as a young lion just roused from his lair.

"Fool, madman! Thou art betrayed. This is the palace of Cæsar. I am made the mock and scorn of his slaves!"

The maidens fled from him shrieking, but he seized one of them—the fair cup-bearer—by the wrist, and held her fast.

"Hold up thy head, minion, let me look at thy face," thundered the enraged barbarian. "Yes, it is so; I know you now—you are Nyssa, my comrade's leman."

Then turning upon the pretended Juno, he added, in a tone of withering scorn—

"And you—you are the consort of Cæsar, the empress of Rome!"

"Strike me, Caractacus," pleaded Agrippina, "if thou hast the heart to injure one who loves thee. I can rather court thy blows than endure the caresses of the vile Claudius."

"Had I sword in my hand I would strike thee dead!" retorted Caractacus. "It would be the best service I could render thee."

Agrippina sank at his feet, and buried her face in her hands.

Caractacus trembled with fury.

"Wanton, where is thy blush? But thou art lost to shame. Let me begone; and let the events of this night be as a dream—forgotten. Off with this frippery, and let me depart."

He tore the chaplets of flowers from his head and neck, and trampled them under foot; he rent the silk robe from his shoulders.

Agrippina stood erect, boldly confronting him. Her face was white as death, but her dark eyes blazed with fury and revenge.

"Barbarian, slave, ingrate, brute, ruffian! do you think to escape me?" she hissed. "Ere thou shalt cross yon threshold to blazen my shame throughout the city I will have thee hacked into a thousand fragments—knowest thou who I am?"

"Yes, Agrippina—all Rome knows who and what you are—the niece and wife of Cæsar," returned the Briton, coldly.

"Death—death!" screamed the empress, and smote Caractacus on the breast.

She bruised her knuckles against his hard firm flesh, and though she struck her hardest, left no imprint of the blow.

The gladiator stood unmoved as a rock, and laughed contemptuously.

"Death, Agrippina," he said. "Death—but not you!"

The empress was stunned, her heart was stilled with awe and admiration at his beauty and impassibility.

She melted into tears.

"Forgive me, brave Caractacus, none but you could move me thus, and it is for you to direct that wild fond passion that urges me to madness," she said, in thrilling accents. "Why should we quarrel? Why should you spurn me? Is it my fault if Rome has crushed your country, has enslaved your noble self? Look: be then kind to me (for midst all my luxury and power I am a wretched woman, lonesome and heart-hungry), and I will be thy slave—thy Roman slave, and I will save thy Britain."

"Perish Britain!" retorted Caractacus. "Let the island sink beneath the engirdling seas rather than I—"

Then touched by her sobs, he added, in a softened voice—

"Pardon my roughness, madam, recollect yourself, and let me go in peace. Forget this scene—I shall not be so base as to betray your confidence. I pity you, I blame you not, for circumstances are stronger than our best nature, but let me bid you farewell. Give me leave to think of you with tenderness and respect."

"I will recollect myself," returned the empress, flashing her pearly teeth. "Thou shalt die."

"Not by a woman's hand."

"By mine!"

Whipping her stylus from its sheath she attempted to plunge it to the Briton's heart.

But he was too quick for her. Seizing her by the wrist he wrested the weapon from her clasp.

At this crisis a lady came rushing into the apartment, her look betokening the utmost consternation.

"Hush, hush, hush!" she exclaimed. "For all the gods, be quiet here!"

"'Tis Portia," cried the maidens. "What is the matter?"

"Where is the Briton?" gasped Portia.

"I am here," said our hero, quietly.

"Fly—escape—conceal yourself!" she exclaimed.

"Fly and escape!—willingly enough—only show me the way," said the Briton.

"What is the matter, Portia? Speak—and speak quickly," urged her fair companions.

"Cæsar is coming. He is at the door."

At this announcement the women shrieked, and dispersed in all directions.

Agrippina sank upon a couch.

"Claudius!" she ejaculated; "then I am lost!"

Waving her hand to Caractacus she went on immediately—

"Go! remember henceforth we are enemies."

Caractacus bowed coldly.

"I am not your friend, madam, nor your enemy," he said. "Farewell."

"This way, this way," urged Portia.

She hurried him through a secret panel, and closed it behind them.

CHAPTER XXXVII.
SIX TO ONE, AND ONE TO SIX.

THE broad moon was floating in the cloudless heavens, when a party of six men gathered under the dark frowning walls of the amphitheatre.

The group consisted of Varro, the gladiator, Zaba, the dwarf, with Caius Licinius, the patrician, attended by three of his myrmidons, armed to the teeth.

"Keep well in the shadow," said Licinius, speaking in a hushed voice, and treading on tiptoe, "where are you going?"

"To watch for him," grinned the dwarf, unsheathing a crooked Moorish dagger.

"Stand close, monstrum horrendum," growled the young noble, clutching him by the arm and dragging him near to the wall; "he is bound to come this way."

"Yes, he must pass through the Flaminian gate on his way back to the palace," answered Zaba.

"Whither does he betake himself?" said Licinius, "I am surprised that he has friends to visit outside the walls."

"He goes to the catacombs, that are the resort of the Nazarenes, the Christians," said Zaba.

"The champion of gladiators a Christian!" rejoined Licinius, incredulously. "It cannot be."

"Wherefore not?" said Zaba. "Such ignorant barbarians are the easiest misled. At any rate he associates with the Christians, and a man is known by the company he keeps. 'Tis enough for me. I have another hold on him if he should escape us now."

"Who talks of escape?" grumbled Varro. "Are we not six to one?"

"Five to one, good Varro," snarled the dwarf; "you count for nothing."

"What do you mean, malice? Is not my sword as good as another?" growled Varro.

"Yes, unless that other is wielded by a better man," hissed Zaba. "Do you remember this place, and how we met here on the night of the storm—the night before the chariot race?"

"Well?"

"Have you forgotten the warning that I gave you?"

"No, you pretended to have seen some omen that portended my death. You said I should die here."

"Yes, by Obi! and what I predicted will come to pass."

"You lie, malignant beast! You say this to frighten me, but I am above your spite. The first blow shall be struck by me."

"It will be your last."

"Silence! No wrangling," interposed Licinius. "Were he Ajax we are too many for him. But, harkye, Varro, when this business is settled I have other employment for you. It is a matter of difficulty, but I will pay you well."

"I am entirely at your service, noble patron."

"Well said. I love the fair Virginia, daughter of Ventidius. She rejects me, but I will have her mine either by force or strategy. We must contrive some means to carry her off from her father's house and— Hist—a footstep!"

"'Tis he," muttered Zaba. "He comes."

"Yes, his eyes are bent earthward, and he is lost in thought."

"Now, braggart! Now for your bold stroke," snarled Zaba.

"One moment. You shall see."

The assassins huddled together under the black shadow of the circus wall.

"Stand fast," whispered Licinius. "Let us fall upon him together."

Caractacus stalked past them, his stately form conspicuous in the full flood of the moonlight.

"Now for it," said Licinius. "Strike home!"

"I strike first!" returned Varro, as he sprang from his ambush.

Immediately our hero was beset.

Caractacus turned at bay.

In an instant one man lay mortally wounded on the ground.

Another staggered bleeding from a gash in his breast.

Varro, with a vengeful shout, sprang upon the Briton.

Caractacus plunged his sword to the hilt in the traitor's heart.

CHAPTER XXXVIII.
CARACTACUS CHALLENGES LICINIUS—THE PATRICIAN'S COMPACT WITH LOCUSTA.

WHEN, with a lunge as sudden and brilliant as a lightning flash, Caractacus drove his sword through the body of his treacherous comrade, Varro, there was a sudden suspension of hostilities.

Zaba gloated over his triumph as a prophet, and, leering at the dying man, pointed to the amphitheatre, and then to the spot where the poor wretch had fallen.

"Outside the walls of the circus," hissed the demoniac little monster, "did I not tell you where it would be?"

Varro uttered a yell of rage and agony, shook his fist at Zaba, then clawed the air with his convulsed fingers.

His arms dropped flat—he rolled over on his back a dead man.

"Down with him!" cried Licinius. "Down with the barbarian! avenge brave Varro!"

The remaining follower of Ventidius sprang at the Briton, while Zaba crept behind him to deal him a treacherous stab in the back.

But our hero was on his guard.

His eyes were everywhere, and his celerity of motion was as quick and keen as his eyesight.

With one downright blow of his sword he fe the dwarf to the ground, bleeding and insensi with a second stroke he cut off the sword-han the more manly assailant, who fled, bleeding screaming.

And now the Briton stood alone with a single assailant.

But Licinius, though by no means a coward, was overwhelmed with awe and dismay at this conclusion of a struggle in which he had justly reckoned all the odds on his own side.

NERO WATCHED THE TERRIBLE-LOOKING PANTHERESS AS SHE PLACED HER PAWS ON THE NECK OF HER MASTER.

He drew back, and even looked around him as though half inclined to take to flight.

Caractacus seized him by the cloak.

"Will you fly?" he jeered.

"No," said Licinius, hoarsely.

"Will you fight, then?"

"You fight not like another man," gasped Licinius. "You deal in magic!"

"So I do," returned the Briton, calmly. "The magic of a just cause, and the skill to defend it."

"Hear me, Caractacus," said the Roman, holding up his hand. "Singly I am no match for you. I am not afraid of death, but I do not care to swell this heap of carrion, to die with base-born slaves, to leave my name a scoff for all the vile plebeians in Rome."

"Are you so proud? You have a strange sense of honour," retorted the Briton, disdainfully. "You attack me, not alone, but like a thief in the night, backed by a gang of cut-throats, braver than yourself, but whom you have the arrogance to despise."

Licinius was a Roman, and his courage returned at these bitter taunts.

"I see you are not the man I took you for," he said. "You do not show that nobility of spirit that might have been expected in the son of the great Caractacus."

"What would you have of a slave or a barbarian?" retorted Caractacus.

"I see I must fight," answered the Roman.

"On guard then!" said Caractacus, "and look to yourself, for I mean to kill you."

But he had no such intention—in that encounter at any rate.

A few rapid passes were exchanged.

Licinius controlled himself, and fought with his utmost skill and coolness.

The Briton's blood was up.

Their swords clashed together.

Agile as a tiger Caractacus sprang upon his antagonist and touched him in the shoulder.

The opponents parried, and thrust with the utmost dexterity.

But the duel did not last longer than a few seconds.

Caractacus with ease performed that most difficult and masterly feat—he disarmed his foe and sent his sword flying over his head.

Then he dashed him against the wall, and pressed the point of his sword to his throat.

"Yield, and confess thyself beaten!" cried Caractacus.

"Never!" replied Licinius. "Despatch, barbarian. A Roman knows how to die."

"I will spare thy life on one condition," said our hero.

"Name no condition—I can accept none," said Licinius. "Kill me, but spare your insults."

Caractacus sheathed his sword.

"I do not intend to insult or even to upbraid you," he said; "but you attribute my victory to my training as a gladiator—will you go into training yourself, and fight me in the arena?"

Licinius turned pale at this challenge.

But it was impossible for him to refuse it.

"Be it so," he said; "from to-morrow I will place myself under the tuition of Phorbus."

"You could not do better," said Caractacus; "he is a good lanista."

He paused, and fixed a steadfast look upon the young patrician.

"You are no coward," he said, "but a foeman worthy of my steel. Therefore, you will lay no more plots to cut me off by treachery."

"No, by the gods!" said Licinius.

"You will promise this?"

"I pledge my knightly word that I will do my best to protect you against your secret enemies," replied the Roman, "Nay more, I will defend you at the risk of my own life, until the fatal hour when we shall meet foot to foot, and hand to hand, upon the sand in the arena."

"It is well," said the Briton; "would that hour were come!"

"Be patient! It will come all too soon for one or both of us."

"Listen," said Caractacus; "in return for this promise I will give you a word of warning."

"Does it concern myself?"

"Yes, indirectly," answered the Briton; "but it chiefly affects your friend and patron, Narcissus."

"Ha!"

"I now live in the palace, and many rumours reach my ears," said Caractacus. "It is said, and I believe with truth, that the influence exercised by Agrippina over her weak-minded consort is greater than ever."

"That cannot be denied. But what follows?"

"Only that she has sworn to ruin Narcissus," replied our hero; "and, mark me, she will be as good as her word."

The young patrician laughed.

"That is old news," said he; "they have hated and opposed each other ever since Agrippina was raised to the throne. But what of that? The poor wretch Claudius cannot dispense with the services of his freedman and secretary, who stands higher than ever in his master's estimation."

"Trust not to that," answered Caractacus. "The power of the empress is not to be slighted—court favour is as fickle as the wind."

Licinius flushed and cast down his eyes.

"You would save Narcissus?" he said, in a low voice.

"Yes."

"I will tell you something," rejoined Licinius, raising his eyes, and regarding our hero with a puzzled look.

"He whom you would save is your enemy—he is the prime mover of all these plots for your destruction."

"I know it," answered the Briton, quietly, "but I would save him none the less. I wish him to learn that I, a Briton, a barbarian if you will, scorn and detest those arts he practises."

"Thou hast a noble spirit, brave Caractacus," said the patrician; "but, farewell, let us part in peace, though the next time we meet in strife."

"A strife that will be mortal," answered Caractacus. "Fare you well, Caius Licinius. Remember your promise."

The Briton waved his hand and departed.

Left alone the young patrician clutched his brow, and stamped his foot with shame and mortification.

"Wretch that I am!" he muttered, fiercely; "is it not enough that I should sink so low as to become a hireling cut-throat, but I must be baffled and vanquished by a rude barbarian, a gladiator, a despised slave? Despised! Oh, no!—hated and feared perhaps, but not despised; he is of royal blood, and has a royal mind."

Licinius glanced around upon the bodies of the assassins, slain by the Briton single-handed.

They lay rigid and motionless, and weltering in their blood.

"What a scene is this!" he muttered. "Surely some invisible power guards that fair-haired boy! He is invulnerable."

He gazed long and fixedly upon the bodies of his fallen myrmidons.

"Not one escaped but my slave Aster," he thought; "'tis so far well that none but he is left to know of my shameful defeat, and I can take sure means for enforcing his silence. He shall not long outlive his companions."

As the patrician was about to leave the spot his attention was arrested by a deep groan.

He picked up his sword, which Caractacus had struck from his hand during the encounter.

"Dead men tell no tales," he muttered. "If any one of these wretches remain alive I will make short work with him."

Turning to see from whom the groan proceeded

Licinius perceived that Zaba the dwarf was recovering from the effects of the heavy blow which had cut him down.

He had raised himself upon his hands and knees, and dragged himself along for some distance, but appeared quite unable to rise upon his feet.

His head drooped low; his hair was matted with blood, which fell from his gashed forehead in crimson drops upon the pavement.

Licinius drew back, and hid himself in the black shadow of the circus wall.

"'Tis the hideous beast-feeder. He lives! He will recover!" muttered Licinius. "I will despatch him."

Zaba had not got far before he appeared to be overpowered with faintness and exhaustion.

He feebly raised his hand to his bleeding brow; then his head drooped lower and lower, and he sank upon the earth, and remained quite still and rigid.

"Is he dead?" thought Licinius. "'Tis best to make sure."

Grasping the sword Licinius crept up to the dwarf, and was about to run him through the body when his hand was stayed.

He felt a small but powerful hand clutching his wrist, and he let fall his sword.

A tall, commanding-looking woman, with sharp-cut features, thin, hard lips, and black, fierce, penetrating eyes stood before him.

She was a woman of about thirty, tall and majestic in stature, and not without a dark, weird sort of beauty.

Her dress was sombre, consisting of a dark grey robe thrown loosely back and fluttering in the wind.

"Hold!" she said. "Do not perpetrate an act of madness."

Licinius appeared thunderstruck.

"You, Locusta!" he exclaimed.

"Yes, it is I," she answered quietly. "What were you about to do?"

"To put it out of that deformed villain's power to betray our secrets—yours and mine," replied Licinius, sullenly.

"Kill Zaba!" retorted the woman, with an angry gesture. "Is it thus you deal with those who serve you?"

"The miscreant knows too much," replied the patrician. "It is better he should be put out of the way—better, I repeat, for your sake as well as my own."

"Do not think it," was the reply; "he is more dangerous dead than alive."

"What do you mean?"

"There is a miserable old wretch, a scrivener, who has taken copies of the letters which have passed between Narcissus and those who are involved in the conspiracy to bring about the divorce of Agrippina, and the exclusion of Cæsar's adopted heir, young Nero."

"True, I know the man," answered Licinius—"one, Pertinax."

"The same," returned Locusta. "While Zaba lives, this fellow, Pertinax, dares not stir; but were the dwarf killed, yourself and Narcissus would at once be denounced to the emperor."

"Let him live then," said Licinius; "but our first care must be to get the fatal documents from him and his confederate."

"I have long studied how to accomplish that," replied Locusta, knitting her brow; "but as yet I do not see how it can be accomplished."

"We must devise some plan between us," said the patrician. "By force or fraud we must get those documents into our possession."

"That is understood," said she; "but tell me how did this affray arise which has resulted in such wholesale slaughter?"

"We laid an ambush for the Briton, Caractacus," was the response.

Locusta started and clutched his arm.

"Is he slain?" she asked, eagerly.

"No," returned Licinius; "his valour is a match against any odds; he is the champion of all swordsmen; he wounded or slew every one of my followers."

"And how did you escape?" she asked.

"I am ashamed when I tell you how I was baffled and defeated," replied Licinius, in a tone of vexation; "the barbarian disarmed me, but spared my life."

"The more fool he," laughed the woman; "but you have no further cause to fear him; he has made an enemy so high-placed and powerful, that his doom is certain."

"Is it a woman?"

"The Empress Agrippina."

Licinius started.

"The gods!" he exclaimed, "can it be possible! But are you quite sure of this?"

"Yes, and I am now on my way to the palace; you may guess what that means," was the reply.

"I know," said Licinius, in a hollow voice.

Locusta laughed harshly.

"O you men!" she said, "what your valour could not accomplish will be done quickly and quietly by a woman's hand."

Now Licinius, though a thorough-paced scoundrel, was not without some of the instincts of a gentleman.

He had accepted our hero's challenge and had promised his future adversary not to countenance any treacherous plots against him.

Licinius was sincerely disposed to keep faith.

"I am sorry for what you tell me, Locusta," he said gravely.

"Sorry that the man you hate should be removed without risk or trouble to yourself?" she asked, in surprise.

"Yes, I have reasons, important reasons, for wishing to save him, at least for the present," answered Licinius.

"He must not die yet!"

Locusta stared at him in wonder.

"Are you in earnest?" she asked.

"Yes, believe me," he replied. "Will you aid me in this matter—will you make an effort to preserve his life?"

"But what has caused this change in your plans?"

"I have no time to explain that now," replied Licinius; "but when the opportunity arrives, I will tell you all about it; meantime answer but this—will you save him Locusta? You have no enmity against the lad, who is a stranger to you."

Again the woman laughed in her cheerless way.

"What matters it to me? I save or slay for gold," she answered. "I have neither loves nor hatreds. I work for those that pay me, and for my victims I am as callous and indifferent in their regard as the fowler who spreads his nets to catch birds."

"You know I am poor, Locusta," he rejoined; "but my patron, Narcissus, will always unloose his purse-strings at my call. I will fill your lap with gold if you will save that youth. Remember, I have done you good service in my time, and will stand your fast friend for ever if you will gratify me in this instance."

Locusta pondered.

"It is difficult," she said. "But nothing is impossible to the crafty and unscrupulous."

"How did the Briton incur the displeasure of the empress?"

Locusta's lip curled with scorn.

"He is a fool, and not worth the coil you make about him," she replied.

"What has he done?"

Locusta looked fearfully around.

"Is it safe here?" she whispered.

"Why not? they will not betray our secrets," answered Licinius, gloomily.

He pointed to the dead bodies that lay around.

Locusta glanced at the mangled corpses of the slain, and recoiled with a shudder.

"Blood, blood!" she gasped; "how I detest this clumsy brutal work! The means I use are swift or slow, at my pleasure, but always sure; they leave no trace behind them."

"Enough of this—we trifle time," rejoined Licinius. "Answer my question."

"I have not seen this lad," said Locusta, "but they say he is very handsome, that he has golden hair, and a complexion soft and white as a woman's"

"It is no more than the truth," replied Licinius. "With the strength and vigour of Hercules he combines the grace and beauty of Apollo."

"So then that accounts for Agrippina's passion."

"How her passion?"

"Yes, she doats on him."

"On Caractacus?"

"Even so."

"A slave and gladiator!"

"As for his being a slave, how many of the imperial favourites are slaves, or for that matter who of them are not?" laughed the woman. "And as for his being a gladiator, it is not the first time the empress has taken a fancy to one of his class."

"But he?"

"The boy! he must be mad, he rejects her love with scorn."

"You amaze me!"

"They say the Gauls and Britons hold their womankind in higher esteem than the Romans," said Locusta. "I think I know the reason why the Briton despises the empress."

"He loves another woman, perhaps," suggested Licinius.

"It is so," replied Locusta. "That poor wretch, Varro, who lies yonder, told me that it is whispered in Ventidius' 'family' that the Briton has fallen in love with his lanista's daughter, Virginia."

The cheek of Licinius grew red, and his brow darkened.

"I know it," he said; "would it were otherwise, for I think she loves him, too."

"Will you pay me well if I win her for yourself?" asked Locusta. "It is not impossible to do so."

"Half I possess shall be yours!" cried Licinius, eagerly. "But how can it be done?"

Again Locusta laughed.

"I must see this milk-faced boy," she said; "I think he is an enchanter, and has bewitched the women—they are all in love with him. Chloris would give her life for one smile or one gentle word from him. She is madly jealous of Virginia—we might turn her folly to advantage."

"So we might!" cried Licinius, triumphantly, catching at the idea. "We can entice Virginia from her home by some strategy, and I will carry her off to my country villa, and there marry her. I know Ventidius; he is too fond of his daughter to nurse any resentment against her very long. She is so good and beautiful, I feel that for her sake I can become a better citizen, a wiser man. But what of Caractacus?"

"We must secure the aid of Chloris, and he must be the lure; for him she would pass through a fiery furnace," replied Locusta.

"It is settled then that you will save him?"

"I will try."

"And the empress?"

"I will beguile her thus," replied Locusta. "I will tell her that I possess a love-philtre that will make the Briton adore her—she will believe me. At the worst we shall gain time."

"And that is something," said Licinius. Then he added—

"But what are we to do with this miserable Zaba? We cannot leave him here."

"No," said Locusta; "my sella is close by; I will have him placed in it, and sent back to my house. But how am I to get to the palace?"

"My chariot awaits me in the Forum," replied Licinius. "Come with me."

The wounded dwarf was placed by the slaves in the sella, and Locusta, accompanied by Licinius, mounted the chariot and drove off to the palace.

CHAPTER XXXIX.
THE CALM BEFORE THE STORM.

CARACTACUS lodged with the Prætorian Guard.

In a very short time, by his frank, soldierly bearing, he won the hearts of the rough veterans amongst whom he had been thrown.

Many of them had fought in Britain, and had learned to esteem their brave and honourable foes, while not a few of them had loved some British maiden.

It was in consequence of his being on such good terms with the all-powerful guard, who had the keeping of every inlet and outlet to the palace, that the Briton enjoyed so many privileges.

When he gave his word that he would return within a certain time they knew they could depend upon him, and therefore would give him the password and suffer him to come and go as he pleased.

More than that, Caractacus shared the plenteous but wholesome fare of the barrack mess-room, and engaged in the drill and exercises of the parade-ground, so that he was, in fact, nearly as well off in regard to his training as he would have been at home among his comrades in the gymnasium of Ventidius.

Honorius the Tribune would often say to our hero—

"You have chosen wisely, my Caractacus, in casting in your lot with us. Here you are safe. Within the interior of the palace you run a thousand risks, and are exposed to a thousand temptations. Many a fine hale lad, with healthful cheek and vigorous arm, have I seen reduced to the condition of the pallid, nerveless minions that crawl about the vestibules and atria, worn out with drunkenness and debauchery, and looking more like ghosts than living men."

Caractacus was pleased to find that he had made so favourable an impression upon the brave and honourable tribune, who was a man universally admired and respected.

When Agrippina heard that the Briton had placed himself, as it were, under the protection of the Imperial Guard, she was enraged.

She knew well enough that he was beyond her reach.

She wanted to get him back into the palace.

She inquired of Nero whether he had seen the British hostage lately, and why the youth did not appear in the presence-chamber occasionally, to pay his respects to Cæsar and herself.

Now, the rumour of the challenge which had passed between Caractacus and Caius Licinius soon got bruited abroad.

At first it was disbelieved.

When, however, Licinius himself avowed the truth of the report, and actually went into training under Phorbus, the excitement amongst the betting fraternity was intense.

The young patrician was known to be an excellent swordsman, and as he was only a year or two older than the Briton, and a man of heavier weight it was thought to be a fair match; or, if indeed there were any difference between the two, the odds were in favour of Licinius.

Young Nero, after consulting with Honorius, had backed the novice for a very heavy sum of money.

He did not want his man to be spoiled by indolence and luxurious living.

"Caractacus is well where he is, good mother," the prince replied to Agrippina's inquiries. "Leave him alone. What do you want with him?"

"He is a splendid youth," replied Agrippina,

"and an ornament to the court. I like to see him in the presence."

"If you mean well by him you will not throw temptations in his way," said Nero. "If you bear him any ill-will you will probably soon learn that he has been duly punished for offending you."

Agrippina flushed to the temples.

"I bear him ill-will! Wherefore should I?" she retorted, rather confused. "What is the barbarian to me? He has given me no offence. I only questioned you about him from motives of idle curiosity."

"Let it rest at that," answered Nero, sulkily. "Your curiosity is gratified. The lad is in safe keeping."

"But you spoke of some punishment to be inflicted upon him."

"You say he has deserved none—do you not?"

"Not from me."

"Why, then, let us pray the gods to crown his arms with victory," returned Nero, "for I have wagered my farm at Tibur upon his skill and prowess, and, as you know, I have been extravagant of late, and have besides lost a good deal of money in gaming."

"You shall have more."

"Thanks, my noble mother," returned Nero; "how much more generous are you than my precious uncle and stepfather, Claudius, who is as wretched a miser as he is idiot."

"Hush, Nero!"

"I am all obedience, madam," replied Nero, "only promise me to leave my novice alone until after the games; then you may crown or crucify him according to his deserts and your own good pleasure."

"Will he then fight in the arena?" said the empress, without noticing her son's jeers; she was used to them, and, though a vile woman, was a doting mother.

"Yes, he will fight for death or freedom on the birthday of our sublime Cæsar," replied the prince.

"Tis a pity," replied the empress; "he deserves a better fate."

"The same might be said of Licinius," rejoined the prince, "who, I hope and believe, will get the worst of it."

"Is he matched against Licinius?"

"Even so."

"I am not sorry to hear it," rejoined the empress; "Licinius is our enemy, and the creature of the only man in the world I am afraid of."

"You mean Narcissus," rejoined Nero; "have patience, my good mother, the end is at hand. Everything is in train to procure his disgrace and banishment, and then we will know what will follow."

"His death!" cried Agrippina, exultingly; "let me but live to see that day, and I care not what may then befall me."

Here the conversation ended.

This turn of affairs was no doubt the saving of the life of Caractacus.

Agrippina abandoned her design of having him poisoned or otherwise put out of the way.

She consulted with Locusta, who gave her the love charm, and told her that it would be sure to bring the handsome youth to her feet.

With little difficulty, one of the common soldiers was induced by a bribe to mix the magic potion in our hero's drink, which consisted of a little wine copiously diluted with water.

Our hero, though reluctantly, was forced to take a little wine now and then, to please his boon companions, the Prætorian guardsmen.

One day, after he had been exercising in the parade ground, leaping, running, and throwing the discus, he came into the guard-room hot and thirsty.

One of his comrades handed him a goblet.

Caractacus drank it off at one draught.

As soon, however, as he had swallowed the liquor, he spluttered and made a wry face.

"Vah! what stuff is this?" he said. "Where did you get this wine, my Corvus? It is enough to poison one."

The man looked rather taken aback.

"The wine is on the lees, comrade," he replied; "the cask is almost empty. We must broach another."

Then he muttered under his beard:

"Nyssa swore to me that it is harmless. If it be poison, woe to her head!"

But he had no occasion to trouble himself in the matter.

The potion, though horribly nasty, was perfectly innoxious.

Had it the desired effect?

Agrippina thought she had reason to believe so.

The fact was that Caractacus was not altogether untouched by the tender pleading of the unhappy woman who had made such a sacrifice for his sake.

His youthful vanity was flattered by his having inspired such a violent passion in an empress, and such an empress—the consort of the Cæsar who claimed dominion over the whole known world.

"After all, she is not so much to blame," he argued; "born and bred in a den of the foulest iniquities, is it to be wondered that her mind has become corrupted? Poor wretched woman, her condition is more pitiable than that of the meanest slave that lives or dies upon her smile or frown."

A few days after he had taken the memorable love-philtre, Caractacus was reposing under a shady tree in the garden, when he was startled in his sleep by the approach of footsteps and the music of girlish laughter.

No less to his annoyance than surprise he beheld Agrippina attended by a large company of ladies advancing towards him.

His first thought was to hide himself, or to make his escape.

But he was too late.

Agrippina had seen him.

She immediately sent two or three of her maidens to tell him the empress desired to speak with him.

Of course our hero could not refuse compliance with a request which was equivalent to a command.

Caractacus was naturally very much embarrassed.

Agrippina made no allusion to the strange scene in which she had played such a prominent part, but discoursed as composedly as if nothing of the sort had happened.

"And it is then true, brave Caractacus, that you intend to fight as a gladiator in the next games?" she said, smiling graciously.

"It is true, illustrious," he replied.

"Mars was in the ascendant when you were born," she answered; "your sole delight appears to be in warfare—you take no pleasure in the amenities of life."

Caractacus smiled ingenuously and shook his head.

"No madam," he replied. "Like the wild, the tameless creatures of my native woods, I cannot bear a cage, though the bars be gilded and the richest viands provided for the captive. This palace is a dungeon to me, this life of ease and luxury distasteful—I pine for freedom."

Agrippina sighed.

"And were you restored to freedom, what would you do?" she asked.

"I would fly far hence, and, returning to my native land, do battle with the invaders."

Agrippina frowned.

"You have no heart," she said—"are without kindliness or gratitude."

"Not so, illustrious," answered the Briton. "In Rome I have many friends, whom I shall always remember with gratitude and affection."

Agrippina raised her black brows.

"Indeed!" she said. "And who are they?—your comrades, the gladiators, I suppose."

"They, and others who have been kind to me."

"Are any of them Romans?"

"Yes, madam."

"Then you are not so implacable after all," she said, with her sweetest smile. "You do not hate us all alike."

Caractacus bowed lowly and gravely.

"Fair and illustrious," he answered, "when I first came hither—like many another traveller—I had a prejudice against the people I was thrown amongst. But experience has taught me that human nature is pretty much the same all the world over—that there is good and evil in all races and conditions of men."

"Then you do not hate all Romans?"

"No, there be those of the Latin race whom I respect and love."

Agrippina started and turned pale.

"And love!" she repeated in a vacant way.

Then she cast down her eyes, and murmured——

"And others whom you hate?"

"Aye, bitterly," was the frank answer.

"Amongst whom I fear I must include my unfortunate self," rejoined Agrippina, in a low pensive voice, that went straight to the Briton's heart, and roused the latent emotions of pity and gallantry.

"The gods forbid, most precious empress!" he replied with fervour.

"You have no cause," she said. "If it lay in my power I would restore you to your native country, and bid you farewell for ever, though I know you would leave me without one pang of regret."

"Not so, madam. I shall not forget your kindness and condescension towards a luckless exile and prisoner of war," replied our hero. "Would I could give you some worthy proof of my devotion to your service!"

"Well, I wish you good fortune both in peace and war, Caractacus."

She gave him her hand to kiss.

Perhaps, unconciously, our hero returned the slight pressure as he raised the little white hand to his lips.

Agrippina smiled radiantly upon him as he bowed and retired.

When he was gone her heart gave a great throb.

"The spell begins to work," she murmured. "His manner was softer, his voice less harsh—he pressed my hand, his stony heart melts, he will love me by and bye."

If she could have known what was passing in the Briton's mind she would have felt less confidence in the effect of Locusta's magic elixir.

"Agrippina is a superb woman—many a man would fall madly in love with her," Caractacus was saying to himself. "But honour and virtue apart, though I pity her from my soul, I could not care for her. What is she compared with the pure, the gentle, the kind-hearted Virginia?"

And what was Virginia thinking of her beloved young hero at that precise moment?

She was sitting alone in the little chamber over the portico, embroidering a crimson scarf with gold thread.

Her tears were falling fast.

"Who knows but I am adorning a shroud for him?" she murmured bitterly. "Who knows but on that fatal day this scarf may be rent and dabbled in blood, and that, vanquished and spurned, his poor body may be dragged with a filthy hook to the awful spoliarium? Does he know I love him so dearly? I cannot tell. Yet his eyes sparkle, and the colour mounts his cheek—he veils his proud look when our glances meet—his words are gentle and tender when he speaks to me."

Then she dried her eyes and smiled faintly.

"But why should I yield to despair?" she asked herself. "Caractacus is braver than a lion—none of the gladiators can stand against him, and more than all he is the favourite of fortune. He will come off conqueror, and then, oh, hope and happiness, he will lay his laurels at my feet, and I shall hear him hailed by thousands as the Champion of the Arena."

At this moment a loud cheery voice was heard shouting on the stairs.

"What, ho! Virginia, where art thou, pretty one, come down! Or stay, I will come to thee."

Virginia rose and hastily put aside her work, and rising went to her mirror and smoothed back her dark glossy hair.

"It is my father," she said to herself; "he must not see these foolish tears."

The next instant Ventidius burst into the room.

"What news, my father?" asked Virginia, putting on a smiling face.

"Good news, glorious news, my darling," replied Ventidius, seating himself by her side, and pressing a fond kiss upon her brow. "Through the interest of my worthy patron, Honorius, I have secured seats in the front row of the equestrian benches. Thus you and your mother will flaunt it with the proudest ladies of the land."

Virginia turned white as death, shuddered violently, and buried her face in her father's bosom.

"I cannot bear such frightful scenes, dear father," she murmured. "Pray do not make me go."

"What! not to see Caractacus," cried Ventidius, buoyantly. "Vah! go to, thou silly wench!"

"But if he should be killed?"

"Killed!" laughed Ventidius. "Who is to kill him, I should like to know—not one of those that will be opposed to him, though they are picked swordsmen of the first-class."

"But since he has sojourned at Cæsar's palace he has gone out of training."

"No, that's the best of it!" chuckled the lanista. Caractacus is the finest of fine fellows—a gladiator born! He neglect his training! He would as soon cut off his right thumb to save himself from being pressed for a soldier."

Again Ventidius hugged his daughter to his breast.

"Fear you not, my birdie," he whispered in her ear, "Caractacus will win. Why, Honorius tells me that our hero, at fencing, running, wrestling, boxing, is a match for the finest warrior in the Prætorian band."

"And who is he to fight against?"

"O, with several challengers," answered the lanista. "But there is one ticklish affair that, I confess, I wish him well out of. A combat of three against three, the palm-crown for the sole survivor. A representation of the combat of the Horatii and the Curiatii, you know."

"And who will fight with him?"

"I have picked two of the best lads in my maniple —Manlius and Lycaon."

"And whom are the opponents?"

"Licinius, the patrician, Arvirargus, the Briton, and Ermanricus or Telamon, one of the lads belonging to the family of Antispas .I know him, too; I killed his father in his twenty-sixth battle. He is a capital swordsman, and grit to the backbone!"

"These are great odds."

"No odds at all, my love," replied Ventidius, "I will back each of my lads against two of any other lanista's, and as for Caractacus he is champion over all."

CHAPTER XL.

THE ARENA OF BLOOD.

VIRGINIA sat crouching in the corner of an equestrian stall in the dread amphitheatre.

She had expressly chosen this corner, nearest to the low partition which divided this compartment from the others, that she might remain as little observed as possible, while she passed through an ordeal, in which she suffered more harrowing torment of hope and fear than even the poor wretches who had to contend for life and death on the sand.

O, how lonely she felt—the poor unhappy girl!

Sometimes she longed to have her father by her side, that she might cling to his strong arm, and whisper her anguish in his indulgent ear.

But no! a second thought convinced her that it was better as it was.

The lanista was away—there, behind the stage on which the fell tragedy was to be performed—admonishing, instructing, encouraging his pupils.

Yes, he was with Caractacus, his experienced eye quick to detect any defect in the young champion's weapons or armour, his skilful hands to make all right.

Virginia felt a pleasant glow at the thought that her father was by the side of Caractacus, to cheer and to advise him; she had such faith in them both; she thought they would be such a stay and comfort to each other, and how she loved them then! How gladly would she have exposed her soft white bosom to the blades of their enemies.

Poor girl, had she but known it—what a waste of sympathy on her part!

While she was sick almost to death with anxiety and tender grief on their behalf, Ventidius and his pupils were quivering with excitement and aglow with that strange, perhaps wicked glee, that men of mental force and animal vigour feel at the prospect of strife, of having something to contend with, something to hunt down and slay, the fiend-like exultation that seems to have its welling-spring in battle, murder, and sudden revenge.

Oh, how lonely she felt, this poor trembling girl—yet, was she alone?

The mother who bore her sat at her side, a warm-hearted woman, and one who loved her child.

Yet, oh, what a gulf was between them!

Lupa, dressed in her most gorgeous array, sat prim, erect, and glancing about her with a proud supercilious air, as much as to say—

"Don't you think that I'm not as good as the best of you. You may think this is the first time I have ever sat in the equestrian benches. You may twit me with being the wife of a common trainer of prize-fighters. I can tell you that my husband is an honest man, and exhibits the finest maniple of gladiators in the empire, and is a rich man into the bargain, while half of you, for all your finery and turned-up noses, are as poor as the beggars under the velarium, and no better than you ought to be. Well, I declare, Honorius the Tribune is bowing to me. I must acknowledge him, he is such a nice, sensible man."

Poor Virginia, how lonely she was! Yet, once again, was she alone?

No, fifty thousand times no! for fifty thousand spectators were assembled to glut their taste for blood and carnage.

The vast amphitheatre rang round with the loud ceaseless hum of the mighty multitude.

The slant beams of the morning sun flooded the stupendous building with a dazzling glare, save where the canvas awnings threw their square crisply-defined shadows, by dusky bluish patches, upon the wavering yet densely-packed fields of faces.

The clear, brilliant sunlight glistened on the fair silvery sand in the arena, so soon to be imprinted with the footsteps of wretches engaged in the death struggle, and to be soddened and stained by the crimson flow from many a gallant heart.

The sunshine glistened, too, upon the rich dresses and ornaments of gold and jewels along the gay equestrian benches, where the nobles of the empire were ranged.

It bleached the lily robes, long and sweeping, of the cold, demure vestal virgins—those chaste nuns of Paganism—in their parted stall.

It glared and sparkled with a rich golden glow upon the pulpit or tribunal of imperial Cæsar.

Claudius himself was already present.

His chair was distinguished by a canopy of velvet.

On his right hand were seated his wife, Agrippina, with her son, Nero, while around the royal group were arranged the nobles, courtiers, eunuchs, slaves, and other attendants.

Virginia saw nothing of all this.

She kept her eyes closed, and leaned her heated, aching brow against the marble partition of her stall.

But her ears were open to every sound.

She heard the loud, fierce, blithesome melody of trumpets.

When this had died away, she heard the editor, in a loud but monotonous tone, reading out the proclamation which announced that the gladiators, with whose combats the exhibition was to commence, were about to enter the arena.

Cæsar, a bloated mass of infirmities, wrapped in Tyrian purple and blazing gold, lolled in his chair, and rolled his eyes about him with a stolid slumberous glare.

He appeared to take little notice of what was going on, but shuffled about with an air of discomfort, as though he would much rather have been at home, sprawling upon a downy couch in his own splendid palace.

Agrippina did not deign to cast a single glance at him.

She sat, her arm leaning on the ivory arm of her chair, less brilliantly white than the moulded limb that rested on it.

Her black, fearless eyes rolled round with a dull wonder, and dazed delight upon the multitudinous faces that packed the amphitheatre.

Two bronze vases, filled with incense, burnt on either side of her throne.

And now the even flow of the editor's recital ceased.

He waved his hand and sat down.

The multitude rent the air with a prolonged shout.

Then came another flourish of trumpets and the clash of cymbals.

Then a folding-door on the right hand of the arena was thrown wide open, and a single trumpet sounded.

The gladiators marched in with slow step a long and seemingly interminable file.

Each man naked, except that he was girt with a cloth about his loins.

Each bore on his left arm a small buckler, and had a short straight sword suspended by a cord about his neck.

They marched slowly and steadily, so that the whole assembly had full leisure to contemplate the forms of the men, and form an estimate of their chances of being victorious.

They made the circuit of the arena three times, and then forming in a double line before the tribunal of Cæsar, they raised their voices in a loud solemn chant.

"*Ave, Cæsar, morituri te salutant.* Hail, Cæsar, those about to die salute thee."

There was a deep hush, emphasised rather than broken by a mournful note on a single trumpet.

Virginia was awake and alert now, and sat with dilated eyes and parted lips, awaiting the coming of Caractacus.

But his turn was not yet.

Presently four men entered the ring.

Two of them were the lanistæ, Ventidius and Phorbus.

They were accompanied by two gladiators.

One was Diomed, the other Ermanricus.

Diomed, the dandy of Ventidius's "family," a tall lissome fellow, was dressed in a short tunic, and carried a net thrown over the left shoulder.

In his right hand he grasped a three-lanced spear or trident.

He was the retiarius or net-thrower.

Though he looked so bold and confident, he was rather heavy at heart, for this was a line of business he never took to kindly since his encounter with the patrician Cornelius, who had so nearly given him his death-blow—though in that case he had acted as secutor.

Ermanricus, the Dacian, who on this occasion acted as the mirmillo or secutor, was a tall, athletic-looking barbarian, with an ugly face, lowering bushy brows, and a mane of tawny hair.

He was armed with a helmet, bearing in silver the device of a fish on the crest, greaves about his thighs, a gorget around his neck, a round buckler and a harpé or long curved scimitar.

The appearance of these men was greeted with a loud jubilant shout.

This sort of combat was very popular among the bloodthirsty rabble of Rome.

There was something grotesque and brutally entertaining in this casting the net for a man-fish.

The retiarius generally gained the most applause.

The place rang with the shout——

"A Diomed! a Diomed!"

After saluting Claudius Cæsar the antagonists took their ground.

The retiarius poised his long trident and unloosened the thong of his net.

The trident clashed against the shield of Ermanricus. But the net flew over his head, and he rolled to the ground. "A Diomed!" yelled the mob. In an instant Ermanricus was on his feet, having cut through the meshes of the entangling net.

Diomed flew upon him, but then staggered back, the blood pouring from his shoulder.

The secutor fled, running with the speed of the wind.

Hisses for Diomed.

But the brave young Greek recovered himself, and, all bleeding as he was, gave chase to the secutor.

Away flew the secutor in pursuit of the retiarius, amid the shouts and jeers of the excited populace.

Virginia was now roused from her apathy, and became interested in the progress of the combat. She sat with her clasped hands resting upon her knees, her eyes fastened upon the contending gladiators, her heart beating violently.

Naturally enough, her sympathies were with her father's pupil, Diomed.

He was one of the finest lads in all the maniple. Though somewhat vain and foppish in his manner, he was a civil-spoken, good-natured young fellow, and very popular among his comrades.

He stopped on a sudden, and bounding upon his adversary, made another cast with the net.

Ermanricus stepped nimbly back, and dodging on one side, escaped being thrown.

The mob cheered him to the echo for his skill and adroitness.

Sinking upon one knee the wily net-thrower waited for his opponent to charge.

Ermanricus rushed upon him, and made a deadly lunge at him with his sword.

Instantly the net was thrown over his head, and in spite of his struggles the loop was drawn tight around his knees.

"A Diomed!" shouted the populace.

The young Greek laughed in triumph, and poised his trident to strike.

But, with a superhuman effort, Ermanricus recovered his footing and dashed upon his foe.

In an instant they fell to the ground together.

A savage and desperate struggle for the mastery ensued.

Diomed fought with hands and feet while the Dacian slashed repeatedly at him with his sword.

Ermanricus now stood up, and bestrode his prostrate antagonist.

The brutal mob cheered the new man, and overwhelmed their former favourite with curses and abuse.

The Dacian glanced around him, and appealed to the spectators for mercy.

But the cruel wretches were infuriated at the defeat of the man upon whom they had laid heavy odds. Not a hand was raised to save him.

The fatal sign was almost universal.

The Dacian plunged his sword to the hilt in the breast of Diomed, who fell back and expired without a groan.

Virginia uttered a wail of horror and anguish, and buried her face in her hands.

Lupa turned very pale, and bit her lips.

"This is a bad beginning," she muttered to herself. "Five sestertia lost at one fell swoop."

But the death of the luckless Diomed did not pass unavenged.

In the struggle Diomed had for a moment got possession of his adversary's sword, and had plunged it into his side.

Ermanricus had got his mortal wound.

He stood for a moment, the crimson blood pouring from the gash under his ribs.

Then he dropped like a stone, and the victor and the vanquished lay dead side by side.

A horseman now rode in from the Gate of Death, a couple of ropes with flesh-hooks attached to the ends trailing from his saddle-girth.

Two Nubian slaves, who acted as ring-keepers attached these to the bodies of the dead gladiators, the horseman plied the lash, and the corpses, covered with blood and sand, were whisked off to the ghastly spoliarium.

Lupa turned sharply to her daughter.

"What are you weeping for, you puling little fool?" she asked, snappishly.

"Poor Diomed!" sobbed the gentle girl.

"Poor Ventidius!" retorted her mother. "Have you no consideration for your father's losses? As for Diomed, he deserved what he got for a clumsy, incapable varlet; though I must say I am glad he gave the quietus to that great hulk of a Dacian."

Virginia made no reply, but turned away her head and closed her eyes, not daring to gaze upon the frightful spectacle.

And now there was a loud flourish of trumpets, and two long lines of gladiators filed into the arena.

They were men of various nationalities, and the diversity of complexion and feature exhibited among these devoted athletes afforded at once a majestic idea of the extent of the empire, and a terrible one of the purpose to which its wide sway had often been made subservient.

The beautiful Greek, with a countenance of noble serenity, and limbs after which the sculptors of his country might have modelled their symbols of graceful power, walked side by side with the yellow-bearded savage, whose gigantic muscles had been nerved in the freezing wave of the Elbe or the Ister, or whose thick strong hair was congealed and straggled on his brow with the breath of Scythian or Scandinavian winters.

Many fierce Moors and Arabs, and curled Ethiopians, were there, with the beams of the southern sun burnt in every shade of swarthiness upon their skins.

Nor did our own remote islands of Britain want her representatives in the deadly procession.

Among the armed multitude were seen two or three gaunt barbarians, whose breasts and shoulders bore uncouth marks of blue and purple, so vivid in their tints that many months could not have elapsed since they must have been wandering in wild freedom along the native ridges of some Silurian or Caledonian forest.

As they moved around the arena, some of these men were saluted by the whole multitude, with noisy acclamations, in token of the approbation with which the feats of some former festival deserved to be remembered.

On the appearance of others, groans and hisses were heard from some parts of the amphitheatre, mixed with contending cheers and huzzas from others of the spectators

But by far the greater part were suffered to pass

on in silence, it being in all likelihood the first—who could tell whether it would not also be the last?—day of their sharing in that fearful exhibition.

Their lanistas paired them.

In succession they began to make proof of their fatal skill.

At first Scythian was matched against Scythian, Greek against Greek, Ethiopian against Ethiopian, Spaniard against Spaniard.

The sand soon became dyed beneath their feet with blood, streaming from the wounds inflicted by kindred hands.

The survivors retired from the arena, which was at once cleared of the mangled bodies of the dying and the dead.

Then the martial music struck up majestically, and the buzz of conversation arose.

Claudius Cæsar, who throughout the late conflict, had reclined on his throne, almost dozing, now roused by the sound of the music, and the hubbub of the multitude, awoke, and stared blankly around him.

He then laid his puffed hand, one blaze of gems, upon the shoulder of his freedman Narcissus, who knelt by his side.

"What were you telling me about Caius Licinius?" he asked; "did I understand you rightly that he was to fight as a gladiator?"

"It is so, illustrious," replied the secretary.

"I thought he had more sense and better taste," answered Claudius, rolling his head to and fro on his velvet pillow, and speaking in a low gurgling voice. "I always took him for a man who could carry his drink well, and one who appreciated the pleasures of the table. He has a nice voice for singing, plays the lyre very well, and writes his own verses. I like such fellows. I meant to invite him to supper to-night, and get him to lull me to sleep, as he has done before. Will you tell him to come?"

"I will, illustrious," answered Narcissus, "though I fear he has a prior engagement to sup with Pluto."

Imperial Cæsar gave a grunt, raised his unwieldy body in the chair, and laid his finger on his bald forehead.

"Let me see, who and what were we talking about? Ah! Caius Licinius! This is the amphitheatre. So Licinius is going to fight—is he?"

"Yes, Cæsar, he has been in training for more than a month."

"The more fool he!" chuckled Claudius; "a month! Imagine that! Of how much exquisite enjoyment he has deprived himself! He has had to work like a slave, and deny himself every indulgence, and what for? To come here and get his throat cut."

"There is no denying the wisdom of my lord's remark," replied Narcissus; "but, considering the men against whom Licinius is matched, he has done well by going into steady training."

He then went on to explain how Licinius, with two others trained by Phorbus, were to be pitted against three of the best swordsmen belonging to the "family" of Ventidius, and that Caractacus was one of the three.

"The worse for the knight," said Claudius. "Caractacus comes of a desperate race, as witness his father's defeat of our legions. We were deceived by Bericus, who promised us an easy victory."

It was by the treacherous representations of Bericus, a Briton, that Claudius was more particulary incited to subjugate our country.

This renegade had unsuccessfully endeavoured to raise a sedition against Togodumnus and Caractacus, who succeeded their father Cynboline.

Aulus Plautius, a distinguished Roman general, was sent into Britain by the emperor.

After fighting various battles, in which each party by turns was successful, Plautius reduced the Britons to a state of great weakness.

The Emperor Claudius came over himself.

The conquest was completed in a decisive victory at Camelodunum, a settlement in Essex.

"It appears to me, illustrious," said Narcissus, "that those daring and obstinate barbarians will never be thoroughly subdued until Mars himself shall take the field against them. Your own invincible arms alone can crush them as it crushed them before."

This was always a safe game to play with the weak-minded Claudius.

No flattery fell so sweetly on his ear as that which ascribed to him the renown of a great and successful warrior.

Not that Claudius had rendered himself so ridiculous as his predecessor, Caligula.

That emperor, in his boasted expedition to Britain, merely gave refuge to one of its banished princes, and this he described, in his letter to the senate, as taking possession of the whole island.

Instead of conquering Germany, he only led his army to the sea-shore in Gaul; there disposing his engines and warlike machines with great solemnity, and drawing up his men in order of battle, he went on board his galley, with which, coasting along, he commanded his trumpets to sound and the signal to be given as if for an engagement.

His men, who had had previous orders, immediately fell to gathering shells that lay on the sea-shore into their helmets, as the spoils of the conquered ocean, worthy of the palace and the capitol.

After this valiant exploit, he ordered a lofty tower to be erected by the sea-side.

As for Claudius he really did visit Britain, though the time he remained there was in all but sixteen days, which were spent in receiving homages.

His conquests were solely attributable to his generals.

None the less was he pleased by the compliment of his favourite.

He waved his hand in a deprecating way.

"You exact too much of me, my trusty Narcissus," he said; "I am tired of the fatigues and alarms of warfare. I grow old, and must leave such cares to younger men; but doubt not, if I find my presence in the rebellious island necessary, I shall be found ready to sacrifice my personal ease for the good of the empire over which I reign."

Narcissus bit his lips to repress a contemptuous laugh at this foolish and arrogant speech.

"The gods be praised that Rome has such an emperor!" he ejaculated, devoutly, casting up his eyes.

At this moment the people gave a great shout, clapped their hands, and rose in their places.

"What does it mean, Narcissus?" asked the emperor; "what is all this shouting?"

Narcissus frowned and looked spiteful.

"It is young Nero, who has just taken his place in front of the pulvinar," he replied.

"And what of that?" asked Claudius, jealously.

"He bows to the assemblage," was the reply, "and the fickle rabble acknowledge his salute with such thundering acclamations as might greet the appearance of Jove newly lighted from Olympus."

Claudius's broad face became suffused with a purple flush.

"I do not like this," he said.

"Yet it is but right and proper that the people should pay such homage to the adopted son and heir of our mighty Cæsar," he said, in an oily tone.

"Humph! that is all very true," grunted Claudius. "But it would become them, I think, to pay some homage to great Cæsar himself."

"Do they not worship the lord of the universe?"

"No! nor do I want them to do that. Have I not forbidden them, by special decree, not to pay me divine honours by sacrifice in their temples, as they did to former emperors?"

"Does not the world ring with your clemency and moderation?"

"I don't know. I wish the amphitheatre would

ring some little chorus of welcome when I enter it," returned Claudius, sulkily. " When I came in, the place was as cold and silent as a tomb. Nay, when I took my place I thought I heard murmurs of disaffection."

Narcissus bowed his head in deep humility, but made no reply.

Claudius folded his fat jewelled hands across his ample stomach and pondered for a moment.

Then he raised himself and asked, with just a flash of spirit and dignity—

" I am Cæsar yet. Where is the empress—where is Agrippina?"

" In the stall yonder, illustrious, with her son, and in attendance are many senators and knights of high distinction."

" Why does she place herself so far from my side?" he went on, yet more angrily. " Did you take her my message."

" I did, illustrious."

" And what was her reply?"

" The empress refused to see me."

" Because you are my friend, Narcissus," returned the emperor; " and, I protest to Jupiter, the only friend I have."

Narcissus glowed with pride and pleasure at this blunt admission.

" O, mighty Cæsar!" he replied, " tall towers are measured by their shadows, great men by their calumniators, a few, the base and criminal may be your enemies, but the wise and the good are your friends, though whatever their wisdom and virtue I make bold to boast that none of them is more entirely devoted to your service than your humble slave."

" I do believe you," returned Cæsar; " and I like you all the better because the empress hates you. Let her beware, Narcissus—I am Cæsar yet. Let her remember the doom of Messalina. It has been my fate to be tormented by my wives, but I have also been their executioner. Let her take care."

CHAPTER XLI.

THE BOXING-MATCH.

THE entertainment which followed was one as brutally stupid as it was cruel, but it seemed to give the immense conclave abundant amusement.

A number of gladiators were brought into the ring, and set in array against each other to fight blindfolded.

That there might be no suspicion of trickery in the matter the helmets they wore were faced with a kind of steel mask that had neither bars nor yet eyelets.

They were mounted on sturdy little horses, and tilted at each other with long spears.

Had it not been for the cruel mischief done, the idea was in itself droll and laughter-provoking.

The whole amphitheatre rang with peals of merriment as the horsemen dashed at each other in wild random charges.

Wheeling round they oftimes turned their spear points upon comrades of their own party.

Again and again one or other would miss his antagonist, and, crashing his spear against the boundary wall of the arena be dashed out of the saddle.

Sometimes one horse would be driven full butt at another, and both horses and riders dashed to the ground, where they would lie kicking and struggling, the men making blind, blundering strokes and thrusts at each other.

When this exhibition was over there was a boxing match between our old friend, Pandion, and a German barbarian, named Balimer.

This rude savage was of herculean stature, and nearly twice the weight and size of his opponent.

His coarse shaggy russet hair was cut close to his bullet-shaped head, his chest incredibly broad and deep, his limbs braced with muscles of iron.

His appearance was hailed with much satisfaction by the multitude, who were pleased the redoubted Pandion was matched against such a worthy antagonist, and promised themselves a rare treat in the approaching encounter.

The noble art as practised among the ancients was very different from the modern style of pugilism, and altogether a much more serious affair.

It is no uncommon thing now-a-days, or perhaps we ought to say until now, for the brutal practice of prizefighting has of late been severely suppressed—it is no uncommon thing for a man, who has been thoroughly trained, to leave the ring after a long and desperate battle with very slight marks of punishment; but the most terrible wounds and fractures, and sometimes even death itself, resulted from the ancient contests.

Boxers did not then, as at present, fight with the bare fists only, but used a kind of glove called the cestus, which had lead or iron screwed into them to make the strokes fall with heavier weight.

The cestus was used by boxers in the earliest times, and is mentioned in the "Iliad" of Homer, but in the heroic times it consisted merely of thongs of leather.

Our hero, Caractacus, scarcely approved of this style of fighting, as it ended the contest too quickly and did not afford that scope for the display of temper and endurance which are a Briton's characteristics.

Ventidius, finding our hero such a matchless fencer, did not compel him to take up the pugilistic mode of warfare.

As Pandion and Balimer stood face to face there was a breathless hush of expectation.

Both men showed the effects of their hard training, their muscular power and lissomeness.

Pandion, though he wore a confident smile, did not like the look of his antagonist.

He had never in his life beheld such a giant of a man.

The German struck the first blow.

After manœuvring about for some time, he rushed in and made a tremendous blow at Pandion's head.

Pandion, however, countered finely.

Warding off the stroke with his left arm, he drove the cestus full against the breast of the huge savage, who staggered back and fell heavily.

The rabble were enchanted.

" Habet!" they roared. " The bully barbarian is down. A Pandion! A Pandion!"

But our old comrade had not escaped without sustaining some damage.

His right arm was fearfully bruised and lacerated by his foeman's cestus.

The German lay so long inert and motionless that Pandion began to think he was stunned, and put *hors de combat*.

Phorbus, the lanista, seemed to be of the same opinion, for he came running up with a pitcher and a sponge to bathe his pupil's wound, and if possible to restore him to animation, in order that he might renew the battle.

But they both reckoned without their host if they believed the sturdy and herculean savage was to be so easily vanquished.

Balimer sprang to his feet.

He stood for a moment, confused and stupefied, then, his little deep-set eyes, flashing viciously from his shaggy brows, he charged with the fury and impetuosity of an infuriated bull.

Pandion slipped aside.

But he was not quick enough to escape a touch on the shoulder, which made him reel, and caused the blood to flow from the gash in a crimson stream.

There was a cheer for Balimer.

Enraged at seeing Phorbus, the lanista, laughing and rubbing his hands with glee, and encouraged by the shouts of Ventidius, the boxer pulled himself together and made another attack upon his powerful foe.

The men fought more warily than they had done before, countered and rallied, advanced and retreated, and made some splendid play.

Though the blows exchanged in this round were comparatively light, both of the antagonists bled freely from the head, neck, and breast, and appeared to be growing exhausted.

At a sign from their lanistæ they at length lowered their arms, and drew away from each other for a moment's rest.

But they were soon called upon to renew the battle. Once more they faced each other.

After sparring, out of distance, for some little time, they closed, and a terrific and brutal scene followed.

They wrestled together madly, trying to hurl each other to the ground, at intervals dealing each other the most frightful blows with their loaded and spiked gloves, inflicting the most shocking injuries upon one another, and causing the blood to spout in all directions.

Amid the cheers, howls, shrieks, hisses, and wild gesticulations of the blood-hankering assembly, the two devoted wretches fought on with all the madness and fury of despair.

But the conflict at length came to an end.

Though battered, bruised, and bleeding, Pandion stood erect, while Balimer lay at his feet crushed and beaten out of all semblance of humanity, unless indeed such as might belong to some poor wretch who had just been broken on the wheel.

The loudest acclamations hailed the victory of the people's favourite.

"Pandion wins!" was the shout; "he has won the palm crown! Vivat Pandion!"

Ventidius snapped his fingers, and laughed exultingly as he jeered his rival, Phorbus.

The colour mantled the cheek of Lupa, and her eyes sparkled with triumph, as seated in her equestrian stall, she clapped her hands and applauded with the rest.

"Look, Virginia! our noble lad Pandion has won the prize," she said, leaning on her daughter and plucking her by the robe; "this will redeem your father's loss on that fool, Diomed."

But Virginia made no reply.

Overwhelmed by the horrors of the scene, she leaned back in the stall—her eyes closed, her face as white as the marble against which it rested.

Meanwhile Pandion was surrounded by his comrades, who heartily congratulated him upon his victory.

But the poor fellow had no voice to answer them—not so much strength left as would suffice to shake them by the hand.

They crowned him with a garland of ivy, and lifting him upon their shoulders, carried him in procession around the arena.

Yet this triumph appeared but a bitter mockery.

He was so frightfully gashed and mangled that he looked as if he had been flayed alive.

His poor blind eyes wandered eagerly round the amphitheatre—the inhuman plaudits came with deadened distant roar to his ear.

He turned his battered face to a certain spot in the upper benches. There, "where he had garnered up his heart," there were his loving wife and his elder children, who had watched, awed and breathless with hope and terror, his desperate fight for death or freedom.

He feebly raised his red right hand and waved it towards the place where he knew they were stationed.

From thence there came a sudden, loud, heart-piercing shriek.

"'Tis Marcia, my wife, comrades," Pandion murmured huskily. "Deal gently with her. I fear it is all over with me, but she will get the pension."

CHAPTER XLII.
CHAMPION OF THE ARENA.

THERE was another long interval. The spectators were seen rising from their places and saluting each other.

There was a buzz of talking, some speaking of this thrust and that ward, and paying and receiving money lost and won.

Some were already discoursing of other matters, as if nothing uncommon had been witnessed.

Others, again, appeared to be entirely occupied with the martial music which ever struck up majestically at such pauses, beating time upon the benches before them, or joining their voices with the proud notes of the trumpets and clarions.

But let us quit the arena, and seek out our brave Caractacus and his two comrades, who were arming to do battle with their three foemen.

They were gathered together in a stone room under the podium or gallery—Caractacus, Manlius, and Lycaon, with their lanista, Ventidius.

The three gladiators, though feverishly excited, were buoyant and eager for the fray.

Not so Ventidius.

His face was flushed, and his brow gloomed with doubt and anxiety.

He nevertheless assumed to be in high spirits, like a good general as he was, knowing that his lads would take their tone from him.

Three slaves acted as esquires to the three gladiators, and assisted them in buckling on their armour and so forth.

"What cheer, my sons?" cried Ventidius. "Look well to your accoutrements, and here's a choice of swords. You will conquer, boys, for never had I such a brave triplet of thorough-bred war-hounds in leash. Here, Manlius, drink from this cup of Cæcuban, and may it fire your heart! Pass it on to your comrades."

Then, turning to Caractacus, he went on——

"Why are you fussing with that buckler? It don't suit you—I see why; the arm brace is too tight. Take another; so, look here, just your size and weight."

The lanista slipped on a shield, and threw himself into a fighting attitude, and moved his left arm about to show that it was in working order.

"Thanks, lanista," answered Caractacus, "I will take your advice."

Then Ventidius glanced at Lycaon, and asked him with some sternness——

"What is that piece of frippery you wear in your helmet?"

Lycaon turned red, and laughed rather bashfully.

"'Tis a riband the Lady Julia gave me, and bade me wear it as her token."

Ventidius frowned and shook his head.

"I like it not," he said. "It has happened more than once in my experience that gladiators decking themselves in such womanish frippery have come to grief. Take my word, lad, it is not a good omen."

"Fear not, my master," answered Lycaon. "I shall fight the better for wearing it."

"Why, then, do as you please," answered Ventidius. "Yet I wish you may not have cause to be sorry that you did not heed my warning."

He then addressed himself to the Briton:

"Euge, Caractacus! you are in splendid form," he said, smiling and clapping our hero on the shoulders. "But be on your guard against a too great eagerness to pick out and to vanquish Caius Licinius."

Caractacus stared in surprise.

"Yet is it not against Licinius that I am specially matched?" he asked.

"Not especially, mark you that," returned the lanista. "You three will be matched against the three trained men under Phorbus, to fight them indiscriminately, to kill whichever of them you can, and then to aid your comrades in destroying the

CARACTACUS TURNED AT BAY, AS VARRO, WITH A VENGEFUL SHOUT OF "I STRIKE FIRST!" SPRANG UPON THE BRITON.

rest. Which of the two parties kills the first will stand the best chance, because that party will be fighting with the odds on its side—three to two."

"I will remember," said Caractacus. "Nor will I permit any private motive of revenge to injure our general interest."

"Very well. When you are paired I will set Lycaon against Licinius," said Ventidius. "Make quick work with him, Lycaon, and, by my head, half the battle is won."

Lycaon appeared delighted.

"You do me too much honour, worthy lanista," answered Lycaon, gleefully. "I shall fight with the better will. The Lady Julia is devoted to her mistress Agrippina, whose enemies she hates—none more than Narcissus and his partisans, amongst whom is Licinius."

"To Hades with the Lady Julia!" growled Ventidius. "Put not your trust in Venus, but in Mars. Think only of the man you must kill, and not of the women you would live for. Put your soul in your sword, or you are a lost man."

Then, once more turning to Caractacus, he looked him heedfully in the face.

"If you do not like this arrangement say so, and speak out boldly," urged the lanista.

"I am sorry that Licinius should escape me, but I consent to your proposal, on one condition," replied the Briton.

"Name it."

"That you will oppose me to that traitor Arvirargus, who betrayed me to the Romans."

Ventidius grinned.

"Your countryman! Trust me. Such was my intention," he replied. "Do I not know that no foes are so bitter against each other, or contend so fiercely, as domestic foes?"

"Then I am satisfied," returned Caractacus.

"And now, my lads," added Ventidius, cheerfully, "fight like Trojans. Remember what you have at stake—your lives and liberties! May you all come off with slight damage. Each survivor earns his manumission and a purse of gold. Remember, freedom! Fight hard for freedom!"

An officer now came to inform them that it was their turn to appear in the ring.

They waved their swords, and answered with a—

"Pluto, befriend thine own!"

There was a little delay in the passage that led to the gate of death.

Here Phorbus was awaiting with his three men—Licinius, Telamon, and Arvirargus.

Arvirargus took an opportunity, while the two training masters were conferring together, to steal near our hero.

The Brigantian was a very handsome fellow, two or three years older than our hero, and, though not quite so tall, was stouter built.

He was finely proportioned, and had blue eyes, and fair hair like Caractacus, but he was neither so graceful nor stately as our hero, and his beauty was of a coarser and less nobler type.

"So, Idris-ap-Caradoc," he whispered, "we meet again."

"Yes, Arvirargus, son of Alvan, and we meet for the last time," retorted our hero sternly.

"We meet as equals here," hissed his rival; "we are both slaves."

"True, but I fell into this condition by the chance of war," replied Caractacus; "you by that treacherous nature that betrays itself. When you and your accursed tribe sold your country to the invader, you should at least have kept faith with him. But no! in turn you would have betrayed your patrons."

"I did but avenge my wrongs."

"Mine remain to be avenged," answered Caractacus.

Ventidius interfered between them.

He saw by their glaring eyes that they were likely to fall foul with each other before the proper time.

It was near at hand.

The doors were thrown open, and in martial array the two parties, each headed by its lanista, marched into the vast arena.

A shout of loud applause rent the air as they came in.

After making the usual salutation to the emperor, they formed themselves in two opposing lines, and in this array—

Our hero was opposed to Arvirargus, Lycaon to Licinius, Manlius to Telamon.

The lanistæ retired.

Then the signal for the conflict to begin was given by the blast of a trumpet.

Now came the shock.

Clashing their swords against their shields the combatants rushed upon each other.

Above all the noise, loud rose the battle-cry of the impetuous Britons.

At the sound Virginia started from her lethargy like one suddenly roused from a trance.

She rose and stood up in the front of her stall, her eyes fixed upon Caractacus.

The two Britons were fighting with the fury and savagery of their Celtic blood, and our hero had already forgotten the sage counsels of his lanista, Ventidius, for he seemed to forget the presence of his comrades, and to think only of his individual adversary.

Their swords clashed together and their countenances blazed with sheer wrath and thirst for blood.

Caractacus seemed transformed, and drove his foe before him with blows that shocked Ventidius by their wild impetuosity—not that they were at all unskilful, but were so reckless.

"He forgets himself, and only thinks of his man," the lanista muttered to himself. "Too rash, though Phorbus' novice stands a poor chance. I was a fool not to match the Briton against the Roman after all; still, perhaps this will be over quickest."

He was right in that.

Caractacus beat his British foeman to his knee, and then, with one swift swish of his sword, struck off his head, and sent it, the long yellow hair in streams, rolling on the sand.

The assembled multitude seemed to have gone mad with excitement.

"Caractacus! Caractacus!" they yelled.

Meantime, how fared it with the others?

Calmly and skilfully they fought together, but the combat was scientific, in regard of the devil's master-art—fencing.

Manlius and Telamon thrust and parried, but as yet had not even touched each other, but Licinius had wounded Lycaon on the sword-arm.

Truth to say the poor Greek's attention had been called off for one fatal instant by a waving scarf from the empress's stall—a signal waved by the Lady Julia.

Still he fought well, though under a disadvantage, for his arm grew weaker and weaker.

Caractacus stood for a moment with the air of a man who had made a fool of himself.

But Lycaon fell.

Then our hero engaged Licinius, and the fencing was cool and perfect.

Their attitudes were most graceful, and their magnificent style won universal admiration.

As they fought on, Licinius seemed to gain confidence, and held Caractacus at bay with wondrous skill and intrepidity.

Manlius had always been reckoned to be the second swordsman in the "family" of Ventidius, poor Lycaon being the first until the matchless Briton came to eclipse them all; and now he was exasperated to find that Telamon was more than his master.

It is true that, so far, not one drop of blood had been drawn, but Manlius had attacked him furiously, striving for the honour of being the first to kill his man, while Telamon had acted simply on the defensive.

But now came the tug of war.

Telamon, having made sure of his power, dashed at Manlius so savagely and swiftly that the Roman was struck to the ground, the blood gushing from his shoulder.

Then, with a joyous cry, he turned his sword against Caractacus, eager to gain renown by slaying such a famous challenger.

The Briton sprang back and stood at bay, and so majestic and lion-like was his look that the amphitheatre rang with applause, and his two opponents looked at him in wonder.

Caractacus stood undaunted.

His right foot rested on the body of Arvirargus, his keen stedfast eyes watching for the first hostile movement on the part of Licinius and Telamon.

The latter made a savage lunge at Caractacus, but our hero caught the point of the sword on the boss of his shield, and in the same moment parried a thrust from Licinius.

The young hero prolonged the contest with desperate valour.

In the midst of this, Manlius, though desperately wounded, raised himself from the ground, and made a feeble attempt to renew his combat with Telamon.   But his strength was gone.

After tottering a few paces he fell, and lay helpless, while a stifled groan escaped him.

Telamon, leaving our hero and the young patrician to settle their difference between themselves, flew upon Manlius to despatch him.

In the same moment Licinius received our hero's sword in the shoulder, and faint with pain and loss of blood, fell to the earth.

Thus released, the Briton hasted to the rescue of his comrade Manlius.

Telamon had levelled his sword at the breast of his wounded and disabled antagonist, and was about to strike home when Caractacus interposed his shield and stopped the blow.

Telamon abandoned his intention of slaying Manlius, and immediately attacked the Briton, and desperate was the fight between them to decide which of the two should survive—sole victor and Champion of the Arena.

They practised every ward, feint, and lunge with the most admirable skill and swiftness, but it was evident to the eyes of the more experienced spectators that Caractacus was the better swordsman.

Soon and fatally their judgment was confirmed. With a masterly thrust Caractacus broke down the guard of Telamon and ran his sword through his body, the hilt striking against the breastbone.

Caractacus stood alone, erect and triumphant. He shook back his golden locks, waved his dripping sword above his head, and uttered his British warcry——

"Iero!"

But Licinius was not slain.

Burning with hatred and thirst for vengeance he crawled on his hands and knees towards Caractacus, with the purpose of stabbing him in the back.

Our hero turned upon him, and was about to plunge his sword into his heart when he felt himself dragged back, and found himself struggling in the arms of the three lanistæ—Ventidius, Phorbus, and Antipas.

"Hold, good lad, enough has been done," cried Ventidius. "You are to spare the life of Licinius; such is the express command of Cæsar."

"I obey," returned Caractacus, sheathing his sword. "He is wounded already. I bear him no further malice; my honour is satisfied."

The victor of this bloody fight received quite an ovation.

He was borne round the ring upon the shoulders of his rejoicing comrades belonging to the "family" of Ventidius; he was crowned with garlands, and presented with the rudis, a wooden foil with a silver hilt, in token that he was emancipated and that henceforward he would not be called upon to risk his life upon that field of blood and guilt—the Roman arena.

CHAPTER XLIII.
THE ABDUCTION OF VIRGINIA.

THREE months have passed away since the terrible and disgraceful scenes we have described were enacted. Ventidius had made a large amount of money by the success of his well-trained and devoted gladiators. But at what a cost of life and noble manhood!

Diomed, Lycaon, Parmenio, and others—the best and bravest of his maniple—had fallen on that fatal day; while Manlius, sorely wounded, languished on a bed of pain; and Pandion, the bluff, kind-hearted bruiser, was crippled for life.

Virginia, too, as delicate and sensitive as she was lovely and amiable, had not recovered from the shock she had experienced while witnessing that climax of horrors.

Caractacus, with the usual good fortune that attended him, had escaped with a few hurts, severe indeed, but not dangerous.

In the course of a few weeks he was sufficiently recovered to go about, though it was long before he regained his former health and strength.

He was no longer a slave, though still a prisoner and a hostage.

The worthy tribune, Honorius, took him in charge, and kept him in his own house, in a sort of honourable captivity, but treated him with the greatest kindness and indulgence.

Licinius fared best of all.

The wound in his shoulder, though a deep cut, had touched no vital part; and as, in consequence of his hard training, he was in perfect condition, the gash soon closed and healed, and he felt very little effect from it.

But his hatred against Caractacus was increased a hundredfold—and this Roman's hatred was deadly.

He was also deeply mortified that he had been rejected by Virginia, and that Ventidius had treated him in a manner so haughty and offhand as almost to amount to contempt.

He had fully made up his mind to ruin and, if possible, destroy the Briton, and was equally determined to carry off Virginia.

With this intent he held many consultations with Locusta and Zaba, the dwarf beast-keeper, the result of which will develop itself in the course of this history.

One evening Zaba sat in the dungeon-like cell beneath the amphitheatre in which he dwelt.

He was caressing his tame pantheress, which crouched at his feet, and licked his hand.

"Thou may'st well make much of me, my Hecate," murmured Zaba, as he stroked her fur, "for I shall soon have another favourite to fondle. Yes, everything works well for my purpose. So Licinius is to carry off the lanista's daughter, and I am to be the mere paid agent in the business. Once I get the lovely one into my power, we shall know how to take care of her—shall we not, my Hecate?"

His reverie was interrupted by three distinct taps at the door.

The pantheress growled.

"Be quiet, Hecate," muttered Zaba; "it is time you knew that signal."

He got up and, shambling across his den, opened the iron-bound door.

A tall woman entered—she was dressed in black and closely veiled.

"So you are come, Locusta," said the dwarf, in a low voice; "I did not expect you yet. What is the news?"

Locusta threw back her veil, and disclosed her white, haggard, wicked face and glittering eyes.

"The deed must be done to-night," she said.

"Ha!" returned Zaba, chuckling and rubbing his hands; "I am glad to hear it—there is no time like the present."

"All is arranged," replied the woman; "the chariot of Licinius will be waiting; either he or you must scale her window, which is not far above the ground, and carry her off."

"I will do it myself," said Zaba, nodding his huge ugly head; "leave it to me."

Then he turned a look upon her so strange and wild that she shuddered.

"I will do it myself," he said, in a husky voice; "no hand shall be laid on her but mine. But there is that fellow, the porter at the gate, a one-eyed, surly watch-dog."

"Hyphax, you mean."

"Yes; how is he to be disposed of?"

"Oh, that is settled; Licinius has bribed Chloris, one of the slave girls. I have given her a sleeping potion, which she will mix with the cup of wine he takes before stretching himself across the door."

"That is well done," said Zaba; "but when Licinius has netted his pretty bird whither will he take her?"

"To his country villa at Præneste."

"He is bold; I should have thought that he would have gone further afield."

"He dares not abandon Narcissus, on whom he depends for money," answered Locusta; "besides there will not be much fuss made about a low-born girl."

"And Licinius will marry her?"

"Yes. That is decided."

"But if she will not consent?"

"She will have no choice in the matter," was the reply; "and never fear, she will consent readily enough to save herself from disgrace."

"And when are we to join?"

"On the instant. He awaits us now."

"I will come then," replied Zaba; "but first let me chain up Hecate and make all fast."

While this conversation was passing between the creatures of Licinius, the intended victim of the base plot, all unconscious of impending danger, had retired to rest.

Before lying down to sleep she had commended herself to the care of that divine power to whom the good Mathias had directed her thoughts, and her slumbers were calm, deep, and dreamless.

The moon poured its silvery beams through the lattice and lit up her soft and beautiful features.

Her white-rounded arm lay under her head, and her raven tresses strewed the pillow.

There was a slight noise as the iron bar, which guarded her window, shook and creaked, but Virginia heard it not.

Nor did she see the hideous face that glared in upon her—the face of Zaba the dwarf.

"All is well, my patron," the little monster whispered, "she is fast asleep, and the bar is loose."

"Stay till I come," answered a voice from below.

But Zaba heeded it not.

He wrested out the bar, and the next instant was in the room.

Immediately Licinius climbed up to the window, where he rested on the sill.

"If she wakes she will scream," he said.

"I will gag her," said the dwarf.

He raised her head and passed a scarf over her mouth.

"This sleep is like death," he muttered; "but 'tis the potion that did it; Locusta never fails."

The dwarf lifted her in his arms, but Virginia, suddenly awakened, struggled madly to escape from his loathsome embrace.

CHAPTER XLIV.

HOW VENTIDIUS MOURNED FOR HIS DAUGHTER.

VIRGINIA struggled desperately to release herself from the dwarf's loathsome embrace and to tear from her mouth the scarf that well-nigh strangled her.

"Despatch," whispered Licinius, from outside the window. "I hear footsteps approaching."

"I am coming, my patron," answered Zaba; "but our bird has awakened, and struggles in the net."

"Wretch, for your life, deal with her gently!" returned Licinius. "Take heed thou hurt'st her not."

"Harm thee, my peerless one," murmured Zaba, clutching her fast in his long sinewy arms; "I love thee too well; thou shalt be my goddess, and I will worship thee!"

Virginia saw his horrid red eyes glaring close to her face; she felt his hot breath against her cheek, and fainted from sheer terror and loathing.

"Quick—are you ready?" urged Licinius.

"I come," said Zaba; "she is quiet now."

And he carried his insensible burden to the window.

"Good," said Licinius; "place her in my arms."

"Anon!" returned Zaba, snappishly; "wait till you get down."

"Lie there," said Licinius, tossing a letter in at the window. "It will be well for Ventidius if he pays good heed to my warning."

He then descended the ladder, and stood on the pavement below, the moon shining full on his upturned face.

Bearing Virginia in his arms, Zaba followed him down the ladder, and joined him in the silent and deserted street.

As soon as he had done so a man, one of Licinius's slaves rushed out from the dark shadows of the porch, seized the ladder and ran off with it.

"I have a covered chariot awaiting at the corner of the Via Nova," said the young patrician. "Locusta is in attendance; we will carry our prize to my villa at Præneste."

"Is it safe to travel so far?" objected the dwarf. "Would it not be better to convey her to Locusta's house?"

"Hold thy peace," returned Licinius, angrily. "Do not proffer advice till it is asked for. All you have to do now is to obey my orders."

While they were speaking a window above was thrown open, and a man appeared on the top of the porch.

He was but half-dressed, and had a mantle loosely thrown about him.

A sword glittered in his hand.

"Ho, there!" he shouted; "who prowls about my doors at this untimely hour? Speak, ho!"

Licinius and Zaba started, and instantly hurried off, keeping close under the shadow of the wall.

"It is Ventidius," whispered the patrician, as he walked beside the dwarf. "The old fool will find his bird flown, and raise the hue and cry against us."

"Quick, then, illustrious—let us get to your chariot while there is yet time."

Upon reaching the corner of the street they found the covered chariot awaiting them.

Around it was an escort of half a dozen men, mounted and armed to the teeth.

One of them held a spare horse for Licinius.

Locusta, who was inside the vehicle, drew the curtains, and received Virginia into her embrace.

"How will you pass the gates, my lord?" asked Zaba.

"The sentinels have been bribed," answered Licinius; "they will not stop my way."

"And whither am I to betake myself?" asked Zaba.

"Go to the house of Locusta, and keep within doors until I send for you."

Locusta thrust her arm through the curtains of the chariot.

"Zaba."

"I attend, mistress—what is your will?" said the dwarf.

"Take this key," she said; "it opens the postern door of my house. You will find no one there but my slave, Chiron, who is deaf and dumb. He will know you, and abide your orders, bring you food, and find you a sleeping-place. And, mark you, Zaba, see that the furnace under the alembic is kept in full blast. But do not approach too near the crucible without you wear the crystal mask; the fumes are as poisonous as exhalations from the Stygian lake.'

Zaba took the key.

"Your behests shall be obeyed, Locusta," he said. "When may I look for your return?"

"Within five days at farthest," she replied. "All depends now upon your caution."

"And you, my lord?"

"I shall not be seen in Rome for some time to come," replied Licinius. "I have given it out that I am still suffering from the hurts I got in the arena, and that I have retired to Præneste for the benefit of my health. Thus no questions will be asked."

"But when Ventidius discovers the loss of his daughter, he will go mad," said the dwarf. "I doubt not he will appeal to Cæsar, and your house will be searched."

"I am prepared for that," Licinius answered, with a smile. Think you I have no crypts, or secret chambers in my country house, where I can bestow my fair captive till the storm has blown over?"

He then mounted his horse, and placed himself at the head of the escort that guarded the carriage.

He then made a sign to the charioteer to drive on.

Locusta dropped the curtain, and the cavalcade got into motion.

Zaba bowed his adieu, and slunk away with shambling gait, but at a rapid pace.

"He has foiled me!" muttered the dwarf, gnashing his yellow fangs, and shaking his huge fists. "Virginia is in his power, but he cannot reach Præneste ere the morning is well advanced. I will be on his heels. The treasonous letters that have passed between him and the other conspirators are in the hands of the empress. Narcissus is a ruined man, and soon the emissaries of Cæsar will be on his track. I will follow on to Præneste, but first I must repair to Locusta's and make all safe."

Loud shouts and outcries now resounded from the house of Ventidius.

"Ha, ha! ho, ho!" chuckled the fiendish little monster, laughing and rubbing his hands. "So, Ventidius, the kite has carried off your dove, and left the nest warm. If the bully prize-fighter saw me now, I should be in evil case. I'll lurk here under this portico, and observe what is going forward."

He concealed himself under a porch, and gazed intently at the house of the training master.

Lights were moving from window to window, while from within came shouts, shrieks, and outcries.

Ventidius came bounding like a maniac to the window of Virginia's chamber, and Lupa's pale face was seen, peering over her husband's shoulder.

Craning his neck out of the window, the lanista glanced up and down the street.

"Help, neighbours—awake!" shouted the gruff voice of the master of gladiators. "Look to your coffers, look to your children in their beds. Thieves and ravishers are abroad."

Then the door opened, and Ventidius came out followed by a dozen of the sturdiest athletes of his family, armed and carrying torches.

They stood for some moments in the middle of the road-way, and appeared so amazed and bewildered, that they knew not which way to turn.

Ventidius looked very haggard, but cool and resolute.

"Demetrius," said the lanista, addressing himself to one of the gladiators, "we will divide our force; you with five others shall hurry on towards the Flaminian-gate, whilst I and the rest hasten to the house of Narcissus, on the Palatine. Question every man you meet, and——"

Here he was interrupted by Lupa, who came running out of the house.

She was wrapped in a dark mantle, hastily thrown on; her black hair hung about her shoulders in disorder; her naked feet gleamed like ivory in the moonlight.

She caught her husband by the arm, and said breathlessly, "come back, Ventidius, I have found something which may give the clue to this mystery.

"Wait here, my lads," said Ventidius; "I will return upon the instant."

He followed his wife into the entrance-hall, where a lamp was burning in a niche of the wall.

Upon the marble pavement lay Hyphax, the doorkeeper, in a state of insensibility.

Upon seeing him the rage of Ventidius broke out afresh.

He spurned him with his foot.

"The one-eyed sluggard, it is all his fault," growled the lanista; "he has besotted himself with swinish indulgence—he is dead drunk. Ouf! shall I trust my dearest interests to such a careless villain? Let him sleep on, for, by the gods! his sleep shall know no waking."

He drew his sword, and would have plunged it through the poor fellow's body, had not Lupa prevented him.

"Are you mad, Ventidius?" asked Lupa, weighing upon his sword arm.

Ventidius laughed a harsh laugh, that had in it something very pathetic and at the same time terrible in its hysteric passion.

"Mad!" he said, "oh, no! I have lost my darling, but it matters not!—she is blighted, I am broken for ever! but it matters not. To her and to me, life, but now so full of present happiness and hopeful promise, has become a shame and a curse. There is no comfort left but the knowledge that death and oblivion must soon blot out this misery! But I am not mad; no, not at all, though I cannot look this disaster in the face as you can, and smile upon its ghastliness. Virginia! Virginia! My dear, my only one! Would thou wert lying dead at my feet."

"Ventidius, are you alone in your trouble?"

"I would I were!" gasped the distracted father. "Now the pitying gods help my poor child; even my sufferings are nothing in comparison with hers."

"You have no feeling for me."

"You have none for your daughter."

"What! I none?"

"No, you wear a smiling face, and there is a kind of triumph in your eye," growled Ventidius.

"How much you mistake me!" rejoined his wife. "Would you have me share the madness that has bereft you of all sense and forethought? I am wounded to the quick, yet not mad either."

Ventidius turned from her impatiently, and vented his spleen upon the unconscious Hyphax.

"'Tis all through this blind, insensate, faithless villain. Let go my sword, for I will have his life."

"Be patient, good Ventidius," cried Lupa, clinging to him; "the man is not to blame. There is foul play. Had he the eyes of Argus he would not be proof against insidious treachery."

"How can you be so calm? How can you teach me patience—you, who in most affairs have shown so much passion and caprice?" returned Ventidius, bitterly.

"Because things are not so bad as you suppose," replied Lupa; "out of evil cometh good. Your daughter will be a lady now, a patrician's wife, exalted high among the matronhood of Rome."

Ventidius stared at her in bewilderment.

"Do I hear you aright?" he asked.

"Licinius ——"

Ventidius interrupted her with a howl of rage and a passionate stamp of his foot.

"Licinius!" he repeated. "Have I not told you that I would rather see her wedded to that little beast Zaba than to the fawning parasite, the heartless libertine you name."

Lupa took a letter from her bosom.

"Is it so?" she said, coldly. "Then I had better tear this."

"No need—leave it to me," said Ventidius, snatching the paper from her hand.

He read it eagerly.

It was couched in these terms; the handwriting beautiful:

"Grieve not, Ventidius, for the loss of thy daughter. She is in safe hands, and will be treated with the tenderness and respect her beauty and virtue claim. You have not lost a daughter, but have gained a proud and happy son."

Ventidius tore the paper into a thousand shreds.

"Are you such a fool as to be gulled by those smooth words?" he demanded of his wife; "you know not the traitor Licinius! Still, I am glad of this—I know where to find the villain, and I will raise all Rome against him."

"But consider, Ventidius, we have no choice in the matter; she is gone, and there's an end," said Lupa, who secretly rejoiced at what had happened. "It will be the worse for her if you exasperate Licinius."

Ventidius did not deign to answer her, except by a contemptuous look.

He hurried to his room, and dressed himself in his best attire, and with some care, though he was in such haste.

Lupa would have spoken to him, but she was checked by his frowning looks.

She dared not tamper with him in his present mood, for she knew that, though mild and placable on ordinary occasions, Ventidius was fierce as a lion when his anger was excited.

"This will pass over," thought the vain and ambitious woman; "meanwhile, our dear Virginia has made a brilliant match, and we may boast of being allied to one of the noblest families in the empire."

Ventidius, when dressed, strode forth into the street and placed himself at the head of his little band of gladiators.

"Follow me, my lads," said Ventidius, in a low sullen tone.

"Whither, Ventidius?" they questioned.

"To the palace of Cæsar."

They passed on, stepping together with military order and precision.

Zaba slipped out from his hiding-place, laughing like a fiend.

"To the palace of Cæsar!" he repeated gleefully; "Why so I would have it. The emperor will be forced to listen to the complaint of such a man as Ventidius, and will be further incensed against Narcissus and all his followers. I will see the end of it. Virginia shall yet be mine."

CHAPTER XLV.

AN UNWELCOME GUEST.

THE pale dawn was breaking in the east, when weary and travel-stained, Licinius and his calvacade arrived at his country-villa near Præneste.

Though Licinius had squandered a large fortune by his extravagances, he still retained possession of the mansion, as also part of the estates which had belonged to his ancestors.

His country-seat was of considerable size and pretensions.

A handsome entrance from the garden led into a spacious atrium, about fifty feet square.

The peristyle was surrounded by columns of the Corinthian order, and adorned with flowers, shrubs, and statuary.

The hangings and furniture were magnificent, but faded and dilapidated.

Several shabbily-dressed, meagre-looking slaves came hurrying forth to welcome their master home.

"Caipor," said Licinius, addressing one of them "is all prepared for the reception of your new mistress?"

"All is ready, my lord," answered the man.

"Good, then. Summon the maids, and let them be in attendance," returned Licinius.

He then turned to Locusta, who entered at the moment.

The tall, stern-looking, powerful woman carried the slight form of Virginia in her arms as lightly as though it had been that of a sleeping child.

"She is still in a trance," said Licinius, gazing upon the fair captive in fond admiration.

"Is not this perilous?" he asked. "How deeply she slumbers!"

"There is no danger, Licinius," answered the woman. "I took care of that."

"But will it continue for any considerable length of time?" was the young patrician's anxious question.

"No longer than I please, Licinius," returned Locusta.

"Then you have the means of restoring her to animation?"

"Yes, and that within a few minutes."

Licinius raised Virginia's passive hand, and pressed it to his lips.

"How beautiful she is!" he murmured. "A sleeping Venus! To you I entrust this priceless treasure, good Locusta. When she awakes, soothe and comfort her. Tell her I am her devoted servant, and that I have no other wish than to secure her happiness."

Locusta bowed assent.

"And hark ye, all!" said Licinius, turning to his slaves. "Let what you have seen and heard be carefully concealed from all outside our own circle. The presence of this lady in my house is a dead secret. Woe to his head who betrays my confidence!"

The trembling servants humbly promised obedience.

"Come with me, Caipor," said Licinius, turning to a handsome youth, much better dressed than his fellows. "I must to my library. I have letters to write. Meantime, get your horse saddled, for you must carry them to Rome."

It may be noted that, among the Romans, persons in good circumstances seem usually to have had only one to wait upon them, who was generally called by the name of his master, with the word "por"—that is puer (boy)—affixed to it, as Caipor, Lucipor, and so forth.

"And now, begone, Locusta!" said Licinius. "Pay strict heed to my directions, and let me know when Virginia awakens."

Locusta, guided by two or three of the slaves, bore her lovely burden from the room.

Licinius, attended by Caipor, then retired to the library.

This study was removed from all noise, and situated in the quietest part of the house.

A lofty window pleasantly illuminated the moderate-sized apartment, the walls of which were adorned with elegant arabesques in light colours and between them, on dark grounds, a troop of dancing figures swept along.

There was a neat couch, faced with tortoise-shell and hung with Babylonian tapestry of various colours.

It was not designed for self-indulgence, or even for rest, but served the purpose of a modern study-table or desk.

The noble Roman was accustomed to recline on

the couch, supported on his left arm, and having one knee drawn up higher than the other, in order to place on it his books or tablets.

By the side of the lectus, lectulus, or couch, was the scrinium, a little case designed to hold books, letters, or other writings.

It was made of wood, had a cylindrical form, as best adapted to that of the books, and was of a size adjusted to the number of books it was designed to hold.

As soon as he had entered this library, Licinius collected his papers and commenced writing.

The slave stood at a modest distance from his master, awaiting further orders.

"Leave me, Caipor," said the patrician. "Make your preparations for the journey. I will call you when I have finished these despatches."

The youth bowed and retired.

Licinius then applied himself with diligence to the task before him.

He was so intent upon his occupation that he either did not hear or did not heed the noise of a quick firm step in the corridor outside.

Suddenly the door was thrown open.

A tall stately figure stood before him.

Licinius uttered a cry of rage and dismay, and quickly snatched up his sword which lay upon the table.

"By the gods!" he exclaimed, "it is Caractacus."

CHAPTER XLVI.

THE FALL OF NARCISSUS.

CARACTACUS stood before the patrician with a calm and undaunted mien.

"You see, Licinius, I am unarmed, and I come upon a friendly errand."

Licinius was amazed.

"Are you alone?" he asked.

"I bring with me one companion," said our hero. "He waits without."

The young patrician looked flushed and confused.

"And your business?" he said.

"To save your life."

"To save my life!" repeated the patrician. "I am in my own house, surrounded by devoted slaves. I have yet to learn that my life is in danger."

"A sword hangs by a hair over your head, Licinius," answered Caractacus. "Your only hope is in instant flight."

Licinius regarded him with a peculiar look.

"Ventidius has sent you hither," he said.

"No," answered the Briton, with a frankness of manner that left no doubt that he was speaking the truth.

"I have not seen Ventidius this month past."

"Nor his wife? Nor his daughter?"

"Neither of them. Nor any one belonging to his household."

"It is plain that he knows nothing—suspects nothing," thought Licinius. "Well for him."

Again he cast a puzzled look at Caractacus.

"But we are foes."

"A Briton knows how to respect an open and honourable enemy," answered Caractacus. "You accepted my challenge, abstained from plotting against me, and met me in the arena hand to hand like a man."

"It is no more than the truth," said Licinius. "I used my best endeavours to protect you against the evil designs of others."

"I acknowledge it," said the Briton, "and it is for that reason I am here."

"You are a strange being, Caractacus," rejoined the Roman, forcing a laugh. "Pray tell me, from what quarter am I threatened?"

"The Empress Agrippina has vowed to have your life."

"That is old news, brave comrade," answered Licinius, with a careless laugh. "She has long

hated and conspired against my patron, Narcissus, to whose fortunes I am bound, and with whom I must stand or fall."

"Aye, but till now the star of your patron was in the ascendant," but it has set in clouds and darkness, never, I fear, to rise again!"

Licinius staggered back, trembling with agitation, and deadly pale.

"But is this certain?" he faltered.

"As certain as that I stand before you and tell you this ill news."

"Great Jupiter, I am staggered by a blow so sudden and so crushing," answered Licinius, pressing his hand to his brow. "Give me a moment to recover myself."

He seated himself upon a couch and buried his face in his hands.

Then starting up wildly he said—

"We must have been betrayed. Tell me, how came this about?"

"My companion will explain all," said Caractacus.

"True, I had forget," said Licinius. "But can I know that he is trustworthy?"

"You will know by this token."

Caractacus held out his hand, on the middle finger of which a gem sparkled.

"Gods! it is the signet ring of my patron, Narcissus," exclaimed the young patrician, quite confounded.

"Hist! It is not safe to mention his name, even here," replied our hero.

"But where is he?"

"In the vestibule, talking with your slaves. He is muffled and disguised, and travelled as my servant," answered the Briton.

"Go, bring him hither," rejoined Licinius. "But be cautious. I think my slaves are faithful, but it is well to be on guard."

"I go, Licinius."

Our hero passed out of the library.

As soon as he was gone Licinius closed the door and bolted it.

Then by another entrance he went into a small enclosed garden, with a fountain in the midst.

Here he found a pretty slave girl watering the flowers and singing to herself.

"Come hither, Celia."

The girl set down her pitcher, and came tripping to his side.

"My lord," she said, "what is your will?"

"Go, Celia, fetch Locusta—bid her come upon the instant."

The girl blushed and laughed, and bounded away.

Licinius awaited, in a fever of suspense and anxiety, until Locusta came.

He waved Celia away.

She pouted her lips, and went off rather reluctantly.

When they were alone Locusta observed with surprise the haggard face of her employer, but she asked no questions, made no remarks.

"Virginia," said Licinius, "is she still sleeping, or have you awakend her?"

"She sleeps still," was the reply. "I thought it better not to disturb her so soon after her long journey, but if you wish it——"

"Let it be as it is," returned Licinius. "I am glad of what you tell me—let her sleep on."

He stood, his eye glaring into vacancy like one in a dream.

Locusta grew alarmed.

"What ails you, my lord?" she asked; "how pale and bewildered you look," said she.

"Not without cause, Locusta," he replied, gloomily. "We are ruined, betrayed."

The woman changed countenance, but maintained her self-possession.

"How ruined, how betrayed, my lord? What does this mean?" she asked.

"This it means. Narcissus is disgraced and proscribed. The myrmidons of Agrippina are in pursuit of him, and he has fled hither for refuge."

"Juno!" exclaimed the woman; "did he tell you this himself?"

"No! I have not yet seen him," was the reply. "The intelligence was brought by his messenger, Caractacus."

"Caractacus!" exclaimed Locusta, utterly astonished.

"Are you not aware that the Briton loves Virginia?"

"I know it," said Licinius.

"But does he know that Virginia is here?"

"He does not dream of such a thing," replied Licinius, "nor must he learn the truth."

"He shall not," answered Locusta. "Virginia herself is safe—I can prolong her sleep for hours if need be."

"That is well," he said. "Yet I am so beset I know not which way to turn."

"Narcissus cannot stay here," said Locusta, hastily.

"No, we must fly together," answered Licinius. "We must embark in some vessel and fly far hence, to Gaul or Britain."

"And what is to become of Virginia?"

"I cannot bear the thought of leaving her behind," said Licinius, bitterly, "yet I fear it must be so. Still, some means may be devised for getting rid of Caractacus, and carrying Virginia aboard the vessel."

Locusta pondered.

"So it has come at last!" she muttered to herself; "but who could have betrayed us?"

"I know not whom to suspect, unless, indeed, it be that villain Zaba," was the reply.

"It could be no other," she rejoined. "But I will wreak my vengeance on him."

"There are other things to think of now," said Licinius; "do you hasten back to Virginia and watch by her side until I send for you again. Hark, I am called, and I must leave you now."

He returned to the library.

He heard Caractacus shaking at the door.

Licinius turned the key in the lock, and admitted our hero and Narcissus.

The latter was muffled in a long black cloak.

When the once powerful but now fallen minister threw back his cloak, and disclosed his face, Licinius was shocked at his altered appearance.

He looked quite ten years older than when his friend and confidant had last seen him.

His cheek and forehead were of a sallow, corpselike hue, and deeply furrowed by wrinkles; the lines about his mouth were drawn down with an expression of mental and bodily suffering, painful to witness. His frame was enfeebled and nerveless.

He tottered to a chair, and sank upon it half exhausted.

Licinius poured him out a goblet of wine, part of which he forthwith drank, and seemed partially refreshed.

"I grieve to see you thus, Narcissus," said the young patrician; "but be of good cheer, you have the start of your foes, and in a few hours will be far out of their reach."

Narcissus shook his head.

"Let them come, Licinius,"he said; "I can fly no further. It is but death after all, and I have long yearned to cease and be at rest."

"Courage, illustrious, talk not so despondingly," urged Licinius; "the world is wide, life is sweet, and Fortune may yet turn her wheel."

"For you there is life and hope, for me nothing but death and oblivion," returned the broken man, sadly; "yet it is hard that I should be robbed of all the wealth I have amassed so painfully, since I prized it chiefly for your sake, my faithful Licinius. I had bequeathed you all to the last drachma!"

Licinius turned away his head to hide a look of bitter vexation.

"And did you save nothing from the wreck?" he asked. "I can but curse my own folly for having dissipated my own fortune in luxury and gaming. In our flight we shall sorely need money."

Narcissus smiled faintly.

"Aye, you say well: no wings are so swift and strong as those that have their feathers gilded," returned the fallen minister.

"Woe is me, our wings are wings of lead," sighed Licinius.

"Nay, we are not such bankrupts as you think," said Narcissus.

He pulled from his bosom a leather bag, of no great size, but full to repletion.

"Do you see that?"

"Gold!" returned Licinius, shrugging his shoulders discontentedly.

"Not gold!" said Licinius, patting the bag, "not gold, my son, not gold!"

Licinius could come to no other conclusion than the very natural one, that trouble had affected the mind of his old friend and patron.

"Not gold!" repeated Licinius, quite chap-fallen.

"No, something more precious," answered Narcissus. "Look to the door!" he added, waving his hand to Caractacus, with an unconscious haughtiness that came of the long-continued habit of command.

Caractacus gazed upon him with a pitying eye, and reflected on the mutability of fortune.

But yesterday he was flattered and fawned upon by princes—was one whose word would have stood against the world—one in whose hands the feebleminded emperor was a mere puppet, and to-day! A hunted fugitive whom no man might harbour, liable to be slain by the vilest slave that crossed his path, for the sake of the reward set upon his head.

With trembling fingers Narcissus loosened the strings of the leathern pouch, and held it out for the young noble's inspection.

The eyes of Licinius glistened with avaricious delight.

"Gems!" he exclaimed, "diamonds, rubies, emeralds, pearls, gems of all kinds. Gods! how they sparkle! They dazzle one's eyes! They must be of immense value!"

Narcissus gave a chuckling laugh.

"Aye, here is wealth enough to buy a province," he replied; "this diamond alone is worth eighty talents."

He held out a large and brilliant jewel that flashed and sparkled with a thousand prismatic hues.

Its value in English money would be about fifteen thousand pounds.

"And whence came all these? How did you obtain them?"

"Some in the form of gifts, and bribes, others by purchase," replied Narcissus. "I have always known the fickleness of court-favour, and resolved to take a bond of Fortune. Gold was too cumbrous to carry, while these jewels, though they occupy small space are of surpassing value. I have prepared for a disaster, which, come sooner or later, must one day befall me."

"In that you have shown the wisest forethought," replied Licinius. "With such riches in your possession, you may well afford to laugh the world to scorn. But is it safe for you to carry them unguarded?"

"I shall travel in a beggar's guise," answered Narcissus; "none will suspect me of possessing an obolus."

"Pardon me, my lord," said our hero; "I am loath to break in upon your discourse, but haste precludes courtesy; 'tis time you were upon the road."

"Noble Caractacus is in the right," said Licinius. "Let us to horse! I will take with me a dozen well-armed slaves to guard the treasure; give me your arm, illustrious."

The Briton smiled grimly at the change of the

young patrician's tone in addressing the man fo broken fortunes, to whom he had formerly been so much indebted.

It is true he had acted respectfully throughout, but before seeing the jewels he was civil—afterwards he became obsequious.

Caipor was summoned.

He appeared in a travelling dress.

He just glanced at the visitor, then bowed low to his master.

"My lord, I attend you," he said. "My horse is saddled, I am ready to start for Rome."

"I have other business for you, my good lad," said his master; "let a dozen of my slaves be mounted and armed as quickly as possible. Business calls me hence—business that will brook no delay."

"It shall be done," said Caipor, leaving the room.

Narcissus sat upon a couch, his hands resting on his knees, his head drooped upon his bosom.

Licinius came to his side, and clapped him on the shoulder.

"Rouse up, illustrious," he said; "you were ever quick of resource, prompt and energetic in action; think then—there is but a little exertion, a few hours' toil, and we are free."

Narcissus rose wearily.

"Black care sits behind the horseman," he said, moodily; "why should I attempt to fly the thoughts that are ever present with me? To fly death, that must overtake the swiftest rider? Nay, let me stay where I am."

"My lord, would you fall into the cruel hands of Agrippina?"

"My life is in my own hands, Licinius," replied Narcissus, tapping the hilt of his dagger.

"May I perish if I leave you!"

"Do you mean this, Licinius?"

"Aye, by the sacred Jove."

"Let me die here, my son," returned Narcissus, regarding him with a strange look. "I cannot endure the journey, I am already outworn with fatigue. I am content to die here. Escape, and live to avenge me!"

All this time Licinius was thinking of the bag of jewels, and was half mad with impatience at this delay.

"For my sake, if not for your own, let us to horse at once," he urged, seizing Narcissus by the arm, and attempting to drag him away. "I set some value on my life if you regard not your own. To stay here is to die."

"Go then, my son," returned Narcissus, "and save your life."

The young patrician's face flushed with ill-concealed rage and mortification, his eyes glared upon his patron and benefactor, and then glanced furtively at Caractacus.

"But for my presence he would cut the old man's throat, and rob him of his treasure," thought our hero.

Caipor came rushing in.

His looks betrayed terror and excitement.

"What now, boy?" asked Licinius.

"My lord, one of your slaves who keeps watch in the north tower reports the approach of a large party of horsemen," he said. "They are riding at full speed, and come in this direction."

"From whence, think you?"

"From Rome, by the Appian Way," answered Caipor. "The man told me that he saw their helmets and spears sparkle through the clouds of dust, and that there could be no doubt that they were a troop of cavalry."

"They are the emissaries of Agrippina sent hither to arrest, perhaps to butcher us," cried the young patrician. "What say you now, my father?" he added, turning impatiently to Narcissus.

"I have no more to say than this. Go and save thyself—leave me to my fate," replied the other, sullenly.

"But will you let the treasure fall into the hungry gripe of your enemies?"

"The treasure, no. You shall take that, my dear Licinius."

"Quick, give it, then," cried Licinius, striving to curb his temper. "Why are you fumbling in your bosom?"

Narcissus drew forth a heavy bag and placed it in his hand.

"There, the gods shield thee. Are you now content?"

Licinius clasped the bag to his breast, and drew his cloak over it.

"Thanks, for your noble gift——"

He stopped short, and turning fiercely upon Caipor, stamped his foot.

"Dog, lead the way," he said. "To horse! There is death in every moments' delay."

"Are you in such haste, Licinius, that you cannot pause for a moment even to bid me a last farewell."

"Farewell!" said the young patrician. "It is by your own act of obstinacy that you remain here, but since you are resolved on such a course I cannot prevent you."

"Nay then, there is something to live for yet," cried Narcissus, starting from the couch. "I have changed my mind, I will go with you."

"It is too late!" growled Licinius, pushing him back.

The selfish and treacherous noble rushed from the library. The next moment the trampling of horses' hoofs was heard. Caractacus flew to the window. He beheld Licinius, attended by a dozen mounted slaves, galloping along the high road that led to the sea-coast. He turned away in disgust.

"So much for courtly gratitude," he said; "no sooner had he got the treasure in his clutch than he cared no more for his friend whose generosity had enriched him. Let him go—bad luck follow him, the traitor!"

Narcissus laughed heartily.

"The fool, he could not stand the test! He was tried and found wanting."

"Not wanting the treasure, however," grumbled the Briton, "and that was all he wanted."

Again the cunning Greek burst in a loud triumphant laugh.

"The fool, the shallow fool, to think he could deceive me!" he chuckled. "I have tricked him finely—look here, my noble lad, and judge between us which is the fox and which the goose."

He took out the bag from under his cloak.

"I am amazed!" cried the Briton; "if I can trust my eyes, I saw you place such a bag in his hands. Is this another?"

"It is, Caractacus. This contains diamonds, emeralds, rubies, the one I gave him nothing but dust and sand, and roadside pebbles."

"He is justly served."

"And upon whom will you bestow this?"

"Upon you, Caractacus, whom I have so grievously wronged—you who have taken such a noble revenge!" answered Narcissus. "Take them—they are of no further use to me, I am a dying man. May this store in your possession be blessed by the sacred gods, and increase and multiply a thousand times."

Caractacus drew back.

"I will not touch one penny's worth," he said; "do not insult me by supposing me so base and sordid."

"Nay, you must accept it."

Our hero shook his head.

Narcissus gave him a penetrating look.

"Is it true that the Christians, the Nazarenes, share all their goods in common, that rich and poor fare alike, and eat at the same table?"

Caractacus turned very white.

"Do you think that I am a Christian?" he gasped.

"I know thou art," returned Narcissus, smiling "and that this very night you are bidden to a love-feast in the catacombs."

"How do you know this?" asked our hero.

"How did I know it?" retorted Narcissus. "Whilst my power lasted I had spies and agents in every corner of the empire. At my command were the eyes of Argus, the arms of Briareus, the tongues of Rumour. Do you think, then, that I should be left in ignorance of what was being carried on by a weak and artless people close to the gates of Rome?"

"Yet there must have been some wolf in sheep's clothing that crept into the fold," sighed Caractacus. "But where is the place into which treason does not creep? It was the serpent in Paradise, the Iscariot among the Twelve."

"Forgive me, Caractacus. I own, with shame, that it was in the hopes of wreaking my baseless grudge against you that I gave the orders that I did."

"What orders?" asked Caractacus.

"Orders that will be carried out in spite of my displacement," continued Narcissus. The matter now rests in the hands of the præfect, who is a zealous man, a staunch pantheist and hater of the Christians. To-morrow a cohort of soldiers will break into the catacombs and seize all on whom they can lay hands. The result will be a fine feast for the lions and panthers."

"To-morrow!" cried our hero, aghast. "I must do what I can to prevent this."

"It is little you can do, for every outlet is guarded, every precaution taken to prevent the escape of the sectarians," answered Narcissus. "Would you be guided by me you would keep clear of all entanglement with these dark, mysterious people. In any case, I bequeath you my wealth, to use it as you please, to secure your own safety, or to share it amongst your associates."

"I will guard it for the present, but only to restore it to you again," said our hero.

"That must be done then on the other side of the Styx, for my end is at hand," replied Narcissus, smiling grimly. "Hark at that shout. It is a summons from Pluto."

The trampling of horses' hoofs, and a hubbub of voices now reached their ears.

Then a stern voice shouted imperiously——

"Open your doors, I command you, in the name of Cæsar."

"There is yet time for flight," said Caractacus. "I will bar the door, and keep your enemies at bay while you retreat."

"You shall not shed one drop of blood in my defence," said Narcissus. But I will die as becomes the dignity of one who was so late a name and power in Rome. Youths of the noblest blood have acted as my chamberlains—do you accept the office for a brief half hour. Go out into the vestibule, demand what these clamourers want with me, and usher them to my presence in due form."

"By the god Beltane!" cried the Briton, who for all his Christianity could not get rid of his habit of using pagan oaths, "I will teach them to pay you some show of respect even to the last."

"Farewell, Caractacus," said the fallen minister. "The gods befriend thee!"

CHAPTER XLVII

HOW AGRIPPINA WAS BAFFLED.

WITH calm step and lion-like mien, Caractacus, his face as impassive as that of a statue of Fate, walked forth into the vestibule.

A number of frightened slaves, belonging to the household deserted by its master, came rushing in.

With loud screams and lamentations they flew to the corners of the room, where they huddled together or crouched upon their knees, the embodiment of terror, whilst others crept under tables and couches, or hid themselves behind the tapestry. Then a rabble of soldiers, their armour gleaming, their spears advanced, came thundering into the marble hall.

They were led on by Zaba the dwarf.

The hideous little villain yelled and capered with fiendish glee.

In his right hand he flourished a long murderous-looking knife.

Caractacus threw himself in their way.

"Keep the peace here!" he cried, in stern, ringing accents of authority. "You degrade the name of Cæsar by this unseemly violence. Stand back, I say."

The soldiers were at once brought to a stand-still by the firm controlling voice of one who was a born commander.

"Ha! is it thou, braggart?" yelled Zaba, the dwarf. "I have thee now. Here's to avenge my wound."

He struck the knife full at our hero's breast.

The keen point of the weapon struck against the hard mass of priceless stones concealed in our hero's bosom, and the blade was shattered like glass.

Zaba drew back with a howl of baffled rage.

"By Obi! it is the fetish," he gasped. "The sardonyx Virginia gave him. He is invulnerable."

A stalwart noble-looking officer came forward, with lowering brow.

"What insolence is this? Art thou some slave of Narcissus that would vainly throw away thy life to give an insane proof of fidelity?" he said. "Stand aside, and tempt not your fate."

Then seeing who it was, he altered his tone.

"You here, Caractacus!" he exclaimed, "what does this mean?"

"Simply this, noble Honorius, I am in attendance upon the secretary of the emperor," said our hero. "I am posted here to keep this door, and you cannot pass until you tell me your business."

Honorius laughed.

"I cannot."

"You will not, I am sure take advantage of your power to commit an offence against good manners," said our hero; "stay but a moment, and I will announce you."

"Meanwhile Narcissus escapes!" laughed the tribune. "This is too much—we have an order from Cæsar for his arrest; keep back, I should be sorry for you to get yourself into trouble."

There was a bustle in the rear of the throng

"Way for the empress!" was the shout.

The throng divided.

With majestic step, Agrippina advanced to the door.

She was accompanied by her son Nero, and the royal pair were attended by numerous slaves, and others.

"Where is this traitor?" she exclaimed.

"He awaits you in the library."

Agrippina started.

"You, Caractacus!" she exclaimed.

"Yes, madam, will you please to follow me?"

"Lead on."

The Briton opened the door of the library.

They passed in—Agrippina and the soldiers of the Prætorian guard.

In the midst of the room, stretched upon his back, Narcissus lay dead—a dagger in his heart.

"He has died by his own hand," said Agrippina, recoiling.

Then leaning upon the arm of Caractacus for a few moments, she contemplated the body in gloomy silence.

"How placid he looks!" she murmured; "sometimes I envy the dead."

Caractacus looked at her fixedly.

"Your vengeance is accomplished, Agrippina," he said; "are you satisfied?"

"No!" said the empress, "he has escaped too easily."

CHAPTER XLVIII.

HOW VENTIDIUS FOUND VIRGINIA.

HE door was now thrown open, and Nero, with several soldiers of the Prætorian guard, rushed in.

"Where is this traitor?" he exclaimed; "ve you secured him?"

Agrippina pointed to the dead body of Narcissus.

"He is beyond the reach of our vengeance, my son," replied Agrippina; "he has perished by his own hand."

Nero scowled darkly.

"This should have been prevented," he said. "The villain should have been scourged to death in the forum."

Then, turning to Caractacus, he gave him an evil look. "What does the Briton here?" he asked.

But Agrippina interfered on our hero's behalf.

"Leave him alone, my son," she replied. "Narcissus was his enemy as he was ours. Let us lose no time but at once search the house. Though Narcissus has baffled us, some of his fellow-conspirators may be hiding about the place."

"If we find not Licinius, we will put some of the slaves to the question," said Nero; "torture will make them confess."

"There will be no need for that," said Agrippina. "Licinius is reported to have been a harsh master, cruel to his slaves, and doubtless there will be some among them ready to betray him."

"Come, Honorius, let us search the house," said Nero; "meanwhile let that carrion be removed. Let his head be struck off, that I may carry it at my saddle-bow as a trophy."

"I will remain here till your return," said Agrippina.

Nero took the lead, and rushed into the innermost chambers of the house.

One of the trembling slaves was seized by the rough soldiers and compelled to act as guide.

They crossed the triclinium, and, entering one of the alæ or wings of the building, mounted a staircase.

Upon reaching the top of it they found themselves in a sort of gallery, at the end of which was a door, closed and bolted.

Honorius knocked, and demanded admission in the name of Cæsar.

He received no reply, but a smothered scream was heard from within.

"He is there!" exclaimed Nero, "break open the door."

The prince's command was immediately obeyed. The soldiers plied their spears and axes, and in very short space of time the door was burst open. Nero, with his myrmidons, burst into the room. It was a small but luxuriously-furnished apartment. On one side of it was an alcove screened y an elegant tapestried curtain, looped up with a cord of gold thread.

In this niche was an ivory bedstead, covered with a purple coverlet, on which the slight, graceful form of the fair captive lay reclining.

Behind the couch lay Locusta. She clung to the wall, and gazed at the intruders with a look of mingled guilt and terror.

The captive girl had recovered from her trance, and, half rising from the couch, leaned upon her hand, and regarded the prince and his followers with a look of wonderment, like one just startled from a deep dream.

She was dressed in a fair white robe, with a broad scarlet fringe or border. Her luxuriant and glossy black tresses were neatly arranged, and bound with a ribbon.

Seldom had she looked so lovely as at that moment.

"Virginia!" exclaimed Caractacus, in a tone of wrath and anguish. "How came she hither?"

Nero stood transfixed with delighted admiration as he contemplated the charms of the beautiful and innocent girl.

"By the sandals of Venus!" he muttered to himself, "Licinius is a man of taste. Where, I wonder, could he have secured such a peerless treasure?"

Virginia rose from the couch, and pressing her hands to her brow advanced a few paces, glaring around her distractedly, while rich warm blushes suffused her neck and face.

"This cannot be real," she murmured, brokenly. "It is all a dream. I shall wake presently."

She sank back upon the couch, and buried her face in her hands.

"What woman is that who lurks yonder?" said Nero. "Drag her forth, and set her before me."

Two of the soldiers seized the woman, and haled her out into the middle of the room.

"Unloose me, ye ruffians!" she exclaimed, struggling fiercely. "How dare you lay a finger upon me? I appeal for protection to the prince and to the empress."

Nero sprang back in amazement.

"Body of Bacchus!" he laughed. "This is a very pretty little drama, I must own. What, you here, Locusta! Then I marvel not that there is mischief afoot."

"No further mischief than this, illustrious," answered Locusta, sullenly. "A patrician of ancient and noble family falls in love with the daughter of a plebeian; he offers his hand in honourable marriage, but from the low-born father receives a churlish rebuff. Being a youth of spirit, what he could not obtain by fair means he resolved to secure by force. Virginia was brought hither against her will, perhaps, but with no other intention than to further her own interest and happiness."

"Else this precious scheme had not received the help and countenance of the respectable Locusta," sneered the prince.

Then, he added, sternly, with one of his terrible frowns—

"Have a care, woman—your nefarious practices will bring you to ruin."

Locusta muttered defiantly, and gave him an evil look that he did not fail to interpret into—

"My ruin will involve yours and that of your mother, the profligate empress."

But Nero pretended not to have observed the fierce and vengeful scowl which darkened the abandoned woman's harsh and evil features.

Caractacus advanced towards Virginia and would have taken her hand.

"Stand-aside," growled Nero; "let the fair one speak."

Virginia threw herself upon her knees before him.

"My lord, I know not what to say," she faltered, "nor can I remember how I was brought hither. While sleeping in peace and security as I thought, within my own quiet chamber under my father's roof-tree, I was aroused in the dead of the night to find myself forcibly dragged towards the window."

"By Licinius?"

"Nay, my lord, by the deformed beast-feeder, the dwarf they call Zaba."

"Ha! is it so? The brutal wretch shall answer for it," said Nero; "but proceed with your story."

"A scarf was thrown over my mouth, to prevent me from alarming the house by my screams. That and the loathsome clutch of the horrid monster with whom I was struggling overpowered me. I must have fainted with horror, for I became unconscious, and recollect no more until I woke to find myself here, and thus surrounded."

"A cursed plot," said Nero; "all concerned in it shall die the death."

Honorius stepped forward.

He grasped by the arm one of the slaves—a miserable-looking fellow, who seemed half dead with fear.

HE POINTED TO THE GHASTLY SPECTACLE, BUT SHE HAD NOT SUFFICIENT RESOLUTION TO DARE THE ORDEAL.

No. 9.

"Who is this dog?" asked Nero.

"One of the household," answered the tribune; "he was found lurking near the stables, the horses were gone, and we extorted from the slave, by threat of torture, the information that Licinius, with some dozen of his followers, have taken horse and fled to Ostia, whence it is their intention to escape beyond sea."

"And when was this?" asked Nero.

"Not more than a hour before our arrival here," was the reply.

"At once give chase, Honorius," was the reply; "mount and away! Detach as many of your men as you think proper, and seize the traitor ere he can set foot aboard."

"He has a good start, great prince; his horses are fresh, while ours are somewhat jaded. I will do my best, but blame me not if we should fail to overtake him."

"We shall not blame you, noble tribune," answered the prince, "but Licinius shall not escape us. The imperial arm is far-reaching. Though he escape to the ends of the earth we will drag him back!"

"I will take this slave with me," said Honorius.

"Do so," said the prince, "and may success crown your efforts! Meanwhile, we will leave some of the cohort in charge of this house, set a seal upon the door, and hasten back to Rome. For the fair Virginia——"

"For me, illustrious, let me return at once to my father, who will be so deeply afflicted at my absence," said Virginia.

"Trust yourself to my care," said Caractacus.

Virginia, with perfect trust, placed herself in his arms.

"Let us go, Caractacus, and quickly as may be, home to my father!"

But Nero took her hand and drew her away.

"Fair Virginia, I will allow no one else to undertake this precious charge. You must remain under my immediate protection."

Virginia looked at him with a half-frightened expression, which told how willingly she would have objected to this arrangement if she dared; but she did not speak.

Caractacus inwardly chafed with anger and apprehension.

"This is all brought about by that treacherous mercenary Licinius," he said to himself, "who deserted his generous master at his utmost need. It is well I did not know it when he was here. I am not sorry though that my hands should be clear of his blood."

Meantime the news of the discovery of Virginia in the house of Licinius had reached the ears of the Empress Agrippina, and she came into the room.

She glanced eagerly at Caractacus, and when she saw his noble, kindly, yet withal stern and thoughtful face turned with a moody yet tender look upon Virginia, she felt her heart sink within her.

"He loves this girl," she thought. "Ah, how I envy her!"

But though at the moment she could have found it in her heart to slay Virginia on the spot, she restrained herself, and dissembled her feelings.

"Come hither, child," she said, in a gracious tone. "Dismiss all fear. You are safe with me."

Though awed by the presence of one so exalted in station, Virginia was glad to have the companionship of one of her own sex.

She made a low obeisance, and placed herself by the side of the empress.

"I thank you, madam," she said, very simply.

Poor Virginia was much surprised, and not a little affrighted, when the empress clutched her hand, and looked down upon her with an eager, searching glance.

"Maiden," said the empress, "this is no place for you. We must get you home to your father."

"I thank you, madam," repeated Virginia, in a faltering voice. It was all she could say, for she was abashed under the ardent gaze of young Nero, whose eyes never left her for a moment.

"If such be your pleasure, madam, the fair Virginia might accompany you to the palace, and there remain until her happy recovery is communicated to Ventidius, who has been clamouring for justice," said Nero.

"She shall go with me," replied Agrippina.

The words were scarcely spoken, when a noise was heard without, and a loud voice cried eagerly—

"I claim my right as a Roman and citizen. Do not bar my way, comrade. I have a petition to present to the prince Nero."

Nero started and frowned.

Virginia clasped her hands, and uttered a cry of joy.

"It is my father!"

"Admit him," said the empress.

The next moment Ventidius rushed into the room.

The girl sprang towards him, and threw herself into his arms.

"Thou art safe, my darling!" he murmured. "Ah, if thou didst but know what I have suffered on thy account!"

Then looking fiercely round, he asked—

"Where is Licinius? Have you caught the villain?"

Nero turned to him with a haughty air.

"What say you, Ventidius?" he asked.

The lanista drew back somewhat confused, and bowed respectfully.

"I crave your pardon, illustrious," he said; "joy at finding my child restored to me, indignation against the man who has injured me so deeply, made me for the moment forget myself."

"You shall have retribution, good Ventidius," said Nero. "But thus far nothing has been done. Narcissus has died by his own hand, Licinius has escaped to Ostia, while the noble tribune there stands pondering how long it will take the fugitive to put miles of sea between his doomed head and the Italian coast."

The hot blood mounted the veteran's swarthy face as he replied—

"Illustrious, I do but wait your final orders."

"Waste no time then, but mount and ride as fast as you can to Ostia. If the villain has already embarked get you aboard a trireme—your own name and authority will suffice to bear you out in such a matter. Go, then, and seek him to the world's end. Challenge and stay each vessel that you meet; only see that you bring his head to Rome."

"It shall be done," said the tribune.

Ventidius here earnestly interposed.

"Let me go too, illustrious! I have most cause to hate this man—let me avenge myself upon him."

Nero, from motives of his own, caught at the suggestion.

"It shall be so," he said.

But Virginia was differently inclined.

She clasped her arms about Ventidius.

"No, no, my father," she said; "do not leave me. Do not rush into needless danger."

"Vah! go to!" returned Ventidius; "I hate the villain for a thousand reasons!"

"Imperial," he added, turning, with a bow, to the empress, "I entrust my child to your care."

"That you may do safely, my good Ventidius," she replied, with much condescension.

Now Caractacus was frank, ingenuous, and easily beguiled, yet for the life of him he could not but wonder that Ventidius should relinquish the charge of his daughter into such treacherous keeping.

The fact was, the lanista was carried away by his spite and hatred against Licinius.

Nero was well satisfied, and expressed his approval of the measure in the warmest terms.

"Hark ye, my Caractacus," said the lanista, pressing our hero's arm; "you worsted me in our first encounter; but on that fatal day, when you met Licinius in the arena, by Pluto! I trembled for you. You shall see, I will give a better account of him than you did."

With this he hastened away to join Honorius, who, with a powerful detachment of the Prætorian guard, rode off to Ostia in pursuit of the fugitive.

Soon after the empress, her son, and their retinue, with Virginia in company, leaving some of the soldiers to guard the house of Licinius, set out on their return journey to Rome.

CHAPTER XLIX.

THE FLIGHT OF LICINIUS.

LICINIUS and the retainers had, in the meantime, quitted Præneste and taken the road to Ostia, the nearest seaport town. They had before them a ride of about thirty miles ere they could reach the coast.

Præneste, now called Palestrina, is a city situated about twenty miles from Rome.

According to Virgil it was founded by Cæculus, son of Vulcan, according to others by Prænestus, son of King Latinus, prior to the Trojan war.

Its elevated position and good air rendered it a point of attraction to the ancient Romans.

It was celebrated also for its Temple of Fortune, restored and enlarged by Sylla, which occupied the whole site of the present town.

Palestrina was destroyed in the fifteenth century, but was rebuilt on the ruins of this temple, when a mosaic pavement was discovered, which is now in the Barberini palace at Palestrina.

This celebrated work represents sundry animals and plants, a tent with soldiers, Egyptian figures playing on musical instruments, others occupied with the labours of agriculture.

Of several interpretations given of this work, the most probable is, that the subject alludes to the festivals established in Egypt under the Greek kings, at the period of the inundation of the Nile.

Licinius and his men avoided the public road as much as possible, preferring the by-ways and bridle-paths through the forests and fields.

Upon reaching the plain below the fugitives slackened their speed.

"So far, so well," said Licinius, as he drew rein and cast a glance behind him. "Hitherto we have pursued our way unmolested. Look, Caipor, at yon terminal stone, and tell me how far we are now from Ostia."

"Ten miles, my lord," replied the youth. "We shall reach our destination within an hour."

"It is well," said Licinius; "I have a commission for you to execute."

"I attend, my lord."

"Do you know the house in the town of Ostia where dwells a certain Jew named Melchior?"

"I do, my lord," was the reply. "The Jew you speak of is an old man, who, though he affects a life of privation and miserable poverty, is reported to be as rich as Crœsus."

"The same, a hard-fisted usurer and money-lender, with whom I have had dealings before now," said Licinius.

"Well, my lord, what is your pleasure in regard to him?" asked the youth.

"It will not do for me to travel through populous towns and villages at this break-neck speed," answered the patrician. "It has too much the appearance of a flight, and may excite suspicion."

"That is true, my lord," said Caipor. "You may be detained and questioned by some meddling provincial quæstor or edile."

"That is my fear," rejoined his master; "so, hark ye, my good boy, do you spur forwards and prepare our way before us."

"I will, my lord; but what of the Jew, Melchior?"

"As soon as you reach Ostia seek him out, tell him that I shall be with him anon, and that I shall bring with me diamonds and other gems that I have for sale. Impress upon him that, though I shall not chaffer with him about the price, that I must have the money paid down upon the instant, else I will carry my wares to some other shop."

"I go, my lord," replied Caipor, shaking his horse's rein.

"Hold, not so fast!" cried Licinius; "do not start with half your errand."

"What are your further commands?" asked Caipor, checking his fiery steed.

"When you have despatched your business with the Jew, go, seek out some merchant vessel about to put to sea, and procure a passage for myself and retinue. Should the man's charges be exorbitant do not hold out, let it be understood that I am rich and travel for my pleasure, and that expense is no object to me."

"I understand you, my lord."

"Away, then!" said Licinius. "Be guarded in all you say and do. Forget not, our lives depend upon your prudence."

"I will use extreme caution," answered Caipor. "But tell me this, my lord. Is it your pleasure that I should use your own name?"

"Oh, by no means!" was the reply. "Call me—well, say, Lucius Valerius, a senator of Rome."

"Farewell, my lord. Where shall we meet again?"

"At the house of Melchior, the Jew."

Caipor bowed, and galloped off.

Licinius and the remainder of his company pursued their way through the lovely and fertile country.

From time to time, the patrician looked backwards, half expecting to find the soldiers of the Prætorian guard in pursuit of him.

But no danger appeared to threaten in front or rear.

As they rode on, and time passed by, the fugitives gained more confidence.

"By this time my ancestral home is in the ruthless hands of my enemies," Licinius mused. "I wonder whether they will fire the place, and put my servants to the sword."

Then he thought of Narcissus, and some slight touch of remorse moved his callous breast.

"So much for pride and ambition!" he muttered. It was a miserable fall, and in Narcissus I have lost a staunch and generous friend. Well, the fool had none but himself to blame. He dallied with his fate until it was too late to save him. Let him go. I have enough to do to take care of myself.

He placed his hand in his bosom, and clutched the heavy bag.

"How fortunate I secured this!" he laughed triumphantly. "I profit by his forethought. Yet it is bitterly hard to lose Virginia. How pure, how beautiful she is! I feel I could have loved her with a nobler passion than I ever knew until we met."

Occupied with such thoughts Licinius hastened on his journey.

His slaves noted his moody looks.

They whispered to each other.

There was discontent amongst them. They did not care to be thus dragged from their country to go they knew not whither.

But dread of their stern master's displeasure kept them passive and silent.

And now the walls of Ostia appeared in sight.

This celebrated town and harbour is situated at the mouth of the Tiber.

It was the seaport of Rome, and was founded by Ancus Martius.

In the course of time Ostia rose, with the rise of Rome, to be a place of great wealth, population, and importance, and engrossed the whole trade of Rome carried on by sea.

But its port had never been good, and, owing to the gradual accumulation of mud and other deposits brought down by the river, it ultimately became inaccessible to ships of heavy burden, which were obliged to anchor on the coast, in an exposed and hazardous situation.

Many efforts were made at different periods to obviate these inconveniences, but apparently without success, and at length the Emperor Claudius constructed a new artificial port at the mouth of the north or right arm of the Tiber, by means of moles projecting into the sea.

Ostia still retains its ancient name, but all traces of its former importance have disappeared.

Licinius and his escort rode through the bustling streets of the busy and populous town.

They stabled their horses at a public inn, and after partaking of some slight refreshment, Licinius, accompanied by two only of his slaves, proceeded at once to the house of Melchior, the Jew.

The dwelling of this usurer was well known to the spendthrift noble, who had frequently been forced to pay it a visit while under the pressure of pecuniary difficulties.

It was situated in one of the lowest quarters of the town.

It was a large, ancient, dilapidated building, but the doors and windows were strongly secured.

As Licinius approached the house he perceived at once that Caipor had faithfully discharged his duty, and that the old Jew impatiently awaited the coming of his client.

He was an old, a very old man, with white beard and hair—a face like a vulture.

He was dressed in a black gaberdine that hung about his gaunt, pinched frame in filthy rags. His restless eyes roamed up and down the street, and he rubbed his lean dirty hands together in a fever of greedy expectation.

As soon as he caught sight of Licinius he turned away his head, as though pretending not to have seen him, and instantly darting into the house, closed and barred the iron door.

Once again Licinius clutched the supposed treasure concealed in his bosom.

Reassured by the conviction that he was possessed of untold wealth, he assumed his haughtiest demeanour, and stalked on towards the house with proud and lordly step.

Arrived under the porch he made a sign to one of his slaves to knock at the door.

The man obeyed, and made the street ring with the heavy blows of the massive knocker.

Licinius and his two attendants were kept waiting on the door step for some considerable time.

The patrician grew weary of waiting, and was about to order the slaves to knock again, when the door was opened.

Caipor appeared.

"So you have arrived," said Licinius. "Is all well?"

"All is well, my lord," was the response; "I have procured a passage in a vessel outward bound for Britain."

"When does she sail?"

"She weighs anchor at sunset."

"I am glad of that," rejoined Licinius. "We will get aboard as soon as possible. But where is this Jew?"

"I am here, illustrious, I am here, and await your commands," said Melchior, in a fawning voice. "Will you be pleased to step this way?"

"I come," said Licinius.

The old man, with tottering step, conducted the visitor into a large and gloomy chamber, and motioned him to be seated.

Licinius took a ricketty chair at the head of a marble table, covered thick with dust.

The patrician beckoned to Caipor, who hastened to his master's side.

"Caipor, there may be treachery," he whispered. "Do you and your fellows keep guard in the vestibule. Remain within call, that in case of accident you may be ready to execute my orders."

"I will, my lord," answered the young man, and left the room.

Melchior showed some signs of alarm at this proceeding

He glanced eagerly at the slaves.

Then turning to Licinius, he asked in a quavering voice—

"Is it my lord's pleasure that we should confer together—alone?"

"It is," said Licinius; "our business is private I cannot command the prattling tongues of my slaves."

Melchior bowed to the ground.

When left to themselves Licinius rose from hi chair, and made a sign for the Jew to approach him.

"Come nearer, Melchior," he said, "time presses; I am in haste, let us use despatch. You can guess what I want from you."

Again the Jew made a low salaam.

"Money, no doubt, great sir," he answered; "many of your order do, but money is scarce in these hard times. I have sustained great losses. Yes, by our father Abraham, I am well-nigh ruined. I am miserably poor."

"Why do you try to foist upon me that old and wretched excuse?" retorted Licinius, in disdain. "Console yourself, I am not here to crave a loan at monstrous usury, but to sell you at a cheap rate that which will repay you tenfold my demand."

"To sell, my lord!" repeated the Jew, shrugging up his shoulders; "'tis seldom that knights and nobles condescend to traffic in merchandise."

"True, old cormorant," laughed the Roman; "there are few who can traffic in such wares as mine."

"May I see your wares?"

"Thou shalt," said Licinius. "I will show you that which will make those old dim eyes sparkle."

"Gems, I think, my lord?"

"Aye, diamonds, rubies, pearls," replied Licinius. "Wealth bequeathed me by one who amassed a fortune such as Lucullus never dreamed of."

"By spoiling the Egyptians, one who was a bondsman in the house of bondage," chuckled the Jew, "I think you mean the favourite of Cæsar, your patron, the high and mighty Narcissus."

"Even so."

"'Twas ever thus," returned Melchior; "one man saves to endow his heirs with the means of squandering."

"'Tis not so with your people—you are a thrifty race."

"Our people are wise, and know that wealth is power," replied the Jew. "The outcasts of Israel maintain their independence though scattered among the heathen nations by whom they are despised. Well, let me see these jewels."

Licinius took the bag from under his toga, and placed it on the table.

The old man was astonished at its bulk and weight, and instinctively stretched his long harpy fingers as though to clutch it.

"Stand off!" said Licinius, "before I disclose my treasure, be it understood I wish to part with only a small portion of it. The rest I shall I take to a better market."

"There is no better market," retorted the Jew. "I am an honest man, and fair in all my dealings. I expect no more than a reasonable interest for my money. It is not so with all my tribe, too many of whom are extortioners—blood-suckers."

Licinius smiled in disdain.

"You have altered your tone since the day you pursued me at law for debt, and would have made me your slave, but for my privilege as a patrician," he said. "But enough of this, let us conclude our bargain; it is time I was gone."

So saying, he poured the contents of the bag upon the table.

Before him there was nothing but a heap of dust and sand, and common pebbles.

Licinius started in horror; his eyes glared upon the worthless rubbish into which his sparkling treasure had been converted; every vestige of colour left his cheek, and with a cry of rage and agony he flung himself into the chair.

"Baffled! cheated! ruined!" he gasped. "It is necromancy."

The Jew looked equally dismayed and disappointed.

He tore his beard and his garments, and stamped, cursed, and raved.

"Am I a dog that thou should'st play this trick upon me?" he snarled. "Are these the gems, the diamonds, the sapphires, the rubies, that you spoke of amassed by the wealthy Narcissus?"

Licinius appeared stunned by this terrible blow to all his hopes.

He sat, his hands grasping the edge of the table, his eyes immovably fastened upon the empty bag, and the little mocking heap of rubbish.

"It was the price of blood!" he gasped. "Aye, those rubies were the petrified heart-drops of many a gallant soldier, sent to perish on the burning sands of Lybia, or the frosty heights of the Caucasus! Those diamonds were the crystalised tears of widows and orphans."

The Jew laughed bitterly and spitefully.

"Even like the spoil the Achan hides in his tent, your treasure has brought a curse with it," he hissed. "Might it not be that this is a judgment upon you for your ingratitude?"

At any other time this hint, betraying as it did the speaker's knowledge of the secret of his flight, would have enraged Licinius.

But he made no answer, and remained with his eyes gloomily fixed upon the ground.

At length he rose and stalked towards the Jew.

The old man slunk away, pale and scared.

Licinius clutched him by the arm.

"Melchior," he said, in a low, determined, and at the same time, unnatural voice, "I am in a desperate strait—I must have money."

"Go then, illustrious, and carry your wares to another and a better market," sneered the Jew; "I am too poor to be the buyer of things so valuable."

Licinius bit his lip in suppressed rage.

"If you are not tired of your life do not provoke me too far," he hissed, between his clenched teeth. "I must have money, and I will have it. If you will help me this once ——"

"You will remain my eternal debtor!"

"No! I will pay you thrice the sum you lend," replied Licinius; "and thereto I pledge my knightly honour."

"You pawned that long ago—it never was redeemed," snarled the Jew.

"Do you hear me, Melchior?" cried Licinius, passionately shaking him; "show me where you keep your gold."

"My gold—I have no gold," gasped Melchior; "or if I had, do you think I should be fool enough to keep it here?"

Licinius drew his dagger and flashed it before the Jew's winking eyes.

"I have no desire to stain good steel in your vile blood!" hissed the desperate patrician; "but beware how you drive me beyond the limits of my self-control. Unless you show me where your gold is hid, I will cut your throat, and this I swear, by Pluto!"

Melchior grovelled on his knees and tried to release himself, but Licinius tightened his grasp upon the wretch's weak, shrivelled arm.

"Good Licinius, most noble sir, why do you use me thus?" whined the Jew. "I am an old man, but the life remaining to me is very precious. I cannot die now. Spare me—have mercy on my white hairs."

"The gold!" cried Licinius, menacing him with the dagger.

"Have patience, noble sir," was the reply. "You shall have gold, only put up your dagger—it blinds and bewilders me like the flash of lightning."

"Its flash is as deadly too, as you shall find, Melchior, unless you supply my need."

He lowered the weapon.

"I must go forth to fetch the money," he said, his teeth chattering, and his knees knocking together. "My neighbour and kinsman, Ahaz, keeps my gold—I will go to him. How much do you require? Do not ask too much. Things have gone hard with me, and I am almost bankrupt."

Licinius dashed the dagger across his face, causing the blood to trickle from his withered cheek.

The poor wretch screamed with fear and pain.

"Dog, you shall befool me no longer," growled Licinius; "your gold is here, and I will have it or take your life."

"Robber, Barabbas! Would you murder me?" shrieked the Jew, "help! Aaron, Shadrach, help!"

Licinius clubbed his fist and smote the wretched old man to the floor, where he lay stunned, bleeding, and quivering in mortal fear.

Licinius stamped his foot.

Caipor and the other two slaves rushed in.

"Quick," said Licinius, "there is a rope in yon corner, gag and bind this wretch to the chair."

The slaves instantly seized the trembling Jew and dragged him to his feet.

The next instant they had him tightly secured. His mouth gagged by a piece of the rope, his arms and legs lashed to the chair.

"Marcus, draw your sword, and when I give the word, run him through the heart."

The sullen ruffian thus addressed, appeared ready and willing enough to perform his brutal office.

Clutching the miserable victim by the shoulder, he levelled the dagger at his breast.

"Now to ransack the house," cried Licinius. "If I find not what I seek, I will set the place on fire."

"His keys, my lord," suggested Caipor; "had we not better secure them?"

"A good thought," said Licinius; "search his clothes, Marcus."

The Jew struggled and moaned, but resistance was altogether useless.

They tore his rags and soon discovered a bunch of keys attached to his girdle, also a very small key of the most complicated make, which was hung round his neck by a gold chain.

Upon being robbed of this the Jew foamed like a madman, and as though, for the moment, endued with superhuman strength, he released one of his arms, and tried to drag himself after Licinius.

But Marcus dashed him to the ground and set his foot upon him, threatening to kill him if he made the slightest movement.

Licinius, with Caipor, proceeded to examine every part of the room.

For a long while their search was unproductive of results.

There were a few amphoræ and other earthenware vessels ranged upon shelves, but these were found to contain nothing but a few preserved dates, dried herbs, or thin cheap wine.

They rummaged every hole and corner but found no signs of money or indeed of anything valuable.

Suddenly Caipor came hurrying to his master, looking flushed and excited.

"My lord," he said, "while examining yon dark recess I found an iron ring-bolt fixed in the pavement. It may be that the treasure is concealed beneath the floor."

"That we will soon ascertain," said Licinius.

They repaired to the spot indicated by Caipor, and found the iron ring as he had described it.

"Lend a hand, Caipor," said Licinius.

They tugged hard at the ring, and presently the square slab of stone to which it was attached loosened and they drew it up.

It swung back like the hatch of a trap door, and disclosed a square black pit like a grave.

"Look, my lord, there is something below," said Caipor.

"Yes, by Plutus, it is a kind of chest or coffer. Let us get it forth."

Calling all hands to his assistance Licinius sprang into the hole.

By dint of great exertion the robbers got the heavy box on the floor above.

They gathered round it, panting and breathless.

"The key," said Licinius.

The small key that had been taken from the Jew's neck was produced by Caipor.

Licinius snatched it eagerly.

He fitted it to the lock and in an instant the lid sprang open.

The coffer was stuffed full of treasure, which in the aggregate must have been of immense value.

Not only was there a large number of fat money bags, but between them were packed gold and silver goblets and platters, with rings, bracelets, necklaces, and every kind of ornament, all sparkling with the finest gems.

"Great Mercury, thou patron of adventures, I thank thee!" exclaimed Licinius. "Never was a gift more timely. Quick, my lads, take as much as you can stagger under, and let us begone."

At that moment he heard a faint groan, and felt a clutch as by a skeleton hand upon his shoulder.

He started, and turned to find himself confronted by the Jew.

The poor old man, driven to a pitch of madness at seeing himself deprived of his beloved gold, struggled so hard with his bonds that he succeeded in bursting them.

Now it chanced that Marcus, when called away from his prisoner to assist in unearthing the treasure had thrown his sword upon the floor.

The Jew snatched it up, and creeping behind Licinius was about to make a vengeful thrust.

He was not quick enough, however, for Licinius feeling his hand upon him, turned round and seized him by the throat.

"Dog of a Jew, thus I repay your insults," he shouted.

He plunged his dagger into the old man's breast.

The Jew tossed his arms into the air, staggered forwards, and fell headlong into the yawning pit where he had kept his treasure.

Licinius sheathed his dagger.

"This is well," said he. "The griping old miser has found a fitting grave. Replace the stone and leave him to rot; dead men tell no tales."

"What is that, my lord?" said Caipor, laying his finger on his lip, and listening intently. "I heard a shouting in the street."

The sound of footsteps was now heard approaching the house.

"'Tis the tramp of soldiers," said Licinius. "We are betrayed."

"The doors are strong, my lord, and will not easily yield," rejoined Caipor. "Perhaps we may find some outlet by which we may escape."

"We must attempt it," replied Licinius. "But we will not go empty-handed."

There was now a loud and continuous knocking, and some one shouting in loud stern tones for admission.

Licinius started and turned pale.

"I should know that voice," he said. "It is the tribune, Honorius."

"Let us fly, my lord," urged Caipor. "If we can get aboard ship all will be well."

"If my hour is come I shall be prepared to meet it," said Licinius, gloomily. "But never will I be taken alive."

He seized some of the money bags, and placed them in his bosom, and made his slaves do the same.

Caipor led the way to the back of the house.

They passed through several large but squalid courts and halls, and at last reached a small garden, overgrown with weeds and brambles, and surrounded by a high wall.

On the side opposite to the house was a little iron-bound door.

They had not forgotten to bring with them the bunch of keys stolen from the murdered Jew.

Among them one was found that opened the door.

Upon passing through this outlet they found themselves standing at the top of a flight of three or four slimy steps, leading down to the edge of the river Tiber.

"Look, my lord!" cried Caipor, in delight. "What could be more fortunate? There is a boat moored at the foot of the steps, let us push out into the midst of the river, and make for the vessel in which we are to embark."

"But can you distinguish her among such a forest of masts?" asked Licinius.

"I can, my lord, by the name painted on her prow, she is called the Centaur."

"To sea then!" cried Licinius. "We shall yet laugh at our baffled foes."

They got into the boat.

Licinius placed himself in the stern sheets, while his three slaves unshipped the oars and pushed off.

The rowers bending to their long sweeps, the little craft shot through the gliding waters.

They soon passed the navalia or docks, with their forests of foreign shipping, the arsenal, the pharos or lighthouse, and other such buildings.

Presently they were riding lightly on the roughening billows of the open sea.

By the direction of Caipor they now pulled towards a galley which lay close inshore, and were soon alongside her.

The sailors on deck challenged the boat.

Caipor responded to the call, and the party were at once permitted to come aboard.

At the very moment that the fugitives had reached the boat, the door of the house came thundering down, and Honorius, with Ventidius and the soldiers of the Prætorian guard, came rushing in.

They entered the room in which Melchior had met his death.

"They have escaped!" cried Ventidius; "see, the furniture has been overthrown, and there is every sign that a struggle has taken place."

"True, and here is blood upon the pavement," rejoined Honorius. "Murder has been done."

"Where is the Jew?" asked Ventidius.

But no one could make answer.

They little suspected that his corpse was lying close under their feet.

"What knave was that who reported that Licinius was about to embark in a vessel bound for Britain?" asked Honorius.

"One of his own slaves whom we caught at the tavern where his master halted," returned a centurion, stepping forward. He said the ship was named the Centaur."

"We will board the first trireme we find in the port, and go in chase of her," said Honorius

"Stay till we have made further search, illustrious," rejoined the lanista; "there is still a chance of finding them hiding in the house."

"No, they are gone."

"Perhaps they have taken to the river—it flows at the back of the garden," suggested the centurion.

"It must be so," returned Honorius; "let us hasten to the port."

They hurried from the house.

The whole of the Jewish community who thronged that quarter—men, women, and children—were gathered in the street, to watch the movements of the dreaded Roman military.

When they learned that Melchior had disappeared,

and that there was reason to fear that he had been murdered, they rent their garments, uttered howls of rage and execration, and rushed into the house to look for him.

Meanwhile Honorius and his party made their way to the docks.

It was not long before they were all embarked on board a large war-galley and ready to put to sea.

Among the Romans ships of war were called naves longæ, because they were of a longer shape than ships of burden, which were more round and deep.

The ships of war were driven chiefly by oars, the ships of burden by sails.

The war-ships were variously named from their oars or banks of oars.

Those which had two rows or tiers were called biremes; three, triremes; and so on.

Each ship had its own peculiar name inscribed or painted on the prow—thus, Scylla, Centaurus, and so on—called its sign, and there was an image of its tutelary god at the stern, whence that part of the ship was considered sacred.

The ship of the commander of a fleet was distinguished by a red flag and a light.

The prows of such vessels were armed with a sharp beak, which usually had three teeth or points, and this beak was covered with brass.

Ships, when about to engage, had towers erected on them, whence stones and other missiles were discharged from engines.

Honorius and his men stood on the deck, eagerly watching for the vessel they were in pursuit of.

At length the pilot pointed to a large sail bearing out to sea, and declared it to be the Centaur.

An exciting chase ensued.

CHAPTER L.

THE FATE OF LICINIUS.

THE good ship the Centaur did her best to escape the trireme that pursued her. Her broad sail was set, and the rowers manned the tiers and tugged their hardest at the long sweeps, whose blades flashed through the green surging billows.

It was from no regard to his passenger that the master of the Centaur made such a supreme effort to save himself from being overhauled by the war-like galley.

He would have had no scruples in giving up Licinius and his attendants to their enemies, but for this reason: he knew well enough that even by doing so he could not escape the consequence of having taken them aboard.

So rapacious and tyrannical, in those days, were all in authority that they never let slip a chance of plunder.

The poor merchant and ship's master would have been accused of harbouring a traitor and rebel proscribed by the senate.

In such a case, even if he had escaped a capital sentence, he might expect to be sold into slavery, or at the best to suffer a long imprisonment, and be mulcted in a fine that would have utterly ruined him.

Neither could he enjoy the questionable satisfaction of throwing his fatal supercargo overboard.

Licinius and his men looked so fierce and determined, and were so well armed, that the united crew were afraid to attack them.

The captain glanced at them with threatening looks, but dared not advance one step to assail them.

But he vented his spleen by cursing his stars, and blaming himself for his folly in ever having taken them aboard.

"By the belt of Orion! I had my suspicions when I first saw that smock-faced boy," he said, addressing the pilot, and at the same time darting a vengeful look at Caipor; "but I was tempted by his gold, and now I am ruined! Like the dog in the fable, I have lost the substance for the shadow."

"'Twas your own fault," growled the surly old sea-dog. "What did the augur tell you? That the day you chose for hoisting sail was unpropitious, and that your voyage would be attended by disasters."

Before a ship set out to sea, prayers were made and victims sacrificed.

The auspices were consulted, and if any unlucky omen happened, as a person sneezing on the left, or swallows alighting on the ships, the voyage was suspended.

The mariners, when they set sail or reached the harbour, decked the stern with garlands.

"Keep a sharp eye upon the master-mariner," Licinius said to Caipor; "he means mischief."

"I think, my lord, that though these fellows may have the will they lack the courage to harm us," replied the youth. "Our danger lies yonder."

"Aye, true, my Caipor," answered the patrician, gloomily; "and it draws nearer every moment."

Such was the fact.

The war-galley, by reason of its superior appliances, its more numerous and more skilful oarsmen, was steadily gaining upon the merchant barque.

Straining every muscle the galley's well-trained rowers pulled strongly and swiftly, and made their long heavy craft fly over the waves as though she were a light skiff.

"The wind freshens," said Caipor, "and our crew are doing their best to keep out to sea. Had I my way I would drive the vessel ashore though she went to splinters. Could we set foot on land we might yet find some chance of escape."

"It would be useless to tender such advice," replied Licinius. "The dogs think only of their ship and cargo, and would gladly fling us into the sea if they dared."

The galley was now within bow-shot of the merchant vessel.

The doomed fugitives could discern the excited faces of the officers and soldiers clustered together on the high stern and on the forecastle.

"All is over!" muttered the patrician. "Narcissus has his revenge—all that remains now is to meet my fate as becomes a Roman."

There came the blast of a trumpet, and Licinius and his men watched with anxious interest the movements of the gubernator.

This was the person who steered the galley. He was sometimes called magister—the master—or rector.

He sat at the helm, on the top of the stern, dressed in a particular manner, and gave orders about spreading and contracting the sails, plying or checking the oars.

It was his part to know the signs of the weather, to be acquainted with ports and places, and particularly to observe the wind and stars.

As the ancients knew not the use of the compass, they were directed in their voyages, chiefly by the stars in the night time, and in the daytime by coasts and islands which they knew.

In the Mediterranean, to which their navigation was chiefly confined, they could not be long out of sight of land.

When overtaken by a storm, the usual method was to run their ships ashore, and when the danger was over, to set them afloat again by the strength of arms and levers.

In the ocean they only cruised along the coasts.

But now another and sterner blast of the trumpet caused the terrified crew of the Centaur to cease rowing, for they knew full well that it was the last summons for them to "heave-to" an order which, if disobeyed, would have entailed their immediate destruction, for, without remorse, the hostile galley would have swept off their oars or run them down with its iron beak.

"Furl the sails!" shouted the master of the vessel, half mad with fright. "Seize those rascals who have brought this ruin upon us."

The first order was more easily obeyed than the second.

The men ceased rowing, the sails were hauled round, and the ship hove to.

But even this act of surrender came too late for the unlucky owner and captain of the ship.

A flight of arrows whistled through the air, and scourged the deck; the captain received one of the winged shafts full in the breast.

He uttered a shriek of agony, sprang upon the bulkwards, plunged into the sea, and instantly sank beneath the waves, and was seen no more.

Several of the mariners were wounded.

The faithful henchman of Licinius sank upon the deck, an arrow quivering in his shoulder.

With a cry of rage and compassion, Licinius stooped and raised the youth in his arms.

"Caipor! my poor boy," he murmured, "you are hurt."

The devoted young slave raised his eyes to his master's face, and smiled faintly.

"It is nothing, my lord," he gasped, trying to suppress the acute pain he was suffering. "But do not draw the arrow, the gush of blood might weaken me, and ere I die I would fain strike one blow in your defence."

The galley was now lying close under the bows of the huge vessel.

With a loud shout the Prætorians came swarming over the decks, their swords and spears flashing in the sunlight.

The crew made but a poor defence.

Some stood paralysed, others shrieked for mercy, while a few, a very few, made some show of resistance, but only to be cut down by the trenchant blades of the veteran warriors.

Foremost and most furious of the attacking party was Ventidius, the lanista.

His quick eye at once singled out Licinius, and with a cry of exultation he dashed towards him.

The devoted Caipor flung himself before his lord and interposed his body to receive the thrust aimed at Licinius by the outraged father.

In an instant Ventidius drew back his sword.

"Vah! you are a mere boy, and wounded too," he growled. "Stand out of my way and let me reach your villain master, who sought to rob me of my child."

Caipor clung to him frantically. It was in vain—the powerful gladiator hurled him off.

He reeled, stumbled, and fell upon the deck.

The stern Prætorian who followed close behind Ventidius showed the poor lad but scant mercy, for while he lay writhing the armed ruffian drove a spear through his faithful heart.

"A prize! 'tis Licinius,—down with the traitor!" was the general cry.

"Hold, I command you," shouted Honorius. "Take him alive."

But Licinius, the skilled swordsman, was not to be so easily mastered.

Striking down his assailants right and left he attacked Ventidius, who encountered him with equal ferocity and determination.

They thrust and parried with such lightning swiftness and matchless skill that neither could reach his opponent.

Presently, however, Ventidius's foot slipped on the swaying deck.

In an instant Licinius was upon him, and shortening his sword, made a vengeful thrust at his breast.

Ventidius warded it with his left arm, which was cut to the bone.

Then swift as thought the gladiator sprang upon the patrician, drove his blade to the haft into his breast, and, whirling him up in the air as lightly as a bison would toss a wolf, threw him over the bulwarks into the galley that lay alongside.

The crew of the luckless vessel were soon overpowered, and indeed the resistance they offered was very slight and only exerted from fear and desperation.

Then the insubordinate spirit of the Prætorians displayed itself.

They searched every part of the ship, and laid hands upon everything valuable that came within their reach.

It was only respect for a veteran officer so much respected as Honorius that restrained them from committing further excesses.

The poor seamen were bound and taken into custody by the Prætorians.

The Centaur was re-manned by a detachment from the galley, under orders to take her to Ostia.

Honorius looked around before leaving the ill-fated vessel.

"Where is Licinius?" he asked. "Have you secured him?"

Grimly smiled the old gladiator as he pointed to the gashed and bleeding corpse of the patrician, that lay drooping over the bulwarks of the galley.

"He is there!" said Ventidius.

"Slain! and against my orders?" retorted Honorius, with a frown; "tell me by whom?"

"By me," replied Ventidius. "None had more right than I to be his executioner."

The tribune laughed and shrugged his shoulders.

"Well, my friend, we will not dispute about such a trifle," he answered. "He was of noble blood, and he died in fair fight, and I'll warrant he fought bravely, for to give him his due, Licinius was no coward."

"Vah! 'twas a stupid affair," returned the lanista. "He was overmatched, and there was no chance for fair sword play. Had we been matched to fight in the arena, we might have shown some sport. But then, my fighting days are over."

"It would not seem so, to judge by your recent performance," answered the tribune, smiling.

Then his manner became grave.

"Was it wise of you, Ventidius," he asked "to leave your daughter as you did, to come on this quest?"

"What do you mean?" asked the lanista, starting.

"That she is in the hands of Nero."

"Of Nero! The gods forbid!" replied Ventidius. "Did not Agrippina promise her protection?"

"Aye—the she wolf promised as much to the lamb that she lured to her lair. 'I'll be a mother to you,' quoth she."

Ventidius staggered back like one struck by lightning.

"Gods! how could I have been so blind?" he exclaimed. "What is this you tell me?"

"I will tell you nothing until we get ashore. Your daughter will be conveyed to Cæsar's palace, but then all may go well; at least, she is not without one protector, shrewd as he is valiant."

"And who is he?"

"Caractacus."

CHAPTER LI.

HOW CARACTACUS SAVED VIRGINIA.

"BUT why do we linger here so long, my Caractacus? Why do you not fly at once from this accursed place?"

"Hist, sweet Virginia!" indeed you must not speak a word; a breath may betray us."

"Footsteps!—hark!"

"'Tis the night-guard going its rounds. Stand close, and pray be silent."

"I will—forgive me, dear Caractacus."

Our hero and the fair Roman were standing beneath the shadow of the wall of the garden of the palace of Cæsar—at a spot where some thickly-planted oaks screened them from view.

The Briton had his arms clasped tight around Virginia's waist, while she leaned confidingly upon his bosom, and clung to him trembling exceedingly.

The night sky was overcast with driving clouds, through which the moon shone fitfully at long intervals.

The wind was blowing freshly through the tree-tops, which made a loud rustling noise as they bowed together.

And now a steady measured tramp was heard, and through the dewy leaves lanterns and torches were seen shining, lighting up with their flare and glimmer the spear points, the golden armour, and the crimson crests of the Prætorians.

Two officers in command of the troop walked beside the file of warriors, and appeared to be seriously engaged in a whispered conversation.

Suddenly one of them stopped in his walk, and turned his head.

"Halt!" he commanded in a stern but low voice. The glittering rank came to a sudden standstill, as though one man.

"Why have you called a halt, centurion?" asked one of the officers of the other, in a tone of surprise.

"I thought I heard a slight rustling among the trees."

The centurion, detaching four of the men, and holding a lantern in one hand, and a drawn sword in the other, advanced into the grove where Caractacus and Virginia were hiding.

"Who goes there?" he demanded.

Of course he received no reply.

There was a long pause.

The centurion advanced a few paces further into the grove and repeated his summons.

Still no answer.

"I could have sworn I heard a voice," he said.

"It was but the wind soughing through the trees, or perhaps the cry of some bird, startled from its roost by the light of the torches," suggested the other.

"It may be so," said the centurion.

"There can be no doubt of it—these glades by night are as voiceful as the groves of Dodona,' replied the centurion.

At Dodona, in Epirus, the responses of the oracle were delivered by mysterious voices, sounding from the sacred oaks and beeches.

The soldiers remained listening a little while longer.

"All's well," said the centurion; "it was a false alarm."

Then he gave the word.

"March! Forward!"

Tramp, tramp, tramp.

The sound of the retreating footsteps gradually died away in the distance, and all was still but the murmuring and sighing of the night breeze.

Caractacus and Virginia stole out from their covert, and with hurried steps moved along a broad path till they came to a flight of marble steps, which they descended.

At the bottom of these stairs there was a sort of grotto, overhung with ivy, and furnished with seats, used as a summer-house.

Caractacus led Virginia into this small building.

"Stay here, beloved," he said; "I will return upon the instant."

"O, must you leave me?" she said, in a tremor.

"I go to seek Philomenes," replied our hero; "he is near at hand."

"But you will not leave me long in this lonesome place?" pleaded Virginia; "I was not wont to be so timorous, but I confess that recent events have shaken my nerves, and I am a very coward in the dark."

"Darkness and light are as one to Him in whose charge I leave you, dear Virginia."

"But you will return soon—very soon."

"Doubt me not, ere you can repeat that brief but hallowed prayer we learned from the good Mathias, I will be with you again."

"You have restored my courage," answered Virginia; "I am fearless now."

Our hero kissed her soft hand, and left the arbour.

He hastened through the gardens till he came to a little hollow, surrounded by umbrageous trees.

It was rather deep, and sunk below the level of the ground for the sake of coolness, and formed a retreat from the ardours of the summer sun, being supplied with fountains, statues, and marble couches.

Here the Briton stopped, and after looking around, uttered a peculiar call, like the note of some nocturnal bird.

Immediately a figure appeared ascending the bank, and stood before him.

It was Philomenes, the sculptor.

"I know by your presence here, my Caractacus, that all goes well," said the Greek.

"Thanks to heaven, Virginia has escaped from the palace," was the reply.

"Where is she now?"

"Close at hand, concealed in a grotto," answered the Briton. "I thought it safest to leave her there until I had found you and made sure that you had met with no mishap."

"You did well," replied Philomenes. "And, to speak the truth, I have passed through many strange and perilous adventures this night. Just now I trembled for your safety—nay more, I thought that all was lost."

"You heard the guard that nightly patrol the palace grounds?"

"They challenged you, did they not?"

"They did, but we lay close, and so escaped their vigilance," returned our hero.

Then he added quickly—

"We are wasting time. Tell me, good Philomenes, have you taken the measures decided upon?"

"I have," was the reply. "Horses are waiting outside the grounds under charge of four trusty fellows, whom Mathias recommended as the most to be relied upon."

"And the ladder by which we are to scale the wall?"

"That and all else is in readiness."

"And should we be so fortunate as to get clear of this place, is it your intention to convey Virginia to her father's house?"

"Oh, by no means; such a course would be far too dangerous," was the reply. "I have sent for Ventidius to meet me at my villa on the Flaminian Way, and thither I propose we should betake ourselves."

During this conversation they had been walking at a rapid pace, and had reached the arbour where Virginia lay hid. Our hero's departure and return occupied a very few minutes.

Upon hearing their voices the poor girl uttered a cry of relief and joy, and came forth to meet them.

The sculptor embraced her and kissed her with fatherly tenderness.

Virginia flung her arms about his neck and burst into tears.

"Oh, Philomenes, you have saved me from a fate more dreadful than death."

Then she continued, with burning cheeks and flashing eyes—

"Not so," she said. "Though a Christian I can never forget that I am a Roman maid; my life was in my own hands."

"Think not of these troubles and dangers that are almost past. Lean upon my arm, and let us hasten on our way."

Guarded on either side by the Greek and the Briton, the fair Virginia was conducted through the gardens, until they came to a place where the wall was not quite so high as in other parts.

Here they stopped, and Caractacus, leaving Virginia to the care of Philomenes, went forward to reconnoitre.

He took up a stone and flung it over the wall.

In answer to the signal, there was a slight noise, as of some one on the outside hammering at the masonry.

The noise ceased, and our hero returned to his companions.

"How goes it?" asked Philomenes. "Did they hear your signal?"

"Yes, and answered it," said our hero. "All is quiet—all has gone well."

"Away then!" rejoined Philomenes. "The sooner we are in the saddle the better."

Caractacus now drew aside the ivy, and shook free a rope ladder, which reached from the top of the wall to the ground.

At the lower end of it were a couple of grappling hooks, which Caractacus fixed to the thick stems of a ground vine, which mantled the soil in rich luxuriance.

Having tugged at it to see that it was properly secured, our hero, by its aid, mounted to the top of the wall.

Then he held down his hand to assist Virginia to mount the ladder.

She sprang lightly up, Philomenes standing below with watchful eyes, and outspread arms ready to catch her if she made a slip.

But Virginia was lissom and agile, and reached the top of the ladder without the least difficulty.

On the outer side another ladder was fixed, which Caractacus descended with Virginia, whom he brought safe to the ground.

Philomenes then followed, and having removed the ladders, rejoined his companions.

And now they found a party of four or five mounted men, with two led horses awaiting them.

A fine-looking young man, tall, broad-shouldered, and of determined countenance, approached them.

To judge by his authoritative manner, and the deference shown him by the rest, he seemed to be the leader.

"You have kept a faithful watch, Marcianus," said the sculptor. "Is the road clear?"

"The road is clear, Philomenes," replied Marcianus. "Not a mouse stirring; the danger threatens not from without but from within."

Virginia clung to Caractacus, while Philomenes looked alarmed.

"What cause have you to think so?" he asked.

"While we awaited your coming I climbed yonder tall tree," said Marcianus. "From my elevated position I could command a wide view of the palace and its gardens. A few moments before Caractacus gave the signal I beheld a light flash from one of the watch-towers—it was answered from another tower by a similar light; then, along the highest of the terraces I saw a number of soldiers rushing along with torches in their hands, as though in pursuit of some fugitive."

"My escape is already discovered!" gasped Virginia. "Oh, let us hasten our flight!"

Even while she spoke a roar of voices came from a distant part of the gardens, and then a stern signal-note on the trumpet.

"They have struck the trail," said Caractacus

"To horse at once!" cried Philomenes.

The led horses were then brought up.

Philomenes mounted one of them, while Caractacus vaulted upon the other, and lifted Virginia to the croup before him.

He felt her soft hand upon his shoulder, and the light touch filled him with the fire and courage of the Nemæan lion.

"Off, my brothers!" he shouted. "Ride for your lives."

The cavalcade dashed off with the speed of the whirlwind, and clattered along the broad Flaminian Way, striking sparks from their flying hoofs.

It was not until they had put a distance of three miles between them and the palace that they slackened their speed, but still kept up a good pace.

Philomenes and Caractacus rode side by side.

"I have yet to learn how you first discovered in what part of yon stately labyrinth the fair Virginia was held in durance," said Caractacus.

"I used every art to find out that secret, but failed. You must understand that upon my return to Rome I received a hint from Honorius, and did not venture my life by going back to the palace. Still, I had friends among the Prætorian guard, and the dying gift of that unhappy man, Narcissus, enabled me to bribe many of the slaves of the imperial household, but none of them possessed the secret which they would have gladly sold at a less price than I offered."

"The credit belonged to Mathias rather than to me," Philomenes answered; "but perhaps Virginia herself, if she will give some account of what befell her after her return from Præneste, can render the affair more comprehensible."

"I will do so in as few words as possible," answered Virginia. "You will remember that after the suicide of Narcissus, and the flight of Licinius, the Empress Agrippina took me under her protection, and that I accompanied her and her train to Rome. Upon reaching the city I expressed a wish to return to my father's house."

"And did she refuse a request so proper and so natural?" asked Philomenes.

"Why, as to that, her manner was most kind and gracious," answered Virginia. "She said she could not part with me so soon, and added that she would have me near her till my father came back with the rest who had gone in pursuit of Licinius"

"Of course you had no alternative but submission," said Philomenes.

"None whatever," she answered; "I was well treated, pampered with the richest dainties, attired in the most costly raiment, and attended upon by a legion of slaves."

"But did the ladies of the court show no signs of envy and spitefulness at seeing you thus suddenly elevated to imperial favour?'

"No," replied Virginia; "at least, not at first. It might be that they saw how loathsome to me was all this empty splendour, how I pined for home and freedom, and the caresses of my dear parents. I know not, but this is certain, it was the empress's will that they should make much of me, and so they did, and never seemed to grow weary of devising fresh amusements to beguile me from my sad thoughts."

"Aye, they mingled the poison with honey," said Philomenes, "that you might be more easily persuaded to swallow the dose."

"One day," continued Virginia, "I was sent for to attend upon the empress in a remote part of the palace, but I found that I had been deceived. I was ushered into a splendid apartment, the door was closed upon me, and I found myself face to face, not with the empress, but with Nero."

Caractacus started and quivered with rage.

"The treacherous monster!" he exclaimed; "Woe to the world if ever he wears the purple!"

"Patience, Caractacus," said Philomenes; "let us hear the rest."

"Had not heaven sent some guardian angel to defend me, I know not how I should have passed through that frightful ordeal so boldly and disdainfully," said Virginia, shuddering. "I felt myself inspired by a spirit of scorn and defiance that I can only ascribe to divine support. Nero flung himself at my feet, he raved of my beauty, his adoration—— let it pass. When he found me deaf to his suit, he changed his tone, and swore his love was honourable, and that whenever he swayed the sceptre he would share his empire with me, that he would lose all the world for my sake even as did Antony for Cleopatra."

"He will never lose the world for 'love's sake,' be assured," rejoined Philomenes, grimly.

"Woman is so weak, her only weapon in such a case is dissimulation; Heaven forgive me if I did wrong in dissembling my hatred and abhorrence."

"You did right," said Philomenes. "By such a course you gained time, and that was something.'

"Though still maintaining a cold and scornful demeanour, I pretended to be rather dazzled by his splendid proffer, and to yield just a little. I told him that I was agitated, and must have time to collect my thoughts, and to consider what answer I ought to make. I asked him to grant me three days, at the end of which time I would see him again. He swore that my wish to him was law, and that he had no other desire than to please me, and so he left me, his face glowing with triumph."

"Poor child, I can well imagine your feelings when left in your loneliness, to realise your helpless, and ~s it might seem hopeless position."

"Not hopeless, good Philomenes," replied the ~man maiden. "I had one last refuge."

"Where and in what?"

"Death, the friend, and the grave, the asylum of all the unfortunate," she answered calmly. "I had found a dagger, which I kept in my bosom, and cherished next to my eternal salvation. But that interview was for the moment too overpowering. No sooner had this insulter left the apartment than I fell into a dead swoon, and recovered only to find myself lying exhausted on a sick bed. They told me I had been delirious for three days. Mathias, that good and holy man, was by my side to heal and comfort me."

"But Nero, what of him?"

"I afterwards learned that when he heard of my condition he laughed, and said that the prospect of becoming an empress had turned my foolish brain, but that I should do well enough by-and-bye—that I was as fair as Helen, and he hoped as frail."

"Gods, do you hear this?" gasped Caractacus. "I will cut his throat in the capitol!"

"I saw what I had done, and, even in my delirium, to hold him at bay, 'to gain time,' as Philomenes so justly puts it (time! that respite craved for by the wretch condemned to the scaffold), I had prated about crowns and robes, and courtiers, and they thought me in earnest—the fools!" continued Virginia, passionately. "No doubt I was mad, but there was a cunning in my madness which brought me safe through!"

"Exult, Caractacus!" whispered Philomenes to the Briton. "This noble creature loves you—her heart is yours."

Caractacus hugged Virginia to his bosom as he urged on his steed in their wild flight.

"As soon as I recovered sufficient strength and calmness to be allowed to talk," she went on, "I consulted with Mathias as to the means of escape; he promised he would do his utmost to deliver me. But here, I will leave the sequel to be told by Philomenes."

"It came about in this way," replied the Greek; Mathias informed me that Virginia was in the power of Nero."

"And did you not report this to my father?" asked our heroine, sharply.

"We did not, for after serious consultation we determined to keep Ventidius in ignorance of our intentions," replied Philomenes. "If you would know why, because we could not trust him."

"Not trust my father!"

"No! he was too hot-headed—too much distracted by grief at your loss to be a match for the wily tyrants and sycophants by whom you were surrounded," explained Philomenes. "He had complained to Cæsar, but had been assured that you had fled the court, and were not to be found. Let me speak out! Caractacus had disappeared about that time."

"And they supposed —," laughed Virginia, placing her arms confidingly round her lover's neck. "But then my father knows me, and he knows Caractacus."

"His trust never failed; but he thought that our champion of the arena had been murdered, and that you had been spirited away," answered Philo-

"And how did you proceed?" asked Caractacus "For all I know is, that you took me into your confederacy merely to do the fighting."

"Which is all you are fit for."

"Thanks for such praise, as I consider it, for I hate these wiles of subtlety—but as for the fighting there has been none yet."

"Thank me for that also," replied Philomenes; "I went a better way to work."

"Claudius is altering, enlarging, and adorning his palace, and I am one of the numerous architects who carry on the work. Learning from Mathias the exact position of the chamber in which Virginia was imprisoned, I contrived to get an opening made by the masons through the thickness of the wall, and thus opened a communication with the fair captive. By the aid of our gallant Briton, and these our worthy brothers in the faith, we have succeeded in effecting her rescue. But enough! We will discourse more fully on these matters when we reach my house."

"It is well," said Caractacus. "We must mend our pace, for the Prætorians have fleet horses, and may overtake us if we do not spur hard."

They rode forwards at increased speed, the gloomy landscape and the dark weird trees hurrying past them like a dream.

The morn was palely breaking in the east when the weary and over-excited fugitives reached the small but tasteful villa of Philomenes.

It lay in the midst of pretty gardens and orchards, a little way from the Flaminian Way.

As they approached the house the doors were joyously thrown open by the servants of Philomenes, who was honoured and beloved by every member of his household.

Philomenes invited Marcianus and the rest of the good fellows who had done such excellent service in the cause of Virginia, to remain for some hours under his hospitable roof, to partake of food and wine and enjoy a few hours' rest before dispersing to their several homes.

But Marcianus respectfully declined the invitation.

"Thanks, good Philomenes; gladly would we take some repose, but we have business in hand that will not brook delay," replied Marcianus. "Our pagan enemies are incensed against us by the slanders of their false priests, and the church is in great danger. We must hasten at once to the catacombs, and take counsel with the elders as to the best means of ensuring our safety."

"You shall not go until you have drunk one parting cup," said Philomenes. "Wine, there—an amphora of my best Falernian."

The slaves bustled about to execute their master's orders.

The wine was brought.

The Christian band, without dismounting, took the wine-cups and pledged the fair Roman maid, for whose sake they had run such a terrible risk.

The murmur ran round—

"Health and blessings to our dear sister, Virginia."

Then, having shaken hands with Philomenes, they prepared to start.

"One moment, my brother," said Caractacus, laying his hand on the leader's rein. "Let our people keep strict watch and ward. For myself inform the good Mathias that I will spend the day haunting the baths, the marts, and fora, to pick up what intelligence I may regarding the designs and movements of our adversaries."

"Do so, my valiant brother," answered Marcianus. "When may we expect to see you amongst us?"

"An hour after sunset," said our hero. "Till then farewell!"

"Peace be with you," replied Marcianus, waving his hand.

The little troop of horsemen dashed off in the direction of the Pontine marshes, and were soon

"VIRGINIA!" EXCLAIMED CARACTACUS, IN A TONE OF WRATH AND ANGUISH; "HOW CAME SHE HITHER?"

No. 10.

lost to view. Philomenes then took Virginia by the hand and led her into the house.

She was received on the threshold by Glauce, once the slave but now the wife of Philomenes, for he had lately married his beautiful country-woman.

With graceful courtesy and womanly gentleness, Glauce conducted Virginia into the atrium, which, in its arrangement and decoration, did credit to the owner's taste as a sculptor and architect.

But Virginia was possessed by one absorbing thought.

She looked eagerly around, and asked—

"Where is my father?"

A curtain was roughly drawn aside, Ventidius sprang into the hall, and in an instant Virginia was locked in his arms.

When the first raptures of the meeting were over, and some degree of calmness restored, Philomenes asked the lanista whither he intended to take his daughter.

"Whither? Where else but to Rome?" replied Ventidius. "Let me have her once safe within my walls, and not all the power of Cæsar shall drag her from me again."

"But you are powerless against his might."

"Not so powerless as you may suppose, my friend," replied Ventidius. "I have a thousand brave lads of the blade and buckler at my beck and call, and, if need be, could raise an insurrection in the city, and like a second Virginius, drive a debauched tyrant from the throne."

"Hush, man! cease this mad talk," said Philomenes, impatiently. "Be reasonable if you can—it is not safe to take her back to Rome."

Ventidius ground his teeth in passionate anger, but answered in sullen resignation—

"Woe the while! I suppose we Roman citizen, once so free and proud, must bear the yoke our tyrants impose upon us," he said. "But it galls me to the quick. Well, I will say no more, but leave this business to your wise discretion."

"Have you no place whither you could send your daughter, and keep her in concealment until better days?" asked Philomenes.

"Yes, I might send her to my country farm among the Appenines," replied Ventidius.

"That will not do, for Nero's emissaries would seek her there."

"I will appeal to Claudius."

"Place not your trust in him," rejoined the sculptor. "He has ruined his health, and enfeebled his mind by excesses; his days are numbered, and Nero will soon replace him on the throne."

"The gods forbid! we have tyrants enough already," growled Ventidius. "But what do you advise?"

"Most gladly would I offer an asylum in my house to the fair Virginia, but here she would not be safe," replied Philomenes. "Have you no friend whom you could trust, and under whose charge you might place her, until the storm has blown over—some one who lives at a good distance from Rome?"

"What say you to honest Pandion the boxer?" asked Ventidius. "He is trusty, and loves me and mine; he would accept the charge, I know."

"Where dwells he now?"

"Since he won the rudis in the last great games, and retired upon his laurels, he has taken a little farm near Baiæ, on the sea-coast," said Ventidius. "Thither I might send Virginia; she would receive the warmest welcome, and would be under the protection of friends who have known her from her childhood."

"You could not have made a happier selection," rejoined Caractacus. "But what says the fair Virginia, herself?"

"Dispose of me as you will, my father," she replied. "'Tis for you to command, for me to obey, but in this case you have anticipated my wishes. There is no one with whom I would more gladly

take shelter than with the brave and faithful Pandion."

"Why, then so it shall be decided," said Ventidius. "I will take you thither this day."

"Not so, Ventidius; your daughter requires rest, and must remain here till nightfall. It will be safer for you to travel after dark."

Glauce now announced that a repast awaited the guests in the triclinium, whither she invited them to follow.

"Come, my hero, why do you stand there looking so moody and downcast?" said Philomenes. "Partake of such humble fare as I can offer; refresh yourself with a cup or two of wine, and you will be the better prepared for the cares and toils of the day."

"Pardon me, my worthy host," returned our hero, "I must to Rome. I will not break my fast until I have reached the house of one of our people, from whom I expect tidings of the greatest import."

"But you will return to-night?"

Caractacus shook his head.

"Heaven alone can tell whether we shall meet again," he said, lowering his voice. "The ædiles have planned a raid against the Christians. I must give them warning of what is intended."

"Go, my Caractacus," replied Philomenes, "I will not bid you stay. You are engaged in a noble cause. I too will share your perils—I will meet you to-night in the catacombs."

Caractacus took an affectionate farewell of Virginia, and tore himself away.

CHAPTER LII.

THE CHRISTIAN MARTYR.

THE horrible persecutions of the Christians during the reigns of Claudius and Nero would seem incredible were they not attested by contemporary and trustworthy witnesses.

What follows is from Tacitus, and the force and value of his statements is so much greater than any imaginary description we could supply that we give it place. Of course the historian wrote from a heathen point of view, and he execrates the Christians from ignorance and prejudice.

He is speaking of the great fire at Rome, which, there is little doubt, Nero was the cause of.

He tells us that the infamy of that horrible transaction still adhered to Nero.

To suppress, if possible, this common rumour, Nero procured others to be accused and punished with exquisite tortures—a race of men detested for their evil (?) practices, who were commonly known by the name of Christians.

The author of this sect, so Tacitus continues, was Christus, who in the reign of Tiberius was punished with death as a criminal by Pontius Pilate.

At first those only were apprehended who confessed themselves of this sect, afterwards a vast multitude, discovered by them, all of whom were condemned, not so much for burning the city as for their enmity to mankind.

The executions were so contrived as to expose them to derision and contempt.

Some were covered over with the skins of wild beasts, that they might be torn to pieces by dogs; some were crucified, while others, having been daubed over with combustible materials, were set up as lights in the night time, and thus burned to death.

For these spectacles Nero gave his own gardens, and at the same time exhibited there the diversions of the circus, until at length these men, though really criminal and deserving punishment, began to be commiserated as people who were destroyed, not out of regard to the public welfare, but only to gratify the cruelty of one man.

Throughout our story we have endeavoured to avoid any exaggeration of the atrocities perpetrated at Rome, during the dark and evil period in which the events we are narrating took place. Indeed, if we have erred it is on the other side; but a graphic description of the state of society would be too horrible, even for the most morbid minds to contemplate.

And so we will return to Caractacus, whom we find standing pale, breathless, fearfully agitated, traversing one of the underground galleries of the catacombs.

He had entered through a low, dark doorway, to an aisle, which, divided into branches, ran in various directions, losing themselves in the gloom and darkness which enveloped objects at the distance of a few feet.

But the Briton was provided with a torch, and proceeded cautiously, though he was well acquainted with the intricate windings of the labyrinth.

The galleries were eight or ten feet high, and from four to six feet in width.

Tombs, their slabs covered with inscriptions, rose tier upon tier in endless succession.

At length Caractacus arrived at a part of the gallery so obstructed with rubbish that he was forced to crawl on his hands and knees.

Then he descended some rough and dangerous stairs, which led to a lower labyrinth of galleries and crypts, and here was a small open space at the junction of branching tunnels.

Here he found himself suddenly seized by four men, who sprang upon him from different directions.

"Stand!"

"Hold, brothers, do ye not know me?" cried our hero, as the torch dropped from his hand, and smoked, and smouldered on the floor.

"Give the word."

"Christ is risen."

"It is he!" cried Marcianus, one of the assistants. "It is our brother, Caractacus, what news—what news?"

"All is lost!" gasped our hero. "The Prætorians are at hand, nothing but flight can save you."

CHAPTER LIII.
ZABA.

NOT even the infamous Nero himself could have derived more satisfaction from the sufferings of the unhappy Christians than Zaba, the dwarf, who, in his capacity as beast-feeder, had much of the bloody work entrusted to him.

No one could have complained that he showed any want of zeal in his diabolical task; for, with a horrible ingenuity, he contrived to add fresh tortures to the dreadful deaths the wild beasts inflicted.

All the arts his long acquaintance with the savage beasts of the forest had taught him were brought into play to inflame their natural ferocity, and he seemed more than ever fiend-like when on the eve of some fresh holocaust.

"Aha, Hecate!" he growled, as he caressed the cat-like head of his pantheress. "Thy time is not yet come. I have reserved a dainty feast for thee, my beauty. Let me but once get Virginia into my power—as I shall do! Let me but once satiate my appetite, and then, Hecate, 'twill be thy turn. How I shall laugh when I hear her dainty limbs cracking in the grip of thy strong teeth and claws! And how she will plead and shriek for mercy from the despised and hated Zaba! Ha! ha! I think I hear her now!"

And the hideous monster set up a shrill eldrich laugh, which was yet more terrible to the ear than the responsive cry of Hecate.

He paused for a while, his huge yellow fangs showing in the wide grin that distended his mouth, and then he resumed.

"These Christians, these worshipers of an ass's head—how I hate them! They preach love and peace and goodwill to all mankind, while I, in the bitterness of my heart, feel naught but loathing for all who wear the semblance of human form. Even Virginia, the love I have for her is so near akin to hate that I would almost as soon give her to thy embrace, Hecate, as strain her to my bosom. But enough of this, we have work to do. More of this accursed sect of Christians die on the morrow, and I have prepared a dainty death for them. Such a death—the applause of the populace—even of Cæsar himself—the gold of my patron; and, above all, the gratification of my own passions. All, all will be gained to-morrow."

The morrow came, and with it the hour for the Christians to die.

They were there to the number of nearly a hundred. Old men, with silvered hair and beards, mothers and their daughters, youths, and even little children, so young as to be quite incapable of understanding the awful fate that awaited them.

They were quite unarmed, and many of them nearly naked—only with their bare hides could they hope to oppose the cruel fangs and claws of Zaba's furious charges.

A shout of demoniac applause went up from the audience gathered in that vast amphitheatre, as the victims approached, driven in like sheep by the guards.

But though they were victims they marched in with the air of conquerors. They were pale indeed, but their countenances were steady, and many of them even smiled. They had no fear of death in the vision of an incorruptible crown of glory that awaited them above.

"Vah!" said Zaba. "We shall see them change their tune presently. They seem now as if they were about to receive an ovation. Wait till my pets are among them, and they feel their limbs gashed and torn by sharp talons and strong teeth!"

So the Christians marched steadily on till the centre of the arena was reached, and there with one accord they knelt down and sent up a chant of praise to the Divine Founder of their sect, who Himself had not disdained to suffer more than they were about to do that day.

But they were not long allowed to continue their devotions, for at a given signal, the cages containing the wild beasts were unbarred, and with a roar, some thirty of the largest and fiercest lions and tigers, imported from the Roman colonies in Africa, and Ind, sprang out upon the sand, and rushed towards their prey.

Involuntarily the band of martyrs shrank back to back, the women and children in the centre, the men facing their savage foes, but ere yet the brutes could touch a single one, they were all checked as if by an invisible hand, and crouched down, growling and roaring terifically.

"It is magic! It is magic!" shouted the audience. "They have tamed the beasts by their arts. Send in the gladiators, and cut them to pieces."

The belief that the Christians dealt in sorcery and other magic arts was very common, indeed universal at that time, but in a moment or two the truth was discerned, for Zaba, with a hideous refinement of cruelty, had confined each of the beasts with a light chain of great strength, so that the martyrs, face to face with the savage beasts, and so close that their fœtid breath could be felt, had to endure the added horrors of suspense.

"Euge! a Zaba, a Zaba!" was now the cry. "See how the accursed Christians shrink and tremble. Ad leones! loose them now."

But Zaba was not to be baulked of his sport by any impatience on the part of the audience.

A few more moments of terrible suspense, and then a huge tiger, who was lashing its sides with its long tail, and growling and straining at the chain that held it back, was slipped from its collar, and like a young hound coursing a hare, it bounded into the midst of the group of victims, and in an instant emerged, bearing in its jaws a beautiful young girl, whom it carried as easily as does a cat a helpless mouse.

That was more than the utmost fortitude could bear. Men groaned with anguish, and struck at the monstrous brute with their bare hands, and sought to tear the prey away, but Zaba, with a howl of delight, now slipped the leashes which held the others, and the horrible work was soon completed.

In little more than a quarter of an hour the sand was strewn with the prostrate forms of that band of martyrs, while, sullen and savage, but sated, the wild beasts crushed and crunched the mangled remains of their horrible meal.

CHAPTER LIV.
CARACTACUS ESCAPES FROM ROME.

MARCIANUS drew back at the warning of Caractacus, and scowled fiercely. He was an old soldier, and his human weakness strove hard with his new faith.

"Let them come," he said. "In these subterranean galleries twenty bold fellows may hold their own against a host."

The Briton smiled.

"Mathias will not let us fight," he answered. "Religion forbids it. They who take the sword will perish with the sword."

"Why let me perish then," growled the Roman. "But I for one will die in battle; I never was made to be a martyr."

"Come, we are wasting precious time," said Caractacus. "Let us warn our people of their danger."

They hurried through the passages, and entered a chapel, where Mathias and his congregation were assembled for prayer.

Mathias stood erect, his hands clasped, his eyes raised heavenwards.

This posture in prayer was common to both Pagans and Christians, as may be seen by a reference to Virgil, a Pagan poet, as well as to Tertullian, a Christian writer.

The latter in his "Apology," says:—

"For the emperor we supplicate the true, the living, the eternal God, in whose power they are; to whom they are second, after whom first. With hands extended because harmless, with heads uncovered because not ashamed, without a prompter, because from the heart we ask long life, and every blessing for him."

"Then while we stand praying before God, let the ungulæ tear us, the crosses bear our weight, let the flames envelope us, the sword divide out throats, the beasts spring upon us, the very posture of a praying Christian—that is, with hands outstretched like a cross—is a preparation for every punishment."

Christians in the catacombs are universally represented as praying in this position, the practice of kneeling in prayer having been introduced at a later date.

No sooner had Caractacus entered the chapel than he shut the door.

"Fly; escape, while there is yet time," he exclaimed. "The Prætorians have entered the catacombs, and all is lost."

The little flock started in terror.

Wives embraced their husbands, children clung to the knees of their parents.

Mathias alone stood firm and unmoved.

"The hour has come, my children," he said, "when we are called to testify to the faith by the outpouring of our blood. Let us not shrink from such a doom, but let us remember the rich blessings promised to those who are found faithful unto death."

The congregation responded with a murmur of assent.

Every eye brightened, and a divine expression of fortitude and hope lit up every face.

The sound of approaching footsteps, mingled with shouts and the clank of armour, was now heard.

Caractacus threw his back against the door.

The soldiers had arrived, and with spears and axes attempted to cut their way in.

The Briton exerted his herculean strength to withstand them, but all in vain.

The wood splintered under the repeated strokes and thrusts of spears and axes, and our hero was thrown down.

A rabble of ruffianly soldiers dashed in.

Zaba the dwarf led them on.

The face of the little monster glared with malice.

In one hand he carried a flaming torch, in the other he flourished a long, murderous-looking knife.

He seized one of the women by the arm, and was dragging her brutally along.

Mathias interposed.

In an instant the villain plunged his knife into the good man's heart.

He fell and expired.

A shriek of horror and consternation rang around.

A man wrapped in a black cloak now entered the chapel.

He flung aside the mantle, and disclosed the fierce, sensuous features of Nero.

He turned a vindictive look upon our hero.

"Arrest that man," he said; "away with him to the dungeons of the Mamertine—he is a Nazarene, and defies the power of Cæsar."

Two of the soldiers immediately laid hands upon Caractacus.

Honorius, who was present, gave the Briton a look, which expressed a sympathy which he dared not give utterance to in words.

The soldiers closed around the Briton.

The Christians were also seized and bound.

Within an hour Caractacus was lying in chains in a stone cell of the Mamertine prison.

The Mamertine prisons still exist, on the descent of the Capitol to the Forum.

They are of great antiquity, and built, like the cloacæ, of large uncemented stones.

The founder was Ancus Martius, as we learn from Livy, who, speaking of that king, says, "He made a prison in the middle of the city overlooking the Forum."

Near the entrance were the Scalæ Gemoniæ, by which culprits were dragged to the prison, or out of it to execution.

A more horrible place for the confinement of a human being can scarcely be imagined.

There are two apartments, one above the other, to which there was no entrance except by a small aperture in the upper roof, and a similar hole in the upper floor led to the cell below. There was no staircase to either.

The upper prison is twenty-seven feet long, by twenty wide, the lower twenty by ten, the height of the former is fourteen feet, the latter seven.

These served as the state prisons.

Sallust describes the place thus—

"In the prison called Tullian, when you have descended a little there is a place on the left, sunk about twenty feet. It is surrounded by walls on all sides; and above it is a room vaulted with stone, but from uncleanliness, darkness, and a foul smell, the appearance of it is disgusting and terrific."

In this terrible place Caractacus lay in chains and gloom.

But our hero, by his frank engaging manner, had won over many friends, who exerted their best efforts to save him.

As we already know, nothing was more irksome to the free-souled Briton than confinement.

Wearily he noted the dawn, the noon, the eve of day, wearily he hoped for the hour which should consign him to his death, for to him life had become a curse and a burden too heavy to be borne.

Several days passed over in this dismal way, and the moonlight was streaming in through the grated window of his dungeon, when Caractacus heard the firm quick step of his gaoler outside his cell.

He sprang to his feet.

He had learned to know when to expect a visit from his stern morose keeper.

He wondered why the man should come at such an unusual hour.

"He is here, illustrious," said the gaoler, in his gruff tones.

"Admit me," answered a woman's voice.

The gaoler threw wide the door, and a tall stately woman entered, bearing a lamp in her hand.

It was the Empress Agrippina.

"Give me the keys," she said to the gaoler.

The man looked at her stolidly, and held out the bunch of keys with a helpless air.

Agrippina snatched them from his hand.

"Take thyself hence," she said sternly.

The fellow sullenly retired.

Then Agrippina set down her lamp in a niche of the wall and approached Caractacus.

"I am here to save you," she said, quietly; "you must fly the land and return to Britain, my brave Caractacus. Nero, my son, has sworn to have your life. What had you to do with those atheists, the Nazarenes?"

Then she moved towards the door.

"I had forgotten," she said; "the knave must be recalled to strike off your chains."

Then she added with a laugh—

"No, none but myself shall free you. Here is a key that methinks will unlock your manacles."

She took a small key from the bunch and unlocked his fetters, which fell with a clash upon the pavement.

Then she looked at him fondly, and laid her hand upon his shoulder.

"How pale you look!" she said. "You, who were champion in the arena, cannot endure the iron that eats into the flesh, that enters the very soul. Poor barbarian, I know you hate me."

"Hate you, madam?"

"And love that cream-faced wench, Virginia," continued the empress, with a laugh and a sigh. "But I exact no favour, expect no gratitude."

The Briton's cheek burnt red—he knew not what reply to make.

Agrippina took up the lamp.

"Come," she said. "Your friends await you—Ventidius and his daughter. The time may come when you will think of me with kindly remembrance."

"I am not ungrateful, madam," said our hero.

"No!" returned Agrippina. "Go to—you are a harsh and hard barbarian, but it matters not. Eros and Anteros! 'twas ever so. One loving and one beloved."

She took up the light and led the way from the dungeon.

Caractacus followed her.

In the stone corridor outside were gathered some half dozen attendants of the empress bearing torches.

They passed through the open doors of the prison.

The empress had her litter, borne by her Nubian slaves, waiting without.

"There lies your road, Caractacus," she said, clinging to his arm. "Farewell, forget me not!"

The Briton took her hand and pressed it to his lips. "Madam, farewell," he said, gravely.

The tears sprang to her eyes.

"Farewell," she said; "Virginia awaits you."

She waved her hand, and with a majestic and Juno-like air, passed on to her litter.

Love is of all passions the most selfish.

Caractacus thought of nothing but Virginia.

He was alone and a free man.

There were the blue marks of his chains around his wrists, the smell of his filthy dungeon was in his nostrils yet, and he could barely realise the situation—he was free!

Not only so, but he knew that a ship was waiting to waft him across the seas to his dear native land, where he would be a prince among his clansmen, where he would hear his native tongue, and would war against the hated Roman.

Caractacus hurried down to the banks of the Tiber.

At some water-stairs he found Ventidius, with his daughter; they were attended by a couple of sturdy gladiators.

A boat was ready to take our hero off to a large ship, that lay out in the broad river.

"Joy to thee, my lad," said Ventidius, shaking our Briton by the hand. "Freedom and life are before thee. Take these papers; they are under the hand and seal of Honorius, the tribune. Should your vessel be overhauled, they will bear you out against all opposition. I am glad to see thee clear of thy foes, yet sorry enough to part with thee."

"But I shall return," said the Briton, smiling.

He passed his arm around his sweetheart's waist.

"I leave my heart behind me," he said.

Virginia burst into tears.

"Fare thee well, Caractacus," she murmured. "The sun has gone out of the world—all will be dark with me now."

"Hope, dearest," replied the Briton, pressing her to his heart. "I shall return."

Demetrius, one of the gladiators, now came running up.

"Do not linger," he said. "There are armed men going towards the Mamertine—they are the emissaries of Nero."

But Caractacus heeded not his danger.

He was occupied by a single thought, which was to console Virginia, who seemed broken-hearted at the sudden and cruel separation.

He whispered a hundred endearments and promises of a happy return.

Ventidius grew impatient.

He tugged the Briton's arm.

"Begone, my lad," he said; "every moment's delay is perilous—get you gone."

But Caractacus was too pleasantly engaged to allow himself to be hurried.

Never before that parting moment did the Briton know how deeply, how dearly Virginia loved him.

At length he tore himself away.

He shook hands with Ventidius, and sprang into his boat.

The rowers pushed off.

Soon the light skiff was under the bows of the merchant barque.

Caractacus went aboard.

He took his station on the high stern-deck of the ship while the crew were weighing anchor.

A dark boat floated past like a shadow in the gloom of the night.

In the stern-sheets a female figure stood erect.

It was the Empress Agrippina.

CHAPTER LV.

CARACTACUS IN BRITAIN.

OUR hero, Caractacus, stood reclining upon the pine shaft, perched on a rock near the summit of a high hill that overlooked the river Isca, or Uske, in Glamorganshire.

His steadfast blue eyes were fixed upon the stream that wound like a vein of molten silver through the valley below.

The sharp mountain breeze whistled through his streaming yellow hair, and fluttered the heavy folds of his rich blue mantle, as the young prince of the Silures advanced to the perilous verge of the deep chasm.

His foot struck against a flint, which clattered and bounded down into the darkness and vacancy below

He heeded it not, but stood boldly confronting the singing blast upon the very verge.

Three eventful years had passed over his head since Caractacus had parted with his Roman friends on the banks of old Tiber.

Three hard years of toil, trial, and warfare, which in their effect had tended only to develope to mature perfection the vigour and symmetry of his manly frame, and the stern beauty of his noble countenance. He had lost nothing of his youthful grace and agility, but had gained a great addition of physical and mental power.

The sun had bronzed his cheek to a darker shade, care and responsibility had imparted to his fine face a graver and more thoughtful cast, but his lustrous blue eyes sparkled as brightly as of yore, though they now beamed with the calmer light of experience and sagacity.

The dress of the young British war-chief, though quaint and somewhat barbaric, was handsome and picturesque, and, in its way, imposing and majestic.

His tunic was of fine-spun cloth, trimmed with red.

His legs were encased in the chequered bry-can, or trousers, peculiar to the Gauls and Britons.

From his shoulders fell in graceful folds his sagum, or blue cloak.

Upon his feet he wore buskins of untanned deerskin.

His flowing hair, turned back from his forehead, and encircled by a plain band or coronet of pure gold, waved down upon his shoulders in a wealth of flaxen curls that a woman might envy.

His arms were his lance, a long, leaf-shaped broadsword, a jewelled dirk, and, strung at his side by a tasseled bawdrick, a round bronze shield, studded over with bosses of solid bullion.

His ornaments consisted of gold armlets and bracelets, a handsome ruby ring—the parting gift of his fair Virginia—and a collar or necklace of gold wires, called a torque, the symbol of his princely rank.

Upon one shoulder glittered a costly gem, set in the fibula or brooch which fastened his mantle.

"'Tis long past the time," young Caractacus muttered, in a tone of vexation. "There is not a coracle on the waters. The spies do not return. They must have failed."

Trailing his spear Caractacus walked to the other side of the rock, and looked down upon the city of Isca Silurum, the capital of his father's kingdom.

Isca Silurum, now Carleon, though a large and important town, was built in the rude style of architecture peculiar to the country, and the period.

It occupied a very strong position, and was surrounded by a rampart of flints and stones.

The houses were little better than huts, placed at short distances from each other, without any order or distinction of streets.

Upon a large belt of moorland that surrounded the town were scattered large herds of red cattle, and flocks of sheep, while on a strip of level ground, enclosed by a thick wattled fence, a number of British warriors were exercising, shooting their arrows at a mark, or hurling their long heavy javelins.

While Caractacus was moodily gazing upon the town, and mentally studying what measures were possible for strengthening its defences, his quick ear caught a slight rustle in a bush behind him.

He turned hastily.

The head and body of a man rose slowly and warily above a bush of heather, and then a tall wild-looking figure glided from behind the covert, and stood before the young prince.

He was a tall raw-boned barbarian, his naked limbs hideously tattooed, and stained with the blue dye called woad.

His immense red tangled moustache mingled with his coarse matted hair, that was rough and bushy as a bison's mane, and hung down to his waist.

His dress consisted of a tight-fitting body-garment, made of the hide of a brindled ox, and a large brown bearskin thrown over his shoulders by way of a cloak.

His body was cinctured with a leathern belt, from which hung his quiver and a bronze, double-headed axe.

In his hand he carried a short bow, and a couple of stone-pointed arrows.

Altogether his appearance was ferocious and terror-striking.

Caractacus stepped eagerly to meet him.

"Welcome, Garvan," he asked; "where is your kinsman, Oswain? I see by your looks that some mischance has befallen him."

Garvan howled, danced, and tugged his red beard with that sudden accession of frenzied rage peculiar to savages of all races.

"Och hone!" he cried. "Behold, son of Caradoc, look at this token."

He took from his bosom an arrow, stained from tip to feather with blood.

Caractacus took the weapon in his hand and examined it.

"This is too well made for a British weapon," he said.

"I found it stuck through my brother's heart—but, my chief, I wandered after him through miles and miles of country—at last I found him. Where, and how? With this shaft through his breast, and the villains had shot him."

"He was a faithful clansman," said Caractacus. "You found that he had fallen into the hands of the Romans, and that having caught him, they held him fast."

"Aye, had they left him so it would have been nothing," answered Garvan, sobbing; "but he was hanging to a tree, pierced through with the arrow."

"But where is the enemy?" asked Caractacus.

"The Romans have landed from their triremes, and are marching into the very heart of the land."

"Who commands them?"

"A tribune of the Prætorian guard."

"Do you know his name?"

"Honorius."

Caractacus smiled thoughtfully.

"Honorius!" he said; "how many pleasant memories that name recalls. But it cannot—it cannot be the same man."

Then, after a few moments' thought, he asked quickly, forgetting his own fancies or recollections—

"How many legionaries has he at his back?"

"At least four thousand."

"In what direction are they marching?"

"Towards Carleon?"

"And where do they encamp?"

"In the Druid's Grove."

"This very night we will surprise them," said Caractacus.

Then Caractacus drew a bugle-horn from his girdle, and blew a loud ringing blast that made the woods and mountains re-echo.

The last throbbing note of the bugle had scarcely died away in prolonged reverberations when its summons was answered from Carleon, by the silver toned peal of trumpets, clashing of shields, and wild uproar of voice.

Then pouring out through the wooden wide-thrown gates a rout of warriors and clansmen, their long hair and heavy sagas or tartaned cloaks streaming in the wind, their spears glittering in the sunlight, came clambering up the rocky height, with eager eyes and inquiring faces.

"Orla," said our hero, addressing a handsome youth, who by his superior dress and gold torque appeared to hold a post of command, "the reinforcements are landed; take forty spearmen and relieve the pickets on the east side of the Druid's Grove."

The youth bowed obedience and retired.

"For the rest of you," he said, "follow me on to Caer-bran."

This place was a strong fortified station on the crow of a high and rugged hill, that commanded a wide prospect of the surrounding country.

This stronghold was of Roman origin, and consisted of a fortified villa, the palace of a Roman præfect or governor of the province.

Over moss and mountain, threading narrow and tortuous passes, under overhanging rocks, marched that gallant little band of British warriors.

From time to time they halted, while scouts were sent on before to reconnoitre

On one of these occasions the scouts brought back with them a grim old warrior, whose clothes were torn and travel-stained, and his right arm slung and bandaged in a piece of blood-smeared cloth.

His haggard looks betrayed his condition.

He was half-fainting with hunger, weariness, and exhaustion.

"'Tis Storno!" cried the young prince. "Where did you find him? How came he hither?"

The old warrior endeavoured to fling himself upon his knees, to do homage to his hereditary chief, whom he, as did almost every other man belonging to the sept or clan, regarded with superstitious reverence.

In this attempt he failed, and would have fallen to the ground, had not our hero put out his strong arm and caught him.

"Bring him food and wine," said Caractacus.

The wounded and exhausted man was placed on a mossy bank.

Two of the soldiers came forward, one with a wine-skin slung over his shoulder, the other with a wallet full of dried deer's flesh and coarse rye-bread.

The old warrior ate with ravenous appetite.

While this was going on, Caractacus interrogated the clansmen who accompanied the veteran.

"We found him," said one of them, in answer to his chief's question, "lying in the valley below; we thought him dying, but we knew he was not dead, for three or four wolves slunk round him; the dog-wolf of the little pack was sniffing at his mouth, while the others squatted on their haunches at a little distance, and with their red tongues licked their gaunt chops in expectation of their meal, whilst above hovered a carrion crow, her black wings winnowing ——'

Caractacus roughly interrupted.

He knew the poetical temperament of his countrymen, their love for long, picturesque description, but his Roman training had rendered him impatient of such discursiveness.

"Enough of this," said our hero. "You found him as you tell me; had he ought to tell you how he became thus prostrate and wounded?"

"A few words only could he gasp out," returned the Briton.

"He said that there had been a battle after the Romans had come ashore."

"And that we were worsted?"

"Too true, Idris-ap-Caradoc," answered the man. "Our men fought hard, but I alone escaped; the rest were either slain or taken prisoners."

"This is evil news," said Caractacus. "But say, was there no treason? Were the Romans alone, or had they any British allies?"

"Chief, those cursed Brigantes had joined them; they betrayed our ambush, and thus our men were outmastered, surrounded, and cut to pieces."

"And the Druids were with the enemy?" rejoined another of the scouts.

Caractacus changed countenance.

"These Druids hate me because I have adopted another faith, and oppose their bloodthirsty rites," he muttered to himself. "'Twas ever so, and ever will be."

And he added in the bitterness of his heart.

"All priests of all creeds are the enemies of mankind"

"——" one asked quickly.

"Did you find out whither the Roman cohorts are marching?"

"Aye, to relieve Caer-bran."

Our hero's eyes sparkled, and his cheek flushed.

"Then there will yet be time," he said, "to take our revenge."

"What shall be done with Storno?" asked one of the scouts.

"Let him be conveyed to Carleon—four of you shall have charge of him."

But the old warrior, who was now refreshed with eating and drinking, arose to his feet.

"I will follow thee, chief," said he; "I can show thee the roadway which these Romans are coming."

"It is impossible, old man," said our hero; "you have done your duty—no more can the best man do."

But the brave Storno pleaded so earnestly that Caractacus was forced to yield to his solicitations.

They journeyed on for several miles, two of the warriors supporting Storno's tottering steps.

Under his guidance they entered a belt of forest that engirdled the mountain.

Here he bade them proceed with caution.

Then there was another halt.

Again the scouts departed, but this time Caractacus in person accompanied them.

Posting themselves under the shelter of a rock, which concealed them from view, our hero and his followers watched the advancing host as it wound through the valley beneath.

Nearer and nearer the warlike calvacade approached.

Snowy-bearded bards, with oak garlands entwined in their silvery hair, and wearing sky-blue robes, led the van, chanting their hymns of victory, their nimble fingers clashing along the strings of their harps in wild accord.

To them succeeded a band of trumpeters.

These were a fine set of fellows, in the most georgeous attire.

They were followed by a troop of mounted British warriors, of the tribe of the Brigantes, with light streaming locks, bright bossy targets, and glancing axes.

After them came about fifty Silurian captives, men belonging to our hero's own people, and every face amongst them familiar to him.

They were pinioned and bound to the saddles of their hostile fellow-countrymen, by thongs made of the sinews of the deer.

After them rode a cohort of Dalmatian cavalry, in their Roman dress.

They formed a splendid array.

In the clear sunshine of the bright autumnal day their spears gleamed, their brazen breastplates glowed, and banners fluttered in the breeze.

Then followed a ruck of rolling chariots, war cars drawn by fiery prancing steeds, four abreast, the hooked cruel scythes attached to the axletrees, with a murderous flash, revolving with the heavy spokeless wheels, leaving their sharp-cut imprints on the springy turf, or striking sparks against the jutting stones of the difficult ascent.

Then followed a seemingly interminable file of archers and spearmen.

Last of all a solitary chariot, in which lay, pale and bleeding, a wounded man.

Beside this chariot, mounted upon a high-mettled charger, rode a noble looking man in full panoply of war.

Even at that distance Caractacus could not fail to recognise him as the tribune Honorius. Behind him, last of all but the rear guard, came a horseman, whose figure seemed familiar to our hero, but whom he could not identify.

But the young chief had little time or opportunity for puzzling his brains on such a subject.

His former friends came now as foes to invade his native country, and, as a leader and a patriot, the son of the great Caractacus was bound in duty to withstand them if he could.

HIS mere immediate concern was to curb the wild enthusiasm of his savage, excitable followers, who with glaring eyes and quivering lips grasped their weapons, and seemed on the point of uttering their shrill slogan and rushing to the assault.

"Steady, my brothers," said he, "wait until they have reached the wood."

The men were calmed in an instant.

Every one of them crouched low in the tall grass, and disappeared like so many sprites vanishing at a wave of the enchanter's wand.

The glittering host had now ascended the heights, reached the first stretch of table-land, and entered the forest.

"Now, give way!—upon them! Take all the prisoners you can—spare the life of Honorius," cried our hero, brandishing his sword. "Follow me. Iero! Iero! Iero!"

With this fierce shout the Britons flung themselves in mass upon the Roman cohorts, and a furious conflict began.

The fight was desperate while it lasted, but that was not long.

The Romans fought with the steady discipline and fervid valour which had rendered their name synonymous with bravery, and had carried their eagles to the utmost limits of the known world.

The Britons charged with that impetuous fury that has carried all before it on many a bloody field.

Caractacus found it a hard matter to restrain the wild, impassioned courage of his men.

With spear, sword, club, and arrow the natives of our dearly-loved island, fighting for hearth and altar, drove their adversaries to the brink of the precipice, and hurled them into the abyss below.

Enraged and mortified at having fallen into the ambush, Honorius fought like a lion.

His horse was slain under him, but rising to his feet the noble Roman stood hacking and hewing amid a swirling mob of antagonists, keeping them all at bay by his superior skill in the use of his single weapon—a short, broad-bladed sword.

His foes fell around him like corn before the reaper's sickle, but he was pressed hard, and the blood flowed from many a desperate gash.

And now the savage Garvan, his face livid with ferocity, wielded his double-bladed axe, and thrusting aside his compatriots rushed upon the Roman commander.

A moment, and the brave Honorius would have been struck dead.

Caractacus flung himself between his enraged followers and their intended victim.

"Hold, I command you!" he shouted, in his stern, authoritative voice.

Before the words had passed from his lips, the axe fell upon his shield, shivering it like glass.

But Honorius was saved.

Awed by the frown of their young chief, the clansmen drew back, and lowered their weapons.

"Yield thee, noble Honorius! Submit to the fortunes of war, to which the bravest must succumb," said our hero, speaking in Latin. "You surrender your sword to a grateful friend."

The tribune started back.

"Caractacus!" he exclaimed.

The Briton smiled, and extended his hand.

The tribune grasped it cordially.

"To no man but yourself, my brave Caractacus, would I give up my sword."

"And few have more reason than I to wish to take it from you, seeing how fatal it is to my cause," answered Caractacus; "but keep it in its sheath, while I will hold your hand instead."

But the tribune tore his hand away, and turned round with an alarmed expression.

"O, for the gods!" he exclaimed, "save him—your old friend—save Ventidius!"

"Ventidius!" cried our hero, in mingled horror and amazement; "where is he?"

The tribune pointed to the chariot in which lay the wounded man.

Around it surged a throng of Britons, eager for revenge and slaughter.

The car was nobly defended by a small remnant of the Roman legionaries, at whose head, and fighting most desperately, was the man whom our hero had observed riding up the mountain side, but whom he had failed at the time to recognise.

"'Tis my comrade, Manlius, the gladiator!" exclaimed our hero, "fighting as he should fight for his old lanista."

Caractacus sped to the rescue.

His stern shouts soon restored order to his wild warriors.

Then Caractacus approached the chariot and gazed with a sad, compassionate look upon Ventidius.

Pallid as a corpse, as still and lifeless, the Roman lay, stretched upon a pile of scarlet mantles.

His broad, black eyebrows were bent in a frown, his white, gleaming teeth were tightly clenched, his war-worn features rigid as marble.

"He is dead!" gasped Caractacus, "he is dead! My friend and benefactor, slain by my warriors. What will Virginia say to this? An impassable gulf seems now to yawn between us. What would I not have done or borne to have prevented this."

CHAPTER LVI.

NEW ENEMIES AND OLD FRIENDS IN BRITAIN.

MANLIUS sprang from his horse and warmly greeted our hero.

"This is a strange encounter, old comrade," he said. "We, who have fought side by side in the arena now meet as foes on the battlefield."

"No longer are we foes, good Manlius," replied the Briton. "The misfortune which has befallen you might have come to my lot. There is no armour against fate."

"Well, comrade, I will thank the Fates that I have not fallen into worse hands," returned Manlius. "But look at your old lanista. I fear me he has got his quittance. Habet! as the mob used to shout when one or other of us gladiators went down. I would you had been there to call off your warhounds."

"I would it had been so," assented Caractacus. "But yet we will not abandon hope. There may be life in him. Our Druids are skilful physicians. If it lies within the range of possibility to restore him, they will effect a cure."

Caractacus gave a sign to his followers.

They gently lifted the wounded Roman from the car, and laid him on a litter formed by interlacing their spears, and placing hides and wolfskins upon them.

"Go, carry him to the Toscar Eubate, who dwells in a cavern of the sacred grove," he commanded. "Beseech him, on the part of Idris-ap-Caradoc to use his best skill to restore the patient, who is my friend, and who once saved my life."

Toscar was a man of great intelligence and the highest attainments, and his clear common sense and benevolence of disposition caused his mind to revolt against the barbarous rites and bloody sacrifices practised by the brothers of his order.

Indeed, the religion of the ancient Britons was cruel and ferocious in the extreme.

We may remind the reader that there were in the Druidical times three orders of the priesthood—the Druids, Bards, and Eubates.

The Druids were held in much veneration by the people.

The chief of the Druids was a sort of pontiff or high priest, who had authority over all the rest.

The Bards, among the Britons and Gauls, were priests of an inferior order to the Druids.

Their business was to celebrate the praises of their heroes in verses and songs, which they composed and sang to their harps.

They continued in being a long time.

There were some even after the Romans had entirely abandoned the island.

A third sort of priests, as well in Britain as in Gaul, were the Eubates, who applied themselves chiefly to philosophy and the contemplation of the wonderful works of nature.

Amongst their maxims and rules, as stated by Marcellinus, were the following, which will give an idea of the barbarities we have mentioned—

"Upon extraordinary emergencies a man or a woman must be sacrificed.

"According as the body falls, or moves after it has fallen, according as the blood flows, or the wound opens, future events are foretold.

"Prisoners of war are to be slain upon the altar, or burnt alive, enclosed in wicker, in honour of the gods.

"All commerce with strangers must be prohibited.

"He that comes last to the assembly of states ought to be punished with death.

"Children are to be brought up apart from their parents, until they are fourteen years of age.

"Money lent in this world will be repaid in the next.

"There is another world, and they who kill themselves to accompany their friends thither will live with them there.

"The moon is the sovereign remedy for all things, as its name in Celtic implies."

A long list of such cruel and superstitious maxims follows. We will add but one more.

"All masters of families are kings in their own houses; they have a power of life and death over their wives, children, and slaves."

Now Toscar, being a man much in advance of his age, had long doubted these doctrines.

He had mixed much with the Roman colonists, and had not only learned to speak, but also to read and write their language.

He delighted in nothing so much as in reading their stately and philosophic literature, thereby greatly improving his mind.

When Caractacus returned to Britain and was cordially welcomed by his father and the other war-chiefs assembled at Carleon, he sought out Toscar the Eubate, who had been his tutor while our hero was a boy.

The aged seer and his beloved pupil had many long and serious conversations about the new and wonderful doctrines which the latter had derived from the Christians.

The upshot was, that Toscar abandoned the priestly brotherhood to which he belonged, and retired to a cavern in the depths of the forest, where he spent his days in study and meditation, diversified by the more active duties of healing the sick and aiding the poor, who resorted to him in their illnesses and troubles, and regarded him with the greatest veneration, dwelling on his lightest words as upon utterances of a sacred oracle.

But to take up the thread of our story.

The little party of warriors departed with their unconscious and apparently lifeless burden, soon disappearing among the umbrageous trees.

Meanwhile, the Britons stood round their captives, scowling vengefully upon them, and only restrained by the presence of their gallant and revered prince from falling upon them, and hacking them to pieces.

"I protest to Jupiter, it is well for us that thou hast tucked us under thy shield, brave comrade," said Manlius, "else there had been a fine feast for the carrion crows and ravens, unless indeed these savages might devour us themselves, as they seem inclined to do."

"Poor creatures, they are not much to be blamed," was our hero's reply, "if they hate the Roman name. They have many and bitter wrongs to avenge."

"That cannot be denied," answered Manlius. "I have known many of them who have been dragged captives to Rome, and sold in the slave-market, some of whom have been lucky enough to find indulgent masters, who fed them well, and treated them with kindness; but it was astonishing to note how even these, so fortunate, pined for their dreary moors and barren mountains."

"I have known the feeling," answered our hero, with a passing sigh. "A cage is still a cage, although the bars be gilded, and these wild hawks of the mountain refuse to be reclaimed."

Then he added, waving his hand to his followers to get into marching order—

"But fear you not, good Manlius, nor you most noble tribune, that any harm will befall you whilst you are under my protection. Rude as my people may appear, they know how to respect the rights of hospitality; the fiercest warrior amongst them would not raise a hand against the guests of his prince." Then he shouted—

"Forward! On to Carleon."

The Britons with their captives began to descend the rugged mountain passes.

Though the town appeared to lie close beneath them, three hours passed by ere the cavalcade had reached the plain.

As they approached the city they were received with loud shouts of triumph and welcome.

Like a swarm of bees rushing out from their hive, a throng of men, women, and children, came pouring out through the gates.

Trumpets were blown, cymbals clashed, the women screamed with vindictive delight at seeing the captives, and altogether the hubbub was terrific.

Caractacus, however, by his authoritative gestures, restored something like order.

Preceded, surrounded, followed by the rabble of wild-looking natives, the Roman prisoners, under the guard of the British warriors, entered the city.

Caractacus at once gave orders to his heralds to make a proclamation, that all the elders should immediately assemble in an open space in the centre of the town, where councils were held, to share the spoil and deliberate upon the disposal of the captives.

When all were gathered, the elders seated themselves in a circle—the women, the young men and maidens, together with the children and slaves, occupied the background.

The trumpets were blown as a signal to command silence.

There was a breathless hush.

On one side of the square was a stone seat, raised upon a flight of rugged steps of rough hewn granite.

On this our hero sat enthroned.

When the flourish of the trumpets had ceased, and a deep and general silence prevailed, Caractacus rose to address the assembly.

In a long and eloquent speech he dwelt with triumph on the success which had so long attended the British arms, and recapitulated the achievements of his own father, their renowned hero-king, Caractacus.

And here, for the better understanding of the events to which he alluded in his address, we will as briefly as possible recount them.

Tiberius, successor of Augustus, neglected Britain, as a country of little consequence, it being unknown to him; as did also Caligula, his successor.

The Britons maintained their independence throughout the reigns of the first four Roman emperors.

Their subjection to the Romans did not commence l the time of Claudius.

This emperor was more particularly incited to subjugate Britain by the treacherous representations of Berious, a Briton, who had unsuccessfully endeavoured to raise a sedition against Togodumnus and Caractacus, who succeeded to their father, Cymbolin.

Plautius, a distinguished Roman general, was sent into Britain by the Roman emperor.

After fighting various battles, in which each party by turns were successful, the Britons were reduced to a state of great weakness.

The Emperor Claudius came himself and completed the conquest in a decisive victory at Camulodunum, a settlement in Essex.

Ostorius Scapula succeeded Plautius.

He found the Britons making continued inroads into the Roman conquests, and resolved to confine them between the Avon and the Severn by means of forts built between the two rivers.

He made Camulodunum a military colony, and, much about the same time, London was also made a trading colony, and that part of Britain lying between the Thames and the sea was reduced into the form of a province and called Britannia Prima.

The Iceni, not yet weakened by the foregoing wars, having from the beginning been in alliance with the Romans, were the first who opposed the designs of Ostorius.

Some neighbouring nations followed their example, and joining their forces under one general they encamped on advantageous ground, throwing up in haste a breast-work of flints to prevent the attacks of cavalry.

Though Ostorius was then without any but the auxiliary forces, he attacked them, ordering the horse to dismount and support those who were to charge first.

The resistance of the Britons was more obstinate than at first expected; nevertheless, their entrenchments were at length forced with great slaughter on their side.

After this victory Ostorius reduced the Cangi and the Brigantes.

But the Silures, the bravest and most powerful of all the Britons, could not be tamed either by clemency or severity.

Their forces were so considerable that the legions were obliged to march against them.

They were headed by their king Caractacus, famous for his great exploits, and universally esteemed by his countrymen as the best general Britain had ever produced.

This prince, whom the nations in alliance with the Silures had made commander-in-chief, retired into South Wales, where he chose a post of very difficult access, from whence he swept down upon the enemy's country and frequently committed great ravages.

Caractacus was in the full flood of his successes.

Leaving this subject Caractacus proceeded to mention the prisoners.

"I know it has been the custom of our forefathers to put their captives to death," he said; "but times have changed, and we ought now to desist from a barbarous practice which gives occasion to the enemy, and affords him a pretext for taking the most cruel reprisals.

"Amongst our prisoners of war several of the leaders are my personal friends, from whom I received much kindness whilst I was myself a captive and a slave in Rome. For the rest they can be retained as hostages, or exchanged for such of our people as have fallen into the hands of the Romans.

"As to the spoil, let that be divided amongst yourselves. I give up my share as a ransom for the lives of the prisoners."

There were a few murmurs of discontent, but the greater part of the assembly expressed their approval by a loud applauding shout.

The council then broke up.

Our hero led his guests, Honorius and Manlius, towards the rude hut which served as his palace.

It was a very simple building, and only differed from the other houses by its superior dimensions, and an appearance of neatness, cleanliness, and order that the others did not possess.

The furniture was of the rudest description—a few pieces of tapestry, some antlered skulls of deer, with trophies of weapons and implements used in hunting and fishing.

Honorius the Tribune glanced around him with an air of curiosity.

"This is but a poor dwelling, my Caractacus," he said, "for one who has sojourned in the palace of imperial Cæsar."

"It is the home of freedom," replied our hero, "which, humble as it is, I would not exchange for the stateliest edifice in your luxurious capital. Here I am master—there I was a slave."

"You have made a wise choice," replied the tribune. "Peace and honour more often dwell beneath a humble roof like this than amid the blaze of gold, ivory, and marble. Speaking for myself I may truly say I have enjoyed more happiness in a soldier's tent or in such a hut as this in winter quarters, than ever I have known in Rome."

Caractacus then invited his guests to seat themselves at his board, and, clapping his hands, bade his attendants bring wine and food.

Meanwhile he continued his conversation with Honorius.

"I doubt it not," he said. "The very splendour of a gaudy palace, when contrasted by the squalor of surrounding hovels, the dens of an oppressed and starving population, is hateful to me."

Then he added, with a slight flush—

"But you must not think that I learned nothing while I was in Rome—that I am insensible to the beauties of art, the refinements of life. Not so: I think I can appreciate the good as well as the evil of your civilisation. Think not I possess no finer abode than this. Not far from hence is a handsome villa, which belonged to a former Roman procurator, but I have turned it into a fort, and dwell here from motives of policy, as much as or more than from taste."

Honorius laughed.

"I think I understand you," he replied. "We have a saying, that while at Rome we must do as the Romans, and I suppose that in Britain we must comport ourselves as Britons."

"Even so," replied Caractacus. "Our people hate the Romans and their customs. I have given offence to the all-powerful Druids, by opposing their barbarous superstitions. Thus I am watched by jealous eyes, and must, at least till the war is over, cleave to a British mode of life."

"In this you act wisely," said Honorius.

At this moment the servants brought in the banquet, which consisted of substantial, plenteous fare, chines of beef, haunches of venison, game, and fish, with cakes of rye-bread, and golden flagons of foaming beer. The vessels were spoil from the Roman foe.

Caractacus once more invited his guests to be seated.

They placed themselves at table, but ere they had time to commence the repast, they were startled by a loud fierce blast of the trumpets, and a great outcry of voices.

"The prince! where is Idris-ap-Caradoc?" shouted a deep voice in breathless accents.

The next instant a Silurian warrior, covered with dust and blood, rushed into the banquet-room and sank at our hero's feet, pale and exhausted.

"Sound an alarm!" cried the prince. "Call our warriors to arms. This man brings news of the Romans!"

CHAPTER LVII.

A THREATENED REVOLT.

CARACTACUS and his guests gathered around the prostrate body of the messenger, who lay as still and stark as though he were dead.

"It is Cathullin, one of the bravest and hardiest warriors of our nation," said Caractacus. "He must have ridden far and fast indeed, to be seduced to this state."

"Your wild and rugged country must be severely trying to your scouts and couriers," remarked the Roman tribune.

"'Tis even so," replied Caractacus. "But their fidelity is beyond all praise. Not many days ago one of them fell dead at my feet."

"Might you not copy our Roman plan, and establish a system of advance-guards and outposts?" suggested Honorius.

"It is not possible," replied our hero; "we are never sure at what part of the coast the beaks of your Roman galleys may touch the shore, nor from what quarter your legions may invade our territories. Besides, there is the hostility and treachery of those of our tribes who have formed an alliance with the empire. Many of our scouts have been waylaid and murdered by such renegades."

With this he gave orders that the messenger should be removed, and that when he had recovered he should be brought back into the chief's presence.

The prince and his guest then sat down to the banquet, which, despite our hero's attempt to appear cheerful, and to disguise the anxiety he felt, passed off rather heavily.

When it was over and the board cleared an attendant entered to announce that Cathullin was restored to consciousness, had partaken of food and wine, and was now strong enough to communicate his tidings.

The man was brought in.

Though ghastly pale and haggard, and forced to lean for support on the shoulder of a youth, he affected indifference to his sufferings, and assumed a calm and self-possessed demeanour.

"Hail to thee, Idris-ap-Caradoc!" he said, in a deep firm voice. "I bring you news of the advance of the enemy."

"Whence come they, brave Cathullin?" asked our hero.

"From their military settlement, the fortified place which they have named Durobriva. They are five thousand strong, and their purpose is to take Carleon."

"To propose is one thing, to perform another," said Caractacus, grimly.

"Receiving information of the movements of the foe," continued the warrior, "the king, your father, who with his forces had retired to his fastness of Caer-bran, sent me with three others to warn you of your danger, and bid you prepare against an attack."

"But your companions, where are they?" questioned Caractacus.

"Alas! my prince, we fell into an ambush of those traitors, the Brigantes," replied Cathullin. "Both my brave comrades were slain. I scarce know how I myself escaped; only this I remember, that amid a storm of arrows and javelins I cut my way through the press, and by a path through the morass, unknown to my pursuers, I reached the foot of the mountains, and arrived here safe."

"And here thou shalt rest, brave Cathullin, until thy wounds be healed, and thou hast refreshed thyself by a few days' repose."

"It cannot be, my prince," was the reply; "I had strict orders from the king to return to Caer-bran as soon as might be after I had delivered my message."

"I will send another man," returned Caractacus. "Go you to rest, Cathullin; I will excuse you to my father, and will find you some post of honour and usefulness here, in the city."

Cathullin bowed deferentially, and retired from the presence.

Caractacus then took care that his guests were lodged in the best sleeping-chamber in his rude palace, and having bade them good-night, threw on his sagum, or military cloak, buckled on his sword, and, attended by a band of chosen chiefs and warriors, walked forth along the ramparts, to see that the sentries were vigilant at their posts, and that every preparation had been made to guard against the possibility of a surprise.

It was a calm, fair night, and the moon shone brilliantly in a cloudless sky, bathing the rude huts, the flint ramparts, the deep and rapid stream, and the surrounding woods and mountains in a silver flood.

Caractacus gave his orders to the different chiefs, and consulted them about the best means to fortify the town against the expected assault.

Stakes were to be driven into the fordable parts of the stream, so as to render the passage as difficult as possible, the walls were to be strengthened at weak points, and the old men, the lads, and even the women in the city, were all to be supplied with bows and arrows, or javelins.

The cattle were to be driven into the town, and the scanty harvest cut and stowed in granaries.

"I will never surrender the town," he said, addressing his chiefs, "rather would I have my people cut off by the sword than dragged into a captivity worse than death."

"The town is impregnable," replied Oswain. "We can stand a siege of months' duration, and meanwhile the king will doubtless march to our relief."

"Idris-ap-Caradoc, what of the prisoners?" growled Jewarth, a sullen, bushy-browed chieftain. "Shall they be allowed to remain in our midst, to devour the provisions we so urgently require for ourselves, to plot mischief, and to be a standing menace? Would they show such mercy to ourselves were we in their power? No! why then should we spare the destroyers? Let them be put to death."

The eyes of Caractacus flashed angrily, and his brows bent.

"I tell thee, Jowarth, that it is my will and pleasure that they should be spared," he said, "and I hold him a rebel and a traitor who dares to dispute my commands."

"I have spoken," growled the rough warrior; "we must do your pleasure, but, by Dis and Samothes! you will bitterly repent your ill-judged clemency."

So saying, he sullenly retired.

Dis and Samothes were the two principal deities of the ancient Gauls and Britons.

But the Britons had a very particular veneration for Andate, goddess of victory, to whom they sacrificed their prisoners of war.

"Would my father were come!" muttered Caractacus. "Should the Romans beleaguer the town, even my influence and authority will hardly suffice to preserve the lives of my friends."

"Look who comes here," said Oswain, pointing; "it is the bard, Caswallon."

As he spoke a venerable old man was seen slowly approaching them.

He was wrapped in a long flowing mantle, of a sky-blue colour; there was a garland of ivy leaves about his hoary head, and a long, snowy beard descended to his waist.

He supported his tottering steps with a long staff, curiously carved.

His brow was wrinkled with the furrows of nearly a hundred winters, his head was bent upon his breast, and he appeared to be sunk in a deep and painful reverie.

Caractacus was secretly annoyed at his appearance at such a juncture.

HE PLANTED HIMSELF FIRMLY AGAINST THE DOOR AS THE SOLDIERS WERE HEARD ADVANCING THROUGH THE CATACOMBS.

He knew the old man to be a staunch upholder of the Druidical religion, and one who bore an intense hatred against the Romans.

Our hero feared, and not without cause, that this venerated seer would inflame the minds of the people against the prisoners.

However, he dissembled his feelings.

"How comes it, O sage Caswallon, that thou exposest thy enfeebled frame to the chill blasts and unwholesome dews of night?" asked the prince, in tones of the most profound respect. "Why do you leave your couch and forego that refreshing sleep so needful to your age and infirmities?"

The old man raised his cold cruel grey eyes with a glare of vindictive fury.

"How can he sleep who knows that his head is resting upon a nest of adders?" returned the old man, in a harsh, husky whisper. "How can he slumber who knows the wolf is sniffing his breath? Sleep! I dare not sleep—the visions of the night render sleep a torment."

'What visions, O Caswallon?" asked the warriors, gathering around him, with pale faces and awestricken looks.

"Dreams of nameless horror," returned the old man, waving his withered hands as though to repel some hideous phantom. "A chaos of fire and blood, a whirlwind of shrieks, cries, and groans, a gulf of blackness and blank despair. Ask me not what I have dreamed, and tell me whether, indeed, I am awake and hear aright, or whether it was a foul slander they spake, who told me that Idris-ap-Caradoc had spared the lives of the accursed Romans who had fallen into his hands."

"It is too true," gasped the affrighted warriors.

"But it is not too late to rectify that error," rejoined the savage Jowarth. "Our foes are at our mercy, let them be destroyed."

"Death to the Romans!"

With this vengeful shout the barbarians drew their swords or brandished their lances.

They appeared to be on the point of rushing into the town and perpetrating a general massacre of the captives. But our hero stayed the storm by a few firm but conciliatory words.

"Say, Caswallon, am I not to obey the orders of my sire and sovereign,—heroic king Caractacus?" he asked the old man, "from whom I had command to keep the prisoners unharmed until his pleasure was made known?"

"Are not the gods above your warrior king?" retorted the bard, contemptuously. "If he offend against the dread Andate, can he hope to prosper in his warfare?"

"Yet hitherto victory has crowned his arms," replied our hero.

"Deceive not thyself, O Caradoc," returned the bard; "even as I speak the eagles have followed his march and are now feasting on the bodies of the slain."

"The gods forbid!" gasped the warriors.

"My father, the invincible Caractacus, defeated!" exclaimed our hero, with a start.

"Aye, by the Mystic Circle, by yon stars that cannot lie, this is true."

As he spoke the old fanatic shook back his hoary dishevelled locks, and upraised his glistening eyes to heaven.

"But whence did you derive this terrible intelligence?" asked our hero.

The old man dropped his arms, and answered in a low solemn tone—

"From a dread source. Ask me no more."

"From dreams," said our hero, "the idle imaginings of an overwrought brain. I must have better proof of what you have averred ere I take action. Meanwhile the prisoners' lives shall be held in pledge."

"Woe to Carleon, woe to all Britain!" cried the old man, bitterly, "when the princes of the earth defy the gods of heaven."

"Shame, Caswallon," our hero remonstrated; "are these the words of the sage who is the light of our council, of the bard whose harp strikes the loudest chords in praise of the noble deeds of virtue and heroism?"

The old man regarded Caractacus with a look of lofty disdain.

"Go! you are a Roman," he retorted. "You wear the torques that have descended to you from heroes like Cunobelin and Caradoc, but your heart is alienated. You wed not the fair-haired daughters of your race, but your thoughts wander back to the black-eyed sorceress you left in Rome."

Caradoc's cheek grew red, and only reverence for the old man's years and infirmity prevented our hero from striking him.

"By the sacred Serpent," continued the old man, shaking his fist, "the Silures have no king, and Caradoc no people. My malediction blight ye all! Dogs that lick your chains and fawn at the feet of a foreign tyrant!"

Folding his blue mantle around his tottering form the inexorable old bard cast a scornful glance round him, and stalked moodily away.

"Now, by the Druid's beard," exclaimed Jowarth, "the old man's reproaches are just. We are women and not men, or ere now the blood of these Romans had been poured out upon the altar of sacrifice."

"Wilt thou, Jowarth, take upon thyself to act in express defiance of my father's orders?" retorted Caractacus. "Or dare mutiny to my face?"

"I have spoken," growled Jowarth. "Pray the gods no worse evil may befall us."

The other chiefs, though less outspoken, showed signs of discontent.

"Who can doubt the wise Caswallon's tidings," said one of them. "Has he not the gift of second sight? If the king has suffered a defeat whilst on the march to our assistance, woe to Carleon!"

"Have patience till to morrow," said our hero. "The morn brings council."

Soon afterwards he dismissed his followers, and retired to his chamber.

He was waited on by his faithful henchman, Oswain. Our hero's heart was heavy with care, suspense, and vexation.

"Hear me, Oswain," he said. "I have ever found thee faithful."

The youth sank down upon his knee.

"My lord, to whom should you look for fidelity but to one whom you have treated rather as a friend than a servant?"

"It is well," replied Caractacus. "I know that I may safely trust you."

Caractacus paced up and down in great agitation; then, suddenly pausing, he took his young attendant by the arm.

"Oswain, the chiefs thirst for the blood of my Roman prisoners."

"Could you not sacrifice a few of them to save the rest?"

"Not a man, by heaven!" exclaimed Caractacus, firmly. "But hark ye, I must get some of the most inveterate of these barbarous chiefs away. I must lead them into action. Meantime, I shall leave the city under your governance."

"I am not worthy of such an honour," faltered the youth, his eyes sparkling.

"Go to! I know your worth, better than it is known to yourself," said Caractacus. "While I am away you will watch over the safety of my prisoners."

"I will defend them with my life!"

"You will swear this?"

"Aye, by my hopes of heaven!"

"You make me happy, good Oswain," said Caractacus, flinging himself wearily upon his couch. "Good night, and peace be with you. Call me at dawn to-morrow, for I must ride over to the Druid's Grove, and pay a visit to my old training master, Ventidius."

CHAPTER LVIII.

THE EVE OF BATTLE.

OUR scene shifts, and we now find ourselves in a spacious and gloomy cavern within the deepest recesses of the sacred grove. The hand of man had evidently assisted nature in giving form and shape to the rocky vault.

The walls, which were composed of massive blocks of granite, had been rough-hewn, projections being rudely struck away, and were covered with inscriptions and diagrams in characters legible only to the initiated—that is, to those of the Druidical order.

The winding of the entrance to the cavern excluded the light from entering in that direction, but a bright shaft of sunshine struck in through a hole in the roof, beneath which smouldered a wood fire, showing it served as a chimney.

On one side of the cavern, removed from the light, lay a wounded man—his body extended upon a bed formed of folded hides and furs.

He lay pale and immoveable as an effigy upon a tomb. His head was thrown back, his features were fixed and rigid as those of a corpse, and looked the more white and ghastly in contrast with his crisp raven curls and bushy black eyebrows.

His breast was tightly swathed with bandages that were saturated with blood.

He appeared to be sunk in profound slumber.

At his feet, seated upon the ground, was an aged and venerable man, wrapped in the ample folds of a dark grey mantle, his head partly enveloped in a hood, from which his long grey elf locks strayed and were moved by the stray draughts that wandered in at the open entry of the cave.

He was engaged in pounding out the juice of certain herbs with a pestle and mortar.

From time to time he would raise his eyes and fix them with a look of interest upon the patient, who was no other than our friend Ventidius, the training master.

Beside the wounded man, and looking down upon him with sympathy and regret, stood the noble form of our hero, Caractacus.

"So, father, he still sleeps," said our hero, laying his hand upon the pulse of the wounded man; "but it seems to me a death-like slumber."

"True, my son," answered Toscar, the hermit, "but when he wakes he will be greatly refreshed, and in a fair way towards recovery."

"Will that be soon?" asked our hero, in an anxious tone, "for I cannot remain here long. I go to join my father. Such business as mine will not brook delay. The king is encamped in a defile of the mountains, and intends to give battle to the Roman hosts. Yet I much wish to exchange a few words with the worthy Ventidius ere I depart—that is, if he be well enough for conversation."

"Have patience, my son," replied Toscar; "in a few moments your wish will be gratified."

He poured some water out of an earthenware pitcher upon the herbs, and when he had steeped them, he bathed the forehead of the wounded man.

The effect was magical. The colour returned to the cheek of Ventidius, his eyes opened, and he glared around him with a wild fierce glance.

"Strike hard, and strike sure, my sons!" he cried. "Our little maniple, if you will stand fast, is a match for a legion of these barbarians."

"His mind wanders," said Caractacus.

"Hush!" returned the Eubate, with a warning gesture, "in a few moments you will find that reason has resumed her sway."

Again he bathed the brow of the wounded man, who ceased his ravings and sank back upon his pillow with a long-drawn sigh.

He lay quietly for some moments and then appeared to rouse himself as from a deep refreshing sleep.

He lifted himself upon his elbow; his body for an instant seemed convulsed by a sharp twinge of pain, and he gave a deep gasp.

"I am hurt," he muttered; "what place is this? Have I crossed the Styx, and is this the Shades? Not so. This pain, this faintness, shows that I still live and suffer."

He cast his bloodshot eyes upon our hero.

"I am a prisoner in the hands of the Britons," he said. "This is their chief, a noble youth, such a one as would have made me a fine gladiator, when I kept my ludus in Rome; but all that is past and over now. Of course he speaks no Latin, and I know not a word of his barbarous tongue, else would I thank him for his clemency, for they have dressed my wounds, and seem to have treated me with gentleness."

Caractacus came to his side and took him by the hand.

"Look upon me, Ventidius," he said, "do you not remember me?"

Ventidius gazed at him with intense earnestness for a passing moment.

"Surely I am dreaming," he exclaimed, "or this is Caractacus!"

"Your novice, Caractacus," replied our hero, smiling, "whom you trained so well, and who may fairly boast that he did no discredit to his lanista when he fought in the arena."

"The gods bless thee, dear lad!" returned Ventidius, flinging his arms about him; "thou wert the best and bravest fighting man that ever I trained—though, for that, little merit was mine, since thou did'st worst me in our first encounter. I behold thee once more, and when I have delivered a message I came all this weary way to tell thee, I shall die content."

The blood mounted to our hero's temples.

"You shall not die, brave Ventidius," he answered, "You are in good hands. Æsculapius himself had not greater lore in medicine or deeper skill in surgery than he who has charge of your health. You will soon be yourself once more."

"I care not now how that may be," replied Ventidius, with a languid smile, "since we meet once more. I always wished to die a soldier's death—my wounds in front, as becomes a Roman."

"Speak not of dying," replied our hero; "your wounds are serious, but under the care of Toscar you will do well enough."

Then he added, in a tremulous voice—

"You spoke of a message from some of my friends in Rome," he said; "from whom, I pray you?"

Ventidius smiled faintly.

"Can you not guess?" he asked.

"Virginia?"

"Aye, from my sweet child," replied Ventidius. "She loves thee, Caractacus, she pines for thee. Many a time and oft hath she had offers of marriage from some of the noblest patricians in the empire."

"Ha!" returned our hero, with a violent start, "and she refused them?"

"Yes; she hath vexed me and enraged her mother by her obstinacy," replied Ventidius, "but she ever answers thus to all our entreaties—'I could give my heart only to one man—he is gone. I shall never see his face again.'"

The face of Caractacus beamed with pride and joy, for never had he forgotten, never had he ceased to cherish a fond remembrance of his beloved Virginia.

Our hero asked many questions concerning his old acquaintances, both enemies and friends; amongst others he mentioned the name of Zaba, the dwarf beast-feeder.

"That villain is dead," answered Ventidius. "He perished by a terrible but well-deserved punishment."

"Was he at last brought to justice?"

"Nemesis is slow of foot, but sure and untiring;

vengeance overtook him at last," said Ventidius. "More than once the wretch attempted to carry off my child, Virginia, for whom he had conceived an insane passion, from the house of your old comrade, Pandion, the boxer."

"O, that I had been there."

"The gods be praised, his vile attempts were frustrated," answered Ventidius. "Failing in his purpose, he thought only of revenge, and tried to poison Virginia, but she was saved through the fidelity of my household slaves."

"Did you not denounce him?"

"I had him arrested and brought before the edile," replied Ventidius, "But what would you? There is no justice in Rome; judges, witnesses and advocates are alike venal and corrupt. Zaba was in the employ of the empress—she saved him, for fear he might betray her secrets. He was confined a few days in the Mamertine—then released.

"What followed?"

"Zaba, to gain favour with the emperor, used all his craft and energy to hunt down those dark, mysterious people, the Christians or Nazarenes, whose society you courted," said Ventidius. "I used to think evil of them, but I know them better now. Zaba was well acquainted with all the intricacies of their hiding place, the catacombs. One night, however, whilst exploring the subterranean galleries in quest of his human prey, he fell into a pit or vault, enclosed on all sides by the sandstone rock, and there perished."

"The wretch, I suppose, was found a mangled corpse," said Caractacus.

"Not so," returned Ventidius. "When his body was found, some days after his disappearance, it was discovered that he had died by the lingering agonies of starvation. His body was wasted away to a mere skeleton- and his teeth were clenched in the fleshy part of his arm, as though he had drunk his own blood to quench his dying thirst."

"A fearful ending of a guilty life," said our hero. "But what induced you to come to Britain?"

"Love for my child, and an intense desire to look upon your face again, my brave one," said Ventidius, pressing our hero's hand. "When I heard that Honorius, the tribune, was about to set forth on an expedition to Britain, I snatched at the vague chance thus offered of meeting you. As you are aware, I have some interest at court, by means of which I obtained a post of command. I got my wounds in a skirmish with your barbarians, who, I must own, fought like lions, though after a wild, undisciplined fashion. I regret not the mishap, since I have fallen into your hands."

Here Toscar interposed, declaring that it was not safe for the patient to excite himself by talking.

He administered a draught, which Ventidius had no sooner swallowed than he sank into a kind of lethargy, which resulted in a deep sleep.

"Is he in fit condition to endure the fatigue of a removal to Carleon?" asked the British prince.

"I can prolong this trance," answered Toscar, "but is it needful that he should be taken hence?"

"It is," replied our hero. "The Romans are on the march, and we know not at what moment we may expect them, for I learn from the scouts that they intend to beleaguer the city."

At this moment the click of a horse's hoof was heard, and a British warrior, hot and breathless, entered the cavern.

Caractacus glanced at him in surprise, for he at once saw that he was not one of the people of Carleon, but a messenger from his father.

The noble-looking warrior bent the knee before young Caractacus.

"Hail, prince!" he said. "I was sent by my lord, the king, to Carleon, to tell you that it is his will that you should at once march to join him at a certain spot on the banks of the Isca, whither I am ordered to conduct you. Not finding you in the city, I came hither to seek you"

"It is well, Morven, replied our hero, "I will obey my father's command, and set forth at once."

The British warrior rose and moved towards the door.

"If so please you, we will waste no time," he said. "The Roman hosts are advancing, and too many of our best and bravest were lost in the last battle with Ostorius."

"Fortune has turned her wheel," muttered our hero. "The fickle goddess has grown weary of her favourite, to whom she has been constant so long. But this is vanity—it is the inscrutable providence of heaven, whose designs are beyond our human understanding."

Then he addressed himself to Toscar:

"I will send some of my men to convey Ventidius to Carleon," he said. "Go you with him, and use your best endeavours for his recovery."

"Pardon, my prince, I have a word to say to you," rejoined Morven "On reaching Carleon, I took upon myself to give certain orders to your people. This is my warrant for what I did."

He held out his hand, on which glittered a valuable ring.

Caractacus turned pale.

"The prisoners!" he gasped.

But his fears were groundless, and he received an encouraging reply.

"The prisoners are safe and well," said Morven. "It is the king's wish that their lives should be spared. It is his pride to show the Romans an example of mercy and forbearance, who brutally ill used their prisoners after the late victory."

Caractacus started.

"Their victory!" he exclaimed. "Then it was true what Caswallon told me—my father has been defeated?"

"There was heavy loss on both sides," replied the warrior, "but the Romans claim the victory."

"Well, my brave Morven, we must endure the fortunes of war," was our hero's reply. "We are yet powerful, and may redeem our losses; but what orders did you convey from my father to our people?"

"It was to save time," returned the chief. "I bade Jowarth muster the forces, and march them forth into the plain; this was done, and there they await your coming."

"You have done well," said Caractacus. "I am armed and in readiness. Oswain attends me. I will mount without further delay."

After giving his final directions to Toscar, our hero took his departure,

Threading the narrow and tortuous rockway that led by a gradual incline up to the level of the earth, he found Oswain waiting with the horses.

He sprang into the saddle, and, with his attendants, rode off to the banks of the river, where he found his warriors assembled in all their warlike panoply.

The appearance of Caractacus, their undaunted young prince, was hailed with a hearty cheer.

CHAPTER LIX.
FATHER AND SON.

WEARY and jaded, their horses flecked with foam, and travel stained, the troop of British warriors, headed by Caractacus, arrived at Caer-bran.

The warriors presented, nevertheless, a very gallant appearance, being the very flower of their clan, chosen for their stalwart proportions.

Tall and stately, they sat their high horses erect, and motionless as a group of statuary.

They were dressed in tunics of fine wool, dyed of several different colours, which, being spun into yarn, was woven either into stripes or chequers.

Here we have the undoubted origin of the Scotch plaid or tartan, which is called "the Garb of Old Gaul" to this day; and, indeed, with the exception of the plumed bonnet and tasselled sporan or pouch, a high and chief in full costume, with his trews, his plaid, dirk, and target, affords as good an illustration of an ancient Briton of distinction as can well be imagined.

The immense tangelled moustaches of the British warriors mingled with their long flowing hair, which streamed down over their black cloaks, while their tight helmets, the only addition they borrowed from the Romans, their glittering spears, dirks, and glaives, and their round bossed targets, completed their warlike panoply.

As our hero sprang lightly to the ground, for the toil which had wearied his companions had taken but little effect upon his iron frame, King Caractacus and a group of his nobles and generals came forward to greet the young prince.

The king's dress was very similar to that of his companions, but of more brilliant colour, and more profusely ornamented.

He wore a gorget of solid gold, his helmet and shield were inlaid with the same precious metal, and no less than five gold torques hung down upon his broad chest.

He was a proud and lordly man, about fifty years of age, with a hooked nose, eagle eyes, and masses of tawny elf locks, slightly silvered, shaggy brows, and a heavy moustache.

He was broad built, yet tall and fairly proportioned, his dark cheek was ruddy with healthful glow. His manners were free, manly, and debonnair; his deep voice suave and conciliating, his looks bland and good humoured, but at the same time highly dignified. The British warrior and patriot looked "every inch a king."

"Hail, my lord and sire!" said Caractacus, bending on one knee. "I bring you tidings of the enemy. On our way hither from Carleon, as we were threading the Druid's Pass, we fell in with the advanced guard of the army of Ostorius. The result was a skirmish, which ended in a complete victory for our forces. The Romans were utterly routed by the furious onset of my brave clansmen."

At this announcement the people gave vent to their joy in a hearty shout.

With kingly grace Caractacus raised the young prince, and, standing by his side, laid his hand caressingly upon his shoulder.

"Idris, my son, thou art as welcome as the glad news thou bringest, and more cannot be said," returned the monarch. "And when, think you, may we expect the approach of the Roman legions?"

"To morrow at latest, I should think, O king," replied our hero, "for they are advancing by forced marches."

"Why then, we must be prepared to give them battle," answered the king.

Then a gloomy look passed over his brow, and he made a sign to his attendants, which they at once understood, and fell back out of earshot, leaving father and son to confer at freedom.

"To you, my son, I will confess a weakness that I should scorn to betray to my chiefs or warriors," he said. "I have a strange presentiment of coming evil. The Druids have consulted their oracles and find them unpropitious, and our recent defeat has somewhat damped the ardour of my people."

"It is, then, true that you have suffered a defeat?" said our hero.

"Alas, it is too true," answered the king. "I had formed a plan for surprising the Roman camp by a night attack, but some traitor of our party must have betrayed our designs to the enemy, for they were forewarned and prepared against our assault. My Britons fought with great bravery, but our efforts were unavailing against the numbers and prowess of our wily and well-disciplined foes. We were repulsed, and that with heavy loss."

"Ah, my brave father, domestic treason is more to be dreaded than alien force," replied the prince.

"But I pray you tell me, who were those Brigantes who lately joined your army?"

"Disaffected chiefs who have revolted against my kinswoman, their queen, Cartismandua," was the reply.

"I doubt not," said our hero, "the traitor was one of their number."

"It might be so," replied the king, the "Brigantines were ever a wily and perfidious people."

"We have had proof enough of that, my father," rejoined our hero; "did not the false Cartismandua take part with the traitor, Beric, who raised a revolt against you when you succeeded to the throne—he who afterwards fled to Rome and incited the Emperor Claudius to invade our island?"

"Aye, she has ever been a firm ally of the Romans," answered King Caractacus; "yet she pretends sincere affection for my person, and solicitude for my safety. Not many days ago her messengers arrived upon a friendly errand; she entreated me, in case of a reverse, to seek refuge in her territory."

"Yes, that she might the more easily betray you to the Romans," answered Caractacus. "Oh, my father, trust her not."

The warrior king gave a deep fearless laugh.

"I will trust in nothing, my dear son, but the courage and devotion of my own people," replied the king.

"And such a trust will never be betrayed," answered the prince. "However fiercely Britons may contend amongst themselves, they are ever found ready to combine against a common foe; their proud souls will not brook the insolence of the most powerful invader."

Then, after a pause, he asked:

"What is the strength of your present force?"

"Undismayed by their former defeat, my people expect no other issue than a total overthrow, or a brave revenge," replied King Caractacus, proudly. "Upwards of thirty thousand men have flocked to my standard, and their number is increasing every day."

"This is brave news," said our hero, his eyes sparkling with a stern joyfulness.

"It is, indeed, encouraging, and gives us good hope of victory," assented the patriot monarch. "The youth of the country pour in from all quarters, and even the men in years, proud of their past exploits and the ensigns of honour which they have gained by their martial spirit."

"Why, then, we are prepared for the conflict, come when it will."

"Good; but your Roman prisoners, my son, you have taken care that they should not fall into the hands of the remorseless Druids?" asked the king, anxiously.

"They are safe," replied our hero; "but I had considerable trouble in protecting them from the vengeance of our chiefs. I had to stretch my authority to its utmost limits to do so."

"You acted with wisdom," said the king. "It has ever been my pride to show those boastful Romans an example of mercy and moderation."

Noise and excitement breaking out among the host, the king sent to enquire the cause, and was told that fresh scouts had come in, bringing news of the advance of the enemy.

"By break of day the Roman banners will glitter in our view," said one of the messengers. "The army has divided, and a large detachment is marching to beleaguer Carleon."

"To whose command have you left the defence of that city?" asked the king, addressing our hero.

"To the brave and faithful Oswain," replied the prince. "He has promised to hold out to the last extremity, and to perish rather than surrender."

"You could not have made a better choice," replied the king. "The city is almost impregnable and Oswain, despite his youth, is prudent as he is brave."

Our hero and his followers retired to take that rest which they so sorely needed, after their long and toilsome march.

The next morning young Idris-ap-Caradoc was roused from his deep slumbers by the blast of a trumpet summoning the British host to arms.

He rose hastily, buckled on his armour, seized his weapons, and rushed forth to greet the eventful day.

Mounting upon the summit of a high crag the British prince gazed long and earnestly upon the picturesque and bustling scene below.

It was, indeed, a grand and heart-stirring spectacle.

Entrenched along the lower heights were the British hosts, with their baggage wains, their cattle, sheep, goods and chattels, with their women and children.

Beyond, upon the plain at the foot of the mountains, were the white tents of the Roman camp, amidst which the legionaries, shining in their armour, were bustling to and fro in all the excitement of active preparation for the coming conflict.

Young Caractacus, attended by his chief and warriors, hurried off to join the king.

CHAPTER LX.

THE BRITONS' LAST STAND.

THE heroic leader was dressed in all his warlike panoply, and presented a noble and majestic appearance. The multitude were gathered round him, eager for action, and burning with uncommon ardour.

The king harangued them to the following effect:—

"When I consider the motives that have roused us to this war, when I reflect on the necessity that now demands our firmest vigour, I expect every thing great and noble from the union of sentiment that pervades us all.

"From this day I date the freedom of Britain.

"We are men who have never crouched in bondage.

"To draw the sword in the cause of freedom is the true glory of the brave, and, in our condition, cowardice itself would throw away the scabbard.

"The Romans are in the heart of our country; no submission can satisfy their pride, no concessions can appease their fury.

"While the land has anything left it is the theatre of war; when it can yield no more, they explore the seas for hidden treasures.

"Are the nations rich—Roman avarice is their enemy. Are they poor—Roman ambition lords it over them.

"The east and the west have been rifled, and the spoiler is still insatiate.

"To rob, to ravage, and to murder, in their imposing language, are the arts of civil policy.

"When they have made the world a solitude they call it peace.

"We must expect no mercy—let us, therefore, dare like men.

"What is this Roman army? or can that be called an army which is no better than a motley crew of various nations, held together by successs, and ready to crumble away in the first reverse of fortune?

"That this will be their fate no one can doubt, unless we suppose that the Gauls, the Germans, and with shame I add, the Britons, a mercenary band, who hire their blood in a foreign service, will adhere, from principle, to a master whom they have lately served and long detested.

"They are now enlisted by awe and terror; break their fetters, and the man who forgets to fear will seek revenge.

"In the ensuing battle be not deceived by false appearances; the glitter of gold and silver may dazzle the eye, but to us it is harmless, to the Romans no protection

"In me behold your general—behold an army of freeborn men.

"Your enemy is before you, and in his train heavy tributes, drudgery in the mines, and all the horrors of slavery.

"Are these calamities to be entailed on us? Or shall this day relieve us by a brave revenge?

"There is the field of battle—let that determine.

"Let us seek the enemy, and as we rush upon him, remember the glory handed down to us from our ancestors, and let each man think the fate of all posterity depends upon his sword."

This speech was received with war songs, with savage howlings, and a wild uproar of applause.

The battalions began to form the line of battle.

The king, his princes, and chiefs rushed forward to the front, and the field glittered with the blaze of arms. The Romans, on their side, burned with equal ardour.

Ostorius saw the impatient spirit of his men, but did not think proper to begin the engagement until he had confirmed their courage by an address.

In his heart-stirring speech he reminded them of their past victories, and of the fact that they had carried the terror of their arms beyond the limits of any other soldiers, or any former general, and that one victory more would make this new world their own, reminding them that a defeat would involve them all in the last distress.

He called upon them to decide whether they would not rather die with honour than live in infamy.

"Here you may end your labours!" he exclaimed, "and close a scene of eight years by one great, one glorious day.

"Let your country see, and let the commonwealth bear witness, if the conquest of Britain has been a lingering work, if the seeds of rebellion have not been crushed, that we at least have done our duty."

During this harangue, whilst Ostorius was still addressing the men, more than common ardour glowed on every countenance.

As soon as the general ended, the field rang with shouts of applause.

Impatient for the onset the soldiers grasped their arms.

Ostorius restrained their impulse till he formed his order of battle.

The auxiliary infantry, in number about eight thousand, occupied the centre.

The wings consisted of three thousand horse.

The legions were stationed in the rear at the head of the entrenchments, as a body of reserve to support the ranks if necessary, but otherwise to remain inactive, that a victory obtained without the effusion of Roman blood might be of higher value.

The Britons kept possession of the rising grounds, extending their ranks as wide as possible to present a formidable show of battle.

Their first line was ranged on the plain, the rest in a gradual ascent on the acclivity of the hill.

The intermediate space between both armies was filled with charioteers and cavalry of the Britons rushing to and fro in wild career, and traversing the plain with noise and tumult.

The Britons being greatly superior in numbers, there was reason to apprehend that the Romans might be attacked in front and rear at the same time.

To prevent that mischief Ostorius ordered his ranks to form a wider range

Some of the officers saw that the lines were weakened into length, and therefore advised that the legions should be brought forward into the field of action.

But the general was not of a temper to be easily dissuaded from his purpose. Flushed with hope, and firm in the hour of danger, he immediately dismounted, and, dismissing his horse, took his stand at the head of his forces.

The battle began.

The Britons neither wanted skill nor resolution.

With their long swords, and targets of small dimensions, they had the address to elude the missive weapons of the Romans, and at the same time to discharge a thick volley of their own.

To bring the conflict to a speedy decision, Ostorius ordered three Batavian, and two Tungrian cohorts to attack the enemy sword in hand.

To this mode of attack those troops had long been accustomed, but to the Britons it was every way disadvantageous.

Their small targets afforded no protection, and their unwieldy swords, not sharpened to a point, could do but little execution in a close engagement.

The Batavians rushed to the attack with impetuous fury, they redoubled their blows, and with the bosses of their shields bruised the enemy in the face ; and, having overpowered all resistance on the plain, began to force their way up the ascent of the hill in regular order of battle.

Incited by their example, the other cohorts advanced with a spirit of emulation, and cut their way with terrible slaughter.

Eager in pursuit of victory, they pressed forward with determined fury, leaving behind them numbers wounded, but not slain, and others not so much as hurt.

The Roman cavalry, in the meantime, was forced to give ground.

The Britons, in their armed chariots, led on by their heroic king, Caractacus, and his warlike son, rushed at full speed into the thick of the battle, where the infantry were engaged.

Their first impression struck a general terror, but their career was soon checked by the inequalities of the ground, and the close-embodied ranks of the Romans.

Nothing could less resemble an engagement of cavalry.

Pent up in narrow places, the Britons crowded on each other, and were driven or dragged along by their own horses.

A scene of the greatest confusion and disorder followed.

Chariots without a guide, and horses without a rider, broke from the ranks in wild disorder, and flying every way, as fear and consternation urged, they overwhelmed their own files, and trampled down all who came in their way.

Meanwhile, those Britons who had hitherto kept their post on the hills, looking down with contempt on the scanty numbers of the Roman army, began to quit their stations.

Descending slowly, they hoped, by wheeling round the field of battle, to attack the victors in the rear.

To counteract their design, Ostorius ordered four squadrons of horse, which he had kept as a body of reserve, to advance and charge

The Britons poured down with impetuosity, and retired with equal precipitation.

At the same time the cavalry, by the direction of their general, wheeled round from the wings, and fell with great slaughter on the rear of the enemy, who now perceived that their own stratagem was turned against themselves.

The field presented a dreadful spectacle of carnage and confusion.

The Britons fled.

The Romans pursued ; they wounded, gashed, and mangled the runaways.

They seized their prisoners, and, to be ready for others, butchered them on the spot.

Despair and horror appeared in various shapes : in one part of the field the Britons, sword in hand, fled in crowds from a handful of Romans ; in other places, without a weapon left, they faced every danger, and rushed on certain death.

Swords and bucklers, mangled limbs and dead bodies, covered the plain.

The field was red with blood.

The vanquished Britons had their moments of returning courage, and gave proofs of virtue and of brave despair.

They fled to the woods, and, rallying their scattered numbers, surrounded such of the Romans as pursued with too much eagerness.

Ostorius was everywhere present.

He saw the danger, and if he had not in the instant taken due precaution, the victorious army would have had reason to repent of too much confidence in success.

The light-armed cohorts had orders to invest the woods.

Where the thickets were too close for the horse to enter, the men dismounted to explore the passes ; and where the woods gave an opening, the rest of the cavalry rushed in and scoured the country.

The Britons, seeing the pursuit was conducted in compact and regular order, dispersed a second time, not in collected bodies, but in consternation, flying in different ways, to remote lurking places, solicitous only for their personal safety, and no longer willing to wait for their fellow soldiers.

Night coming on, the Romans, weary of slaughter, desisted from the pursuit.

Ten thousand of the Britons fell in this engagement ; on the part of the Romans the number of the slain did not exceed a thousand, amongst whom were a good number of officers.

Caractacus and his son, finding all was lost, at length, covered with wounds, abandoned the field.

The Roman army, elated with success, and enriched with plunder, passed the night in exultation.

The Britons, on the other hand, wandered about, uncertain which way to turn, helpless and disconsolate.

The mingled cries of men and women filled the air with lamentation.

Some assisted to carry off the wounded, others called for the assistance of such as escaped unhurt.

Numbers abandoned their habitations, or in their frenzy set them on fire.

They fled to obscure retreats, and in the moment of choice deserted them ; they held consultations, and having inflamed their hopes, changed their minds in despair ; they beheld the pledges of tender affection, and burst into tears ; they viewed them again, and grew fierce in their resentment.

It is a fact well authenticated, that some laid violent hands on their wives and children, determined, with savage compassion, to end their misery.

Thus was the last battle fought by the hero Caractacus against the invincible foes of his country lost and won.

CHAPTER LXI.

CÆSAR'S CLEMENCY.

ALL Rome was astir, and its thoroughfares were crowded with citizens, who lined the various streets, or thronged to the capitol to witness the triumphant entrance of Ostorius into Rome.

The capitol, we may remind the reader, was a celebrated temple and citadel at Rome, on the Tarpeian rock—that rock from which, in earlier times, persons guilty of treason were thrown.

　　" The steep
Tarpeian, fittest goal for treason's race,
The promontory whence the traitor's leap
Cured al ambition.

The temple was dedicated to Jupiter, and was adorned with a lavish splendour almost incredible.

Its gates were of brass, covered with large plates of gold, the inside wall was all of marble, adorned with vessels and shields of solid silver, with gilded chariots and other splendid trophies.

This temple was the principal sanctuary of Rome.

The consuls and magistrates offered sacrifices there when they first entered office, and the processions in triumph were also conducted to the capitol.

Amongst the numerous groups of the more privileged spectators who occupied windows and balconies that overlooked the grand esplanade on which the triumphant procession was to draw up and salute the emperor, there was one group, each member of which we recognise as an old friend.

Ventidius, Lupa, and their daughter, our hero's loved Virginia, honest Pandion, the boxer, our hero's old comrade, with his wife, Marcia, and the children.

Opposite them, at the top of a flight of wide marble steps that led up to the gilded arch of the capitol, Claudius Cæsar sat enthroned, his consort, Agrippa, on his right hand, young Nero on his left, behind them a crowd of senators, patricians, priests, and prætorian guards.

Around the wide area were dense masses of the populace, kept back by mounted soldiers.

The hum-dread in its combination of myriad voices, throbbed in the still summer air—broken now and then by a shout or a shriek, and at intervals drowned by the blare of trumpets and the clashing of cymbals.

At length there was a stir amongst the dense mass of humanity, and every face was turned in one direction.

Then, like a roll of thunder, pealed the eager cry—"They come! Ostorius! Ostorius!"

Virginia turned faint, and leaned her head upon her father's shoulder, while, with trembling hands, she clasped his arm.

"Oh, my father," she murmured, "you have seen him, how does he bear himself?"

"As becomes a free-born prince," answered Ventidius, "and a brave man, suffering bravely the buffets of malignant fortune—he suffers as he fights, like a hero."

"He is wounded, they tell me," sighed Virginia.

"Aye, he carries scars upon the front; but he wears them rather as badges of honour—his fine condition has rendered them harmless," answered the old training master. "Mehercle! though his chains were so heavy that an ordinary man could scarcely lift them, he stood as erect and walked almost as nimbly as though he were just stripped for the arena."

Virginia turned pale and faint.

"Is he in chains?"

"Aye, poor lad, he and all his fellow captives."

"What think you, husband—will they spare his life?" asked Lupa.

"The gods alone can tell, not I," answered Ventidius. "He has one powerful friend who may save him."

"Who is that?" asked Lupa.

"The Empress Agrippina," replied her husband

A hot, jealous flush for a moment suffused Virginia's cheek.

"That creature," she retorted indignantly, "the noble Caractacus would scorn to owe his life to her intercession."

"Yet it was she, sweet mistress, who delivered him from prison, and found him the means of escaping from Rome," remarked Pandion.

Then he added, after a brief pause—

"I heard, worthy Ventidius, that you and the other Roman prisoners had a narrow escape of your lives while in the hands of the barbarians."

"True; but for Caractacus we should have been butchered to the last man," answered Ventidius. "After Ostorius had won his great victory, a small body of the routed Britons, under the leadership of the young prince, Caractacus, escaped to Carleon, where we were held in captivity. He arrived just at the moment when the citizens, having revolted against their governor, a youth named Oswain, were about to sacrifice their captives to the gods

It was only by the exercise of the greatest courage and determination that he succeeded in pacifying the enraged multitude."

"Did Ostorius take the city?"

"No," replied Ventidius. "Rather than suffer it to fall into the hands of the enemy, the despairing inhabitants set the town on fire, and fled into the woods and mountains."

"And what became of the famous Caractacus after his defeat?" asked Pandion.

"After the battle," replied Ventidius' "Caractacus, with his wife, daughters, and brothers, fled for protection to Cartismandua, queen of the Brigantes, and by her they were delivered up to the Romans, for fear of drawing a victorious army into her country should she think of protecting her kinsmen."

"Hush! Ventidius," interrupted Lupa, "the procession is in sight"

This fact was confirmed by the loud acclamations of the populace.

The gorgeous procession now filed into the vast square before the capitol.

First went the musicians of various kinds, singing and playing triumphal songs.

Next were led the oxen for sacrifice, having their horns gilt, and their heads adorned with fillets of ribbon and garlands of fresh and lovely flowers.

Then, in carriages, were brought along the spoils taken from the enemy.

The titles of the vanquished nations were inscribed on wooden frames, and the images or representations of the conquered countries, cities, and the like, were carried by slaves in gorgeous liveries.

The captive leaders followed in chains, with their children and attendants.

Conspicuous amongst them stalked the lordly figure of King Caractacus, who gazed about him in simple wonder.

After the captives came the lictors, having their fasces, or bundles of rods, bound with laurel.

These were followed by a great company of musicians and dancers, dressed like satyrs, and wearing crowns of gold.

In the midst of these a jester, or pantomime, clothed in a female garb, whose business it was, by his looks and gestures, to insult the vanquished. Next followed a long train of persons carrying perfume.

Then came the victorious general, Ostorius himself, dressed in purple embroidered with gold.

In his right hand he held a branch of laurel, in his left an ivory sceptre with an eagle on the top, having his face painted with vermilion, in like manner as the statue of Jupiter on festival days.

A golden ball hung from his neck on to his breast, with some amulet in it, or some magical preservative against envy.

He stood in a gilded chariot, adorned with ivy, and drawn by four milk-white steeds of purest breed and faultless beauty.

He was attended by his retinue and a great crowd of citizens, all in white, a slave, carrying a golden crown sparkling with gems, standing behind him.

After the general followed his relations and friends, the consuls and senators, on foot.

The victorious horse and foot brought up the rear, rending the sky with exultant shouts of—

"Io triumphe!"

The procession passed round the square, and the ceremony of the presentation of the victorious general to the emperor commenced.

Claudius received the conqueror with gracious smiles and compliments, and placed him on his right hand.

Then the chief captives were brought to the foot of the throne.

Caractacus, the British king, all undaunted and seemingly forgetful of his misery in his contemplation of the splendid scene, gazed around him with bewildered eye

"How is it possible," he exclaimed, "that a

people possessed of such magnificence at home could envy me a humble cottage in Britain?"

Confronted with the Roman emperor, the patriot Briton looked upon him with a proud and independent air that inspired the spectators with sympathy and respect.

Claudius put on a frown, and sternly demanded why Caractacus had dared to revolt against the Roman Government, and had so long and desperately opposed the Roman power.

To this question Caractacus returned a bold but conciliatory answer—

"If my moderation had been as great as my birth and fortune," he said, "Rome had seen me this day her ally and not her captive, and perhaps she would not have disdained to rank in the number of her friends a prince royally descended, and who commanded many nations.

"My present condition is as dishonourable to me as it is glorious to you.

"I had arms, horses, riches, and grandeur.

"Is it strange I should part with them unwillingly.?

"Does it follow, because you have a mind to rule over all, that therefore everyone must tamely submit?

"Had I sooner been betrayed to you, neither your glory nor my misfortune had been rendered so famous, and my punishment would have been buried in eternal oblivion.

"But now, if you preserve my life, I shall be a standing monument of your clemency to future ages."

Claudius sat revolving these words in his mind, his eyes fixed upon the ground.

The hapless captives awaited the emperor's decision in dead silence and heart-sickening suspense.

Agrippina, in the meantime, sat gazing intently upon the face of our hero, young Caractacus, for whom she still entertained a deep and passionate affection.

She laid her hand upon the emperor's and looked up into his face with a smile of resistless fascination.

"Great Cæsar," she whispered, "spare these noble barbarians. Such an act of magnanimity will cost you nothing, yet will render your name for ever illustrious. The noble bearing of this hero has won the sympathies of the populace, while nothing is more likely to tame the fierce souls of his people than by winning their hearts in sparing their king, to whom they look up with a feeling akin to admiration."

"You counsel well, my Agrippina," answered Claudius. "But it will not do to yield too easily."

"Nay; let your act be spontaneous, of a free heart—it will be the more generous and more deeply appreciated," urged the empress.

Claudius rose, and with real dignity, for it was one of his lucid moments, he performed an act that makes amends for many of his vices and follies.

In a brief, generous speech he accepted the brave captive's vindication, pardoned him and his fellow-captives, and ordered that their chains should be struck off, and that they should at once be set at liberty.

CHAPTER LXII.
FAREWELL !

THE glare, the noise, the music, the multitude, the cruel excitement of that terrible day were over. All had passed like a wild, wild dream, and the calm holy hour of evening had come.

Our hero, the brave, the patiently-enduring Caractacus, was seated in the vestibule of the house of Ventidius, at Baiæ.

Beside him knelt the fair and gentle Virginia, her beautiful head nestling upon his bosom, her white arm thrown about his neck, her glorious dark eyes raised to his, and beaming with unfathomable love, her face radiant with happiness.

"Forgotten, dear Caractacus!" she murmured, in accents of tender reproach. "When wert thou absent from my thoughts? I have spent the weary time since we parted in wondering about you, how you fared, what triumphs you had won, what defeats you had suffered. Yet, believe me, through all this torment of suspense, that sweet new gospel which we learned together brought me peace and comfort; I knew that, whatever might befall us in this vale of tribulation, that there—beyond the grave, above, in Elysium—in Heaven, we should be united."

"Light of my eyes," returned Caractacus, kissing her smooth white brow; "and thou didst never doubt my constancy?"

"Nay; I will confess that sometimes I have doubted," replied Virginia, lowering her glance. "I have thought that, in the turmoil of statecraft and warfare, the prince of a brave and free nation must have forgotten the daughter of his humble master, under whom, by a cruel destiny, he was bound to serve as a slave and a gladiator. It was this grief made me sick at heart."

"By Heaven, you did me wrong, dearest Virginia!" replied Caractacus. "Your image was ever before me; at night I never lay down to sleep without invoking a blessing upon you; in the morn I never rose at the sound of the trumpet, to buckle on my armour for the field, but I kissed the talisman you gave me, which I have ever worn close to my heart."

"The sardonyx!" returned Virginia, laughing and blushing. "Indeed, when I gave it you I believed sincerely that it was a charm against evil; but now I am wiser, and scorn the superstition."

"Superstition!" repeated Caractacus. "No, by Heaven! Your gift has proved a true and holy charm. It cheered me in my darkest hours, it added a lustre to my most glorious victories, for it was a token that the being whom I love and prize above all earthly objects was still my own, still cherished a remembrance of the poor slave whose body and blood had been purchased by her father."

Virginia clasped her arms closer around him, as she murmured—

"And must we part so soon?"

"Too soon, my dear one," replied Caractacus. "It is the emperor's pleasure that I should return to Britain. The ship sails to-morrow, and I may see thee no more."

"But why should we part?" said Virginia. "Why should I not go with you?"

So lovely she looked, her cheek dyed with maidenly blushes, while her dark eyes beamed with the fearless and frank expression of devotion, that Caractacus pressed her to his heart in a fervour of passionate love.

"It may not be, dearest," he said. "Thou art too fair and frail a flower to be torn from thy native soil and planted on the rough strand of my rugged island. Amid the rude scenes of our barbarian life you would pine for the bright skies, the comforts and luxuries of Rome."

"A desert shared with thee is paradise," returned Virginia. "Without thee, paradise were a desert. Leave me not, but take me with thee."

While she was speaking, Philomenes and his wife, Glauce, entered the vestibule.

They were accompanied by their children, a boy and girl, who might have been taken as models of an infantile Cupid and Psyche.

The first cordial greetings over, Philomenes shook our hero by the hand.

"Great and good news I bring you, brave Caractacus," he said. "Your royal father has made a treaty of alliance with Cæsar. In a few days he will sail for Britain, restored to his throne and kingdom. You are to go with him, and to take your princely rank as his eldest born, and heir of his dominions. Be faithful to your pledges, and peace and prosperity will bless your reign."

"So will I, by my hopes of Heaven!" exclaimed Caractacus. "Thus will I prove how Britons, proud and martial, ever may be led by kindness, when they cannot be driven by tyranny and oppression. 'Render unto Cæsar the things that be Cæsar's'—I will render him all that allegiance he has won by force of arms, but only so far as is compatible with the happiness of those over whom I am to rule. He has behaved generously in this. I leave him, whom I have so long hated, with a new feeling—gratitude."

"You leave him in bad hands," said the Greek sculptor. "The empress——"

"Peace, good Philomenes," interrupted Caractacus; "I am not bound to defend her, but am precluded from breathing one word to her disparagement. I owe her much."

"'Tis strange," murmured Philomenes. "As the sun gilds the most squalid objects, so love throws a halo even round the vilest criminal. I know the Briton's secret—the empress loves him, purely and disinterestedly. Strange inconsistency! The pure, the bestial, the gold, the clay, how they are mingled in poor human nature! But he is right, he is not her judge; she was good to him."

By the glad consent of her parents, Virginia, wedded to our hero Caractacus, departed with him for Britain.

All the young Briton's friends and comrades gathered in the mole at Neapolis to see him embark.

Pandion and his wife were there, Ventidius and Lupa, the tribune, and Manlius, the gladiator.

It boots not to tell with what splendour and ceremony the British king and prince embarked in the vessel that was to bear them to their island home, accompanied by quite a fleet of Roman war-galleys.

Amid the acclamations of the multitude, the flotilla sailed away.

The crowd dispersed.

A solitary female, muffled in a black hood cloak, sat watching the sails of the departing fleet till they faded away in the far distance.

She was weeping bitterly.

She raised her pale face and wofully wrung her hands.

"He is gone!" she moaned. "The sun has set, the light has gone out of the world, all is crime and foulness, all is darkness and despair. Oh, the gods! what might have saved me has departed for ever!"

There was a sentry on guard near the spot.

He approached and laid his hand roughly upon her shoulder.

"Ædepol!" he growled, "what mad woman is this? What is she muttering? I have orders to keep away such baggages. Woman, ho-hoa," he shouted in her ear. "Do you mark me? You must get home, this is no place for you."

The black-robed figure rose majestically, the black hood fell back, displaying a face as fine and haughty as the face of Juno.

"Slave!" cried the woman; "take off your base hand, I am the Empress Agrippina!"

THE END.

HOGARTH HOUSE LIBRARY—Continued.

All to be had in Penny Weekly Numbers.

ROBIN HOOD;
Or, the Archers of Merrie Sherwood.

In three Vols. at 1s. each, or complete in one Vol., handsomely bound in cloth and gold, 3s. 6d.—In telling this well-known story of England's celebrated outlaw, the author has closely followed the soul-stirring old ballad of Robin Hood and his Merry Men, so well known to all English-speaking boys.

WILL DUDLEY; or, the Scarlet Riders.

Complete, price 1s. 6d.—This is the story of a more modern outlaw than Robin Hood—told by the same author. The adventures are, however, quite as thrilling, and the descriptive passages quite as accurate, as those depicted in the preceding story. The daring deeds of Dick Turpin are herein outdone.

TYBURN DICK; or, Take Me Who Dare!

Four Vols. at 1s. each, or complete in one Vol., handsomely bound scarlet and gold, 4s. 6d.—This is one of the most stirring stories of the Road ever written, and details the life and exploits of an unfortunate but gallant young nobleman, who was hounded almost to allows by his unnatural relatives, and who, after many struggles, ned his position and estates, thus entirely defeating his enemies.

THE OUTLAWS OF EPPING FOREST.

Complete, price 1s. 6d.—This is a sensational narrative (founded on fact) of the daring exploits of a band of outlaws, who, under the leadership of the celebrated Batswing, took up their quarters in a cave in Epping Forest.

SHAW, the Lifeguardsman.

Complete, price 1s. 6d.—This is a faithful story of the life of the gallant Shaw, the Lifeguardsman and Pugilist, and takes the spell-bound reader through the stirring times of Waterloo, when England, almost unaided, defeated the mighty Napoleon.

FOR VALOUR;
Or, How I Won the Victoria Cross.

Complete, price 1s.—Every boy has read of the recent gallant struggles of our soldiers in Afghanistan. The scene of this story is laid in the same country, in the days of Akbar Khan. As we have seldom met foemen more worthy of our steel, so this book stands almost unique amongst military romances.

THE KING'S HUSSARS.

Complete, price 1s.—This story takes us from the snow-clad steppes and plains of Russia to the torrid climes of India during the heart-rending period which will be known to all time as "the Mutiny." The writer of this work took an active part in all the scenes which he so graphically describes, and was present at the Siege of Lucknow.

CAPTAIN JACK;
Or, One of the Light Brigade.

Complete, price 1s. 6d.—Since the days of Thermopylæ, no such heroic deed as the Charge of the Light Brigade has been witnessed by an admiring and awe-stricken world. In this soul-stirring story of the Crimean War a full account of the glorious charge is given by one who passed through that Valley of Death.

DEATH OR GLORY;
Or, the Uhlans of England.

Complete, price 1s.—This is also a story of the glorious adventures of our countrymen during the Crimean War, the fortunes of the Death or Glory Boys—the gallant 17th Lancers—being followed in the story.

KARL THE UHLAN;
Or, the Cast of the Die.

Complete, price 1s.—This is a story of the last Franco-German War. So realistic is the account of the furious struggle between the two countries, that Prince Bismarck and Marshal Mac Mahon have alike pronounced eulogiums on it. Treating of a period which has entirely changed the map of Europe, every boy should read this story of our own times, dealing as it does with the deeds of still living characters.

SHOT AND SHELL.

Complete, price 7s. 6d.—Comprising the preceding six Volumes, forming an entrancing historical novel, containing a complete History of the Indian Wars, including the Great Mutiny, and a graphic and entertaining narrative of the Franco-German War. Handsomely bound in cloth and gold, making a splendid presentation or prize volume.

RED HUGH, the Backwoodsman.

Complete, price 1s.—This story, by "Silvershot," a well-known hunter, is a faithful narrative of life in the backwoods, and should be read by every boy who has an Englishman's love of adventure implanted in his breast.

TOMAHAWK AND RIFLE.

Complete, price 1s.—By the same author as the last-mentioned work. This stirring story tells of furious combats with unfriendly Red Skins, and of the doings of the mighty hunters of the almost unexplored prairie and backwoods.

WHIP THE WIND;
Or, the White Horse of the Prairie.

Complete, price 1s.—This is no fiction, but is an actual narrative of the experiences of the author during his sojourn in the boundless wastes far from the habitation of civilised mankind.

YOUNG WILL WATCH;
Or, the Smuggler King.

Complete, price 1s.; fully illustrated.—Every boy enjoys good tales of adventure on sea or land; this book is replete with soul-stirring incidents in the career of a bold smuggler, who, together with his gallant crew, defy all comers by sheer clever stratagems and bravery—a book that every boy ought to read.

DASHING DUKE;
Or, the Mystery of the Red Mask.

Complete, price 1s.; fully illustrated.—This story professedly illustrates the career of a disinherited young nobleman, who, in the course of his reckless life, upturned some very extraordinary scenes, and was also the hero of wonderful adventures during his successful attempts to establish his right to the title and estates of his father.

The HOGARTH HOUSE HARKAWAY SERIES *is the* ORIGINAL EDITION *fully Illustrated.—The cheapest, most complete and entrancing edition published.*

JACK HARKAWAY IN AMERICA.

Complete, price 1s.; fully illustrated.—This stirring story of adventures in America is from the pen of the original "Jack Harkaway," and should be read by every boy who wishes to know anything of life on the great Continent which claims Old England as its mother country, and between whose sons the bonds of friendship are daily strengthening.

JACK HARKAWAY OUT WEST AMONGST THE INDIANS.

Complete, price 1s.; fully illustrated.—From the pen of the same author. This story carries the reader out into the boundless prairies, and tells of the adventures of the hero amongst the Red Skins, who in their various tribes unite the highest with the lowest attributes of mankind and the brute creation.

JACK HARKAWAY IN SEARCH OF THE MOUNTAIN OF GOLD.

Complete, price 1s.; fully illustrated.—In this stirring narrative the reader is taken still further away from the civilised portion of the United States; but it will be found that this, the third volume of the "Harkaway" Series, loses nothing by comparison with its two exciting predecessors.

JACK HARKAWAY IN SEARCH OF HIS FATHER.

Complete, price 1s.; fully illustrated.—In this book the reader will find young Jack at a boarding school; some of his adventures there. —Old Mole on the scene.—How the under master, Canker, kills his nephew.—The gold teeth of the idol; the Malay on the track.— Young Jack and Mole start in search of his father.

JACK HARKAWAY AMONG THE PIRATES.

Complete, price 1s.; fully illustrated.—Young Jack sees his father in a cage.—Is taken prisoner by the pirates; their cruelties to prisoners.—He escapes to the prairie.

JACK HARKAWAY ON THE PRAIRIE.

Complete, price 1s.; fully illustrated.—Life on the prairie.—Encounters with Indians; taken prisoner; meets old friends; escapes again; on the pirates' track; meets with friendly tribes; starts for the haunt of the pirates.

JACK HARKAWAY AND HIS FATHER AT THE HAUNT OF THE PIRATES;
Or, The Last of the Black Flag.

Complete, price 1s.; fully illustrated.—A friend in need.—Hunston's retreat on the Isle of Refuge.—Murder will come out.—Given to the Sacred Serpent.—The man-monkey.—The battle of the lake; young Jack's peril.—The snake charmers.—Hunston's tactics.—Harkaway and Monday on the yacht.—The Shum.—Jack visits the skeleton.— The fate of the Pirate King.

HOGARTH HOUSE, BOUVERIE ST., FLEET ST., LONDON, E.C.

www.ingramcontent.com/pod-product-compliance
Lightning Source LLC
Chambersburg PA
CBHW081153170626
46813CB00009B/3180